JACKIE COLLINS

"Sinners" is one of my early books, and has been through two title changes. Originally called "Sunday Simmons & Charlie Brick", the title got changed to "Hollywood Zoo", eventually ending up as "Sinners." And I cant remember why!! Actually I like "Sunday Simmons & Charlie Brick" best, the names of my two main characters.

I think it is one of the first long books I wrote, & I enjoyed developing the characters of Charlie — an English movie star. And Dallas — a former American call girl. Have fun getting to know them! Jackie C.

Jackie Collins

SINNERS

**SIMON &
SCHUSTER**

London · New York · Sydney · Toronto · New Delhi

A CBS COMPANY

First published under the title *Sunday Simmons and Charlie Brick*
in Great Britain by W.H. Allen & Co. Ltd, 1972

This edition published by Simon & Schuster UK Ltd, 2012
A CBS COMPANY

1 3 5 7 9 10 8 6 4 2

Simon & Schuster UK Ltd
1st Floor
222 Gray's Inn Road
London WC1X 8HB

Simon & Schuster Australia, Sydney
Simon & Schuster India, New Delhi

www. simonandschuster. co.uk

A CIP catalogue record for this book is available from the British Library

ISBN 978-1-47113-415-9

This book is a work of fiction. Names, characters,
places and incidents are either a product of the author's imagination
or are used fictitiously. Any resemblance to actual people, living or dead,
events or locales, is entirely coincidental.

Typeset by Hewer Text UK Ltd, Edinburgh
Printed and bound by CPI Group (UK) Ltd, Croydon, CR0 4YY

SINNERS

Chapter One

Herbert Lincoln Jefferson stared disgustedly at his wife, Marge. She sprawled on a couch in front of the television, legs apart, displaying fat white thighs, eating an orange so that the juice dribbled down her chin, and holding a beer can from which she took occasional swigs. She was wearing a blue cotton dress which was so tight that it had split under one arm. Her huge bosom hung in a dirty white bra which peeked through the split. A stranger seeing her would have found it hard to judge her age, and perhaps assessed her as ten years older than she was. Actually she was thirty-five.

'I'm going,' Herbert announced.

Marge didn't shift her eyes from the TV set. She crammed some more orange into her mouth and mumbled, 'OK, hon.'

Herbert left the faded pink house, one in a row of many faded houses. He kicked viciously at Marge's cat which wandered under his feet, and started the walk to the bus stop. It was early evening and particularly hot. Herbert felt enraged that he had no car. Everyone had a car in Los Angeles. Last week he had had a beautiful shiny grey Chevrolet, but they had taken it away as he hadn't kept up the payments.

Herbert was of medium height, a thin man with brown hair and sharp features. He wasn't good-looking, he wasn't ugly, he was just perfectly ordinary-looking. He was the sort of man

1

you never remembered, that is unless he stared at you with his oblique brown eyes, and then suddenly you would get an odd sort of shudder. His eyes were mean and cruel and grabbing.

There was a young Mexican girl at the bus stop in front of him, and he appraised her quickly. Too skinny and too young, but a virgin, he was sure of that. He pressed up against her as they boarded the bus, and she turned round and gave him a startled look. He ignored her and took a seat next to a plump matron, probably some rich movie star's housekeeper. No, if she was, she would have her own car.

There was a musty smell of dried sweat in the bus, and Herbert wrinkled up his nose in disgust. He had taken a shower before coming out. Sometimes he showered four or five times a day. The man he really admired was Tiny Tim, because he had read somewhere that he showered every time he took a leak. Herbert really admired such cleanliness.

The plump matron shifted in her seat. She didn't like the pressure of Herbert's leg beside her. But he stared straight ahead with his ordinary face, and she was sure he couldn't be doing it purposely.

The old bag's wearing suspenders, Herbert thought. One of them was digging into him. He moved his arm so that it nudged against the side of her bosom. She squashed nearer to the window, and Herbert stared impassively forward.

At the next stop the woman got out, and Herbert shifted his knees so that she had to squeeze past him. He felt the outline of her big buttocks against his knees, and he laughed silently. Old cow, give her a thrill. They all loved a thrill, even the old ones.

He thought lovingly about the letter he had sent to sexy red-headed film star, Angela Carter. He had mailed it the previous evening, and she had probably read it by now. He had managed to get her home address; that was an advantage of doing the job he was in now. They had a file in the office of most of the film stars' addresses. He was working for a chauffeur service employed by Radiant Productions. It was most important when writing to people that you were sure they would open the letter themselves. That was the whole point.

To Angela he had written lovingly in glowing and explicit terms about what he would like to do to her. No detail had been spared and he enclosed a small plastic bag into which he had proudly masturbated.

It was one of his better literary efforts, and he hoped that Miss Angela Carter appreciated it.

The bus arrived at his stop and he walked the short distance to the Supreme Chauffeur Company.

Chapter Two

The woman caressed the man beneath her, and in return his hands stroked her arched naked back.

She was beautiful in no conventional sense. Long wild hair, framing a tanned, almost animalistic face. Eyes a mixture of brown and yellow. Mouth wide and sensual.

They lay on a bed with black silk sheets, one sheet covering the woman just below her waist. She had a marvellous body, a combination of long limbs, curves and fine muscles.

She sighed and bent to kiss the man. He was also naked. A brown hard body with hairs on his chest and a fine display of muscles.

As they kissed she reached down to the floor, and from under the bed produced a small gun which she stealthily brought up to his head.

Ending the kiss she whispered, 'Goodbye, Mr Fountain.'

In one quick movement he threw her off him and twisted the gun from her hand.

Furious, she crouched on the floor glaring at him.

He laughed. 'Better luck next time, baby, you're not dealing with a Boy Scout.

She brought up her arm to try to strike him, and a voice shouted, 'Cut.'

Sunday Simmons's hands flew to cover herself. Quickly a wardrobe lady appeared and threw a robe around her.

Abe Stein, the director, strolled over. He was fat, and chewing on an ancient, stinking cigar. He spoke to the man lying on the bed. 'Sorry, Jack, too much tit.'

Jack Milan grinned. He was a well-preserved forty-nine, with jet-black hair and a smile that had kept him hot at the box-office for twenty years. 'There's never too much tit for me, Abe old boy.'

Everyone within earshot laughed, except Sunday who huddled miserably on the floor, clutching the robe around her.

Why had she ever agreed to do this film? In Italy, in fact in most European countries, she was regarded as almost a star; and here in Hollywood, she was treated as a nothing.

Abe addressed himself to her. 'Look, honey, I know you got a gorgeous pair of boobs there, but just keep them pointed at Mr Milan, huh?'

'I'm sorry,' she said stiffly. 'When he throws me to the floor it is very difficult. Perhaps if you let me wear some sort of covering, as I wanted to . . .'

'No, those things look worse than nothing.' He was referring to 'patsies' which some female stars insisted on wearing in any kind of nude scenes. They were round flesh-coloured pads which stuck over the nipples. Sunday had asked to wear them, but her contract for the film stipulated she had to do what the film company wanted, and they wanted no patsies. So here she was, exposed, except for a brief pair of panties, to the entire unit, which seemed to have doubled itself on this day.

She dreaded having to remove the robe again.

As if reading her thoughts, Abe said, 'Get on the bed, let me show you what I mean. Do you mind, Jack? Shall I get your stand-in?'

'Do I mind? Just get me a Scotch and a cigarette, and I'll shoot this scene all day!'

More laughter, and Sunday reluctantly took off her robe.

She tried not to care, tried to blank out the grinning faces watching her.

She got on the bed, partly under the sheets, and half lying across Jack Milan.

'Now let's take it in slow motion,' Abe said. 'Show me how you throw her off you.'

Jack's strong arms lifted her slowly and edged her sideways. Abe's fat arms brushed across her until both men were holding her.

'Try and keep her towards you like this,' Abe said. 'That's it, marvellous. Now on the floor, dear, when you go to hit him, just make sure your back is to the camera. Like this.'

Once more he handled her body, and this time she was sure his fat hands didn't slide across her breasts by accident.

'We'll break for lunch now.' He turned to Jack Milan who climbed out of the bed, wearing orange jockey shorts and matching socks. 'Everyone back by two p.m. sharp. Come on, Jack, I'll buy you that Scotch.'

Sunday walked slowly to her dressing room. She was close to tears. It was so humiliating to be treated like this. She had thought a Jack Milan film would be a good thing to do, but it had turned out to be just another girl in a multi-girl spy film. She had been so anxious to leave Rome that she had hardly even looked at the script. And she had wanted to see Hollywood; the nearest she had been before was Rio, where she was born.

Sunday had had a happy childhood. Her father was South American and her mother French, and the two nationalities were very compatible.

By the time she was sixteen she had decided to be an actress, and she persuaded her parents to send her to a dramatic academy in London. It was the best, and arrangements were made for Sunday to stay in London with her mother's elder sister, Aunt Jasmin. Of course, she was to return to Rio for all vacations, and immediately if she didn't care for England.

It didn't make any difference whether she cared or not. Her parents were killed in a car crash two days after she left.

Sunday was heartbroken. She blamed herself, reasoning that if she had been there it might not have happened.

Her father left hardly any money at all. Generous, he had lived big, spending and lending in every direction.

After the funeral, Sunday decided to stay in London and continue her studies. She had a few thousand pounds left to her by her mother.

It was a far different life for her to adjust to. A small apartment in Kensington, the cold weather, and Aunt Jasmin, who thought it a sin to show any affection.

Sunday found this strange and worrying. She needed love and affection, and it seemed there was no one she could turn to.

She threw herself into her work at the academy.

One day after she had been there a year and a half, she met Raf Souza.

Raf was a dynamic young man, currently the most in-demand fashion photographer and very aware of it. He turned up at the school with three thin model girls, a hairdresser, a battery of equipment, and three huge dogs. He had permission to use the interior of the academy for a *Vogue* lay out with students in the background.

At that time, Sunday wore her hair flattened down and scraped back. She dressed for the cold, wearing at least three sweaters and baggy trousers. She wore no make-up.

Raf picked her out immediately, made her loosen her hair, and had her kneeling with the dogs looking up at the three model girls.

She was secretly delighted, but to the other students she pretended it was an awful bore.

When Raf left he handed her his card and said, 'If you want to see the pictures, drop around tomorrow about six.'

Raf's studio was the wrong end of Fulham Road, and it took her ages to find it. He hardly gave her a glance when she arrived, just threw the contact sheets at her.

She studied them intently. How blank her face looked beside the models. How lumpy she appeared in her loads of sweaters.

7

'How old are you?' Raf asked casually.

'Nearly seventeen. Why?'

'Just wondered. I had an idea you might be good for. You want to try some test shots?'

'Yes, I'd like to.'

'If they're any good it will mean a week abroad plus all expenses paid and a hundred quid.'

Raf was no fool. He was getting paid a thousand for the job, and if he took a really good professional model it would dig deeper than a hundred. Anyway, he saw great potential in this girl. That fabulous skin would photograph a million dollars in colour, and with the right make-up and hairstyle she would be a knock-out. He was fed up with the usual faces. They all looked the same. This girl could be quite a diversion.

Raf, in his short career, had been to bed with many of the top photographic models, lady editors of magazines, and generally any female who could do him some good. He was stocky, untidy, with a little-boy smile that turned women on.

He tried it now on Sunday. 'What do you think? Could you make it with no family problems?'

She thought how nice he was. 'Yes, I'm sure I could. Term ends tomorrow and I didn't have any definite plans.'

'Great! Let's get started. You'd better get out of your clothes. I'll give you a shirt to put on. Oh, and take your hair down, it looks terrible scruffed back like that.'

She had second thoughts. What sort of pictures did he want to take anyway? She hesitated when he threw her a shirt.

He noticed her hesitation. 'They're going to be fashion shots, darling, beach jazz and harem gear, I've got to see if you've got a body underneath all that. Get changed upstairs if you like.' He busied himself with a camera.

She took the shirt, went upstairs, and put it on over her bra and pants. It looked quite decent. Then she loosened her hair and padded quietly downstairs.

Christ! Raf thought, he'd picked a winner this time. The girl was magnificent. She had the most incredible long legs, and he imagined the wild shots he could do with her. Her breasts jutted through the shirt, and she had a special kind of walk. Very, very sexy.

He spent an hour taking photographs. She fell into poses naturally. He couldn't wait to get her out of that shirt. Apart from fancying her, she was going to make this assignment really good.

Arrangements were made, and they went to Morocco.

Raf, who used women purely as a convenience, found himself completely fascinated by Sunday.

Because of the situation with her aunt, Sunday found herself spending more and more time with him. On her seventeenth birthday he made love to her, and shortly afterwards she moved into his studio.

Aunt Jasmin accepted the move as she accepted everything else in life, tight-lipped and silent.

'I'll keep in touch,' Sunday promised.

Aunt Jasmin just shrugged her disapproval.

Raf was the first person Sunday had been really close to since her parents died. They lived together for several months, Sunday finishing her last term at the academy, and Raf getting on with his work. Then the pictures of Sunday in Morocco appeared, and the magazine was inundated with calls wanting to know who she was. There were offers for her to do a hair commercial, a toothpaste commercial, and a film company wanted to test her.

Raf withdrew into a black mood. Sunday was thrilled.

The magazine wanted Raf to arrange another session with her immediately. He talked her out of doing the commercials, although the money was excellent. But she insisted that she wanted to do the film test.

Raf took her to Rome, and while they were taking the photographs she fell in love with the city. It reminded her of Rio.

When they got back she did the part in the film she had tested for.

9

Raf brooded, extremely jealous about having to share her. For the first time since she came to live with him he had other women, got drunk before she came home, and took to insulting and ridiculing her in front of their friends.

She couldn't understand why Raf had become so bitter towards her. What had she done?

But he couldn't explain how he felt about her success, that he was terrified of losing her.

She did a couple of other small parts, and then the first movie appeared and she received an offer to do a film in Rome.

'Take it,' Raf said bitterly, 'we're about through anyway.' And to settle the matter he told her he had found someone else.

Sunday was quite successful in Rome, appearing in a string of movies that usually showed off her more physical charms.

All thoughts of becoming a 'serious actress' were pushed to the back of her mind. She enjoyed the excitement and attention she seemed to create wherever she went.

The Italian men chased after her in full force, but her thoughts remained with Raf. He had been her first man and she had loved him. She had *thought* he loved her.

Then Paulo appeared on the scene. Count Paulo Gennerra Rizzo. He was to bring nothing but trouble.

* * *

'Miss Simmons.' There was a knock on her dressing-room door. 'Miss Simmons, you're wanted on the set please.'

Automatically she checked herself in the mirror and vaguely realized she hadn't had any lunch. Oh well, back to the charming Abe Stein and delightful Jack Milan, who hadn't addressed one word to her. What a way to start one's first day's work in Hollywood.

On the set there was much activity. Word had spread about the nude scene, and little groups of men whom she hadn't noticed before were dotted around the sidelines. She also noticed several men with cameras who hadn't been there before. Neither Jack Milan nor Abe Stein was present.

A makeup man with whom she had argued that morning approached her. It had been a silly argument as far as Sunday was concerned. She had asked to do her own eye make-up, as she always did, and the man had refused. That annoyed her, as she knew her face a lot better than someone who had merely glanced at her for five minutes. She insisted, and the man stamped out of the room in a fury, muttering about 'Dirty foreign starlets.'

Now he approached her with a cake of make-up and a sponge. He said, 'Take your robe off. I've got to check your body make-up.'

She glared at the man who had gathered a bunch of mates to watch the fun. 'Where is the woman who did it this morning?' she asked.

'On another set. Don't be bashful, everybody's seen your big tits already!'

She felt her face blaze, and turned to leave the set, bumping into Jack Milan and Abe.

'Where are you rushing off to, honey?' Abe asked, gripping her arm with his fleshy hand. 'Let's get this scene in the can, come on.' He pulled her back to the set.

She had a sudden feeling that she wasn't going to be able to take her robe off in front of this whole group. She said to Abe: 'In Italy when we shoot such a scene, the set is cleared until only the essential technicians remain. I would like that done here, please.'

'Oh, would you?' Abe coughed and spat. 'This isn't Italy, honey, and all these guys are needed around here.'

Sunday, who rarely lost her temper, was burning now. 'In that case you can shoot the scene without me. I am not an animal to be stared at. I am an actress.'

'Ha!' Abe snorted. 'An actress, huh? One that can't even keep her tits out of the camera. Don't get high-hat with me, baby, you've got a contract, remember?'

'Yes, I am well aware of that. However, I cannot work under these condition. I'm so sorry.'

And with that, she walked off the set.

It was the first time anyone had walked off a Jack Milan movie.

Chapter Three

Charlie Brick and the girl sat side by side in the dimly lit restaurant overlooking Park Lane. Several waiters hovered nearby, ready to spring forward at the slightest sign from the man.

They sipped coffee, the girl eagerly, bright eyes darting all over the place. She was pretty and young. Charlie was much older, nearing forty. He had a long sad face, and wore heavy horn-rimmed glasses.

'I wish my mum could see me now!' the girl said suddenly.

'What, my darling?' Charlie leaned closer towards her, groping for her hand under the tablecloth.

'My mum,' the girl continued brightly. 'She just wouldn't believe it, me sitting here in a place like this with you.'

'Why not?' He gave her hand a tight squeeze.

'Well, y'know.' She giggled. 'They could hardly believe it when I won that beauty competition and came to London; they're a bit square where I come from. So you can imagine what they would think if they knew I was sitting in some posh old restaurant with a real live film star!'

'You're such a pretty little thing.'

She looked pleased. 'Do you think so?' She covered his hand with her own. 'My mum always said I should be in the movies.' She looked at him hopefully. 'What do you think?'

He let go of her hand and summoned one of the nearby

waiters. 'I think it's time we were going. I have a very early call in the morning.'

'Oh.' She looked disappointed. 'I thought you were going to show me your new stills back at the hotel.'

'Some other time.' His attitude had changed; it was distant, hurried.

The head waiter came rushing over. 'Everything all right, Mr Brick?'

Charlie stood up. 'Thank you, Luigi, it was fine.'

'I saw your latest film last week, Mr Brick, sir. It was funny, very funny indeed. It's a pleasure to have you here tonight.'

'Thank you, Luigi.'

They moved out into the cold London night; it was spitting with rain. The doorman sprang to attention. 'Evening, Mr Brick, sir, your car's just coming.'

A long black Bentley rolled into sight. They climbed in.

'Thank you, sir, thank you very much,' the doorman said as he was handed a large tip.

The car slid silently off.

'Where to?' the chauffeur asked,'

'Drop me back at the hotel, George, and then take Miss Marymont home.'

'Yes, sir.' George allowed himself a fleeting smile. Another choked bird to deliver home!

They drove to the hotel in silence. The girl too nonplussed by his sudden change of mood to know what to say.

'Are you sure you don't want me to come up?' she asked upon arrival.

'That's very sweet of you, love, but you know, it's the old five a.m. up bit. I'll call you some time next week.' He got quickly out of the car. 'Bye.'

He stood and watched the car thread its way slowly back among the traffic. Foolish little girl, he thought. Was that really the only reason they went out with him? Did they honestly believe that he could be used to get them into the movies?

How many times had he heard it now? How many different

ways? The direct approach: '*Do you think you could get me a screen test?*' The oblique hint: '*I've always wanted to act.*' The actress's approach: '*My agent says I'm perfect for the girl's part in your next film.*'

Lorna had warned him, laughed at him. 'Oh yes, sure,' she had said, 'you'll have tons of little girls just lining up to jump into bed with you. But ask yourself, my darling, is it *you* they want? Or is it Charlie Brick?'

The divorce had been final just one month now. Twelve years of marriage shattered. Lorna with another man. The children shuttled back and forth between them. And a terrible loneliness that couldn't be filled, however many people he was with.

He walked into the hotel. The desk clerk immediately sent a bellboy rushing over to him. 'There is a call coming through from Hollywood for you, Mr Brick, sir.'

'I'll take it in my suite,' he said.

The liftman was pleased to see him. 'My little girl was thrilled to bits with the photo, Mr Brick. She's seen your last film four times now.'

Charlie smiled, always pleased to hear praise.

The phone was ringing as he entered his suite. It was his agent, Marshall K. Marshall, calling from Hollywood to check certain details about his arrival the following week. He was due to start work on his next film.

They had a short chat about things, and Marshall concluded by saying, 'Charlie, we'll be looking forward to seeing you on the twenty-eighth. Everyone will be at the reception.' There was a slight pause, then: 'Do you want me to line up any broads for you?' He named a couple of well-known bit players. 'No? All right then, I'm sure you can manage on your own.'

They said their goodbyes and Charlie hung up.

He paced around the room restlessly. There seemed to be a conspiracy on everyone's part to annoy him with sly little digs. He could hardly imagine Robert Redford or Michael Caine being asked if they needed to be fixed up with a date. Why him? Oh yes, he knew he wasn't exactly a matinee idol, but he had his own teeth and hair, and a pleasant enough face, rather distinguished-looking really. And since he had lost all that weight for his last picture he was in rather good shape. After all, he was still quite young, and he never had any trouble getting girls to go to bed with him. As a matter of fact it was a job to get rid of them later. A quick look at the watch. 'My God! Is that really the time? I had no idea!' – and eventually they would take the hint and go.

The penthouse suite was cold and impersonal in spite of the wealth of possessions strewn around. Cameras, books, scripts, an elaborate stereo set and stacks of records.

He wouldn't be sorry to leave it: a hotel room never gave one any feeling of permanence.

The phone rang again. He picked it up.

'I dropped the lady home,' said his chauffeur. 'She didn't seem too pleased. Do you need anything else tonight?'

'No.' He yawned. 'Think I'll get into bed. Make it about eight in the morning. Night, George.' He hung up. Almost immediately the phone rang again.

The voice on the other end was female and heavily accented. It said reproachfully, 'Darling, you didn't call, what happened?'

Kristen Sweetzer, a large-bosomed would-be actress he had met at a party the night before and had a scene with. He had been quite smashed, and only vaguely remembered her.

'Oh, hello, love,' he said. 'Sorry, did I say I'd call today?'

'Yes, darling, but I'll forgive you just this once.' There was a short pause, and then, 'Well, darling, when am I going to see you again?'

He suddenly remembered that he couldn't stand her. She reminded him of a bossy gym mistress, always talking in her unattractive guttural accent. 'We'll go back to my place,' she had stated the night before. Not would you like to? Or shall we? And he had gone.

'Listen, love,' he said, 'let's go out to dinner later in the week. I'm a bit tied up these next few days, but I'll call you soon, all right?'

She sighed. 'I was looking forward to seeing you more quickly.'

He stood his ground. 'Thursday or Friday; I'll speak to you then.'

'Very well, but I think you're a naughty man!'

He shuddered at her choice of adjective. 'Yes, love, you're probably right.' He put the receiver down quickly, before she could continue the conversation.

Women never failed to disappoint him. For as long as he could remember they had always managed to let him down. Even his ex-wife Lorna, after all the years they had been together, had finally proved herself to be like all the rest.

The bitter memories of the last few months came rushing back. The accusations on both sides, the days of long silences followed by interminable rows. And worst of all, the utter hate and lack of interest Lorna seemed to project towards him.

He bought her presents, jewellery, furs, a new car. She accepted them all in a cold unthrilled way, the way she accepted him in bed. She had never been of a very passionate nature, but in the last months, before the end, forget it. His very touch seemed to make her shrivel away from him. One memorable night he had been lying on top of her, trying to do what he had to as quickly as possible, when she had started to cry, long stifled sobs. He had withdrawn quickly, and felt there could be no greater distance between them than this.

When he thought of Lorna he imagined that perhaps she was all the things a woman should be. But had he really behaved so badly that she couldn't find it in herself to forgive him?

In the end it had been she who had ended it, not he.

He stopped thinking about the past, and put his mind to the future.

Charlie Brick, a name well-known to millions. He had made a lot of films. A lot of money. Not bad after starting his career touring the variety halls as a comedian for fifteen pounds a week. If he didn't want to, he need not work for the rest of his life. It was a comforting thought.

His mother lived in a handsome house in Richmond with two servants, a car and chauffeur. His two children had money in trust for them. He had insisted. Lorna had not wanted a penny from him, but he had seen that the children were well looked after. On the material side, things couldn't be better.

The new picture should be interesting. The director was an old friend of his. His co-star, Michelle Lomas, was also an old friend, although in a different way. Michelle was a big star, a big voluptuous woman. Discovered in the south of France wearing a bikini at the age of nineteen, now, ten years later, she had an international reputation, both as an actress and a woman. Charlie had first met her five years previously, when his career as a film actor was jogging along nicely and hers beginning to smoulder.

For the first time in a film, instead of being just a comedy actor, he had been given the romantic interest as well. Women everywhere took to him immediately in his new role as lover. If he was good enough to make love to Michelle Lomas, then he was good enough for them.

The letters started to pour in, and his career started to zoom.

It was the beginning of the end as far as Lorna and he were concerned.

The start of his affair with Michelle had changed his life a great deal. In the beginning he just couldn't believe that a famous sex symbol, probably the most famous European sex symbol of that time, could possibly fancy him. But fancy him she had. Most of the arrangements had been manoeuvred by her. She had a husband who conveniently stayed in Paris and appeared only occasionally.

'You are a wonderful man,' she used to purr at him. 'A wonderful lover, the best.'

No one had ever said anything like that to him before. He had always felt inadequate, or, at the very most, average in bed. But Michelle had changed all that: she made him feel like a king.

Of course his marriage suffered. He would return home

from the studio later and later. At weekends, he would always say he had to work. In the end he hardly ever saw Lorna; they just happened to live in the same house.

Occasionally they saw each other long enough for a brief exchange of insults.

Lorna: 'I know you're screwing that big French cow.'

Charlie: 'I don't understand you, how can you say that?'

Lorna: 'You're like a dog after a bitch in heat. What a fool you're making of yourself.'

And so it went on, fight after fight, insult after insult, until one day things really came to a head. Charlie was planning to follow Michelle back to France. She had been gone two weeks following the completion of their film, and they spoke on the phone every day.

'My husband will be away in the south for ten days,' she told him at last. 'He will be leaving tomorrow, you can come then.'

It was unfortunate that this should have coincided with his daughter's birthday, and Lorna had arranged a party. He told her he had to leave immediately for discussions about a film.

She stared at him very long and very hard. 'If you go to her,' she said very slowly, 'then hold yourself responsible for the consequences.'

When he returned things were different. There were no more fights, because Lorna was very rarely there to argue with. She seemed to manage to be just going out whenever he came in. She stayed away from home at night, not even bothering to say where she was.

He didn't question her. He was too involved with planning to see Michelle an often as possible.

His career continued to progress in the best possible way. He found himself in the enviable position of being able to pick and choose what films he would do. His notices were always the best: 'CHARLIE BRICK SHINES AGAIN'; 'BRICK SAVES THE FILM'; 'THE COMIC GENIUS OF CHARLIE BRICK'.

Lorna and he decided to move from their country home to a penthouse in Knightsbridge. The affair with Michelle had more or less finished, due to the fact that they were both working in different countries, and meetings became impossible to arrange.

Of course he realized he had been a fool. It had all been his fault. But the actual thing of making it with Michelle Lomas had been too much for him to miss. He felt, in a funny sort of way, that maybe he and Lorna would be closer because of it.

She didn't feel the same. She was cold and unfriendly in spite of his attentiveness.

He decided to buy the penthouse in the hope that new surroundings would bring them together again.

Lorna did not become enthusiastic about it. She insisted they hire an interior decorator, and left the whole thing to him.

Two weeks after they moved in, Charlie had to go to Spain. When he returned, Lorna had moved out. She had left the children, and a short note saying: *This is all your fault, don't ever blame me.*

She had vanished, and it took Charlie two weeks to find her. A private detective discovered her in a hotel room in Bayswater, in bed with an out-of-work stuntman. The detective took photos, and that was that. One divorce coming up.

At first Charlie couldn't believe that Lorna would leave him for a 'nothing', a 'nobody'. Why, the man wasn't even good-looking.

But Lorna didn't seem to care about anything. 'Go ahead and divorce me,' was all she said, 'it will be a pleasure.'

He was left with the children, a nanny, his chauffeur, and a huge penthouse.

He could hardly believe it. He had finished with Michelle. He wanted Lorna. She was his wife. Couldn't she understand that? He was prepared to forgive her for the stuntman. Surely she should forgive him? For the children alone she should be prepared to try again.

But she didn't want to know.

She moved in with her boyfriend, and shortly afterwards her

lawyer demanded the children. The law being what it was, she got them, but Charlie had ample access.

He sold the penthouse and moved into a hotel suite. He spent long evenings alone, sometimes just staring blankly at a wall, sometimes getting stoned on pot.

There were many girls. One night he would be with a stripper, the next with a married woman whose husband just happened to be out of town.

And they all let him down. One by one they tried to use him in some way or other.

With all of them he told his story: how unhappy he was; how his wife had left him for another man; how life and success only meant something if shared.

The women he saw more than once all half-expected him to propose. He hinted at it all the time. He made them each feel as if she were the only woman he wanted. But he treated them badly, stood them up, never called when he said he would, contacted them only when he felt like it, sometimes at two in the morning. He felt, in a way, he was getting his own back on Lorna. A different woman every night. But none of them meant anything.

It was a big change from the days when he had gone after Lorna. *He* had been the chaser then, and she had certainly given him a hard time.

They had met at a party in Manchester. He could remember his first impression of her very clearly as she was so unlike any other girls he had met. Her hair was pale yellow, pulled severely back into a bun, and she wore huge National Health glasses, which made her face look strangely small and pathetic. She wore no make-up, and was a bit on the short side. No raving beauty by any means, but to Charlie she was lovely.

Within a year they were married and spent their wedding night in the best hotel in Manchester, an extravagance they could hardly afford but which Charlie decided would be worth it. It wasn't.

Although he had been seeing her for nearly a year, it hadn't been an every night thing. Most of the time he was travelling round the country, and their time together had been limited. She lived with her family and had told him firmly and clearly, early on in the relationship, that there would be 'none of that' until she got married.

It was one of the reasons he decided to marry her. He was getting plenty of 'that' elsewhere, and the thought of a 'nice' girl he could marry and have children with was appealing. Besides, she really seemed to care about him. And he certainly cared about her.

At twenty-one Lorna was still a virgin, and from the way she carried on, it seemed she planned to stay that way.

She had undressed in the bathroom, and then refused to come out until all the lights were out. She then made a quick dive into bed, and by the time Charlie had washed and cleaned his teeth, she appeared to be asleep, bundled up beneath the covers with her dressing-gown still on. He slid into bed beside her.

After ten months of seeing each other as often as possible, they were still complete strangers as far as their bodies were concerned.

'Are you asleep?' he whispered, trying to work his hands beneath her tightly tied dressing-gown.

No reply.

After a struggle he reached her breasts. He played with them gently. She lay as if still asleep, eyes tightly shut.

It was very exciting for him to fondle this strange motionless body. After a short while he became so excited that he pulled all the bedclothes away and roughly yanked her nightdress above her waist.

She opened her eyes rapidly and started to protest.

She was the only virgin he had ever been with, and he became so carried away that he forgot about the fact that it was her first time. He bore down, harder and harder, until at last he came to a shuddering, shattering halt, and fell off her exhausted.

She lay there sobbing until gradually the sound of her crying got through to him. He lazily reached out and put his arm around her. 'It's all right,' he said tenderly. 'Nothing to worry about.'

'It's not all right.' Her voice was harsh between her sobs.

'What are you talking about?' He was genuinely surprised. 'I love you. I know it's not good for you the first time, but it's best to do it quickly, get it over with. Next time you'll love it, you'll see.'

But the next time didn't happen for months, and when she finally did consent, it was only under protest.

On the few occasions they made love she lay beneath him as stiff and as still as a board. Perhaps if she had liked it better Michelle would never have happened . . .

Things improved when Charlie got a job in London. It was only in a run-down nightclub, but it was better than trudging from town to town week after week.

Lorna was pleased. They rented a small flat in Old Compton Street. It was no more than one large room, but it was somewhere permanent, more or less. Apart from their unsatisfactory sex life things were fine.

Charlie stayed at the nightclub for three years. He was sort of MC and comedian rolled into one, and although it was a clip-joint, it was a good steady living.

He was seen there one night by an American producer, who arrived backstage. 'I want you to come to my office tomorrow and read for the part of Bernie the Pimp in my new show. It's a small cameo, but important, very showy.'

Charlie started to protest that he wasn't an actor, but the producer thrust his card at him and said it didn't matter, he was just right.

The next day he read for the part and got it.

After six weeks of touring, the show finally came to London, and Charlie with his 'small cameo' part walked off with all the reviews. The show was panned, but he came out of it glowing.

He got himself an agent, and slowly but surely things started to happen. Another show, in which he again stole all the reviews. A small part in a film. A television appearance which turned into a highly successful series. A play. Several more films, and then the big break – a major British comedy film in which he was the star. From there he never looked back.

After his success in the first show, Lorna became pregnant and they had a son – Sean. Then two years later, a little girl – Cindy. They moved into a big house in Wimbledon, and everything was fine until the film with Michelle.

* * *

Charlie wondered how Michelle would greet him. It had been nearly two years since they had last met. He was so fed up with the endless procession of girls who were only too willing to jump into bed with him at the mention of his name or the thought of being seen *out* with him. A woman like Michelle was different. Thank God.

He reached for one of the many scripts stacked on a table. He liked to read everything sent to him. That way there was no chance of missing out on anything good that might go to another actor.

He started to read. Thinking about Lorna had depressed him, but he soon became immersed in the script, and fell asleep while reading.

Chapter Four

Carey St Martin was a tall attractive black girl of twenty-eight. She wore her hair in a sleek Vidal Sassoon bob, and her clothes were smart and gave the impression of being expensive. She smoked twenty cigarettes a day, drove a pale beige year-old Thunderbird, and lived in an elegant three-room apartment high above the Strip.

Carey had done very well for herself.

It was a hot June day and the smog hung like cobwebs over Hollywood.

Carey yawned. What a drag for the agency to pick her to go and persuade Sunday Simmons to get her ass back on the picture. These starlets were all the same. Cute dumb bits of fluff, who had finally laid enough guys to get on film. Carey was proud to think that she had never laid anybody in her career to get where she was today.

She stopped at a red light, and a man in a Lincoln tried to catch her eye. She ignored him, and turned the air conditioning higher. Wow – it was *hot*!

Carey worked for Marshall K. Marshall, one of the biggest agents in town. She had started as a secretary seven years ago, and now she was, and had been for two years, a personal representative, looking after some of the clients he handled. Actually for some time now Carey had been seriously thinking of branching out on her own. What she really wanted to do was personal management. *Carey St Martin, Public Relations & Management*. Incredible!

She parked her car near the Château Marmont where Sunday was staying, and picked up the contract lying on the seat beside her. It stipulated that Sunday Simmons was contracted to work three weeks for Milan Productions from June 3rd to the 24th. Clause three mentioned a nude scene from the waist up, as written in the script.

Carey wondered what Sunday's problem was. She must have read the contract before signing it.

Marshall had told her, 'Get the silly little broad back to the studio – and fast. If she's not back by four she's off the picture, and they'll probably sue. Anyway she won't be able to work anywhere else – stupid bitch!'

Carey put on green-tinted sunglasses and walked into the Château. She was wearing a green linen two-piece dress purchased at Orbach's, a Paris copy.

'Yes?' The little old lady at the desk glanced up.

She asked for Sunday's room. It was funny how the lobby of the Château always seemed like a piece of Hollywood long gone. Shades of *Sunset Boulevard*.

Sunday had a suite on the fifth floor and Carey took the newly decorated elevator. Her mind was dwelling on an office building nearby where she had looked at space the previous week. She really meant to break with Marshall soon.

Sunday answered the door. She was dressed in a short orange muu-muu, her feet were bare, and she still had on her film make-up.

Carey felt a jolt at the sheer magnetism of the girl's face. She held out her hand and said, 'Hi, I'm Carey St Martin. Marshall K. Marshall sent me over to see if we can get things sorted out.'

'I suppose you had better come in.' Sunday's big eyes were cloudy.

She led Carey into the living room, which was strewn with

clothes and half-opened suitcases. Carey couldn't decide if she was packing or unpacking.

'Would you like a Coca-Cola? I'm afraid there's no ice.'

'Lovely. Can I get it?'

'No, that's all right.' Sunday padded into the kitchen.

Carey sat down and opened up the contract. She wondered if Marshall had seen this girl.

Sunday came back in and handed her a glass. 'I'm sorry about all this,' she said quickly. 'I know it makes me look like I'm being difficult, but really, I must explain it to you.'

'Yes, sure,' Carey replied, slightly taken aback. She hadn't expected the apologetic bit, rather the ranting and raving scene. 'By the way, if we can get you back on the set by four, all will be well.'

'I'm sorry, I can't go back. Not unless things are different.'

'You signed a contract, you know.'

'I do know. Everyone keeps on pointing it out to me. But I have certain principles, and one of them is to be treated like a human being – not a piece of prize meat. Let me tell you about it. I'm sure, as a woman you will understand.'

Carey was fascinated by Sunday's low husky voice, and the way she seemed to pick her words so precisely. She sat back and listened as Sunday related the whole story.

At the end she felt quite sorry for her. What a bunch of rat finks most guys were. However, it didn't really merit the walking off the film bit. After all, she wasn't a star, and only stars could get away with action like that. Besides which, there was still the contract to consider.

'Look, honey, I know it's tough. But the guys don't mean any harm, and you did agree to take your clothes off. Now how about if I take you back to the studio, have a word with Abe Stein, and stay there with you?'

Sunday shook her head stubbornly. 'No, I am definitely not going back. Not unless I get a formal apology from Mr Stein and a closed set.'

Carey sighed. 'You're asking the impossible.'

The phone rang and Sunday picked it up. The operator said, 'The *Hollywood Reporter* is on the line, dear, and three other calls from papers holding on.'

She covered the mouthpiece. 'The newspapers. What shall I tell them?'

Carey took the phone. 'Let me deal with it.' How the hell had they picked it up so quickly? She answered questions smoothly. No, Miss Simmons wasn't available for comment. Yes, it would all be sorted out. No, she had not had a fight with Jack Milan. Yes, Miss Simmons would be back on the set later on today.

'Why didn't you tell them the truth?' Sunday questioned after Carey had dealt with all the calls.

'Because, sweetheart, if you're smart we'll take off for the studio right now. You don't want a lawsuit on your hands, do you? And I gather you have plans for working in this town again. After all, everyone takes off their clothes today, there's nothing wrong with it.'

Sunday suddenly laughed. 'Carey, you're a nice girl, very helpful, but we obviously are not going to see eye to eye on this, so I don't think I should waste any more of your time.'

Carey looked at her in surprise. Was she being dismissed? What a laugh! She had expected to walk in here, deal with some hysterical attention-grabbing actress, dump her back at the studios and that would have been that. Instead she was faced with a girl, who seemed to know exactly what she was doing and went about it in a cool and calm fashion.

The phone rang again, and this time Sunday picked it up and kept it.

'Yes, this is she. Yes, that is correct. No, I will not be returning unless I get a formal apology from the director and Mr Milan. I feel that as a woman I have every right to be treated with respect and that . . .'

Carey listened in amazement. She had a funny feeling that Sunday Simmons was going to be a big star. She just felt it.

The interview was perfect. Carey could see it in print now.

Abe Stein and Jack Milan were going to appear as the villains, and Sunday a put-upon innocent.

Oh boy, she had done her duty for Marshall K. Marshall; now how about looking at it from Sunday's point of view, and becoming her personal manager?

This girl was a natural.

Chapter Five

London was going through a once-in-a-blue-moon heatwave, and Charlie was delighted that he had insisted on having a swimming pool built in his mother's Richmond garden.

It was the weekend, and he had arrived to spend the day with his children, who were staying with their grandmother for a few days. It seemed to him that Lorna was only too anxious to get rid of Cindy and Sean whenever she could. It was a bloody shame that the judge hadn't given *him* custody of them. Sean, at eight, was sturdy and tough, and Cindy, two years younger, was a prettier version of her mother.

Charlie lay on a beach-chair next to his mother, watching them splash in the pool. She was a bird-like woman, clad in a two-piece swimsuit that showed off gnarled flesh and drooping bosom. She wore vivid make-up, heavy rouge, green eyeshadow, and a splash of carmine for her mouth. Her hair was mostly hidden beneath a cyclamen scarf, and a cigarette drooped permanently from her mouth.

'I look wonderful for nearly sixty,' she would often proudly announce. And indeed there was always a 'gentleman friend' around.

Charlie adored his mother. Such a character, always happy, living life to its full potential. Serafina Brick, exile from the variety palaces of England.

Charlie had brought a girl with him. Her name was Polly Quinn. At least she didn't talk too much.

She emerged from the house wearing a polka-dot bikini. Bouncy breasts and baby rolls of fat around the middle. She settled herself on the grass, next to Charlie. 'Isn't this weather super?' she stated, and lying on her stomach she unhooked her bra strap. Not another word was heard out of her until lunch.

Natalie and Clay Allen and their three-year-old child arrived at twelve. Clay was one of Charlie's best friends, an ex-actor, now a successful screenwriter. They had known each other from the days of Charlie's first film. Natalie Allen was thin and attractive. She and Charlie had a sort of unspoken 'thing' going. He knew she fancied him, but she being Clay's wife and everything, nothing had actually been done about it. Once at a party when they had both been drunk, they had necked, but Charlie was rather ashamed of this one lapse.

'Hello, my darling,' Natalie said. 'What a divine day. I've simply got to strip off and collapse in the pool.' She kissed him on the cheek and set off for the house to change.

Clay squatted on the grass and indicated the lifeless body of Polly.

'Asleep,' Charlie explained.

Clay winked. 'Hard night, I expect,' he said with a chuckle.

Serafina cackled knowingly, as Cindy and Sean came running over to say hello.

Lunch was served in the garden.

'Who needs Hollywood?' Natalie said, spooning in mouthfuls of strawberries and cream. 'This is heavenly. Clay, darling, why can't we build a pool?'

'Because, my sweet, for the two weeks of summer we get a year it's just not worth it.'

'Charlie thought it was worth it. If he can do it, why can't we?'

There were times, Clay reflected, when Natalie was a pain in the bum.

'I wish you would sit down,' Charlie said to his mother. 'The maid will clear away.'

Serafina gave him one of her girlish smiles, revealing rotten teeth. 'I have too much nervous energy,' she trilled. 'I must keep on the go. That is my secret.'

'What secret?' asked Natalie.

'Eternal youth, my dear. Joy and vitality.'

Natalie looked at Clay, who quickly looked away. He knew she wanted to send the poor old lady up.

'Can we swim, Daddy?' asked Cindy.

'Yes, come on. Want a dip, Poll?'

Polly had finished her lunch. She jumped up and obediently joined Charlie and the children as they raced for the pool.

'What a fat tub of lard,' Natalie remarked. 'Charlie really goes through all the scrubbers.'

Clay had just been admiring Polly's retreating bottom. 'Do you think so?' he asked mildly.

Natalie snorted. 'I suppose you fancy her. You would. Just your type, big breasts and fat ass.'

Yes, not bits of skin and bone like you, Clay thought. Since the birth of their baby, Natalie had dieted away to nothing.

In the pool Cindy sat on Charlie's shoulders, squeaking with joy. He dropped her into the water and she squealed for more. Polly leisurely swam the length of the pool and back again. Then she got out and flopped on the grass.

Charlie joined her. 'Where do you want to eat tonight?' he asked.

'I'm easy.' She spread her arms to the sun.

I know that, he thought. 'Well, let's have a bite at my hotel, then. I'll get them to arrange something on the terrace.'

'Fine.' Her eyes were closed.

Actually he had already arranged everything before leaving. Champagne on ice. Caviar and sour cream, steak and asparagus.

Natalie came walking over. 'What day are you leaving?'

'Wednesday.'

'Only two weeks and we'll be there with you. It seems a shame to leave England with this wonderful weather.'

Charlie grimaced. 'I'll be glad to get away.'

Natalie put a sympathetic hand on his shoulder. 'I know. It's been rough for you.'

His eyes misted over. God, it was good to have friends. 'Yes, you do understand, don't you, love?'

'Of course I do. And anytime you want to talk about it, just don't hesitate to phone me. Clay is always so busy. I have lots of free time. If you want to have lunch or something before you go, call me. Really, Charlie, it would do you good to get it all off your chest. Actually I'm free tomorrow. I'll tell you what, I'll come by the hotel about twelve and we'll have a good old heart to heart.'

'I'm having lunch with my agent. It's awfully sweet of you but—'

'You know,' Natalie stared thoughtfully into space, 'I think I'm one of the few people who actually knew Lorna. We talked quite a bit; she confided a lot in me.'

'Did she?' Charlie was at once interested. 'What about tea tomorrow? I could be back at the hotel by three.'

'I think I could manage that.' Natalie glanced at Polly who was breathing evenly and seemed asleep. 'Only don't mention it to Clay. I'm supposed to be visiting his parents and he'll go all stuffy on me if I get out of it.'

The weather stayed hot for the whole day, and it was past seven by the time Charlie and Polly left.

At the hotel Polly collapsed in a chair and announced, 'I'm absolutely exhausted!'

Charlie looked at her in surprise. As far as he had seen she had spent the day flaked out on the grass, not moving a muscle.

He put on a new Sergio Mendes tape and rang the desk for his messages. His mind was half-occupied wondering if Polly would indulge in a little pot-smoking. He needed something to relax him.

The switchboard told him Mrs Lorna Brick had telephoned twice, and would he please return her call.

Charlie sat quite still by the telephone. Lorna had phoned him. Lorna, who hadn't even spoken to him, except through lawyers, for months. All thoughts of Polly, getting high, and dinner were forgotten.

Perhaps Lorna wanted to come back.

Perhaps he would take her back.

They had been through a lot together, and there were the children to consider. He had known all along that Lorna would see sense. She could fly to Hollywood with him, a sort of second honeymoon.

He glanced over at Polly, sprawled in a chair with her eyes closed.

'Listen, love, I'm rather done in myself. All that sun. Let's take a raincheck on dinner tonight. I'll call you a cab.'

Her eyes flicked open. 'I'm not *that* tired, Charlie.'

But he was already on the phone ordering her a taxi. With Polly gone, he paced the room, wondering how to play it.

Should he be hard and unforgiving, softening as the conversation progressed? Or should he acquiesce immediately and say something like, 'We've both made our mistakes. Let's just forget about it and start afresh.'

He had a moment of doubt as to why Lorna was calling him, but the moment passed and he was sure it could only be for one thing. He dialled her number, feeling elated. It was almost like calling a girl you fancied for the first time.

A man's voice answered, which threw him. Hadn't the berk left yet?

Lorna got on the line, her familiar flat accent cool and impersonal. 'Hello, Charlie, thank you for phoning back.'

'That's all right.' He paused awkwardly, waiting for her to say something.

'How's everything?'

'Well, y'know, fine, I suppose. I just left Cindy and Sean.'

'Oh. Listen, Charlie, I want to ask you a favour.'

Here it came. He breathed deeply. 'Yes?'

'I would have asked your mother but she hardly talks to me any more. The thing is I'm getting married.'

'You're *what?*'

Her voice went very cold. 'Getting married, and I wondered if the children could stay with you in America on July 15th instead of the 29th. You see, I'm going to Africa on location with Jim, and I won't be here when they break up from school. I thought it would be better for them to be with you.'

Charlie was stunned. 'You're not actually marrying that – that stupid prick!'

'Let's not resort to childish insults, please, I can't stand it. Now that we're no longer connected with each other, can't we at least be civil? Can you take the children on that date or not?'

'Yes, I bloody well can. I can take them for good and all, get them out of your clutches.'

Lorna sighed. 'They'll be returning at the end of August as arranged. I shall be back by then.'

'You silly cow. What are you marrying that layabout for? Is he a good screw? You don't even like to do that – so what for?'

'Goodbye, Charlie. My lawyer will take care of the details.' She hung up.

He stared blankly at the receiver. Rotten bitch! How could she possibly marry a lousy stuntman? It just wasn't logical, not when he was prepared to forgive and forget and have her back. Christ Almighty, why had he sent Polly home? Her body was just what he needed now.

It was great being a movie star, wasn't it? Just great. Sitting in a hotel suite all alone and no one anywhere Who gave a fuck. Charming! Perhaps it would have been better if he had stayed plain Charlie – not *the* Charlie Brick.

The phone rang and he wondered abruptly if it was Lorna ringing back to apologize.

It wasn't. It was Kristen Sweetzer.

'I thought you was going to call me?' she said reproachfully. 'We had such a good time together. When shall I see you?'

'Soon, love, soon. But this week's been impossible. I'm going away tomorrow. I'll call you when I get back.'

He wondered why he found it necessary to lie, to try to be nice. He had no intention of ever seeing the big horse again.

'Charlie, you are a *very* bad boy. But I shall forgive you. How long will you be away?'

'Not long. I must rush now. See you soon. Bye.' He replaced the receiver. He hated these women who chased him. They either gurgled with the thrill of being with a film star, or they tried to put him down, insulting him and his films in the hope that this would make them more interesting.

Damn Lorna and her stupid stuntman!

He wondered what Natalie would have to tell him tomorrow, something of interest he hoped. Determined not to spend the evening alone, he phoned his chauffeur and told him to get hold of a good movie they could run.

George, who was enjoying his day off, relaxing in bed with a plump secretary, reluctantly sent her home and did as his boss asked. He had a great job, more a sort of friend than an employee. He had been with Charlie six years, and he prided himself on always being available. With Charlie Brick you never knew what he would want, and whatever it was, George did his best.

Chapter Six

Sunday liked Carey immediately, so when Carey asked if she might become her manager and press representative, Sunday was only too pleased.

She *didn't* want to stay off the movie, and she certainly *didn't* want to go back to Rome, but she was determined that Abe Stein and Jack Milan should apologize.

Once Carey realized that this was something about which Sunday was serious, she suddenly switched sides and came around to her way of thinking.

And it worked. Oh, how it worked.

The next day, Sunday was headlines. Nothing much else was happening. The papers were short of stories, so they played it up. Sunday was the hard-done-by heroine, and Abe and Jack were the big bad villains.

Carey arranged everything. She gave out brief ladylike press releases, arranged the right TV talk-shows, and by the end of the week Sunday was back on the film.

Abe Stein had sent her a short stilted letter, expressing his concern for her feelings and asking her forgiveness. He was furious about having to do it, but realized it was for the best.

Jack Milan threw a huge press party and was exceedingly charming to Sunday. Privately he said to his wife, 'The little bitch could really screw up my reputation.' He had read some

37

of the letters from his fans who were shocked at his treatment of her.

Meanwhile Sunday's part in the film was enlarged, and the nude scene took place on a closed set, with Carey nearby. Abe ordered it printed after one take.

In spite of the fact that Carey had been telling Marshall for some time that she was going to leave, he was nevertheless upset. 'At least give a couple of weeks' notice,' he said. 'What am I supposed to do with Charlie Brick coming in any day, and the deal you were arranging for Salamanda Smith? I'm up to my ears with the TV package.'

'You're the one that taught me to be tough in this business and grab all the chances when they come,' Carey said, perching on his desk and swinging her long legs. 'Sorry, Marsh, but I'm grabbing. Send me Charlie Brick as a client if you like.'

'Listen, baby, who are you kidding? You can't buck the big outfits here, they've got everyone tied up. You'll flop right on your nice round ass.'

'We'll see.' She smiled. 'By the way, now that I'm Sunday Simmons's manager, how would you like her as your exclusive client?'

'Forget it. I have enough to handle. She's just another broad. You'll learn your lesson and come wiggling back for your job.'

'Oh yeah? Don't be so sure. Well, I have lots to do, so I'll be on my way.'

Marshall got up and put his arm around her waist. He was a wide-faced man in his early fifties and he wore the best that Cy Devore had to offer. Nothing could hide the fact that one leg was shorter than the other and that he dragged a heavy club foot.

'You know I wish you luck, sweetheart,' he said. 'And believe me, you're going to need it.'

* * *

When the film was finished, Jack Milan decided to throw a party at his Bel Air mansion. Sunday was invited.

She hated parties. She didn't really enjoy drinking, social small talk, and sly passes from drunk old men whose wives stood not five feet away.

The Hollywood wolf-pack would be present. Following her publicity, she had been approached by various well-known actors for a date, but had turned them all down.

'Who needs it?' she said to Carey. 'I don't enjoy going out unless it's with someone I really want to be with.'

Carey shrugged. 'Your personal life is your own. Do what you like.'

So Sunday did just that. She bought herself a Yorkshire terrier and a stack of books, and each evening she stayed home reading. She remembered her last experience with a man, her husband, and she didn't feel able to cope with any new relationships – however casual. That was why she had fled from Rome.

It all seemed like yesterday, not three years ago, when she was first introduced to Count Paulo Gennerra Rizzo. She had been in Italy seven months, and still thought often of Raf. But Paulo had finally made her forget.

He was a romantic, an expert in the art of making a woman feel completely beautiful. He flattered her constantly, showered her with flowers, looked only into *her* eyes adoringly. When they walked into a restaurant, people stared. What a couple they made! How the press loved them, and how Paulo adored the publicity. They were married three months later.

A few weeks afterwards Sunday discovered the truth about Paulo. She found him in the bathroom one day, his leather belt tied tightly around his arm, his eyes bulging, just about to stick a syringe in a waiting vein.

She cried out in horror. His eyes bulged even further, distorting his arrogant Roman features, then the needle was safely in, and he sucked in his breath quickly and turned his back to her.

She rushed from the room.

When he emerged his face was perfectly composed.

'Don't be frightened, my little one,' he said. 'It is correct for me to inject myself daily under my doctor's orders. I did not wish to tell you before, however now . . .' He shrugged, perfectly at ease.

'But why?' Sunday asked, still horrified by the sight she had seen.

'Oh, depression you know, nothing very serious.'

'I've never seen you depressed.'

'That is because of my good doctor. You see? There is nothing to worry about.'

'Yes,' she said uneasily, 'but why do you have to inject yourself? It's horrible.'

'I could not bother the doctor every day, could I now? So he showed me what to do, and I just do it. See, it is simple. Come, let me take you to the beach for lunch. Make yourself even more *bellisimo*.'

Later they left their apartment and drove in Paulo's Lamborghini to the beach, where they lunched with friends, and then played miniature golf and lay on the sand at Freggenni. Paulo had put her mind at rest. After all, if his doctor had told him to do it, then it must be all right.

She enjoyed the afternoon. She was due to begin work on a film the next day, and it was good to relax.

The new movie started, and this time her voice was not dubbed. She spoke her part in Italian, which took up all her time and attention. Paulo fetched her in the evenings, and they dined with friends. Once home she would collapse into bed, exhausted. It only occurred to her after the film was finished that Paulo no longer made love to her. She also noticed that at night, when he thought she was asleep, he would creep from their bed and prowl around the apartment.

The first night she realized this she fell asleep soon after. But the next night she forced herself to stay awake, and an hour later crept out of bed to look for him.

The apartment door was wide open, and Paulo was nowhere to be seen. She knew he couldn't have dressed without her seeing him, and he couldn't have gone very far with just his pyjamas on, so she waited by the door and surprised him when he came back. He was carrying a package, which he dropped when he saw her, spilling the contents – box after box of glass ampoules, three syringes and two bottles of large green pills.

They stared at each other. 'Why are you up? Why are you spying on me?' he asked coldly, as he bent to pick up the things.

'The door was open,' she stammered. 'Where have you been? What do you need all that for?'

He slammed the door in a fury. Then, eyes narrow and mean, he hit her across the face and screamed, 'Spying bitch!' With that he marched off to the bathroom, locking the door.

She was stunned. Her face blazed red where he had hit her. She bent to the bathroom keyhole and peered in. He was giving himself an injection. Frightened, she ran to bed.

The next morning he appeared charming and gay as if nothing had happened.

Sunday found out who his doctor was and went to see him. The doctor was as shocked as she was. Paulo had never been under orders to administer drugs to himself.

Together they planned to catch him. The next afternoon Sunday went out, only to return immediately with the doctor, who had been waiting downstairs by arrangement. They caught Paulo in the bathroom, the door open, injecting himself in the leg.

In a way he seemed relieved to have been caught. He was giving himself up to five intravenous injections a day, plus massive doses of sleeping pills to calm himself down.

The drug he was taking was methadrine, which after a time could become as addictive as heroin.

The doctor ordered him straight into a private nursing home, and there for the first time Sunday met the man she had married. He lay in bed day after day, his eyes glassy and blank, hardly talking, completely passive.

She visited him every day, and after a few weeks he begged her to get him out, to let him come home. He assured her he was completely cured.

The doctor said no, it was too soon. But she felt so sorry for him just lying there. She felt sure that at home he would become his old self.

She persuaded the doctor to release him, and within two days at home he had made a miraculous recovery. He was his old charming assured self.

Of course he was back on the drug.

The next two years were a nightmare. She became his nurse, enemy, spy, welfare visitor, and jailer. And he went from doctor to doctor, hospital to nursing home, with intervals in between at home – supposedly cured. But she would always discover the truth, and back to another doctor he would go.

Her life became an existence of visiting him, or if he was home, watching him. She also had to work as much as she could, for suddenly there was no money, and his family didn't care to be involved.

The end came one morning when she awoke uneasily. Paulo had been home a week, off the drug, just lying in bed staring at the ceiling, his once-handsome face unshaven and drawn. Now he was not beside her.

She ran first to the bathroom. The door was locked. She knocked and called his name, but there was no reply. She looked through the keyhole, he was lying on the floor quite still.

Panic stricken she called the doctor, and together they broke the door down.

Paulo was dead. Killed by a massive overdose.

At the inquest they called it accidental death. In her own mind Sunday wasn't sure.

She endured the gossip for a few weeks, and then the opportunity to go to Hollywood arose and she leaped at the chance.

Rome no longer held the same magic for her.

* * *

'Look, I really think you should go to this party of Jack's,' Carey said for the second time.

Sunday was staring out of the window cuddling her little dog. 'Did you know my husband killed himself?' she asked.

'What?' Carey looked at her in amazement. They had never discussed Sunday's former life although Carey knew all about it from newspaper clippings.

'Yes.' Sunday nodded dreamily. 'How will that fit into my big publicity build-up?'

'Look, honey,' Carey put a hand lightly on her shoulder, 'I know about your past and that's what it is – past. It's not normal for you to shut yourself up here. You're a beautiful girl, you've got to get out and enjoy yourself. Apart from which, it will be good for your image to be seen. Just Jack's party to start off with, huh?'

'I suppose you're right,' Sunday said. 'OK, I'll go.'

'Great! There's a good girl. Now what are you going to wear that will knock 'em all cold?'

Chapter Seven

Herbert Lincoln Jefferson polished the faded crinkled leather of his best brown shoes. He had had them eight years but they still gave good service.

Marge shuffled into the kitchen to fetch herself a beer from the fridge. She was chewing on a chicken leg.

'You want me to do that?' she asked mouth full of chicken.

Herbert shook his head. She asked him every night, and every night he said no.

Marge pulled the ring on the beer can and some of the liquid sprayed out over Herbert's shoes, which he was cleaning on the table.

'Gee, I'm sorry, Herbie,' she said nervously, grabbing at a corner of her dress and attempting to rub the shoes.

He gave her a shove.

She looked at him with hurt eyes. 'I'm sorry, Herbie, I said I'm sorry . . .' She took her can of beer and left the kitchen.

Muttering under his breath Herbert finished polishing the shoes. He put them on and admired them, one foot at a time. Then he put on his jacket, patted the letter in the inside pocket, and left the house on his way to the bus stop.

He liked working nights for the Supreme Chauffeur Company. He hated the daytime jobs, boring trips to the airport and back.

He wondered who he would be driving tonight. The previous week had been very dull, just old married couples. He liked to get single actors with their dates. They were the interesting ones. They were the ones that kept you waiting outside the girl's house or apartment at the end of the evening while they screwed her. Once he had managed to watch; the girl lived on a deserted hill in a big glass house, and she and her date had gone inside and started right at it in the middle of the floor. Herbert had crawled to the bottom of a glass pane and seen the whole thing. He wrote to that girl regularly once a week.

The bus arrived and he climbed aboard. It was a hot sweaty ride and he was pleased to get off. He hurried to his place of work, posting the letter on the way.

'Hello, Jefferson.' The man behind the desk nodded to him. 'Tonight you're driving Sunday Simmons. She's to be picked up at the Château Marmont at eight and taken to a party at Jack Milan's. You know his house in Bel Air?'

Herbert nodded.

'You're to wait. Take the number four black Caddy. It needs gas and a wash.'

He nodded again, pleased with his assignment. He had read about Sunday Simmons. She was the one who wouldn't show her tits or something. Now he would have a chance to look her over and see if she was worth writing to.

Chapter Eight

Charlie got back to his hotel just after three. Natalie Allen was waiting in the lobby.

'Sorry, love,' he said. 'You know the Elephant at lunch-time, it's like a meeting of Equity. Come on up.'

Natalie had been to the hairdressers, and her short dark hair hugged her head like a cap. She was wearing a yellow linen suit, and Charlie couldn't help thinking how attractive she was. Clay was a lucky fellow.

'You must have heaps to do before you go,' she remarked.

'Not really. I'm all set. George will pack everything.'

'Oh yes, the trusty George. Are you taking him with you?'

'Of course. I don't know what I'd do without him.'

'Lorna didn't like him, you know.'

'Didn't she?' He looked surprised. What was there not to like about George? And Lorna had never said anything to him about disliking George.

'Yes, she was jealous. I mean he's more like your closest friend than a servant.'

He winced at the word servant. He didn't like it. As far as he was concerned George worked for him because he wanted to, not because he had to.

'Do you want some tea or a drink or what?'

They were in the suite, and Natalie took off her jacket and

sat on the couch. 'A drink, I think. A Pernod with masses of ice.' She leaned back. 'Do you know this is the first time we've been alone together since that party?'

He had not been aware of that fact, but was embarrassed thinking about it. Clay and Natalie had had a fight, and Clay had gone off in a fury. Then Charlie had tried to console her, and ended up kissing her. Fortunately, Clay had come back, but Charlie felt badly about the whole thing. You didn't go around grabbing other people's wives, especially your best friend's.

'I'm sorry about that night,' he said, 'let's just forget about it. I was drunk, and so were you.'

She smiled thinly. 'But I don't want to forget it. I enjoyed it, didn't you?'

'Of course I did. But you know, love, it's a bit tricky, Clay's my friend, and I want it to stay that way.' Charlie was disturbed at the direction the conversation was taking. He had thought Natalie was going to talk about Lorna.

'Clay's a shit,' Natalie said firmly. 'A lousy, egotistical shit! I know all about the little girls he bangs. Why shouldn't *I* have some fun? You do fancy me, don't you, Charlie? Well, of course, I know you do.' She got up slowly and came towards him.

He backed away warily.

She wound her arms around his neck and started to kiss him.

How the hell did he get out of this?

'I've always liked you,' she whimpered. 'Lorna was never any good for you. I always felt something between us – something special, didn't you?'

The phone rang, and with relief he untangled himself and went to answer it.

It was George, phoning from the lobby. 'I thought if you didn't need me for an hour I'd pop round to Hayward's and pick up your suits.'

'What, *now?*' Charlie said loudly in an annoyed voice.

'I don't have to, I just thought—'

'Oh, God. All right. I suppose I'll have to. I'll be right down.'

He hung up on an amazed George.

'What's the matter?' Natalie asked.

'Business. Some bloody appointment I clean forgot about. Sorry, love, what a drag.'

'Shall I wait?'

'God knows how long it will take, you'd better not.'

She sighed. 'Whoever invented phones should be shot.'

'You're right.' He helped her on with her jacket and hustled her to the door.

'About us,' Natalie said. 'What's going to happen?'

'We'll figure something out,' he replied, making a mental note never to be caught with Natalie Allen alone again.

'Goodbye, darling.' She kissed him. 'Don't forget, we'll be in Hollywood two weeks after you. Wait for me.'

He nodded. Charming! Clay wasn't so lucky after all.

* * *

At the airport Charlie was stoned. He was petrified of flying and could only board a plane completely out of his mind. Before leaving for the airport he had smoked two joints, and the plane now looked like a beautiful big bird ready to receive him. He smiled benignly at the photographers, pantomiming funny faces for them, and waving his horn-rimmed glasses in the air.

George hissed at him. 'You know you don't like photos without your glasses on.'

'Oh, yes, very very factual,' Charlie replied in his best Indian imitation.

'Bye, Charlie – good luck,' one of the photographers called.

A pretty air hostess arrived to escort them to the V.I.P. lounge.

'The flight will be boarding in ten minutes,' she said. 'Can I get you a drink?'

He nodded. 'A double scotch, my dear.' He needed it.

Once airborne he fell into a deep sleep.

Chapter Nine

Jack Milan's house stood in acres of grounds, surrounded by electrified fences. At the entrance there was a small guard-house. Nobody had access to the main house unless the guard said so. This was due to the fact that Jack had five children, and in the past there had been several kidnapping threats. Although the kids were all grown up now, he was taking no chances.

Sunday sat nervously in her car while the chauffeur thrust her invitation at the guard. Then the car swept up a long drive to a big white colonial mansion.

Sunday felt nervous. First she had decided Carey was right, and she should have brought an escort. Second she was sure she wouldn't know anyone. And third, since Paulo's death, she hated to be among lots of people. In fact, she dreaded the whole evening.

She looked quite fantastic in a long black sequin outfit that she had had made for a film in Italy. She wore nothing underneath, and her body was shown off to great advantage.

A butler greeted her, and led her through the house and out onto the sloping floodlit terraces at the back.

'Miss Sunday Simmons,' he announced through a loud-speaker system, and left her standing there.

The many people drinking on the terraces all turned to stare. Her name was already known.

A plump fortyish woman came over extending her hand. 'Hi, Sunday dear, I'm Jack's wife, Ellie. It's lovely to see you. Come along, and I'll introduce you around.'

Sunday immediately liked the warm plump Ellie. She followed her to a group of people and soon found herself mingling easily into the small talk.

It wasn't going to be too bad. After dinner she could slip quietly away. She would have done her duty.

She was chatting to a bleached-blond actor, a well-known queen and an elderly red-headed woman who kept one protective hand on the queen's arm in case he should flit off, when a girl said, 'Sunday. How great to see you. How *are* you?'

She looked at the girl. Very trampy with long blonde hair, and a busty figure crammed into a shiny red dress. Sunday knew she had seen her somewhere before, but she couldn't for the life of her think where.

'Hello,' she said.

The girl laughed. 'Don't you remember me? Dindi Sydne – Prince Benno's friend. We all used to go to the beach together in Rome. You and Paulo – gee, I'm sorry, I guess I shouldn't mention him. It was so awful what happened. Benno was heartbroken. Anyway, you remember me, don't you?'

'Yes, of course.' Vaguely she remembered her.

'Well, here I am. Back in my home town,' Dindi continued. 'It just didn't work out with Benno. Anyway, I was offered a movie, so here I am again. Would you believe I had to go all the way to Rome to get a job *here*? Ain't life funny? *You* look great. Are you having a good time? Your publicity's wonderful. Hey, did you see Steve Magnum yet? I'd love to meet him. Do you know him?'

Sunday shook her head. She knew who he was, of course. A film star, swinger, four-times married (all to famous ladies) millionaire. At least that's what one read about him.

'He's a great friend of Jack Milan's,' Dindi said, 'so I guess *you'll* meet him. I haven't even met Jack yet. My date is a real creep cameraman. Doesn't know anyone. I don't know how the hell he got invited in the first place. By the way, where are you staying? Let's get together.'

'The Château Marmont. But I really don't go out much and—'

'We'll soon change that. I can fix you up with some live ones. Things can get a little dull around here if you just mix with the importants. Agreed, that's a good scene, but a little action on the side doesn't hurt. I'll call you, must rush now, there's a director over there I've had my eye on for weeks.'

Dindi wriggled off in her tight dress, and Sunday found herself standing alone. She looked around. The party was in full swing. Soon, she hoped, they would serve dinner and then her ordeal would be over.

She felt very much alone, but that had been a constant feeling ever since Paulo's death. In the few months beforehand, she had watched him degrade himself. Would she ever forget the lengths he had gone to in hiding the drugs from her? Burrowing beneath the tiles in the bathroom like a dog, hiding little stores under the mattress, in the light fixtures, even on the narrow ledges outside the windows of their apartment. In the end she had been thinking about divorce, and the week before he died had threatened him with it. He had cried like a baby, making her fervent promises of how good he would be, how this time he was cured.

'Sunday, dear,' Ellie Milan bore down on her, 'I'm putting you at a table with Jack. Table number two, you'll see a place card for yourself. I'm trying to get everyone seated.'

She smiled. 'Thank you.' She followed the groups of people drifting towards the tables.

Dindi was sitting earnestly at a table, her hand laid casually on top of a fat man's arm. His eyes were glued firmly down her neckline.

'Hi there, Sunday.' Jack Milan waved at her from table two.

She went over, returning his smile and shaking hands with the people already sitting there, to whom he introduced her. Abe Stein was among them, with a horse-faced wife who glared.

She was seated next to Jack on one side, with two vacant chairs on the other.

'You look wonderful,' he said. 'And great in the dailies too. I understand Radiant are giving you a contract.'

'Well, they have offered me one, but I'm not taking it. I don't believe in long-term contracts, they're too restricting.'

There was a short shocked silence from everyone.

Abe said, 'I'd take it if I were you.'

'*I* haven't done too badly,' Jack said mildly. 'I've been with Radiant seventeen years.'

'No, the kid's right.' Steve Magnum had appeared, accompanied by his latest steady, Angela Carter. He sat down next to Sunday. 'Forget it. Long contracts are a thing of the past. Radiant's about the only studio left who sign people, and they don't know their ass from a hole in the ground. Don't let them talk you into anything, kid.'

'I won't,' she replied, trying to stop herself from staring at him. His face was so familiar. Back in Rio, when she was still at school, he had been her favourite film star.

Steve Magnum had aged well. At fifty he wore his years with style. He barely made five foot eleven and he was very thin – his unkinder critics described him as scrawny – but his face still had the same bony, hungry quality that had made him a huge star some twenty-five years before. Steve Magnum was a legend in his own time. Women were mad about him. Even his four ex-wives never tired of saying they would always have him back. He had been single eight years now, and the newspapers and columns were always speculating about who would be the next Mrs Magnum. There were many candidates, but most people in the know bet there wouldn't be another Mrs Magnum at all. Some said he might even go back to his first wife, by whom he had three children.

'Hey now,' he looked Sunday over with his famous pale blue eyes, 'you've handled yourself pretty well so far. Came into town and caused quite a stir. Even told old Abe and Jack where to get off.'

Jack laughed, but Abe scowled and tried to ignore his wife who was nudging him to say something.

'Carey St Martin is looking after me. She's terrific. I'm sure I have her to thank for all the offers I'm getting. If it wasn't for her I'd probably have been out of here on the next plane to Rome.'

Angela laughed prettily. 'How sweet. All because of some itsy-bitsy nude scene. Darling, they're all the rage now. If you want to get on in this business, you have to learn to take your clothes off.' She snaked an arm around Steve and gazed at him adoringly.

'Yeah, honey,' Steve said, 'and you *certainly* know how to do that. On *and* off the screen.'

During the meal Steve kept on talking to Sunday. She was well aware of Angela on his other side, listening to every word and trying to join in.

Angela had been his steady girlfriend for three months and she had high hopes of continuing the role, perhaps even making it permanent. She was infuriated by Steve's interest in Sunday. What idiot had sat him next to her, and what the hell was all that slop she was coming out with about principles and good scripts?

She could hardly believe her ears when she heard Steve say to Sunday, 'You know you'd be great as the rich sexy broad in my new movie. Want to test?'

Angela had hoped that Steve was going to let her do that part. It wasn't a star role, but it was good. She had hinted that she would like to do it, but Steve had brushed her off. And now he was practically offering the part to this unknown bitch! And the unknown bitch was replying, 'I'm sorry. I don't test. There are quite a few Italian films I am in that you could run. I don't believe in testing.'

Steve looked at Jack, and they both burst out laughing.

'Sonofabitch!' Steve said. 'You were right. This broad is different.'

Chapter Ten

Marshall K. Marshall left his custom-built white Rolls Royce with the doorman at the Beverly Hills Hotel, and limped into the lobby.

Actors – lousy actors. They were becoming so damn demanding. They seemed to want to have a say in everything. He remembered the days when all they did was sign their contracts and get on with it.

Marshall had arrived at the hotel to be present at a meeting between Cy Hamilton, Jnr – producer of *Roundabout* – and Charlie Brick, star of said picture. The meeting was due to the fact that they could stall Charlie no longer. He certainly wasn't a fool, and it was becoming increasingly obvious that Michelle Lomas was not going to appear.

Already they were shooting around her, and the previous day Charlie had stalked off the set, leaving a message for Cy that unless Michelle was there he wasn't doing another day's work. So the time had come to tell him that Michelle Lomas was pregnant, a fact confirmed yesterday. She was confined to her house by Lake Lugano and wouldn't be budging, on doctor's orders, for nine months.

Marshall carried a small briefcase in which were photographs and brief biographies of his ideas for replacements.

The main thing was to convince Charlie that it was

worthwhile to go ahead with the picture without Michelle. He had every contractual right to walk out if he wanted to. It was up to Marshall as his agent to persuade him not to.

* * *

In his tastefully decorated pale beige suite with two colour televisions going full blast, Charlie paced the floor wearing a white towelling bathrobe and brown Gucci slippers.

George hovered respectfully in a corner, one eye on the television and one on Charlie. A rented secretary sat at a table, day-dreaming about being discovered. And another table held a spread of eggs, toast, fruit and coffee, all untouched.

'You should eat something,' George said mildly.

Charlie grunted, still pacing. His work was more important than anything else, and he was incensed that they should have done this to him. Without Michelle the film wouldn't be the same. Where the hell was she? Why had she backed out?

He wasn't going to do it. He would go back to London and screw 'em. They weren't going to fob him off with some replacement.

Six boring days he had been waiting for Michelle, and apart from a press party, where he was asked a string of inane questions, he hadn't been anywhere except to the studio.

Of course, he had had a stack of invitations. Hollywood was always delighted to see a new face in town. Any excuse to throw a party. Several well-known hostesses vied with each other to be the first to have a dinner party for him. This time they were out of luck. He said no to everything. He didn't believe in a social life until the film was under way.

There was a knock at the door and Marshall K. Marshall limped in. In spite of the air conditioning he was sweating profusely. He rarely left his office during the day, only in emergencies.

'You look great,' Marshall said. 'Even thinner than last week.'

'Yes, I am managing to keep the old weight down.' Charlie smiled. He knew it was only supreme willpower that kept him looking as good as he did. Four weeks of normal eating and he would be back to the fatty he once was.

'You're not going to like this,' Marshall said. 'Cy's not exactly ecstatic about it. But Michelle is expecting a baby. She's got us by the balls.'

Charlie slumped into a chair. That was the last thing he'd expected.

'We got a doctor's written confirmation yesterday – so that's why there's been all the shillyshallying. Who would imagine Michelle would get herself knocked up? Not only knocked up, but thrilled about it. Cy wanted her to go ahead and do the movie anyway – after all, it won't notice for another four or five months – but no, she ain't taking no risks. Sorry, Charlie, that's it. Look Cy's in a bind, if you walk out it will be bad, and I know you *can* walk out, and personally I wouldn't blame you. But listen, baby, if we can find a replacement – someone you OK, and you stay, then I reckon it will be another ten per cent of the gross, and that ain't chicken feed. What do you think?'

The rented secretary sat straight in her chair, trying to listen over the noise of the television. George still lingered in the corner.

Charlie closed his eyes and tried to think. Another ten per cent. Not bad. But who could replace Michelle?

As if reading his thoughts Marshall said, 'We could have a re-write. Instead of the parts being equal, build yours up and cut hers down. It would be your movie, all the way. Can we turn that goddam television off?'

'George, turn it off,' Charlie said, his mind racing. 'And I don't need you, dear' – to the secretary – 'come back tomorrow, same time.'

The rented secretary got up, smoothed down her mini, and wriggled past Marshall. Perhaps he would discover her. He didn't even give her a glance.

At the door she paused, trying to decide whether to tell

them she was an actress, but George blocked her path and ushered her out.

She wriggled off, angry at not having been discovered.

Charlie said slowly, 'It sounds good. What about Cy? Has he agreed?'

Marshall felt relief. 'He will.'

* * *

By the time Cy Hamilton Jnr arrived, fresh from an argument with his recent third wife, Charlie and Marshall had sorted everything out.

Cy was a likeable man, but he had a steely temper that appeared on occasion.

'You bastards – you're holding me to ransom,' he said. But eventually he agreed.

All that remained to be settled was a new actress for the role, and they all had different ideas.

'Magda Seal,' Charlie said.

'Forget it, she's booked solid.'

'Mirielle Montane from Cy.

'No tits – skinny, useless.'

'Anna Karl.'

'Too old.'

They discussed the possibilities, eventually running out of foreign actresses and deciding that the girl could be any nationality.

'How about a new girl?' Marshall suggested, opening his briefcase and bringing out pictures. 'Sunday Simmons.'

'Sunday what?' asked Charlie.

'Simmons. You've seen her, Cy, haven't you? Great body, big boobs, good publicity potential.'

Cy nodded. 'Not a bad idea. Can she act?'

Marshall shrugged. 'Who knows? We could run some film of her – she's in the new Jack Milan.'

'I don't want an unknown,' Charlie said.

'Take a look at her pictures,' Marshall replied. 'She's a wild-looking broad.'

Charlie thumbed through the stills, lingering on one that showed Sunday in the nude scene with Jack Milan. He felt suddenly aroused. My God, he realized it was at least two weeks since he'd had a woman. Have to do something about *that*.

'She's gorgeous,' he said. 'What's her phone number?'

'Yeah, what is her phone number?' Cy asked, smiling slowly.

Marshall laughed. 'Shall we run film on her?'

They both nodded.

'Now another idea I had,' Marshall said, 'and don't blow your stacks – is Angela Carter.'

'Angela Carter!' Cy exclaimed.

'Yeah, Angela. She's a name. I think I can get her to test.'

Charlie nodded. 'OK with me. It sounds like a good idea.'

They decided on another three possibles, and since time was at a premium, they arranged to meet at eight o'clock at Cy's house, where he would have film on all five girls to show in his private screening room.

As Marshall was leaving, Charlie called him to the side and said something he hadn't wanted to. 'Can you fix me a girl for later?'

'Sure. Any preferences?'

Charlie shook his head, already regretting asking Marshall. But after all, he didn't know anyone in town and he didn't want someone from the studio sending him a hooker.

'Leave it to me,' Marshall said, limping off, relieved to be on his way back to the office.

Chapter Eleven

'I love drive-ins!' Sunday exclaimed, examining the menu on a stand by the car window. 'I want two hamburgers and a chocolate malt.'

Carey laughed. 'You'll get fat.'

'I don't care. I think I'm beginning to like it here.'

'I'm not surprised.' Carey pressed the buzzer on the carside speaker and gave their order. 'If I was in your position I'd be crazy about it. I mean, let's just consider things. You get into town with a small part in a Jack Milan movie. You march out of that like a star, grab all the headlines – march back in again, plus apologies all round. Meet Steve Magnum at a party. He showers you with roses and invitations all week long. You refuse to even date him – Mr Number-One Hollywood Catch. And now today a firm offer for you to be in his new movie. Six glorious weeks in Acapulco. Wow – no wonder you're beginning to like it.'

Sunday smiled. 'Thanks to you. If it wasn't for you I would have gone back to Rome.'

'Thanks to *you*, kiddo, I got myself out of that agency job, and now things are really swinging for me. I'm picking up new clients every day. Do you know Angela Carter called me yesterday and wants to know if I'd be interested in handling her. She must hate you.'

Sunday frowned. 'I don't know why. Life is too short to go around hating people.'

A waiter in tight white jeans came bearing two trays with their order. 'Aren't you Sunday Simmons?' he asked in a feminine voice, peering through the window.

She nodded.

'Lots of luck, dear, my friend and I think you're lovely. We saw you on TV the other night.'

'Thank you.'

Carey waited until the boy had gone, then said, 'Fame, baby, that's fame.'

Sunday munched on her hamburger. 'Delicious!' she exclaimed.

Carey picked daintily at her cottage cheese and fruit salad. 'You really are an unusual girl. I ask you out for a celebration lunch, thinking maybe the Polo Lounge or Bistro and where do you want to go? A drive-in! I shall be glad to pack you off to Acapulco.'

'When am I supposed to leave? And when do I get a copy of the script? And don't forget the clause about no nude scenes.'

'I'm hardly likely to forget that. They're sending a script to your hotel today. You start costume fittings, hair and make-up tests next week. They want you to leave July tenth. What are you going to do about Steve Magnum?'

Sunday smiled sweetly. 'Nothing.'

'Oh God, you're too much. Why not go out with him? He's not going to eat you – and even if he was – wowee, baby, I hear he's the greatest!'

'I don't want everyone saying the only reason I'm in his movie is because I'm having an affair with him. If he's that anxious to go out with me he'll just have to wait until Acapulco, and then we'll see.'

She spoke calmly, but she had given a lot of thought to Steve Magnum. She *was* attracted to him, but she knew his reputation with women, and instinct told her that the only way to hold his interest beyond a few dates was to play it very cool indeed. Also she was frightened of what a relationship with Steve Magnum would involve. There had only been two men in her life – Raf and Paulo – and she wasn't yet sure if she were ready to cope with a third.

'I think Stevie the lady-killer has met his match,' Carey said with a laugh. 'Only don't under estimate him – he's been play-ing the boy-meets-girl game for a long long time. Whatever you do, don't *ever* take him seriously – there are more hearts broken by Magnum than convertible cars in Southern California!'

'I've got the message, thank you.'

They called for the check and Carey drove her car down La Cienega to Sunset, dropping Sunday at the Château.

'When you get back from Mexico we should really find you a house or apartment, and you've got to get a car.'

'I think I'd like a little place at the beach.'

Carey shrugged. 'You're impossible. That's just not chic. However, knowing how definite you are, I'll ask around and see what's available. Talk to you later. Oh, by the way, we'll break this to the press about the movie tomorrow, so stay avail-able.' She waved and drove off.

Sunday walked slowly inside. She had decided to spend the afternoon by the pool. It was so hot that her thin cotton trou-sers and shirt were sticking to her body.

The old lady at the desk beckoned her over. 'There's more flowers for you, Miss Simmons. And a letter from England. I wonder if I might have the stamp? My grandson collects them, you know. And there's a young woman here for you, she's sitting over there.'

Sunday looked over in surprise and saw a girl, flopped out in a chair, sunglasses shielding her eyes. 'Who is she?'

The old lady reached for a message pad. 'Dindi Sydne.'

'Oh!' Sunday remembered her from Jack Milan's party. The girl who had known Paulo. What on earth was she doing here?

Sunday took the flowers and letter, carefully peeling off the stamp and handing it to the old lady. It was from her aunt; she would read it later.

The note with the two dozen roses read: '*When are you going to change your mind? S.M.*'

She walked over to the girl in the chair and nudged her gently.

The girl sat up like a startled rabbit. 'Shit!' she exclaimed loudly. 'Sunday! Oh, and you've brought me flowers – how nice!' She stood up. She was wearing tight hipster orange pants, and a brief sweater. Her exposed midriff was very tanned. 'Guess what happened to *me*? I was driving along Sunset in my beautiful T-Bird and the frigging little monster goes and blows up! Fortunately it happened not two blocks from here, right by a gas station, and this adorable mechanic with muscles like Superman is fixing it for me. I remembered you lived here, so I figured I'd while away the afternoon with you. He's going to drop it back here when it's fixed. You should see him – a real sex machine!'

Excuses leapt to Sunday's lips, but she hated to lie, and anyway, the girl was only trying to be friendly.

'That's fine. I thought I might sit by the pool, you're welcome to join me.'

'Yeah, great. I'll borrow a bikini. My tan could do with a booster.' She examined her stomach.

'I'm just going upstairs, I'll bring you down a bikini.'

Dindi linked arms with her. 'I'll come with you.'

Upstairs, Limbo, Sunday's little dog, came bounding to greet them. The rooms were stuffy and Sunday turned up the air conditioning.

Dindi wandered around, picking up everything to inspect. 'Who are all these flowers from?' she asked.

'Just a friend,' Sunday replied shortly.

'A very good friend,' Dindi said with a chuckle. 'I adore good friends. I once made it with a guy on top of six dozen red roses. It was the end, very sexy. Only he couldn't come, said the smell put him off. Some guys are so weird.'

'Here.' Sunday handed her a green and-white bikini. Dindi stepped out of her pants and sweater, revealing that she wore nothing underneath. She put on the bikini. 'Man, you've got big boobs – give me some cotton wool to pad this thing out. I wish I had a big pair, guys really dig that.'

Dindi was not exactly flat-chested, Sunday had observed.

They rode down in the elevator and walked the short distance to the pool. It was nearly deserted except for an aged woman in a huge flowered hat, and a muscle-bound man stretched out and covered with oil.

'Not much happening here,' Dindi said, a note of disappointment in her voice. 'You should move to the Beverly Hills, the pool there is always full of action.'

'Listen, Dindi, let's get one thing clear. I *am not* looking for any action. I enjoy peace and quiet.'

Dindi lifted orange-tinted sunglasses and stared in disbelief. 'Sorry, I didn't realize I was with such queenly company. For someone who doesn't want to swing, you certainly look the part. Do you want me to go? Buzz away and leave you to your peace and quiet?'

'No, of course not. I just wanted you to know, that's all.'

'So I know. Hey, I'm going to ask that guy to lend me some of his oil.' And she was off.

Sunday decided she quite liked her. She was loudmouthed, nosey, and obviously a pushover with men, but she had a certain honest charm.

She came back after ten minutes, triumphantly bearing a bottle of sun oil. 'That's Branch Strong,' she announced. 'He's in from New York to do a test. He swings both ways.'

'How do you know?' Sunday asked curiously.

'I have a feeling for these things. Anyway he was brought in by Sam Plum who is *the* faggot agent.'

Sunday rubbed some oil on her body and lay back. It was good to get to know people. Carey had said she was strange because she stayed alone all the time. Well, Carey didn't know the full story about Paulo. About the hurt he had left behind,

63

and the lingering guilt – which she knew she had no reason to feel, but couldn't help.

Soon Branch Strong (formerly Sydney Blumcor from the Bronx) came lumbering over. He had a smooth good-looking face without a trace of character.

'Hello there, little ladies,' he said. 'Hot enough for you?'

'Yeah.' Dindi grinned. 'Hey, Branch, this is Sunday Simmons.'

'Pleased to meet you,' he said, rubbing oily hands over his muscle-bound stomach. He thought he had never seen such a beautiful girl as Sunday, and the body on her – wowee – what a couple they would make!

'When do you test?' Dindi asked.

'Tomorrow,' he replied nervously. 'Keep your fingers crossed.'

'You bet.' she giggled. 'I'd cross my legs too but that would be *too* boring.'

Sunday stood up. 'I think I'll swim.' She walked to the deep end of the pool and dived off the low board. Then she swam a length under water.

Branch watched admiringly. 'She's really something,' he said with a note of awe.

'Yeah,' Dindi agreed. 'But a bit uptight – no action – you understand?'

'Huh?'

'Forget it.' She decided Branch Strong was a big good-looking hunk of blond idiot. He was still watching Sunday in the pool, his mouth hanging slackly open, his tongue nervously jumping up and down, Dindi had to admit that Sunday certainly was a fantastic-looking girl, but she didn't seem to have much personality, a bit of a drag really. Dindi wondered what she would say if she told her about the scene she and her Roman boyfriend, old Prince Benno, had had with her faggy husband, the one who had knocked himself off. Three days locked up in a Rome hotel room. What a time that had been. Only a few weeks before he killed himself.

Sunday emerged from the pool and lay down. 'It's absolutely lovely, you must go in.' She draped her wet hair over the back of the chair and closed her eyes. The sun was hot, and as it dried the tiny rivulets of water on her body, she fell into a light sleep.

Branch didn't take his eyes off her.

Chapter Twelve

Herbert Lincoln Jefferson smiled contentedly, displaying one black tooth amongst a row of off-white ones. For someone so obsessed with bodily cleanliness, he held the inside of his mouth in complete disregard, cleaning his teeth only when he remembered, which wasn't often.

He stood under the rusty shower, soaping his thin hairless body and grinning all the while.

It had taken him two weeks but at last he had done it. He had written a letter to Sunday Simmons of such poetic obscenity that the mere thought of it excited him – in spite of the fact that he had only five minutes previously ejaculated into a plastic bag to be enclosed with the precious letter.

He stroked his fine upstanding member with soap and felt very proud of himself. What a man he was! What joy and thrills he could give to any woman!

The wait had been worth it. As soon as he saw Sunday he had realized that this was the girl for him. To hell with Angela Carter and all the other past recipients of his letters. This was the woman he dreamed about. Perfect, from her tawny mane of hair to her rounded sensual body. Even her feet, peeking at him through gold sandals, were sexy.

On the drive to the Milan house he watched her in the rear-view mirror. Once her big browny-yellow eyes met his, and he coughed unobtrusively, making some remark about the weather.

Since that night he had hoped to be assigned to drive her again, but no such luck. So he had started to compose a letter. His early efforts did not meet with his approval. The first letter had to be something special, something that would intrigue and excite her so much that she would want to meet the man who could write with such explicit passion and know-how.

And now, at last, he had written such a letter. A masterpiece. The crowning touch being instructions as to what she should do with his plastic-bag offering. Tomorrow he would sit and imagine her reading it and following his instructions. He would fill another plastic bag and write another wonderful letter, explaining how the second bag was filled as he thought of her lovingly dealing with the first.

'Herbie.' The whiney voice of his wife was accompanied by a knock on the bathroom door and a rattling of the handle. 'Herbie, I wanna go to the john. Can I go to the john, please? You've been in there an hour.'

The big fat cow *would* have to spoil these few pleasant moments for him.

'Just a minute, dear,' he called back mildly. He wrapped a towel around himself and unlocked the door.

'I don't know why you have to always lock the door,' she complained. 'Makes me feel like an intruder.' She lifted her skirt to sit on the toilet and Herbert rapidly left the room.

Heavy thighs, Marge had thick heavy thighs. She forgot to shave her legs for weeks on end and they were covered in an unpleasant ginger stubble. They had been married ten years, and glancing at the photo on the dressing table, Herbert could hardly believe that the pretty red-head with the slim figure and big breasts was now the slovenly, fat, Marge, squatting on the john. Did he know he was marrying an eating maniac? A woman to whom six eggs and a loaf of bread for breakfast were not unusual?

She had been so lovely. Their first meeting near Los Angeles airport, in a bar at lunchtime, had been so romantic. He had

gone with a friend for a beer and a sandwich – at that time he
was driving trucks – and Marge had come forward to serve
them, looking girlish in a short fringed cowboy skirt, white
boots, and a stetson hat. It was a topless bar, and her large
bosoms had bobbed tantalizingly at him, a sheriff's star cheekily covering each nipple.

'What'll you have?' she had asked, standing by his table, a
pad in her hand, and a sheriff's star nearly in his mouth.

Herbert would never forget that first meeting. They married
a few months later, Marge already pregnant. But she had lost
the baby, and then another. Shortly afterwards she started to
eat, and Herbert started to write his letters.

'Hon,' Marge came shuffling into the bedroom, 'what do
you think I should wear?'

'Wear?' He looked at her in surprise. 'For what?' This was
about the time she always settled in front of the television.

She was wriggling her fat body out of her shabby house-
dress. 'I told you, hon, I'm gonna go to a movie with our new
neighbour. She asked me two days ago. I told you.'

'Oh, yes.' He remembered now. A married couple had
moved into the yellow house next door, and Marge, on her
daily trip to the supermarket, had met the wife. The two
women had arranged to go to a film. Marge was thrilled. She
had no friends and Herbert never took her anywhere, so to go
to a movie was a rare treat.

Marge was trying to struggle into a blue sailor dress that no
longer fitted. She grew larger every year.

'We're gonna see a movie,' she repeated, 'it's supposed to
be a real weird movie – y'know, weirdy weird, and dirty too.'
She abandoned the struggle with the sailor dress and chose
instead a loose polka-dot shift that she had bought for her
sister's wedding the previous year. She managed to squeeze
into that, although it was no longer a loose shift.

Herbert said, 'What time are you going?' He wasn't sure
that he liked the idea of his wife roaming around enjoying
herself at dirty movies whilst he was out working.

'Louella's calling for me at seven. She's got a car.' She pouted at herself in the mirror, applied a jammy red lipstick and touched her cheeks with it, wiping the residue on her dress. 'It's so hot,' she sighed, running a comb through her scraggy red hair.

'Yes,' Herbert agreed, but his mind was no longer on Marge. His mind was on the letter waiting to be posted.

After Marge went downstairs he would pocket his prize and set off lovingly to post it.

She splashed cheap cologne over her fat freckled arms and put on a pair of white scuffed shoes. 'There. How do I look?'

She looked like a ginger elephant in a polka-dot dress. 'Very nice,' he said, noticing that the back of her hem was hanging loose. 'Don't you two girls do any flirting.'

She cackled. 'Herbie!' She lumbered off downstairs and he quickly pocketed the letter.

Oh, Miss Sunday Simmons, what a treat you have in store for you!

Chapter Thirteen

Charlie was pleased at the way things worked out. He stood to make a great deal more money, he would be the main star of *Roundabout*, and they would pick a leading lady of his choice. After all, were he truthful with himself, the main reason he had wanted Michelle was personal. His ego had taken a bad beating with the divorce, and he had needed the reassurance that a sex-symbol, a woman most red-blooded men would give their right arm to possess, desired him – and not as a star, but as a man.

Michelle's defection was a great personal disappointment. But he had to admit that professionally it was probably better.

He dressed prior to leaving for Cy's house. His clothes reflected the new Charlie Brick, the free, divorced Charlie Brick, the *thin* Charlie Brick.

He wore brown slacks, and a loose Indian-type shirt. He adjusted his horn-rimmed glasses and, peering at himself in the mirror, decided that maybe he should try some tinted lenses, something a bit newer.

George was waiting in the red Maserati at the front of the hotel.

'I think I'll drive myself tonight,' Charlie said. He felt good. So good in fact that he had sent Michelle a telegram of congratulation.

'Are you sure?' George asked doubtfully. The car was always in terrible shape after Charlie drove it.

'Of course I'm sure. You take the Mercedes and go and have some fun. I'll see you in the morning.'

'All right.' George was quite pleased at the prospect of an evening off. He was bored with sitting around the hotel each night trying to keep Charlie cheerful. He stepped out of the car. Charlie climbed in and revved the engine, loving the sound of unleashed power.

A pretty girl, leaving the hotel with a small poodle, turned to stare at him. He winked, she winked back. Why the hell had he told Marshall to fix a girl for him? He could manage very nicely on his own.

*　*　*

Cy Hamilton Jnr's wife, Emerald, was a lush. She was attractive, with long straight black hair parted in the middle. She wore gold patio pyjamas, and drank straight Scotch on the rocks while directing bitchy put-downs at her husband's every other sentence. She clung onto Charlie's arm, swaying slightly and breathing lethal alcohol fumes in his face.

Marshall caught Charlie by the arm as they were going into the Venetian dining room. 'Take no notice of Emerald,' he whispered, 'She's always smashed. She'll probably try to grab your cock under the table. Just pretend not to notice.'

'What?' Charlie found the thought of Emerald making a grab for him highly amusing, and also improbable with her husband sitting right there.

'I should have warned you before,' Marshall muttered, 'only Cy gets very steamed up if you say anything. She makes a play for everyone, it's her way of getting at him.'

'Why?'

'It's a long story. To put it in a nutshell, once he marries them he can't get it up any more. He's in analysis about it.'

'Yes, I should think he would be.'

71

Charlie felt an immediate rapport with Cy. What an awful position to be in. He had always harboured a secret fear that one day it might happen to him.

The four of them sat down to dinner served by two Mexican maids wearing starched black and white uniforms.

Emerald immediately knocked over a glass of wine and accused Cy of having pushed her elbow. They squabbled like two children, ignoring the melon and Parma ham put before them.

Marshall and Charlie ate, trying to ignore the bickering.

Marshall said quietly, 'There'll be a young lady coming to your hotel at eleven. She's a nice kid, a big fan of yours. As a matter of fact, she's quite an up and coming actress. She doesn't usually go on blind dates, but as I said, she's a fan of yours. You'll like her, her name's Dindi Sydne.'

'Great.' Charlie raised his eyebrows. 'Does this go on all through dinner?' He indicated the battling couple.

'No. She'll throw something at him in a minute and walk out. She'll be back for dessert.'

Sure enough, Emerald suddenly got up, called Cy a string of four-letter names, threw the bread basket at him and stalked out.

'Broads!' Cy exclaimed.

True to Marshall's prediction she re-appeared at the strawberry shortcake stage. She had changed into a silk jersey floor-length dress which clung to her like a second skin, and was split from the neck to the navel, showing off lightly tanned skin and an almost flat bosom.

She smiled at everyone and sat down, sipping at a large glass of Scotch she had brought with her.

Cy continued talking about a recent production of his.

Is that a hand creeping up my leg? Charlie thought. My God, it is! Light fingers were stalking past his knee and fiddling with his fly. He was thankful that these new trousers had buttons instead of the usual zipper. Marshall certainly knew the order of events!

Emerald was making no progress with the buttons, and her fingers started to rub impatiently. To his embarrassment he started to get an erection.

Emerald smiled and sipped her drink. Cy droned on. Charlie uncomfortably spooned a mouthful of strawberry shortcake and tried to think of other things.

At last dinner was over, and Charlie excused himself quickly and went to the bathroom. What an unbelievable scene! And Marshall said she did it to everyone. The woman must be insane, and Cy even more insane to put up with it.

He cleaned his teeth with a gold Asprey's toothpick, washed his hands, and returned to the others.

'I thought we'd have coffee in the screening room,' Cy said. 'Are you going to come and watch, darling?'

Emerald shook her head and made some crack about having better things to do than watch a load of dumb starlets – only she didn't use the word starlets.

Cy's viewing room was done entirely in red leather. Even the screen was fitted into a red leather surround, studded with gold horseshoes.

Charlie admired it, and thought to himself that when he was finished on this film, he must buy a home for himself somewhere. It was important to get out of hotels. Now that he knew he was staying to do the movie, he would send George out to rent a house tomorrow. The children would be joining him soon, and they deserved the best.

The first girl came on the screen. She was blonde and curvaceous, but she lacked a certain something. All three of them said no. The second clip was Angela Carter. She was tall, with a particular gamine quality that appealed to Charlie. The scene was backstage at a theatre and she was wearing a leotard that made her legs appear six feet long.

'Y'know, I don't think she'd be bad at all,' Charlie mused.

'Yeah,' Marshall agreed. Angela was bugging the life out of him to get her a part. 'After all, it's a comedy – no big dramatics. I think it would be a clever bit of casting.'

JACKIE COLLINS

'She looks like a Pekinese,' Cy said.

'But a sexy one,' Marshall continued, 'and there's talk around that she and Steve Magnum might even get married. What a publicity natural that would be!'

'Let's see the others before we get carried away.'

The next girl was a new English discovery who had just starred in her first film. Rumour had it that she had screwed everyone on it from the star to the clapper boy.

'No,' Charlie shook his head, 'she speaks like she's got a plum in her mouth.'

'Maybe somebody left their prick there!' Marshall said with a dirty laugh.

Girl number four was Sunday Simmons, in the bedroom scene with Jack Milan.

'Now *that's* what I call sensational,' Cy said, sitting up very straight. 'I don't know about using her for the movie, but I have to meet her. Fix it up, Marsh. That is *all* woman.'

Charlie agreed. She *was* gorgeous. But who had ever heard of her? Angela Carter was certainly the best bet as far as he was concerned.

It was the first time Marshall had seen Sunday on the screen, and he suddenly understood what Carey was so excited about. This girl had it. He must phone Carey first thing and sign her up. His bad leg tingled, a sure sign that he was on to something good. 'It wouldn't be such a bad idea to use an unknown,' he said slowly. 'She's done a lot of Italian films.'

'No.' Charlie shook his head. 'She's not right.'

'She's got a wild pair of tits!' Cy said, running the scene again.

'You don't judge an actress by the size of her tits,' Charlie replied coldly. He refused to be fobbed off with an unknown just because Cy wanted to lay her.

'Let's run the last girl,' Cy said.

The last girl was a young television actress. She was appealing and nice. Not sexy enough, all three men agreed.

'I'm happy to decide on Angela Carter,' Charlie declared.

74

Cy nodded. 'I guess she's the best choice. Is she free right away, Marsh?'

'Free as a bird. What about Sunday Simmons for the other girl, the small part?'

'Not a bad idea. What do you think, Charlie?'

'Yes – fine with me.' He glanced at his watch. It was ten-thirty, time to be getting back to the hotel and preparing for his date. He got up and stretched. 'Thank your – er – um – wife for a lovely dinner.'

'Pleasure.' Cy stood too. 'I hope we didn't disturb you with our little tiff. Emerald's alone all day and she gets very bored. Our fights are just her way of letting off steam.'

'Of course. Well, I'll leave you two to discuss details.'

'Charlie – the re-write was started today. All being well we can start shooting again next week.'

* * *

Back at his hotel Charlie changed into a black track suit. He then decided he didn't like it, and was just struggling back into his original outfit when Dindi arrived.

She had dressed carefully for the occasion. Nothing too far out, she didn't want to frighten him off with some wild outfit. After all, each star was a golden opportunity, and one of these days she was going to strike it rich.

Of course she had heard of Charlie Brick – who hadn't? And when Marshall had called her about entertaining him, she had jumped at the chance. Marshall had promised to see she got a small part in *Roundabout*. They had a good working arrangement.

She remembered with amusement her first encounter with Marshall. Seeing he was such a big important agent and all, she had thought she had better put out for him. But he hadn't wanted to know, practically fell under his desk with embarrassment when she unzipped her dress and wriggled her bare ass at him.

In moments of idleness, which were few in Dindi's life, she tried to figure out what the agent's sexual hang-up was. He didn't swing with girls. Boys? She didn't think so. Anyway, she entertained his more important clients, and he got her a small contract and plenty of walk-on speaking parts; so as far as she was concerned it was a good arrangement.

Charlie Brick was thinner and more attractive than on the screen. Not her type at all though. She liked them big, young, and good-looking. Maybe he was sensational in bed. The English were pretty wild in that department.

She played it sweet and friendly.

'Hi, I'm Dindi Sydne. What a fabulous suite. I'd *love* a frozen banana daquiri.'

Charlie thought her a charming girl, obviously not a hooker – exceedingly pretty, with silky blonde hair pulled back and tied with a big blue bow that matched the sleeveless dress she was wearing. The dress clung in all the right places and had diamond patterns cut around the midriff which showed off her glowing tan.

'Marshall tells me you're an actress,' he said, wondering why on earth he had brought up *that* subject.

'Trying to be, but I'm not terribly ambitious.' She smiled disarmingly.

He ordered drinks from room service, put on a José Feliciano tape, showed Dindi a book of stills from his latest film, and reminded himself to thank Marshall for sending him such a delightful girl.

Dindi admired pictures of his children, sipped her drink like a lady, enthused over his stills, and carefully and unobtrusively saw to it that her skirt hitched its way up, showing lots of naked tanned thigh.

Several frozen banana daquiris later she pretended to be ever so slightly drunk. Actually they didn't affect her at all, but she was smart enough to know when to play it tough, and when to play it Baby Girl. Charlie was definitely Baby Girl. Already he was telling her about his wife, the divorce, and how lonely he was.

She made sympathetic clucking noises, and secretly thought here was a goose good and ready to be plucked.

After he had complained bitterly about all women being after his money, fame, or both, she said, 'How awful. I guess people just use you, and girls hope you can get them in your movies.'

'That's right, love, that's absolutely right.' What an intelligent girl, he thought, hardly aware of the fact that he had been doing all the talking. 'Y'know, if I ever get married again, one thing I'll be sure to do, and that is see my wife has a separate bedroom. I understand that she wouldn't want to be with me all the time.'

This guy is a nut, Dindi thought, an out and out nut. 'I understand how you feel,' she said softly, 'although if I was your wife, that would be the last thing I'd want.'

Charlie suddenly grabbed her and kissed her. What a wonderful understanding girl. He moved his hands over her breasts and she gave a little gasp.

'Listen, love,' he said quietly, letting her go and moving over to the desk drawer. 'There's something I want you to try with me.'

Oh goody – action at last, Dindi thought.

'Yes?' she said, her voice barely a whisper as he lowered the lights and turned up the music.

'I want you to smoke a little grass with me. It will make you feel good, you'll enjoy it. Here.' He lit the joint and passed it to her. 'Just drag deeply and inhale very very slowly.'

She choked back a laugh. She had been smoking pot on and off since she was fourteen. Gingerly she took the brown cigarette and puffed, manufacturing a small frightened cough. It was weak stuff, had no kick to it.

'There's a clever girl.' Charlie was pleased. He took the joint from her and dragged long and hard. It was the only thing in the world that really relaxed him.

They lay back on the couch and shared the rest. Dindi despaired of him ever making a move. But at last he began to kiss her again and run his hands over her body. She sighed and moved and moaned and said, 'I feel so wonderful, you make me feel so wonderful.'

Then he was gently pulling her dress off, and manipulating her bosom over the top of her bra (a Fredericks special – black lace and pink ruffles), and kissing her nipples until they stood up firm and hard. She suppressed a desire to scream at him what to do next. He was so slow. After five minutes of playing with her breasts she wanted him to shove it into her good and hard, but he was making no move in that direction. Shit! she thought – shit! shit! shit! And she squirmed uncomfortably until at last she came to an unsatisfactory climax.

Unaware of this, Charlie continued to play with her nipples. By this time she was a mass of raw nerve-edges silently screaming at him to stop.

Could a Baby Girl reach for his prick?

Why not, if she were a stoned Baby Girl?

She deftly moved out of his grasp and felt for his fly. What the hell were all these buttons?

'Can I touch you?' she asked shyly.

'Of course, darling, of course.'

He got up quickly, feeling a bit guilty at having made her turn on, and struggled out of his pants.

Before he could sit down, she fastened her mouth on him like a limpet, forcing him to a quick climax.

He gave a long and anguished moan.

She let him free, and fell back on the couch murmuring, 'Oh Charlie, I've never done that before. You're so sexy. So great.'

He smiled. Yes, he could give women a good time. Movie star or dustman, he was a good lover. Hadn't this sweet girl just said so?

The phone started to ring and he padded to answer it, feeling stupid in just his shirt, socks, and horn-rimmed glasses.

Dindi lay back, feeling pleased with herself. She was definitely playing all her cards right. With any luck she would get a good cameo part in *Roundabout*, plus maybe a spell as Charlie Brick's girlfriend. It was always good to go with a star, got you around to all the right parties and premières, where important people noticed you. He obviously liked her. She could see his big bag was flattery, and man, she was the best at that. The main thing with any guy was sweet-talking him about what a stud he was.

Charlie was surprised to hear Clay Allen on the phone. It was early morning in London, and since Clay was arriving in Hollywood the following week, he wondered what he wanted. He hoped to God that Natalie hadn't said anything. Not that there was anything for her to say, but you never knew with women. They had a way of fabricating things.

They exchanged pleasantries, then Clay said, 'Look, old boy, I think there's something I had better tell you before some smart reporter blurts it at you. It's about Lorna. As you know, she's marrying that berk, and what is more, my friend, she's pregnant – five months.'

'Is it his?' Charlie blurted foolishly, in a state of shock.

'Well, it certainly isn't yours. Anyway, Natalie found out and we thought you should know.'

'Yes, yes, thanks, Clay.' He replaced the receiver.

Lorna had really gone and done it. Now there was no hope of them getting back together, no hope at all. His Lorna. Pregnant with another man's child.

He gazed blankly at Dindi lying on the couch. Blonde hair spread around her pretty face, bosoms peeking at him over the top of her bra, long brown legs. She was at least ten years younger than Lorna, a real little beauty. One whom all his mates back in London would really fancy.

'Hey,' Charlie said. 'Let's get in the Maserati and drive somewhere – anywhere. How about Las Vegas? I've never been there. Let's get married.'

Chapter Fourteen

'Smile,' Carey whispered to Sunday, 'you look like a girl who's just had bad news.'

Sunday obediently manufactured a smile for the photographers buzzing round her and Steve Magnum. Actually the last thing in the world she felt like doing was smiling. She had had a terrible morning.

First, the pornographic letter with its sickening contents. Then, in her confusion, her little dog, Limbo, had somehow or other got lost. She had visions of it being trapped on Sunset Boulevard, and couldn't wait for the press conference to end, so that she could get back to the search.

'You've done a pretty good job of avoiding me,' Steve said, putting his arm around her for the photographers.

'Thank you for the flowers,' she replied dutifully.

'Is that all you've got to say on the subject? Why don't we discuss it over dinner tonight?'

'I'm sorry, I'm busy.'

He looked at her quizzically. It was such a change to meet a girl who played hard to get. He had a reputation as a lady-killer and most of the ladies couldn't wait to get killed.

In the whole of Steve's life there had only been two women who had actually turned down the opportunity of going to bed with him. One was a girl in high school who had called him skinny, and the other his mother's best friend. He bet they were sorry now. They were shrivelled-up old bags by this time anyway.

Still, it was refreshing to meet a girl like Sunday. She was so unlike the usual Hollywood actresses, and really great-looking, not your hairpieces and false-eyelashes type of beauty. Jack Milan had been right when he said, 'There's a broad you've got to meet. I'm sitting you next to her.' Angela was getting to be a habit. Sunday had appeared at just the right time.

'What's the matter, am I too old for you?' he said with a smile. He knew that at fifty he was not too old for anyone. Not with the fame, the millions, the various homes around the world, the private plane, and the reputation – especially the reputation.

'How old *are* you?' Sunday asked sweetly, wondering if maybe Limbo had got shut in a closet somewhere.

Carey, watching on the sidelines as the photographers jostled for good shots, wished that Sunday would ease up just a little. She was really uptight. The best thing in the world for her would be an affair with someone like Steve Magnum – although those movie stars were such unpredictable bastards.

'That's enough, fellows,' Steve said, 'you'll be seeing a lot more of Sunday in our new movie.' He turned to her, fixing her with his famous pale blue eyes. 'The dinner invitation is open any night you care to pick it up. Otherwise I'll see you in Acapulco.'

'OK.' She did find him attractive, or was it that his face was so very familiar?

It was quite an achievement for Steve Magnum to appear at a press reception to introduce his latest leading lady. It made the whole thing more important.

Carey was delighted. 'You looked great, honey. It will make every front page tomorrow.'

'I must get back to the Château. Can we leave now?'

'Sure. Don't worry, Limbo's probably safely asleep under the bed.'

But he wasn't. Sunday searched her suite again, and wandered around the hotel, looking everywhere. She hired a taxi and cruised up and down Sunset. She called the police. By six o'clock she gave up hope and went home.

It took some time for the knocking on the door to get through to her. It was past seven, and her eyes were red-rimmed, her cheeks streaked.

Branch Strong stood there, Limbo barking cheekily under his arm.

'Er – Miss – er, I guess this is your dog, huh? Found him jigging about outside, down by the pool. I think he must have fallen in a few times 'cos he's wet through.' He handed the tiny dog to Sunday and it immediately covered her face with wet licks.

'Oh yes, yes. Come in.' Her face lit up as she muttered to the dog half scoldingly, half lovingly.

Branch walked in, swaggering unconsciously in his very tight blue jeans and thin white T-shirt. He was really quite knocked out with Sunday.

'I can't tell you how grateful I am. I've been going mad with worry. I was imagining the most awful things.'

'Yeah.' Branch stood awkwardly, his hands dangling beside him. 'I guess it was a good thing I found him.'

'You bet it was. Honestly, I am so relieved. If there's anything I can ever do for you – just name it.'

'I'll name it,' he hesitated. 'That is – er – I thought maybe you might like to have a bite to eat with me tonight.'

He paused hopefully, then quickly added, 'Nothing fancy – there's this great health-food place I found. What do you think?'

'Can we take Limbo?'

'Sure, yeah, sure. You mean you'll come?' His big boyish face beamed. 'That's great. I guess I'd better go and wash up, and I'll fetch you in half an hour. Is that all right with you?'

'That's fine.'

She took Limbo in the kitchen and gave him a dish of meat

and some water, then watched as he wolfed the lot down. Then she changed into a pair of white slacks and a sweater, brushed her hair and cleaned her face. Branch seemed nice; there could be no harm in having a quiet dinner with him.

In the bedroom she noticed the revolting letter she had received that morning, still lying in fragments in the waste-paper basket. She shuddered. It was so vile, so obscene. Carey had laughed when she told her about it. 'You'll be inundated with pieces of garbage like that. Don't even bother to read them; it gives some poor sick guy somewhere his jollies. Forget it, they never do anything else but write.'

Didn't they? In spite of the fact that they seemed convinced that they *would* do the things described?

Of course they didn't. Only it gave Sunday a bad feeling to know that somewhere, someone knew where she was and had such thoughts about her.

Chapter Fifteen

Charlie tried to get hold of George but couldn't locate him. George, taking advantage of his night of freedom, was sitting in a strip club admiring the scenery.

Charlie was very stoned, and completely carried away with the idea of running off to Las Vegas with Dindi.

She was sceptical. Could this nut really be serious about getting married? But if it came off, what a break!

Charlie thought: *Screw you, Lorna. Screw you, Michelle. Screw you, Natalie. I'm going to show the lot of you.* They would all see how much he cared when they read their papers tomorrow.

He told Dindi they wouldn't bother picking up any of her things, she would have everything new in Las Vegas. Then, throwing a few clothes in an overnight bag, they headed for the Maserati and took off.

It was an easy ride, freeway all the way, and Charlie really put his foot down, revelling in the sound of the powerful engine. He played his new stereo tape equipment and they shared another joint.

Dindi hoped to hell they wouldn't get stopped for speeding or anything. If they got booked for smoking pot it would ruin a beautiful scene.

She contemplated giving him a little going over while he was driving, but at the speed they were travelling it was probably unwise. Anyway, she didn't want to appear too forward – yet. Maybe it was her supposed innocence that he went for. She lay back in her seat and listened to the music.

It was around four a.m. when Vegas loomed ahead. It was a mass of blazing neon signs as they drove through the downtown section. In spite of the hour the streets and gambling halls were crowded. It was a waste of time to go to bed in Vegas – unless of course that was the business you were in. Charlie had never been there before, but he had had the desk clerk at the Beverly Hills phone through to the Forum hotel to alert them of his arrival. It was the latest hotel to be built on the main strip.

Dindi had fallen asleep. Charlie woke her. 'Which way to the Strip?' he asked.

She had already told him she had been there before, although not in what circumstances. She had been dating a small-time hood at the time who had dumped her there without a cent, after three glorious days together. She had hung around and worked as a cocktail waitress and made it with a few fantastic swimming coaches, and had then got a ride back to L.A. with an up-and-coming actor – the only trouble was he was up and coming practically the whole trip! That was before Rome.

'Just keep on this street and take a right at the top.' She thought a minute, then added, 'Hey, there's a fabulous new hotel – the Forum. I'd love to go there, it's supposed to be wild, TV in the john and fruit machines in the elevators.' She had decided it was better to go somewhere she might not be known. It wouldn't be cool to have half the croupiers greeting her by name.

'That's just where we're going.'

The Forum was approached through a driveway of marble Roman soldiers – very impressive. Several bleached-blond boys in short togas surrounded the Maserati as it arrived at the entrance. They opened the doors, took the one bag, and escorted Charlie and Dindi inside.

Charlie asked for the manager, who appeared almost

immediately – a dead ringer for a young George Raft. He appraised Dindi with a flick of his eyes, greeted Charlie profusely, and organized the biggest suite in the hotel. He was no slouch at recognizing celebrities, and was used to dealing with all their peculiar requests. However, it did shake him a bit when Charlie said they wanted to get married right then and there. 'Give me an hour,' he said.

Charlie nodded. It seemed quite reasonable in his present state of mind that a marriage could be arranged at four a.m. in Las Vegas.

Dindi was starting to feel shaky. The sonofabitch was actually serious.

Charlie indicated the arcade of shops around the lobby. 'Miss Sydne would like to buy a dress, and I'd like to get in the jewellers.'

'Certainly.' By this time the manager was unflappable. Charlie had slipped him a large tip, and as far as he was concerned he could have what he liked. 'I'll send a selection of dresses to your suite: size ten, Miss Sydne?'

She nodded. The manager was just the type of good-looking, smooth bastard she could fall for.

'OK, Mr Brick, as soon as I've located the jeweller I'll put him in touch with you. Meanwhile, leave everything to me. Will there be any guests?'

Charlie shook his head.

'Do you have any objection to publicity?'

'None at all.' The whole point as far as Charlie was concerned was to have large photos of himself and gorgeous blond Dindi spread all over the newspapers for everyone to see.

* * *

The preacher was a southern cracker. Hurriedly dressed in a shiny blue suit, he peered at the couple before him and drawled out his version of the wedding ceremony.

Dindi noticed that his fly was undone and tried to stifle a

giggle. She was wearing a pink frilled dress, and her blonde hair fell loosely around her shoulders. She looked like a lovely innocent doll. On her finger she wore a huge cluster diamond ring, a present from Charlie.

He had also noticed the preacher's undone fly, and couldn't keep his eyes from straying there. The funny old chap had probably been fast asleep. What an accent! He listened intently. This would be a great voice to use in some future film.

The manager had arranged the wedding in the penthouse, with the hotel photographer, press man and two representatives of the local newspaper, with their photographer, present. The manager and his girlfriend were the two witnesses.

* * *

The preacher pronounced them man and wife, belched unobtrusively, and shook Charlie's hand. Then there was champagne, photographs, and congratulations all round.

The preacher sidled up to Charlie – 'Here's my card if you need me again.'

Charming – Charlie thought – only just married and he's asking me if I need him again!

It was seven a.m. by the time they got back to their suite. Charlie was beginning to feel the strain. His eyes hurt behind his glasses, and the beautiful high he had achieved was beginning to wear off. For the first time he thought about the sanity of what he had just done. He had married a girl he didn't even know. It was the most ridiculous insane thing. She was very pretty, but he didn't even *know* her.

It was all Lorna's fault. He had done it to spite her. What would Serafina say?

Dindi was dazed, but for different reasons. So suddenly and unexpectedly she was someone. She had married a movie star!

She took off her dress and caught Charlie staring at her with a puzzled expression.

She giggled. 'Hey, lover, now we can do it legal!'

Chapter Sixteen

Sunday was as amazed as the rest of Hollywood when Dindi and Charlie Brick appeared on the front of all the newspapers – married in Las Vegas. She couldn't understand why Dindi hadn't mentioned it to her, as she wasn't exactly the sort of girl to keep a secret.

Carey was laughing. 'I tell you, honey, Marsh is fit to be tied, but beside himself! Seems he fixed her up for Charlie to get himself laid, and the schmuck ups and marries her. Can you imagine? That chick had really been around – but I mean *really*.'

'Maybe it was love at first sight,' Sunday replied, always a believer in romance.

'Maybe, my ass. She must have cast one hell of a mean spell on him.'

'She's very pretty, and she certainly has lots of personality. Why couldn't it be love at first sight?'

'Oh, Sunday, baby. Sometimes you are so naive. It's times like this I realize you're only twenty, and not the cool forty-five-year-old you usually come across as. By the way, they pushed you and Steve right off the front pages, but there's still good coverage inside.'

'Anyway, I think it's wonderful for Dindi, I really do. I'm going to send her a telegram.'

'Save your money. I don't give it two weeks. When Charlie comes to his senses and finds out what a hooker she is – then – like – the party's over.'

'Carey, you're much to cynical.'

Carey hooted with laughter.

'By the way, I just turned down a part for you in *Roundabout*. The timing was wrong. Marshall suddenly accepted the fact that you exist and flipped. He saw a clip from the Milan movie.'

The two girls were talking over an ice cream. Sunday spooned peppermint into her mouth and said, 'I wonder how Branch will do with his test.'

She had told Carey about her date with him the previous evening and how pleasant it had been.

'Listen, kid, I know you think I'm always putting people down, but I checked up on Mr Branch Strong, and he is purely fag time. It's not a good scene for you to go out with him.'

'According to you, everyone is either a hooker or gay. I don't intend to go to bed with him. He's just very simple and straightforward, and I like him purely as a friend.'

'Simple is the right word. All right, as long as you're not planning a grand love affair, although while we are on the subject, about your sex life—'

'Look, I appreciate everything you're doing and have done for me, but my sex life is my own business, and if I don't care to have one, that's also my own business.'

Carey smoothed her hands over her sleek cap of black hair. Sometimes Sunday could be very cold.

They finished their ice creams in silence, then Carey said, 'I'll drop you off for your fittings.' She noticed that everyone in the place turned to stare at Sunday as they left. When this girl was really exposed to the public, when her films came out, she wouldn't be able to travel around alone. She was destined to be a Monroe-Sinatra type of celebrity, the kind they wanted to mob and touch. Marshall's reaction to seeing her on film had been an indication. He never got excited about anything.

Carey thought of Marshall fondly for a few moments. She missed being with him, missed his sudden bouts of temper, and his gammy footsteps as he stamped about his office. He was a real character. Although she had worked with him for seven years, she knew practically nothing about his personal life, nor apparently did anyone else. There was a wife, long ago divorced and now living in Pasadena. The only reason she knew about her was because of the alimony cheques that were sent every month.

'You want to go to a movie tonight?' Carey asked, when she dropped Sunday at the costumiers.

'Thanks, but I think I'll study my script.'

'Talk to you tomorrow then.'

*　*　*

The fittings were perfect: a white leather micro dress with matching bikini; a startling fall of white jersey folds to the floor, plunging to expose most of her bosom; a white linen suit with huge cowboy hat.

Steve Magnum had decided her wardrobe should be all white to complement her golden skin and tawny mass of hair,

'You'll adore Acapulco,' Hanna said. Hanna, a gaunt English lady wearing a mannish suit and unappealing flat brogue shoes, was doing the fittings.

'I'm sure I will.' Sunday shivered slightly as Hanna's stubby fingers delved across her bosom, adjusting a button.

'There,' Hanna stood back and surveyed her work. 'You look quite ravishing.'

'I love the clothes,' Sunday said. 'Who should I talk to about buying them for myself after the film?'

Hanna looked at her strangely. 'I would think you'd have no difficulty with Steve Magnum. He's very generous, especially to close friends.' She allowed herself a fleeting private smile, which Sunday understood only too well.

'Thanks. But I don't think I shall be asking Mr Magnum for favours like that.'

'Really?' Hanna's arch smile said: Who are you kidding?

So that's what they all thought. Sunday was furious, and furthermore she resolved to keep her relationship with Steve Magnum absolutely and utterly professional.

Let them all see just how wrong they were.

Chapter Seventeen

Herbert pissed a perfect arc, which landed delicately in Cy Hamilton's horseshoe-shaped swimming pool. He zipped up his fly with pleasure. One more Hollywood pool had the addition of his wine. What a blow he was striking for the poorer classes!

Herbert had been in the habit of relieving himself in the best pools in Hollywood during the two years he had been working for the Supreme Chauffeur Company. The opportunities were not to be ignored, and as long as there were no nosey servants hanging around, he usually managed it while waiting to pick up his parties. He was always kept waiting, and it gave him a thrill when his passengers finally climbed in the car, all dressed up, to think of them the next day swimming around in his piss.

He had driven the Hamiltons before and he loathed them. The drunken woman with her steely eyes and skinny body, purposely giving him a good flash of her intimate parts as she got in the car and the man, so obviously rich and powerful, sitting and listening to the woman nag and whine and bitch her way to wherever they were going.

Tonight it was a party. The woman was wearing skintight leopard-printed chiffon trousers and hardly any top.

Herbert thought it disgusting the way some men let their wives go around. As a matter of fact, he was rather concerned about Marge – dear fat old Marge, who for so many years had been simply content to squat in front of the television and eat. Since her first outing with Louella Crisp – the new neighbour – she had changed. She was always popping over to visit the house next door, and her dresses actually looked clean. She made up her face, and had even gone to the beauty parlour to have her scraggy hair styled.

Herbert was amazed, and not pleased at all.

The final straw had come that evening, before he left for work.

'Louella's having a little party next week,' Marge announced. 'She wants to know if you can come. It will be awful good fun, games and things. Her husband's gonna be there too. *Will* you be able to come, hon? I'm gonna get myself a pretty new dress, *and* go on a diet.'

Herbert regarded his wife's elephantine form coldly. 'I don't want you going to no party.'

Marge's eyes brimmed full of tears, which, mixing with her mascara, dribbled down her cheeks. 'But Herbie, hon, she's my friend, my only friend . . .'

'She's a bad influence on you. I don't want you seeing her no more. Look at yourself – made up like a whore.'

She chewed on her lower lip, the tears ceased, and a crafty expression passed across her fat face.

'If you don't let me go, I'm gonna tell about you writing those dirty letters. I'm gonna tell the police and they'll put you in jail for being . . .'

She trailed off as Herbert fixed her with his eyes. They were the meanest eyes she had ever seen.

'What letters?' His voice was very controlled, but inside he was shaking with fury. *Nobody* knew about his letters. He wrote them upstairs, locked away in the little box-room. Marge was always busy watching television. 'What letters?' he repeated, taking her fleshy arm in a tight grip.

She was frightened. Herbert got so strange at times. She wished she hadn't mentioned the letters, after all she had only found two, and she certainly didn't mind if he wanted to write to those fancy movie stars.

'Angela Carter,' she gulped, 'it was torn up, and I stuck it together. It's all right, Herbie, I was only joking. Herbie, you're hurting my arm – Herbie . . .' She screamed as his nails raked into her soft skin and drew blood, then she sniffled quietly as he paced up and down the room, beside himself with anger.

How could he have been so careless? He usually tore up, and flushed down the toilet, any unfinished efforts.

'Get them,' he demanded.

She scurried off immediately and fetched the two letters, hidden carefully under the mattress. She was reluctant to part with them. They had kept her company many a long and lonely night. She handed them over.

'I wish you'd do some of those things you write about to me,' she whined. 'You never do anything to me any more.'

She rubbed her vast bosom up against him. 'I'd like to do all those things again, Herbie. Can we start doing them again?'

He pushed her away. 'You're too fat,' he muttered. How could he ever consider touching that gross body again when he had someone like Sunday Simmons?

'But, Herbie.' In desperation Marge was unbuttoning her blouse and releasing a mammoth bosom from the confines of a dirty white bra. 'Look what I've got. I've got beautiful titties, you used to love my titties.'

He glanced at her with disgust. Big fat floppy bosom. He turned his back. 'Get dressed, you whore. And see you stay in tonight.'

Then he grabbed his jacket and marched out.

* * *

Yes, the whole episode with Marge was most disturbing. Especially the sexual part, the exhibiting of herself to him. Didn't she realize that that part of their life was over? It made him feel unclean and disgusted just thinking about it.

'Hey, driver,' the woman was leaning drunkenly forward from the back seat, a cigarette dangling from her painted scarlet lips, 'got a light?'

'Emerald, sit down please. I'll light your cigarette.' Cy's voice was tense.

'I wouldn't dream of bothering you, my sweet. You don't want me to smoke. *You* don't think it's the done thing for a lady to arrive at a party smoking. Well, fuck *you*.'

'Emerald, please.'

She waved the cigarette at Herbert. 'Light me up, Sam.'

Furious with the man in the back for letting this woman get away with such foul talk, he silently handed her the automatic lighter.

She threw it down on the front seat when she was finished, and Herbert burnt his fingers returning it to the dashboard. Then the man in the back pressed a button, and the glass partition slid up, cutting off the rest of their conversation.

Herbert resolved to pee in their swimming pool again on the return journey. He would drink plenty of beer and piss another perfect arc . . .

Chapter Eighteen

Charlie wasn't sure when he first realized he had made a terrible mistake. Was it the day after his Las Vegas wedding – or the day after that?

Viewing things in the cold light of reality, he couldn't imagine how he could have done it.

Dindi was just as pretty as ever, but an idiot, a pretty little unintelligent idiot. Every time she opened her pouty lips it was to ask for something.

Even after two days it was beginning to drive him mad.

'Baby, can I have some money for roulette?' 'Sweetie, can I have those *marvellous* diamond and turquoise earrings?' 'Pussycat, what about a little mink to keep off the cold night air?'

He gave her everything she wanted. After all, it was their honeymoon.

Public reaction to their wedding was mixed. The newspapers made the most of it: *Beautiful starlet marries Charlie Brick*, and similar headlines all over the world.

Personal acquaintances were another matter. George arrived by plane, and he and Dindi seemed to become instant enemies. Marshall on the phone was positively rude; he talked business and ignored the marriage until the end of the conversation, when he mumbled something about lots of luck, you're going to need it.

From England came a long telegram from his mother. 'Son, what have you done? Couldn't you have waited? Will arrive soon. Serafina, your loving mother.'

It irked Charlie that everyone wasn't going around saying how lucky he was to have married such a gorgeous young girl. He was infuriated that there had been no word from Lorna.

Serafina was merely upset because she had not been present. She hated to miss anything, and was looking forward to her forthcoming trip to Hollywood. A new daughter-in-law wasn't exactly what she had been anticipating.

Dindi was immediately jealous of George. He arrived, summoned by Charlie after the wedding, and as usual, stayed near Charlie, available for all his requests.

'Is he going to come everywhere with us?' she questioned, a little put out because George had hovered near them at the swimming pool all day, and was now back in their suite setting up stereo equipment.

'He doesn't bother you, does he, darling?' Charlie asked mildly.

'Oh no,' she shrugged, 'I guess I'll go downstairs and have a looksee through the shops. Can I have some bread?'

Charlie was beginning to be irritated by Dindi's constant use of what she considered to be hip phraseology.

He gave her yet another stack of dollars, she seemed to go through money like confetti. She left and he went to watch George at work on the stereo.

'How long will we stay here?' George asked. He had already summed up the marriage as a dead loss, and couldn't understand how Charlie had been so foolish.

'A few days, maybe longer. I was thinking of having you drive the Maserati back and coming to fetch us in the Mercedes. There's a couple of houses you can look at for me. I've got to get something settled before the children arrive.'

* * *

Downstairs, Dindi bought three new bikinis, and a big straw sunhat. The rest of the money she took over to the roulette table and covered number twenty: she bit her lip with excitement as she watched the wheel spin, and hey presto – twenty came up. She gave a little squeak of joy, and then the manager was beside her and muttered, 'Let it ride.'

She looked up at him. He smelt of a very funky aftershave. She let the money ride, and twenty came up again. She had won a bundle.

Laughing, he took her arm. 'Take it all off.'

She smiled at him. 'The money?'

'For now.'

They understood each other.

Dindi felt a tingle of excitement. Charlie didn't excite her: she didn't feel free to be herself. With him she was still playing Baby Girl.

'Listen, if you want to count your money, I have an apartment on the eighteenth floor, apartment E.' He winked at her and walked off.

Well, the sonofabitch was certainly sure of himself, but so what, she had nothing to lose. She was a married lady now, and fun was fun. She scooped up her chips and went off to change them. Then she took the elevator to the eighteenth floor.

* * *

They stayed in Vegas five days, at the end of which Charlie was bored stiff and couldn't wait to get to work. Angela Carter had been signed for *Roundabout* and the new script was completed. They were still looking for another girl, as Sunday Simmons was unavailable. It was only a small part and presented no major problem.

Unbeknown to Charlie, Dindi had plans to grab the role for herself: a little chat with Marshall, a few hints to Charlie, and the whole thing should be a cinch.

George had chosen a house in Bel Air which he thought

would meet with Charlie's approval. It was a two-storey ranch with indoor and outdoor swimming pools, tennis courts, a guest house, and numerous bedrooms and entertaining rooms. It had been a choice between that house or a glass and steel modernistic effort up in the Hollywood Hills. George had instinctively known Dindi would prefer the modern house, so he had picked the other one.

Charlie was delighted with it. There was more than enough room to assemble all his stereo equipment, records, tapes, cameras and other toys that took his fancy. He was a great collector, getting a bug about something for months on end, then abandoning it and going on to something else. At the moment it was stereo and cars, but he was just starting a photography phase.

Dindi was impressed with the house. She had had a great time in Las Vegas, and had returned to Hollywood loaded with clothes, jewellery and a movie-star husband. What more could a girl want? She didn't even bother to collect her things from her old apartment, just instructed the landlady by phone to find her passport and mail it on to her. Who needed old things when she could have everything new?

She opened charges everywhere, and, the first day back, went on a wild spending spree.

* * *

Clay and Natalie Allen arrived in town.

'Why don't we have a little dinner party, a sort of celebration?' Charlie asked Dindi. 'You can ask some of your friends, as many as you like. We'll have it catered by Trader Vic's.' He had decided to make the most of his mistake. After all, Dindi was very young, and surely it would be a fairly simple matter to make her into the kind of girl he had thought he had married. She was bound to be willing to improve herself.

'Yeah.' Dindi nodded thoughtfully. Who of her so-called friends could she possibly invite? All the guys she had screwed.

And as for her girlfriends – well, who needed those big mouths? The only person she could think of was Sunday Simmons.

'Really, I don't have many friends here,' she said. 'Most of my close friends and all my family are in Philadelphia.' Dindi had never been to Philadelphia in her life, but she figured it sounded like a pretty respectable town to come from. Actually she had been born in Arizona and hadn't been back since she zoomed out of town with a travelling salesman at the age of fifteen.

'It doesn't have to be a big party,' Charlie said. He didn't want to present his new wife to the Allens on her own; she seemed more intelligent among people. 'We'll make it small – just Marshall, Cy and Emerald Hamilton, Clay and Natalie and a few others.'

'My best friend is Sunday Simmons, I'd like to invite her.'

'Fine. Make out a list, and we'll try and arrange it for the weekend.'

He went off to study his new script. Everything was going to work out. At least now he wouldn't have to go running after little ding-a-lings. He could concentrate on his work, and Dindi would soon have the children arriving to keep her occupied. Maybe she and Natalie would become friends. Natalie could teach her a lot. He just had to remember she was seventeen years younger than himself and hadn't been around. It would all work out.

Chapter Nineteen

Sunday found herself spending a lot of time with Branch. He was easy-going, and pleasant. She didn't fancy him sexually, she thought of him as a big brother, and hoped that he regarded her with the same feelings. She hadn't forgotten that both Dindi and Carey had said he was gay and since he hadn't made a pass at her, she was prepared to believe he was.

He was a strange boy in many ways. He hated to talk about himself or his past, was very nervous about the outcome of his test, and dreaded the thought of having to return to New York if it was unsuccessful.

It was good for Sunday to have a male companion. With Carey, when they had gone out together at night, they had been constantly bothered by men: now, with Branch by her side she was never pestered.

Carey was most put out by the whole situation.

'If your name has to be linked with someone, at least let it be Steve Magnum, not some little unknown schnook.'

Sunday just laughed, and she and Branch were soon regarded as an item.

Steve Magnum was unamused. It was not often he was turned down for some muscle-bound nothing. Just wait until he got Miss Sunday Simmons in Acapulco!

Branch's test was successful. He was signed for a cowboy

movie that was to start shooting in Mexico almost immediately. He was delighted.

The night before he left, Sunday took him to Dindi and Charlie's party. She was looking forward to seeing Dindi again, and hearing about the wedding. She was also excited about meeting Charlie Brick. She was a fan, and considered him to be a brilliant comedy actor. It was a shame she hadn't been available to do the part in *Roundabout*, but Carey had said it was a small part anyway, and *Cash* was more important.

* * *

Dindi was playing Hollywood Hostess to the hilt. Her blonde hair was joined by a long fall of ringlets cascading down her back, and she wore a full-length green chiffon dress that laced Roman-style down the front to her waist. Around her person she wore every bit of jewellery that Charlie had bought her.

'Darling!' she greeted Sunday, her voice high and strained. 'How wonderful to see you.' She flashed her diamond ring and leant forward to exchange kisses, whispering in her normal voice, 'Thank Christ you're here. This is the draggiest crowd ever!'

'What a marvellous house,' Sunday said. She looked around the huge living room, the walls covered with interesting paintings. There were about twelve people standing about drinking and talking. 'You remember Branch Strong, don't you?'

'Of course.' Dindi smiled brightly at him. 'I read where your test was fantastic'

He looked embarrassed.

'Come and have a drink. Sunday, you look great. When do you start the movie with Steve Magnum? I'm green with envy. I understand he's one of *the* great Hollywood lays.'

Dindi hasn't changed, Sunday thought, looking around for Charlie. She was intrigued to see what kind of man he was. Branch was dragged off by Emerald Hamilton, who trapped him in a corner.

Marshall arrived accompanied by Carey, and Sunday spent

all her time chatting to them. She was surprised to see Carey, who hadn't mentioned coming to the party.

'It was a last-minute thing,' Carey told her. 'Marsh called and said he had some important things to discuss with me, so I blew out my date and came here. Business before pleasure, you know. Anyway I wanted to catch this scene.'

Sunday thought how chic and attractive she looked, her dark skin setting off the white lace dress she was wearing perfectly.

Charlie came over then. Thinner than Sunday expected. A long sad face with heavy horn-rimmed glasses. Black hair. He smiled at Sunday, a slightly crooked smile, almost boyish. His voice was very warm. She liked him at once, and wondered why his eyes behind the glasses were sad.

'Dindi's spoken a lot about you,' he said, struck at once by her strange browny-yellow eyes and wide sensual mouth. She was far more beautiful than she had seemed in that short piece of film.

'Has she?' Sunday smiled.

Marshall said, 'Charlie, you never met Carey, did you? My ex-right hand. Took a powder to make it on her own.'

'Very wise too.' Charlie appraised her. 'Anyone who sets up on their own has the right idea. Especially if it means escaping from old Marsh. He must be a bastard to work for.'

Carey grinned. 'He is.'

Charlie found his eyes wandering back to Sunday's and she met his stare. He wondered if the gossip about her and Steve Magnum were true. Probably – most actresses were the same; just mention a part in a movie and they would sell their mother.

Sunday thought: he's not a happy man.

'I love your house,' she said, to break the stare.

'Do you? Thank you. It's only rented, but I'm quite pleased with it.'

Dindi appeared then and pushed her arm through his. 'Baby, the head waiter's getting all uptight about serving dinner. You want to tell him it's OK?'

'All right, love.' He gave her an absent-minded kiss and went off to organize things.

Dindi winked at Marshall. 'It's something, huh? Little old me finally made it. Hey, girls, would you mind if I grabbed Marshall for a private tête-a-tête?'

'Be my guest,' Carey said, picking up her martini and sipping it slowly.

Dindi took Marshall off.

'Well?' Carey said. 'What do you think?'

'About what?' Sunday replied.

'This whole scene. Do you still think it's love at first sight?'

'I don't know, how can anybody know? Dindi seems happy enough.'

'And Charlie?'

'I don't know Charlie.'

'No, but he'd like to know you.'

'What do you mean?'

'You *know* what I mean. The two of you had your own private electricity line buzzing between you.'

'Sometimes I think you're nuts.' But Sunday knew exactly what she meant.

'Hi, Carey.' Cy came strolling over. 'How about introducing me to your client?'

'Sure. Sunday, this is Cy Hamilton, my favourite producer.'

'Hello.'

'Hello, there.' Cy took her hand in a clammy grip and didn't release it. His eyes probed beneath her silk jersey top, and lingered on her naked bosom.

She pulled her hand free.

'I'm disappointed you're not available to do *Roundabout* for me,' he said, 'but I'm sure we'll fix something together soon.' He glanced at Carey. 'I think Sunday and I should have a meeting to discuss future projects. Maybe lunch on Monday?'

Sunday said, 'Carey arranges everything for me, I just follow her advice. She's the one you should have lunch with. Carey, Branch is trapped in a corner by some woman. Who is she?'

'Cy's wife.'

'Oh!'

Cy laughed. 'Jealous?'

'Of course not. I just wondered who she was.'

'And for your information your muscle-bound boyfriend is the one that has my wife trapped. You know something, you're a snotty broad.'

With that he walked off.

'Honestly!' Sunday exclaimed.

'Take no notice,' Carey replied, 'he's just annoyed cos you turned down his lunch invitation. It's not often he gets a no. He's banged practically every actress that ever set foot on a movie of his. His wife's a boozer and screws everything in sight. They're a beautiful couple.'

Chapter Twenty

Natalie and Clay were suitably impressed with Charlie's house. They were also renting, but on a more modest scale. They arrived an hour before the party was due to start, and Charlie sat with them in the study and heard all the London gossip.

He hadn't seen Natalie since that day in his hotel, and it was to her credit that her attitude towards him was exactly the same as before. He felt relieved, and hoped that now he was married again she would just forget all about it.

'Where's your wife?' she asked. 'I can't wait to meet her. Did Clay tell you he knows her?'

'Knows her?' Charlie was incredulous.

'Only vaguely,' Clay said quickly, shooting Natalie a glance that said, Why don't you keep your big mouth shut? 'I met her in Rome a year or so ago. I'm sure she won't remember me.'

Clay was banking on the fact that Dindi would definitely prefer not to remember him. They had met at a party, and he and some Italian producer had both screwed her one after the other, while she had shrieked with laughter and said, 'I hope this gets me the part!'

Of course Clay hadn't told Natalie the whole story, in fact he wished he hadn't mentioned it at all. But he had been so surprised when he had picked up his morning paper and found a large picture of Dindi and Charlie on the front page, that he had exclaimed, 'My God! Where did he ever dig up *that* one?'

'Yes, Dindi spent some time in Rome with her parents,' Charlie said. 'She's finishing dressing, she'll be down in a minute.'

'I hope you didn't mind my inviting Max Thorpe,' Clay said quickly to change the subject. 'His television show is a big hit here.'

'Not at all,' Charlie replied. Actually he couldn't stand Max Thorpe, a half-assed clairvoyant palm-reader who had got lucky by foretelling a couple of world events that any fool knew were bound to happen, and had ended up with his own show from Hollywood called *I Predict*. Charlie knew him from his struggling days when they had both been performing in Soho. One drunken evening he had read Charlie's palm at a party and had said a lot of things Charlie didn't like.

'You know it must be three years since I've seen Max,' Clay remarked. 'He told me then I'd be doing a lot of travelling.'

'Have you seen Lorna?' Charlie tried to sound casual, although even now it was difficult to say her name without feeling she was still his wife.

'Yes, as a matter of fact we bumped into her at a little restaurant in Hampstead,' Natalie said. 'She's absolutely huge, although she claims she's only six months. Frankly she looks like she's going to pop at any minute. I think they're getting married this week.'

'That's nice.' He tried to keep his voice emotionless. 'Did she mention me?'

Natalie and Clay both spoke at once, Natalie said yes, and Clay no.

Charlie laughed nervously. 'It's all right, I'm immune to any of her comments now.' He poured himself another Scotch, with a shaky hand.

'She said she was glad you had married again so soon.' Natalie smiled slightly, savouring the next remark. 'She said it would serve you right marrying a girl so much younger than yourself.'

'Why the hell did she say that?'

'Oh, you know Lorna. Always full of cryptic remarks.'

Dindi walked in, kissed Charlie, and smiled brightly at the Allens. The smile froze on her face when she recognized Clay. Dindi had screwed, two hundred and twenty-three men, and remembered the faces – though not the names – of all of them.

Clay bridged the gap quickly, but not before Natalie had noticed the girl's look of shock.

'We met in Rome,' Clay said, 'remember? At Claudio Finca's party. I was teasing you because you were with your mother.'

'Oh, yes.' Dindi's smile unfroze. This was one smart guy. 'Mummy's back in Philadelphia now.'

Charlie said, 'This is Natalie, darling. Clay and Natalie are two of my oldest friends.'

'Now, now,' Natalie chided gently, 'be careful when you say oldest, I'm very sensitive. How are you, Dindi? I've been so looking forward to meeting you.'

The two women took stock of each other.

Natalie saw a pretty blonde girl with too much hair and too much bosom on show. She noted that the blue eyes were sharp and bright, and she didn't underestimate her.

Dindi saw an attractive thin dark woman in her late twenties, very sure of herself, and very possessive of Charlie. It was possible that she might have screwed him.

'Charlie's talked lots about you,' Dindi said, 'I feel I know all about you.'

'Oh, good,' Natalie smiled thinly. The girl thought she and Charlie had had an affair.

'You look lovely,' Charlie said, patting Dindi on the bottom. 'Isn't she a little darling?'

'Adorable,' Natalie said.

'Yes,' Clay agreed, remembering what a little darling she had been with her pants down. It occurred to him that maybe he should have been truthful with Charlie. After all, they had been close friends for many years. But he had married the girl, so what was the point?

Later in the evening Marshall K. Marshall felt the same way. He had fixed Charlie up with Dindi in the first place. How was he supposed to know that the idiot was going to blow his mind and marry the girl? Now that he *was* married to her, it certainly wouldn't be the time to tell him that she was a semi-hooker, accepting film parts instead of money – although Marshall could remember the one occasion when he paid her five hundred dollars to spend a weekend in Palm Springs with a German midget who was up for a Best Supporting Actor award. Anyway, it certainly shouldn't take long for Charlie to see the truth.

Dindi approached him during the evening and told him she wanted the other girl's part in *Roundabout*.

'You can convince Charlie,' she said. 'It will be great publicity for the movie, and I know I'll be good in it: all I need is a decent chance.'

'Ask Charlie yourself,' Marshall replied. 'You got him to marry you, you shouldn't have any problem getting in the film.'

'Oh, Marsh it's got to come from you. I don't want him thinking I married him to get in his movie. Please, just give me a chance. Now I'm Mrs Brick I'm a changed girl, I really would be just right for the part.'

In spite of everything he liked Dindi, and it would be a natural publicity break to put her in the film, and she *was* right for the part. It was a simple role that would just require her to look pretty and sexy, and that she could certainly do.

'I'll talk to Charlie.'

She gave him a kiss on the cheek. 'You're a doll. You won't be sorry. I'll become a big star and you'll make a fortune off of me. And Marsh, anytime I can return the favour,' she winked, 'just give me the word.'

* * *

Max Thorpe was a plumpish man of Charlie's age. He had a bright red suntan, and had recently bleached his mousy brown hair with vivid yellow streaks. He wore a black and white striped cotton suit with matching shirt and tie.

'All he needs is a straw hat with "Kiss me quick" on it, and he would fit straight into a Brighton day trip,' Charlie remarked to Natalie.

However, Max Thorpe was the hit of the party. Nobody could resist knowing what good things the future had in store for them, and it was Max's policy only to predict good things. He was soon surrounded by anxious outstretched palms, but the hand that really interested him was that of Branch Strong.

Max, like Charlie, had come a long way from the Soho joints where he had first appeared. And along the way his tastes had changed from flat-chested long-legged girls to muscle-bound beautiful young men. Branch was a perfect specimen.

Max felt his heart pounding as it hadn't done since he had met a fake Indian at Disneyland. He recognized a kindred spirit in Branch immediately, and holding his hand tightly, he foresaw great fortune and success, and that someone with the initial 'M' would become most prominent in his life. He advised the young man to follow his natural inclinations, and asked whether he would like to appear on an *I Predict* television show?

Branch listened intently, a wide grin on his perfect features. Fame, fortune and success were just what he wanted, and then perhaps he could get rid of all the perverts who swarmed around him. 'M' must stand for Mother. He had been too ashamed to go home and see her for two years. Follow your natural inclinations must mean tell all the queer boys to stay away from him. As soon as he achieved the fame, fortune and success, he could do just that, including getting rid of his agent, whose demands were the most demeaning of all. Then perhaps he could have a real relationship with Sunday. He didn't feel it would be proper to touch her until all his past associations were finished.

'How about appearing on my show?' Max persisted.

'Yeah, well, I'm off to Mexico tomorrow. Got me a great

little part in a cowboy movie, but when I come back, I'd sure love to.'

Max asked anxiously, 'When will that be?'

'They reckon I should be there six or seven weeks.' Branch pushed a lock of fallen blond hair off his forehead.

'We could pay in advance.' Max lowered his voice and said this quickly. 'In fact I could pay you tonight if you could come back to my house and collect. Fifteen hundred dollars.'

'Yeah?' It slowly dawned on Branch what Max Thorpe had in mind. If he had fame, fortune and success he would punch him right on his burnt-up red nose. But he didn't have any of those things yet, and fifteen hundred dollars was an awful lot of money. 'Is that so? Well, I guess I could meander by later. First, I have to take a little lady home.'

'Fine, fine. Any time will do.' Max felt his whole body slump with relief. 'I'll let you have my address.'

* * *

Later in the evening Charlie found himself the object of Max's interest. 'Remember what I told you, old boy. You didn't like it at the time, but it's all come true.'

'Some of it,' Charlie admitted reluctantly.

'Pretty accurate I was.' Max chuckled at his own cleverness, and also because he knew he was annoying Charlie, whom he disliked. 'Broken marriage. New marriage across water. The initials "R" and "S". Well, "S" is your wife's second initial, isn't it? Two more children.'

'Yes, yes,' Charlie interrupted, 'but what about all the things that didn't happen? An accident or illness. A scandal. The initials "H.S." What about them?'

'Oh, don't worry about them,' Max said tartly, 'there's plenty of time for them. As far as I remember you have rather a good lifeline. Shall we have another reading?'

'No, thanks.'

* * *

After dinner Carey said, 'What was the business you wanted to talk about, Marsh?'

He was smoking a short fat cigar and didn't answer.

'Hey listen, I gave up a hot date for tonight, don't brush me off with your agent's stare.'

He took the cigar out of his mouth and studied it. Then he suddenly said, 'I'm fifty-six years old, a cripple – and don't give me any bullshit about a club foot not making me a cripple – *you* try dragging it around for a few days. I've been married once and made a mess of it. On the good side I'm rich, powerful in my own little way. I don't gamble, drink too much or screw any good-looking piece of ass that comes my way. I'm kind, generous and clean. I don't give a shit about the black so-called problem and I want you to marry me.'

Carey looked at him in amazement. 'What?'

'You heard me right. I want to marry you. You're a very sharp broad, you should jump at the chance.' He was trying to play if funny, but the way he was shredding the leaves of tobacco, on his cigar with nervous fingers made it quite plain he was serious.

Carey recovered her composure. She had never even considered Marshall in a romantic sense. He had been the boss figure in her life for seven years, and during that time she had watched and learnt from him, and pulled herself right up from being a dumb little secretary to where she was today.

'You don't have to answer me at once,' he said. 'Take time to think about it. I know it's a shock for you, but I've been thinking about it for the last year. We'd be good for each other. If you like, I'll romance you a bit, take you out to dinner, send you flowers, although Christ knows I'm a bit too old for all that. But if it's what you want, I'll do it.'

She put her slim hand over his. 'I'm very flattered, Marsh. I'm sort of speechless though. I never thought, well, I mean, what I want to say, well, Oh God, I told you I was sort of speechless.'

He stood up. 'Think it over. We'll talk about it later, or not at all. See how you feel.'

He limped off to join the crowd gathered around Max Thorpe.

* * *

'I predict,' Max was saying to Natalie Allen, 'two more beautiful babies, could be twins, and plenty of travelling; it seems you're always on the move. It looks like you and Clay are going to have a long and happy life together.'

Natalie pulled her hand away and covered her irritation with a charming smile. It wasn't what she had wanted to hear at all.

'Who's next?' Max enquired, enjoying himself immensely. 'How about you?' He addressed himself to Sunday. She started to protest, but found herself propelled towards Max by an enthusiastic Dindi.

'You have very delicate hands,' Max remarked. 'You are not married but perhaps you have been. Yes, I see a definite indication that you have been. It was not a happy marriage. I see signs of great stress – very great stress. Your parents are dead – a crash – perhaps an aeroplane? You are on your own, you are very quiet. I see many lovers, another marriage.'

Sunday sat quite still, listening intently. This man was uncanny. He knew everything. She forgot about the other people listening too.

'You're right,' she whispered. 'What else do you see? Will I be happy?'

A strange question, Max thought. Usually they asked, Will I be rich, famous, successful?

He said, 'I would have to do a proper chart to tell you that. I see an extremely strong career line, fantastic success. I see – a letter, a letter. You must not ignore the letter. Your lifeline broken – no, no, no, I mean marriage.' He stopped abruptly. 'I can't see any more.'

'Oh, please!' She wondered if Paulo had left a letter she had somehow or other missed. She pushed her hand back at Max. 'Please tell me more.'

His eyes clouded over and his head ached. Sometimes this happened and he got carried away and went too far. He had gone too far with this girl. He should never have mentioned a broken lifeline. It was so strange, this power he had. 'I'm sorry, dear. There is no more. I can see nothing else.'

Charlie noticed how upset she was and he broke up the gathering around Max to tell a funny story. Then when everyone was drinking again, he went to find her. He had noticed her slip out onto the patio.

She was standing beside the pool, but as he went to join her, Branch appeared and from the shadows he watched them chat for a while and then turn and walk to the house. Charlie went quickly back inside.

* * *

Once home, Max Thorpe changed into a silk dressing gown, hand-embroidered with the signs of the Zodiac. First he washed and liberally splashed his round pink body with a musky-smelling perfume. He put on some Japanese music – so soothing – and opened a bottle of champagne in preparation for Branch's arrival.

Then he sat on a pile of cushions and let his mind drift back over the evening. It had been another triumph for him. Practically every party he went to now came under his spell. The great Max Thorpe held court, and all the most important people gathered around him. He made it a firm rule never to tell them anything bad; they were only interested in hearing the good things. Sometimes it was difficult though. Sometimes, when their faces became mere shadows and words poured forth from his mouth, words he found hard to control. He remembered the year before when a very famous actor had sat beside him, and in the man's palm he had only seen emptiness. He had talked fast about new deals and triumphs and successes.

The man was pleased. Two days later he died in a plane crash en route to Spain. Such was life. Max would certainly have made him no happier by telling him he had no future. With the girl tonight he had seen strange things, not necessarily death, but something strange.

The doorbell chimed and he hurriedly got up. What a marvellous physique Branch Strong had. What a wonderful night lay ahead.

He turned the Japanese music louder and answered the door. Branch shuffled from one foot to the other, making no attempt to enter. 'Hi,' he muttered.

'Come in, dear boy, come in.'

They went together into the living room and Max gestured for Branch to sit on the cushions. Then he poured him a glass of champagne and waggled a short pink finger at him. 'Tonight, I predict, *you* are going to get fucked!'

Chapter Twenty-One

The next two weeks passed quickly for Sunday. She was busy with fittings, interviews and publicity photos. She heard from Steve Magnum only once. He telephoned to know if she would like to use his private plane to fly to Acapulco. She politely refused.

Carey had lined up some houses for her to look at, and she rented a car so that she could get around without having to depend on Carey or cabs.

The houses were not what she wanted – either too big and ornate, or not near enough to the sea. Finally she found a beach house at Malibu which was available for a year.

It was situated on a private road right by the beach and, although small, was just what she wanted. She loved the small patio at the back, with wooden steps leading practically into the sea. The house would be vacant by the time she returned from Acapulco, and she rented it at once.

Branch had written her one long scrawly letter. She missed him and their dinners at his favourite health restaurant.

Since the party at Dindi's, she had tried in vain to see Max Thorpe. It seemed imperative to her that she talk to this man. Perhaps he could tell her more. Anyway it became an obsession that she have a meeting with him.

He was impossible to get hold of. His secretary said on the phone that he no longer gave private readings. She tried to contact him at his television studio, but he was unobtainable. She wrote and received no reply. Finally, she asked Carey's advice. Carey said, 'Forget it, he's an old faggot quack. But if you really want to see him, get your boyfriend Branch to arrange you an appointment – *he'll* have *no* problem.'

She called Branch in Mexico. It took three days to locate him, and although unenthusiastic, he promised to see what he could do.

The next day Max Thorpe's secretary phoned and said an appointment had been made for her on Saturday at twelve o'clock. It would cost her a thousand dollars and please bring cash. In the meantime, what were her time and date of birth?

* * *

Max Thorpe rarely did personal charts any more. It was too time-consuming and he had other things to occupy him. His television show took up most of his time, and then he wrote a weekly column of horoscopes which was syndicated to one hundred and forty newspapers. He had various other forms of activity also. 'I Predict' T-shirts and badges and posters. In fact, he was involved in negotiations to open a chain of 'I Predict' shops throughout the country.

Max Thorpe was doing very well indeed.

He only agreed to see Sunday because of Branch's phone call. For days, he had been trying to reach the boy. He had sent cables and letters and tried to get through on the phone, but all to no avail. After the one night at his house, Branch had collected his fifteen hundred dollars and taken off for Mexico. He hadn't even acknowledged the cables. Then suddenly out of the blue he had telephoned. Max was delighted and asked if he could come up to see him for a weekend.

'Sure,' Branch drawled, 'only we'll have to meet away from the location, and I want you to do me a favour.'

'Anything,' Max declared. Branch had far surpassed the fake Indian from Disneyland.

So that was how Sunday got her appointment.

* * *

She appeared at Max's house promptly at twelve. The thousand dollars cash had come as a bit of a shock, but she wanted to see him, and if that was what it cost – well, that's what she would have to pay.

He kept her waiting twenty minutes in a strange dark room with the sunlight curtained firmly out.

He swept in finally, wearing a Zodiac shirt and black leather trousers that emphasized his plumpness. He then talked for half an hour about himself, his show, and his talent.

Sunday was beginning to despair about him ever getting around to her.

At last he said, 'I think we shall start with the cards. I have a chart for you, but perhaps you would care to take notes.' He handed her a notepad embossed at the top of each page with 'Max Thorpe – Predict'.

He started to speak very rapidly in short unfinished sentences, things about her that she knew no one could have told him. It was incredible.

He covered her past briefly until he came to the time of her marriage. Then he talked for quite some time about how she should not blame herself for what had happened, that it would have come to pass anyway.

He stared at her with watery eyes. 'You must forget all about it. It is a closed period of your life. You are not to blame. You must close it from your mind and think no more of it. Look to the future with a light heart, for I see much success.'

He told her initials of people important to her future. Of contracts, of advice from an older man to which she must listen. Then he stopped. He could go no further. There was something strange, something he couldn't fathom – not death, just something.

He stood up. 'Sunday, you are a very lucky girl. Yours will be no mediocre fame. Take great care of yourself and always behave with caution. But believe me, you must forget the past.'

He had been talking to her for over an hour.

'Thank you, Mr Thorpe. I really appreciate your seeing me.' She felt lightheaded and relieved. He had been right about everything else, so perhaps he was right that the whole thing with Paulo wasn't her fault. She fumbled in her white shoulder bag. 'I have the money, the cash.'

He held up his hand. 'No. I have changed my mind. I don't want your money. Feel free to see me again. We shall be friends.' He had decided payment was a petty gesture, and perhaps it would disturb Branch. After all, he certainly didn't need money, and anyhow, he liked the girl, they *would* be friends. And if he were right about her future, she would be a friend worth having.

* * *

Sunday flew to Acapulco feeling much better. Somehow the session with Max Thorpe had relieved her immensely. The fact that he had told her she must forget the past seemed to change things. She would forget. She would forget about Rome and Paulo and start afresh. She *would* go out and mix and date and do all the things that Carey had been nagging her to do. Acapulco and the new film would be a starting point, and then she had the beach house to look forward to on her return.

Carey was delighted with the change in her. 'That Maxie boy must be one hell of an analyst,' she said. 'Maybe I should see him myself.' Since the party and Marshall's proposal, she was confused. She had never thought of Marshall as a potential boyfriend, let alone a lover. Her life was very well organized – several boyfriends at a time, one of whom she would be sleeping with. Then, when it looked even vaguely serious, on to the next. She had worked too long and too hard to put her job second to anything or anyone.

However, Marshall was different. She had always looked up to him, admired him, copied him, even been a little bit in awe of him. His proposal had come as a great shock. She had decided to fly to Acapulco with Sunday and stay a few days, think things out.

They sat in the black Cadillac sent to meet them at the airport, the air conditioning going full blast and a glass partition separating them from the young Mexican driver allocated to Sunday.

'What am I going to do?' Carey asked for the fifteenth time.

'It's simple,' Sunday replied patiently, 'if you love him, marry him, and if you don't love him, don't marry him.'

'Oh honey, what the hell has *love* got to do with it? It's far more complex than that. I might hate him in bed, he might hate me if we should have black children, I might—'

'That's a healthy sign, at least you're considering children.'

'I'd love children,' Carey's eyes clouded over, 'only they might be little black cripples.'

'Carey, shut up. Is that your problem? Are you worried because of his leg?'

'Not really. I don't know. I'm frightened. I've never been involved with a man like him before.'

'Sleep with him then. Maybe that will help you decide how you feel.'

'Listen to you – Miss Anti-Sex!'

Sunday laughed. 'I never said I was anti-sex, just anti-everything.'

'Hmmm, it's going to be interesting to see the new you with Steve Magnum. He'll eat you for breakfast in your present frame of mind.'

'I'm not going to leap into Steve's bed. I may have changed, but not that much.'

Carey grinned. 'They say he's the best.'

The driver pressed a button and the glass slid open. 'Your hotel, Miss Simmons. Very beautiful, yes?'

'Yes.' It reminded her of Rio. Pale pink bungalows perched on a hillside, each with their own pool. 'I'm going to love it here,' she said to Carey.

Carey nodded. 'Who wouldn't?'

Chapter Twenty-Two

Not one decent job. Not one good screw to watch. No action at all. And Marge shuffling around at home, nagging and watchful.

Herbert felt well and truly frustrated. He hadn't even been able to follow up his first and glorious letter to Sunday Simmons. Was she wondering what had become of him?

He had finished his job for the evening, driving an old-time horror star on a personal appearance at a supermarket opening. No one had turned up, so Herbert was finished three hours before he expected to be. He decided to use those three hours to his advantage – the Supreme Chauffeur Company would never know.

It was nine o'clock when he left the Beverly Hills area. He drove slowly along the Strip, the big black Cadillac easy beneath his touch.

The hippies were gathered outside their usual haunts, sitting huddled on the sidewalk or wandering aimlessly about.

Herbert spat out of his window. Let the little long-haired morons get some discipline. The girls were all whores, four-teen- and fifteen-year-old whores with flowing hair and weird outfits. One of them sidled up to the car as it waited at a light.

'I'll screw for ten bucks,' she mumbled.

Herbert looked her up and down. She was about eighteen,

skinny, with a pointed ugly face and freaked-out hair. She wore a shabby multi-coloured robe to the ground, and many rows of black beads.

He started to sweat. It had been a long time. 'Get in,' he said harshly.

The girl ran round the car and jumped in. She began to bite her nails, and surveyed Herbert with blank red eyes. 'Don't go too far,' she said, 'just drive up in the hills a couple of blocks. For a straight screw it's fifteen – anything special it's more.'

He didn't say anything, just swung the big Cadillac up Miller Drive and kept going.

'Not too far,' the girl said sharply.

He remained silent.

'Christ! What are you – deaf and dumb?'

He had found a suitable side-turning and pulled the car to a halt. It was dark and all that could be heard was the chirping of crickets.

The girl started to pull off her robe.

He watched her. She had a flat chest like a boy.

'OK. Hand over the bread and let's get it done.'

They were all whores. They all wanted money and sex in that order. Sometimes in the other order. All of them. 'Come on,' she whined, 'I haven't got all night.' She reached for his fly and started to unzip it. 'You can pay me after. I'll give you a special for twenty. You look like a nice john.'

All the while she was manipulating him out of his trousers. He sat behind the steering wheel, staring straight ahead. She smelt. He could smell various body odours as she leant down and tried to push his limp member in her mouth.

'Stop it,' he cried, bringing his hand down and smashing it on her head. 'Get your filthy mouth off me. Stop it – stop it – stop it.'

He didn't cease hitting her until she crumpled to the floor of the car and lay there very still.

He was sobbing with rage. The bitch. Why had she picked on him?

He struggled and kicked her out of the car, throwing her robe after her.

He adjusted his clothing and calmed down. Then he thought of Sunday Simmons, and miraculously he was hard and virile, a real man. If only he could write to her now and enclose his precious offering. There was no other way for him, not with Marge, not with anyone. The ultimate delight was only possible with pen in hand.

He left the girl lying there and drove off. To hell with Marge poking and nosing around. He was going home to lock himself in and write a masterpiece. Then he would have a long, cleansing shower. Later he would take the car back and mail the letter.

* * *

Marge was out.

'Bitch!' Herbert muttered. He had told her quite clearly that she wasn't to go out at night. He supposed she was with their neighbour. Well, he would soon put a stop to *that*. After he'd written his letter he would go next door and drag her home, *and* tell the cow neighbour what he thought of her.

He went in the kitchen and poured himself a glass of milk. A large moth fluttered around the light. Quietly he caught it, and tore off both its wings before throwing it in the garbage can.

Then he went upstairs into the box-room. He picked up his pen . . .

* * *

It was a wonderful letter. So full and explicit, and there was a plastic bag to go with it. He was satisfied. Perhaps one day Sunday and he would read through his letters together and do everything that he had written about. She was sure to save them, perhaps bound with pink ribbon. After all, they *were* love letters.

He sang in the shower, in a flat toneless voice that he liked to think sounded like Perry Como's.

Then he dressed and carefully put his letter in the glove-compartment of the Cadillac, locking it up before setting off to find Marge.

* * *

The front yard was a mass of overgrown grass and weeds. The Crisps had not touched it since moving in.

Herbert could imagine what kind of people they were – slobs, like Marge. Uneducated coarse slobs. Well, they weren't getting their dirty hands on *his* wife.

They were obviously home, as lights peeped from every room, although the drapes were closed.

He edged up to the house, intending to surprise them. Round the side there was a small gap in one of the drapes. He bent down and peered in. It was difficult to see as the gap was so small he could only focus with one eye.

Marge was spreadeagled on a sofa, stark naked, and around her stood ten nude men and women, who appeared to be singing; Marge was joining in, and she was smiling. There was some sort of paint – or was it blood? – all over her breasts.

Herbert froze. One of the men, fat and balding, stepped towards Marge. He was wearing a black mask. One of the women handed round black candles, and when they were lit, the lights were turned out, and the fat man fell onto Marge, heaving back and forth, while the others knelt down and watched.

Herbert could not believe what he was witnessing. It was disgusting. But it was exciting him and he stayed quietly where he was.

One by one the men in the group stepped forward and fell upon Marge, and only when they had all had their turn were the candles extinguished and the lights turned on.

Marge got up, quite happy, and accepted a glass of something and an affectionate pat on the back from a tall woman with straggly white hair and stringy breasts.

Herbert remained frozen to the spot. His eye hurt and his mouth was dry.

Finally he made his way home. He eradicated any sign of having been there earlier. Then he got in the Cadillac and sped silently away.

Chapter Twenty-Three

Serafina adored Hollywood. She arrived dressed from head to toe in crimson, with a slinky silver-fox fur, complete with crafty face, draped around her shoulders.

Charlie was proud of her. She was one hell of a mother who acted like a woman half her age.

His two children were solemn and respectful, almost as if Lorna had told them to be on their best behaviour.

'Daddy, we don't have to call your new wife Mummy, do we?' Sean asked in the car from the airport.

'No, you can call her what you like,' Charlie replied. There were a few names he would like to call Dindi himself. She had refused to come to the airport, claiming a headache. A headache indeed. More like a bellyache because he had turned down the idea of her being in *Roundabout*. He realized that if Serafina and the kids were going to have any sort of decent holiday, he would have to relent and let her be in the picture, although the last thing he wanted as a wife was an aspiring actress.

'It's wonderful here, wonderful, Charlie. Where's your wife?' Serafina asked, bright bird eyes staring him down.

'She thought it would be better to meet you at the house.'

'Did she now, did she? Pretty little thing. Sharp, I bet. Smart as a button. I don't know why you wanted to go tying yourself-up again so soon. You can take your pick now, have a bit of fun. Is she – you know?'

He laughed. Trust Serafina to think the worst. 'No, she's not pregnant. You'll like her.'

'I hope so.' Serafina rescued several straggles of bright red hair escaping from her crimson beret. 'I'd like to have been here for the wedding. I love weddings. I'd like to have seen that Lost Vega.'

'Las Vegas,' Charlie corrected. 'We'll go there, maybe next weekend. Natalie and Clay might come.'

'Can we go to Disneyland, Daddy?' Cindy enquired. She looked exactly like Lorna, much to Charlie's annoyance.

'We can go wherever you want.'

Sean supported his sister. 'Mummy said we should go to Disneyland. She said it's super.'

'Mummy's never been there,' Charlie retaliated.

'No, but Uncle Jim has, and he says it's terrific, with real Indians and cowboys and a showboat and wagons and—'

'We'll go, I said.' Charlie was furious at the reference to Uncle Jim.

Back at the house Dindi was nowhere to be seen. George was sent off to find her.

Serafina said, 'A nice cup of tea, that's what I'd like. There's nothing as good as a nice cup of tea. Show me where the kitchen is. I brought six packets of Lyons Quick Brew with me.' She fumbled in her handbag and produced a packet.

'You can't start messing around in the kitchen, the maid will do it.' When on earth would his mother realize that he was a big star and had people to do everything?

'I wouldn't trust an American to make *my* tea,' Serafina huffed. 'Show me the kitchen.'

* * *

Dindi was shopping. She had so far spent two and a half thousand dollars and was still going strong. She was trying on a skimpy orange silk jersey dress and preening in the mirror. 'What do you think of this?' she asked the salesgirl.

The salesgirl, wearing a similar dress, stifled a yawn and said, 'Great.' She was bored with watching Mrs Charlie Brick buy everything in sight.

'OK. I'll take it. What other colours does it come in?'

'White, black and a sort of plum.'

'I'll have it in all colours.'

'Dindi?'

'Yeah. Oh – hi, Natalie.'

'Hello, I was told this was the place to buy clothes. What a terrific dress.'

'Yeah.' Dindi wished she had stayed in the fitting room instead of coming out to inspect herself in the main room.

'I thought Charlie's mother and the children were arriving today.'

'Yeah, well I guess they are. I figured they'd want to be alone.'

'Oh.' Natalie smiled. 'Very thoughtful of you. You haven't met Serafina yet, have you?'

'Nope.' Dindi shook her head, edging back to the fitting room.

Natalie followed. 'She's quite a character, idolizes Charlie of course, and he adores her. I do hope the two of you get along.'

'Why shouldn't we?' Dindi shrugged off the dress, revealing red bikini pants – and that was all.

Natalie felt her eyes drawn jealously to the girl's pointy young breasts. 'No reason really, but she is difficult. She's quite old and yet she still wants to have men . . .'

Dindi giggled. 'She sounds like a swinger. I expect I'll still want to have men when I'm quite old, won't you?'

Natalie flushed. 'I just thought I'd warn you about her.' Oh God, Charlie had married a real little bitch. She would have to move swiftly to get rid of her.

'Yeah – well, thanks for the warning. I'll fix Charlie's mom up with a live one! Oh, by the way, how's Clay?'

'He's fine,' Natalie replied stiffly. 'Did you know him long in Rome?'

Dindi winked. 'Long enough.' She giggled as Natalie opened her mouth to reply. 'I'm kidding. Are you jealous?'

'Not at all. In fact I'm quite used to the fact that Clay will go to bed with any silly little tart that gives him the green light.'

Dindi's eyes narrowed.

'Well, bye bye, dear. I do hope we'll all get together soon.'

'Bye bye, Natalie dear.' Furious, Dindi put on her clothes and called to the salesgirl. 'For Christ's sake hurry up with my things, I haven't got all day.'

* * *

'Where have you been?' Charlie didn't relish playing the jealous husband, but having made excuses to Serafina all day about Dindi's absence, he was in a mild fury.

'Shopping. I get so bored just sitting around.'

'But you knew my mother was arriving today. You knew I'd only gone to the airport.'

She looked sulky. 'I guess I forgot.'

'I guess you did.' Angrily he marched to the window and stared out. Cindy and Sean were splashing in the pool. Serafina was upstairs, taking a nap. 'Look, if you want the part so badly, it's yours,' he blurted.

Her face lit up. 'Honestly, baby? That's marvie. I'll be terrific in it, you won't be sorry.' She rushed over to him and hugged him from behind, rubbing herself against him.

He turned round and she slid her hands under his shirt.

'I didn't want to marry an actress,' he remarked.

Her hands wriggled their way under the waistband of his trousers and grabbed hold of him. She felt him harden and sank to her knees.

'Not here, Dindi,' he muttered.

'Why not? We're married, aren't we?'

* * *

'The secret of eternal youth, my dear, is keeping busy,' Serafina announced at dinner. 'I myself have never been idle.'

'I can believe that,' Dindi replied, quite exhausted at just watching Serafina darting off to the kitchen every five minutes.

'When I was in the theatre, I was known affectionately backstage as Miss Vitality.'

'Really?' Dindi looked interested. Since Charlie had told her she had the part in *Roundabout* she had gone out of her way to charm Serafina and his rotten kids.

'Yes, Miss Vitality. Oh dear me, those were the days. I can remember the line of gentlemen friends waiting at the stage door, all well-to-do and handsome, and then I met Charlie's father – God rest his soul – a fine man. We had a wonderful life together.'

Charlie looked at his mother in surprise. She must be getting old. His old man had been a right bastard and had walked out on her. A fine life indeed.

'Has Charlie told you of his early days?'

'Nope.' Dindi shook her head. 'I guess he was figuring you would.' She stifled a yawn and smiled brightly. How she longed to say 'Has anyone ever told you you're an old bore?'

The phone rang and Charlie reached for the dining-table extension. When he hung up he said, 'Clay and Natalie are going to drop by for coffee.'

'That's nice,' Serafina said. 'Anyone else?'

Charlie knew she was wondering if he had picked out any potential 'friends' for her. When he had first asked her to come to Hollywood with the children she had wanted to bring Archie, her current beau. But Charlie couldn't stand Archie, so he had said that Serafina would meet plenty of more interesting men if she came on her own. It was a problem fixing up one's mother. Not that she liked young men, she preferred them older than herself, but in Hollywood finding an older man prepared to take on a nearly seventy-year-old woman was impossible. Hollywood was full of young available women. It was a problem Charlie had decided to ignore, and when Serafina got too fidgety he would send for Archie.

'Er, I don't think so. By the way, I thought perhaps next weekend we might fly up to Las Vegas. Would you like that?'

Serafina nodded. She didn't plan to spend her holiday closeted up in Charlie's house. She was still an attractive woman, she must get out and be seen. Just because Charlie was jealous of introducing her to men, fancy, her own son jealous. Well it was understandable really.

'I am sixty-three years of age,' she announced to Dindi, cleverly deducting six years, 'and I feel like a girl.'

'You look wonderful,' Dindi murmured, thinking she might look a bit better if she cleaned off all that terrible theatrical make-up and false eyelashes at her age! Really!

'Yes, people find it hard to believe, but it's the truth. And you my dear, how old are you?' Serafina fixed her with a penetrating stare as if daring her to lie.

'Twenty,' replied Dindi, smiling sweetly and knocking off three years. If the old bitch could lie about her age so could she.

'Oh, twenty,' Serafina fluttered. 'Twenty. In my day girls of twenty—'

'Did I ever show you the pictures I have of Serafina when she was twenty?' Charlie interrupted.

'No,' replied Dindi, thinking, so this is how one spends one's evening when married to a movie star.

'I'll have to show you. She was a real knockout, weren't you, love?' He put his arm around his mother.

She smiled, and Charlie thought – I must get her to a good dentist while she's here.

'Do you remember the good old days, Charlie son?'

Yes, he remembered. The fading old theatres, stale smells and Serafina's boyfriends.

'Those were the days.' A tear sprang to her eyes. 'Those were the good times. Just your father, you and me.'

131

What good times? Charlie thought. Stuck outside a pub in some asshole of a town with a packet of crisps and a lemonade while Serafina and her latest 'beau' lived it up. Anyway – so what. No good looking back. He loved Serafina. She was his mother. She had kept him with her when he was a boy, and that was the main thing.

'I always knew Charlie would be a star,' Serafina said sharply. 'I encouraged him in everything he wanted to do. He's got my vitality and drive. I could have been a star myself, but I gave it all up to look after him.'

Dindi yawned openly. People's pasts were a bore. As far as she was concerned, Charlie was a big movie star, and before that she didn't want to know.

'Tired?' Serafina questioned.

'Yes,' Dindi replied, 'I had a job to do this afternoon that tired me out.' She shot a secret smile at Charlie.

He smiled back. She looked so pretty and innocent. He could hardly believe that she was the same girl who had made love to him earlier.

'You pop on up to bed, love, if you like,' he said. 'Serafina won't mind, and I'll explain to the Allens.'

'Are you sure, darling? I *would* like to.' She wanted to go upstairs and try on her new clothes and read the script of *Roundabout* now that she had the part.

'You go ahead love, see you later.' He watched her say goodnight to Serafina, then peck him on the cheek. She had such a compact, sexy body. It made him feel good to think that she was all his. It might not be such a bad idea having her in the movie after all. Other men could look but not touch. Let the world see what Charlie Brick had.

Chapter Twenty-Four

Acapulco was hot. After the first day's shooting in the mountains, Sunday was a wreck, the heat was impossible.

She had been working hard, surrounded by a mostly Mexican crew, and three Americans – the director, Woody, the cameraman, Mike, and the continuity girl, Marisa.

Woody and Marisa were having an affair. He was a pleasant, thirtyish man whom Steve Magnum had picked personally. He had not directed a movie before, only television. Marisa was twenty-four and pretty.

Sunday liked them both. As a director Woody was quiet, considerate and extremely encouraging. There was a great difference between him and Abe Stein. Abe represented the old-style Hollywood. Woody the new.

Upon arrival, she had received a huge basket of flowers from Steve, with a note saying 'Welcome'. Apart from that, no word from him at all.

'You had your chance and blew it,' Carey said. 'He's probably shacked up in that mansion of his with a beautiful Mexican virgin.'

'I hope he is,' Sunday replied. She was secretly glad. Now that she had reached the stage of deciding to get involved, there was no need to.

For a week she and Carey had done nothing but loaf around, sunbathing and swimming.

The day before she started work, Carey left, saying, 'Well, I guess it's decision time.'

She found it lonely with Carey gone. The Las Brisas Hilton Hotel was very beautiful, but somehow Sunday felt it was the sort of place one should be with a man.

She spent a quiet evening on her own, sending out for food, and studying her script. The next day Steve was due to appear for a scene in the mountains where he was supposed to rescue her. In the script she had escaped after being kidnapped. It was also a love scene, and she looked forward to it with a mixture of anticipation and uncertainty.

* * *

'Ha!' Marisa exclaimed. 'How about that bundle of goodies?' She nudged Sunday, who was sitting in the canvas chair next to her, reading a book.

Steve Magnum was approaching accompanied by a young curvy Mexican girl, with long black hair flowing to her waist and green hungry eyes.

'Hello, ladies.' Steve waved casually from a distance, and patting the young girl on the bottom, shoved her towards them. 'Keep an eye on Enchilada for me, Marisa baby.' He then went off in a huddle with Woody.

'That man!' Marisa said, shaking her head and laughing. 'He's too much!'

The girl, nicknamed Enchilada, came over with sulky suspicious eyes.

'Hi,' Marisa said, 'grab a chair and make yourself at home, it's going to be a long hard day. I'm Marisa and this is Sunday Simmons.'

The girl nodded briefly and sat in a chair several yards away. She then turned to stare at Steve and Woody.

'Friendly,' Marisa remarked. 'Sunday, I think they're going to be ready soon. You want to get dressed, I'll send wardrobe in to you.'

'Good idea.' It was eleven in the morning and Sunday was becoming bored just sitting around. The Mexicans seemed to take much longer to get started than the Americans. She had arrived at eight, spent two hours in make-up and hairdressing, and then had a long wait. Steve had now disappeared into the make-up caravan, so perhaps they would start soon.

In the scene she was wearing white trousers and a skimpy white top. A matching jacket was around her shoulders. She was supposed to appear dishevelled and distraught.

'You look great,' Steve said, when they were in front of the camera. 'How do you like Acapulco?'

'It's nice.' She smiled at him with her eyes. 'Thank you for the flowers.'

'You're always thanking me for flowers. How about sending some?'

They both laughed while Enchilada glowered from the sidelines.

'Took myself a little insurance,' he said.

'Insurance?'

'Against you, baby – against you. My little Mexican tomato is only sixteen, so I guess that should keep my greedy hands from grabbing you. That's the way you want it, isn't it?'

She just smiled. She wasn't sure at all that that was the way she wanted it. Steve was magnetically attractive, and it had been a long time between men.

Woody came over and chatted to them about the scene.

The rest of the morning passed quickly. Steve and Sunday worked well together and they finished three short scenes with hardly any retakes.

When the lunch break came, Steve grabbed Enchilada and took off in his helicopter. Sunday had her lunch with the rest of the crew from a mobile canteen. She sat with Woody and Marisa. She was beginning to be a little piqued by Steve's apparent uninterest.

The first scene after lunch was the love scene. It started with Steve pulling off her jacket, laying it on the ground and

135

pushing her down on it. In the film she was supposed to fight him, struggle, and then submit.

'Look,' Woody explained, 'when you're on the ground I want him to pull your top down. That's when I want you to lie very still and just stare at him with those eyes of yours.'

'How far down?' Sunday asked suspiciously.

'Well, off, sweetheart. The camera won't see anything, Steve will be covering you.'

'In that case my top won't have to come right off.'

Woody laughed. 'I'm not looking for a free show, but sure the top will have to come off. When I say the camera won't see anything, I mean we're not going to pan in for a great close-up on your bosom. But it's quite obvious that you can't have the top down a little; it will look messy and awkward. He's got to get it off and throw it out of shot. Then you'll be in an embrace with him, so all we're going to see is arms and sides and things.'

'Woody, I have a clause in my contract that says no nude scenes. Didn't you know?'

'No, I didn't,' he, snapped. 'Christ, you make me feel like a dirty-minded little schoolboy trying to glimpse a lady's boobs. I'm a director and I hope a good one, and in these days of truth and realism you're going to look mighty silly clutching a top around you to preserve a little old-fashioned modesty.' His tone changed, becoming persuasive and soft. 'Trust me, honey. I know what's going to look right.'

She sighed. 'I don't understand what difference there is whether I keep the top on or not.'

'There, you see,' he was triumphant, '*you* don't understand the difference, but I do. So please believe I'm right.'

'I had a horrible experience with Abe Stein on—'

'I am *not* Abe Stein. Well send everyone who's not needed home. OK, sweetheart, OK?'

'If you really think it's necessary.'

'I really think.'

She wished that Carey were still there. Why was there this

obsession with nudity? Why didn't she have the strength to stick to her decision? Was it because she liked and trusted Woody? Or did she know in her own mind that the scene would be more realistic the way he wanted it.

Steve returned in his helicopter, Enchilada sulky by his side.

Woody was getting rid of crew members whose presence was not strictly necessary.

Marisa entered Sunday's caravan and offered her a stick of gum. 'Believe me,' she said, 'I'd be the first one to yell if it wasn't right for the scene. Do you think I want my boyfriend getting an eyeful of what I'm sure are a beautiful pair?'

* * *

They rehearsed the scene first.

Steve grabbed her from behind, snatched the jacket off her shoulders and forced her down, pinning her arms to her side. Then he kissed her.

'The mechanics are fine,' Woody said when they had got that far.

'Yeah!' Steve agreed. He was lying on top of Sunday and she could feel his thin hard body, and shivered in spite of herself. His lips had been insistent and demanding.

'Now,' Woody said, 'I want you to keep holding her with one hand and edge the top down with the other. We'll take it from the beginning and shoot.'

Steve smiled at her as he got up. 'One take, huh?'

She smiled back at him. 'I'll try.' She felt elated and excited in spite of herself. She knew Steve would be impressed with her body. She became unaware of the crew, Woody, everybody, and immersed herself in thinking only of Steve.

The scene started smoothly, but then Steve fluffed a line and Woody shouted, 'Cut.'

They began again, the small Mexican clapper boy saying in his fractured English – '*Cash*, scene 31. Take two.'

Everything went well. Steve started to kiss her and pull off her top. 'Mamma mia!' he muttered under his breath as he looked at her briefly, and then embraced her tightly.

His shirt was open and she felt a cool film of sweat between them. Her fingernails raked his back.

'Cut,' shouted Woody. 'Cut,' he repeated as they made no move to separate.

Steve drew slowly off her. She was breathing heavily and staring at him.

'I think I just blew my insurance,' he said.

Chapter Twenty-Five

Roundabout was going well. The new script favoured Charlie, and even Angela Carter's part had become minor in comparison.

He threw himself into his role completely, enjoying himself. He knew he was giving a good performance – the dailies told him that, and the way the crew laughed after certain scenes. It was notoriously hard to get any reaction from a crew. They were there to do their job and nothing ever moved them.

Angela and he were casually friendly. Since her break-up with Steve Magnum, she had started an affair with Cy: it occurred to her that professionally Cy was a much better bet. So she concentrated on playing her part effectively, and getting Cy to dump Emerald.

A rush of publicity resulted from Dindi joining the cast. The newspapers started to refer to her as film star Dindi Sydne or Mrs Charlie Brick. She posed for countless stills and enjoyed it all thoroughly.

On the screen she came over as surprisingly fresh and appealing, and Angela started complaining to Cy that her part was too big.

In a way Charlie was pleased, but it didn't please him when reporters visited the set and took more interest in her than in him. After all, he was the star of the family.

Eventually he insisted that all reporters be banned, and a

feud between him and the publicity department began. Dindi was on the publicity department's side, and she and Charlie had a series of fights about his attitude. They also had fights about the money she was spending. And about Serafina and the children, who had been with them nearly a month.

Charlie complained that Dindi spent no time with them at all. *He* was busy at the studio every day, but *she* was only needed a couple of days a week, so she had plenty of time to spend with his family if she wanted to.

She *didn't* want to. She loathed Serafina and thought the children a couple of brats.

Charlie was furious, especially because he had only agreed to her appearance in *Roundabout* so that she would be polite to his family. Secretly he tried to get her taken off the film, but that was one request he wasn't granted. It was too late.

He fully realized now that he had married a tough, money-grabbing, ambitious female. Just the sort he had been running from.

One lunchtime he confessed his mistake to Clay.

'I don't know what to do, love, I don't know what came over me. I must have been bloody mad. I don't even fancy her any more.'

He didn't tell Clay that the reason he no longer fancied her was because in a recent argument she had yelled at him, 'You might be a good actor, but you're a lousy lay.' The remark had stayed with him. He was extremely sensitive about his sexual prowess.

Was he a lousy lay? Michelle Lomas hadn't thought so.

He brooded on it and finally went to bed with a pretty extra, who assured him that he was 'fantastic'.

Clay was embarrassed. He was in two minds whether to tell Charlie about Rome. He decided not. The marriage was floundering anyway and Charlie might be choked that he hadn't mentioned it before.

Serafina had fortunately found herself a boyfriend. He was a gardener on the estate, a former character actor, about the same age as she was, and very charming. They made a colourful pair.

Charlie suggested that they went on the trip to Las Vegas which he had promised Serafina. She would be returning to London with the children in two weeks, and he wanted to be sure she enjoyed herself. He hired a private jet for the short journey.

Dindi was unenthusiastic about going, but it was either that or staying in Los Angeles with the children, so she agreed to go. It would only be a two-day trip, and perhaps she could fit in a little session with the George Raft-type manager.

Clay and Natalie came along, and Serafina's friend, whose name was Morton, and whom Dindi had cruelly nicknamed Mortuary. She was especially furious that he was accompanying them. 'A fuckin' gardener, only your mother would pick a gardener!' she moaned.

* * *

They stayed at the Forum, arriving early on Saturday morning.

Clay, Natalie and Charlie relaxed round the pool, while Serafina and Morton, armed with six hundred dollars given to them by Charlie, set off to try their luck at the tables.

Dindi complained she was tired and left to take a nap.

'This is the life!' Clay exclaimed, as a toga-clad redhead served him a giant Planters Punch beside the pool. 'What a great place!'

'Any place would be great for you where they have girls sticking their bottoms in your face,' Natalie said tartly. She smiled at Charlie. 'Coming for a swim?'

'No, love, I'm just going to relax.'

Two women in multi-coloured flowered bathing-caps were arguing nearby. 'It is him, Ethel, I know it is.' 'No, it's not, he's much *fatter* than that.' 'Ethel, I'm telling you it's him.' They stared pointedly at Charlie until the one called

141

Ethel suddenly approached and said loudly, 'Are you Charlie Brick?'

He lapsed into his Indian voice, 'I'm very sorry, madam, but you are quite mistaken.'

Clay joined in and said, 'This is the very famous Swahili poet, Señor Charles Bleakworth.'

'Oh!' The woman's mouth dropped open. 'I told my friend you weren't anyone.'

The woman departed, leaving Charlie and Clay in fits of laughter. It was a game they had been playing for years, making up names, characters, confusing people. For a movie star, Charlie was very infrequently recognized – a fact that both disturbed and delighted him. He became so immersed in each role he played that he became that character on the screen and as each role was different, the real Charlie Brick became very hard to spot.

* * *

By lunchtime Charlie wondered if he should phone the room and wake Dindi.

'I'll get her,' Natalie said, 'I have to go upstairs anyway.'

'We'll find Serafina and meet you in the Orgy Room,' Charlie said.

'The *what?*

'It's a restaurant, great food and near-naked waitresses.'

'Oh, Clay will *love* that. I'll see you there in about twenty minutes.'

* * *

'She's a great girl,' Charlie remarked, watching Natalie's slim figure out of sight. 'You're a lucky man.'

Clay laughed. 'I suppose I am. You know it's going to be seven years this month. Seven years!'

'Lorna and I would have been married thirteen years this

year. December's our anniversary. December the fifth.' He sighed. 'You know, with all I've got now, the money, the fame, everything, all I really want is Lorna back.'

'Oh come on, Charlie, it's over, finished. She's married to someone else now, and so are you. For Christ's sake don't keep thinking about her. You've got a world of cooze at your feet.'

'Is that all you ever think about?'

Clay laughed. 'Give me something better to think of. I've knocked off two beautiful little pieces since I've been here.'

It irritated Charlie when Clay talked about his sex life. It was a known fact that he was well hung, and the thought made Charlie extremely jealous. He always made a careful point of never going to bed with a girl with whom Clay had slept.

'Doesn't Natalie mind?' he asked, thinking of the embarrassing scene he had had with her in London.

'She doesn't know,' Clay protested, 'just suspects sometimes. In fact, she only ever caught me once, and that was with the German au pair. Terrible fight. I told you about it, didn't I? When she chased me bollock-naked into the garden and I fell in the pond?'

'Yes.' Charlie laughed, remembering the story well.

'That German bit had the biggest pair of knockers I ever saw. It was Natalie's fault for hiring her. She knows what I'm like about tits. By the way, while we're on the subject, that friend of Dindi's – Sunday Simmons – what wouldn't I give for a piece of that!'

'Hmm . . .' Charlie thought about Sunday reflectively. He had thought about her several times since the party and decided that she was one of the most beautiful women he had ever seen. He remembered her eyes, strange browny-yellow tiger eyes.

'I wonder if she fucks,' Clay said.

'They all do,' Charlie replied shortly. 'You offer them a job and they all do.'

* * *

Natalie went upstairs and changed into pants and a shirt. After lunch she thought she would try the hairdressers, she wanted to look particularly attractive for that evening. She knocked on Dindi's door; they had adjoining suites. There was no reply.

Blast the little tart! She wasn't about to go searching the hotel for her. The bitch would just have to miss lunch.

Natalie walked slowly to the elevator. Things were going well between her and Charlie. She had noticed the small intimate looks he kept giving her. She smiled to herself. It wouldn't be long.

The elevator arrived and she stepped in. It was going up. A tall brunette in a short toga said, 'You musta pressed the wrong button, people are always doing that. It's a drag, you'll have to come right to the top, and then it'll stop at every floor down.'

The elevator zoomed silently up, finally stopping at the eighteenth floor. The girl in the toga got out, and two girls got in, pressing the hold button for another girl hurrying to join them.

Natalie, standing at the back of the elevator, saw Dindi emerge from a room with a good-looking dark-haired man. Then the elevator doors closed and she saw no more.

The girls were talking. 'Well, he grabbed my thigh and I said, "Knock it off, jerk."'

'Honestly, some guys have such a nerve.'

'You can get black and blue just walking around here!'

'Excuse me,' Natalie said. 'What's on the eighteenth floor. Is it part of the hotel?'

The three girls all stared at her. 'Offices,' said one.

'Steam room, staff rooms, management suites. Are you English?' said another.

'Yes.'

'Charlie Brick's staying here, you know,' the third girl confided, 'and Tom Jones came in here one night when he was playing Caesar's. Hey, I've a cousin in a place called Leeds, maybe you know her? Her name's Myrtle Long, she's a model.'

'No, I don't know her.' Natalie shook her head.

'I *looove* English actors,' the first girl said, 'Roger Moore, Peter Sellers, Omar Sharif. Oh, boy!'

'Omar Sharif's not English,' said the girl with the cousin, 'he's an Arab.'

'Well, I dig Arabs too.'

Natalie smiled. Steam rooms, offices, staff rooms, management suites was definitely where Dindi must have been. She wondered with whom. But whoever it was, she planned to find out.

* * *

'I think Dindi's still sleeping,' Natalie remarked, arriving for lunch.

Serafina scowled, furious at having been dragged away from the roulette wheel to eat. 'That girl will sleep her life away. A truly fit person needs no more than six hours a night.'

Morton yawned, as if to confirm the fact that Serafina needed only six hours a night.

Clay was grinning at a statuesque lady, poised with pencil and pad, ready to take their order.

Charlie wished he were back at the house in Los Angeles quietly getting stoned. He didn't feel social. It wasn't right for him to be forced to spend an active weekend when he was working. He should be resting, studying his script. He wished he had brought George, instead of leaving him with the children.

'What's on for this afternoon?' Clay asked.

'I'm going to the hairdressers,' Natalie announced.

'Morton and I shall be returning to the tables,' said Serafina. 'The sun saps your vital energy and ruins your skin.'

'I think I may sleep,' Charlie said.

At that moment Dindi appeared, flushed and pretty. 'Hi there. I thought this is where I'd find you. Charlie, sweetie, I'm doing stills this afternoon. Can I have some bread? I've seen some things I want to buy.'

'Stills for what?' Charlie asked, unaware that the studio had arranged anything for Dindi that weekend.

She pouted. 'For a magazine.'

'What magazine?'

'Just some magazine, I don't know.'

'Well you had better know, otherwise just forget it.'

'Forget it?' Her blue eyes narrowed. 'What do you mean, forget it?'

Charlie realized the whole table was listening – Clay embarrassed, Serafina spiteful, Natalie sympathetic, Morton uninterested.

He smiled coldly. 'Dindi, love, be a good girl and run along and find out what magazine it is. Now that you're such an aspiring actress it wouldn't do for you to appear in the wrong sort of publication.'

His voice was mild, but Dindi realized she had pushed too far. 'OK, honeybunch,' she said, tossing blonde curls. 'See you later, gang.' And she wriggled off in tight jersey slacks and cutoff sweater.

Charlie sighed. He didn't want it and he didn't need it. After the movie Dindi was out.

He went upstairs after lunch and phoned George.

'Send me a cable immediately,' he said. 'Say – meeting imperative on *Roundabout*, urgent. Return at once. Sign it Cy Hamilton.'

An hour or so later the cable arrived, and full of apologies, Charlie showed it to Serafina, now playing black-jack.

She looked dismayed. 'Does that mean we have to go too?'

'No, love, not at all. I'll leave you credit, and you can stay as long as we planned. Dindi will stay too, and Clay and Natalie. You'll be fine.'

Serafina didn't argue.

Next, he located Clay by the pool, chatting up a showgirl. He showed him the cable. 'Sorry, love, it's a real drag. You'll keep an eye on Serafina for me, won't you? I've left her plenty of credit but if she needs any money, give it to her.'

Clay nodded. 'What about Dindi?'

'She's staying too. I don't know where she is, but I've left her a note. Just make sure she stays, and see she's nice to Serafina.'

'Yes, boss!'

'I don't know what I'd do without you and Nat.'

Clay grinned. 'You'd manage.'

Charlie was on a plane half an hour later on his way back to Los Angeles.

Chapter Twenty-Six

The item read: '*Steve Magnum and ravishing eye-stopping Sunday Simmons seem to have found each other on the sunny shores of Acapulco where they are filming* Cash *together. Do we hear wedding bells?*'

The item read: '*Sexsational Sunday Simmons and much-married Steve Magnum constant companions on location for* Cash.'

The item read: '*Steve Magnum seems to have bewitched lovely newcomer Sunday Simmons. Friends say they are inseparable. They are working on* Cash *together.*'

* * *

For once the Hollywood gossip columns read correctly. Sunday and Steve were constantly together.

She found him charming, easygoing, and very attractive. He was so unlike anyone she had ever met before. Always in command of any situation, always laughing and joking. She wasn't sure if she was in love, so she refused to sleep with him.

He couldn't believe it. 'Honey, it's not like you're a virgin. How long has it been for Chrissake?'

She smiled in reply. 'Long enough. I don't want to be another Steve Magnum conquest. Let me be sure.'

So she waited.

'I'm in shock,' he confessed to friends. 'This broad's put me in shock!' But he laughed when he said it, and he respected her and didn't push her into bed. What he did was install Enchilada in a nearby hotel, and she visited him when Sunday returned at night to Las Brisas. It seemed like a fair arrangement. What Sunday didn't know wouldn't hurt her, and as soon as she overcame her doubts, Enchilada would be sent packing with a couple of thousand dollars to soothe her ruffled pride. Actually, it rather pleased Steve that Sunday wasn't prepared to leap straight into the sack; at least it suggested that there hadn't been a long line of guys in front of him. She told him, and he believed her, that there had been no-one since her husband. What a change it made from the usual Hollywood scene which was like a bizarre game of Change Partners.

* * *

Cash was nearing completion. The film Sunday had made with Jack Milan was released, and although her part was only small, she was mentioned favourably in the reviews and started to receive an avalanche of fan mail.

Carey phoned her every day to report the offers she was getting. There was a movie in Europe. A *Bonnie and Clyde*-type film in Texas. A comedy in Hollywood.

Steve advised her not to accept anything. 'Keep 'em waiting and your price will rocket. When they see you in our movie you'll be able to name any terms you want.'

Sunday wasn't sure. It would be months before *Cash* came out and she didn't want to wait that long. It was too much of a risk with the industry in its present state.

Carey was persuaded. 'OK, let's strike while you're hot.'

So Sunday signed for the comedy.

Steve sulked. 'Wouldn't listen to me, huh?' he complained. 'Five minutes in the business and you know it all.'

'I haven't been five minutes in the business. Anyway it's a very good script.'

They were sitting by the pool at his house. It was early evening and they had just finished the day's shooting.

'I'm going for a swim,' she announced, and went to a cubicle and changed into a white bikini.

'Hey, listen, do an old man one favour at least and swim in the raw.'

'What?' she asked laughing. 'You're as bad as all the directors I work with.'

'Listen, baby, it's enough not having you yet. If anyone knew my reputation would be shot to hell. So give me a cheap thrill, huh? Just for kicks.'

'Steve, I can't. You've got a house full of servants. Anyway, I don't think—'

'OK.' He shrugged. 'OK, if you don't even care that much about me. You know we're completely secluded from the house.' He turned away, staring at the pink uneven walls surrounding the pool area and wondering what it was about her that had him so hooked.

There was a splash, and then she called him.

She was floating in the pool, her hair wet and streaming out behind her, and her naked breasts outlined clearly in the opalescent blue water. She wore only the bottom half of her bikini.

He was pleased. 'Hey, baby, that's really something.'

She waited for him to dive in, but he just smiled his famous smile and said, 'Baby, *you are beautiful.*' So conditioned was he to not having her that it didn't occur to him that she might be ready. Besides, he had had a three-hour session with Enchilada the previous evening, and at his age it was exhausting.

She swam slowly around the pool. Soon the film would be finished and she had to decide about herself and Steve.

'Listen, baby,' he said, 'I promised we'd go to a party tonight. OK with you?'

She climbed out of the pool, covering her breasts with her hands. 'Fine.'

* * *

The Acapulco Film Festival was in full swing, and Sunday and Steve had already attended several parties together.

Sunday enjoyed them. It was interesting meeting the foreign contingent, and she had run into two or three people she had worked with in Rome.

'You're quite a celebrity,' Steve said with a mixture of jealousy and pride when an important Italian director greeted her with a stream of praise about a film they had made together.

'I did exist before Hollywood,' she said with a smile.

'You bet your ass you did, and I don't want to hear about it.'

Claude Hussan, the French director, was brought over to be introduced by an anxious publicity girl. Claude was a tall angular man with dark emaciated features, black eyes and long straight hair. He was the current rage in French film circles, and married to a French actress who had starred in his latest film. The film was collecting a series of awards, and his wife was being acclaimed as a young Garbo.

Sunday was excited at meeting him, but he greeted her with bored eyes and a great lack of interest, talking only to Steve. It upset her. She couldn't understand why he was so rude. She had seen his new film and admired it greatly. Secretly she harboured the wish to work for him. She knew that he was in the process of preparing his first American film, although no one seemed to know much about it.

On the way home Steve said, 'What did you think of Claude?' She shrugged. 'Full of his own importance.'

'Yeah, he's a cold fish. I hear he's a bastard with the ladies.'

'Yes, well you're not exactly Little Boy Blue.'

He told the chauffeur to pull over and stop. 'Listen kid, you have no complaints. I'll tell you what I was thinking. You want to try the marriage bit?'

'What are you talking about?'

'Marriage baby. Let's get MARRIED. Then maybe I can

151

score a little sex around here.' Memories of Sunday swimming half-naked gave him his first hard-on of the day.

'You're not serious, are you?'

'I'm serious. When do you want to do it? Jesus, I thought the days of a broad holding out until after the ring was on her finger were over, but I guess they're not. When, baby? You name the day.'

'I – I don't know.' A proposal of marriage was the last thing she expected. She certainly hadn't been holding out for that reason. I mean are we compatible? Do we like the same things?'

'Take off your clothes, sugar, and we'll soon find out.'

'Steve, don't joke. I'll have to think about it.'

His voice echoed disbelief. 'You'll have to think about it. What is there to think about? My God, I've met difficult broads but you beat the band.'

'I can't just rush into a decision. It's a little more complicated than that.'

'Jesus, Sunday. Do you think now that we're practically married I can get on with my sex life? I feel like a goddamn monk, it's been so long.'

'Is that why you want to marry me, just for sex?'

'Don't talk like an idiot.'

'I'll tell you what. We'll go to bed together and then we'll see.'

'We'll see what?'

'We'll see if we want to get married.'

He shook his head. 'You know, you're a nutty broad.'

'I'm not a broad.'

'No, I guess you're not.' He lit a cigarette. 'So when do I get lucky?'

She smiled. 'Soon, I promise.'

The next day, without asking her, Steve announced their forthcoming marriage. Journalists started to flow into Acapulco from all over the world. *Cash* received a million dollars' worth of free publicity. Sunday Simmons became a household name.

She was angry. 'You should have waited. This isn't fair.'

He grinned his famous grin and presented her with a flaw-less square-cut diamond ring. It was difficult to stay angry with him, he was so pleased.

She phoned Carey, who was delighted about the whole thing. Then she phoned Max Thorpe. He hadn't predicted an immediate marriage.

'I'd like to see you,' she pleaded. 'We're having an engagement party tomorrow night. Can you possibly come?'

'I'd love to,' Max said. 'Will Branch be there?'

'I hope so.'

'So do I, my dear, so do I.' Max chuckled and envisaged himself in his pink frilled evening shirt.

* * *

It seemed all of Acapulco turned out, plus a certain section of Hollywood, and most of the wandering jet-setters.

Sunday was amazed at Steve's wide range of friends.

Her guests were few – Carey, with Marshall, smiling all over her face and whispering, 'I want to hear the whole story.' Branch, strangely quiet and morose. Max Thorpe, telling fortunes, in particular that of an eighteen-year-old rock idol. And Dindi, alone and pretty in the skimpiest dress, which showed off every one of her assets.

'Where's Charlie?' Sunday asked, slightly disappointed by his absence.

'That man is such a drag,' Dindi said. 'All he has on his mind is work. I'm seriously thinking of trading him for a newer model now that I'm making it on my own. Did you know I'm starring in *All the World Loves a Stripper*? It's a fabulous part. Lots of nude scenes, but it's very artistic, and absolutely imperative to the story.'

'That's terrific, I'm sorry that things aren't too good with you and Charlie.'

'Good, schnood, who cares.' Dindi peered closely at Sunday. 'Say, is it all true or what?'

'Is what true?'

'The sexy Mr Magnum. Is he where it's at or not? I mean does he swing like they say? Is he *that* good?'

'Er, Dindi, I'll see you in a minute, there are some people I must talk to.' Sunday hurried off.

'For a great-looking girl she sure is dull,' Dindi muttered. 'Bet she wouldn't know a good screw if it was staring her in the face.'

Dindi was particularly disturbed by the engagement. She had got herself lumbered with a moody English actor, and Sunday had picked the plum, Steve Magnum himself.

Steve was talking to a well-known senator when Dindi zeroed in. 'Hi,' she said, 'I'm Dindi Sydne, Mrs Charlie Brick. I'm Sunday's best friend. I guess she told you about me.'

'If you give yourself any more billing, you'll own the studio!' Steve said with a laugh.

Dindi laughed too, as did the senator, who said, 'My wife is a big fan of your husband's.'

'You don't say,' Dindi replied. 'How nice. I'll tell Charlie. Great house you have here, Steve.'

'Thank you.' Where had Sunday found this ding-a-ling? If indeed she was a friend, for Sunday had never mentioned her.

'I may get Charlie to buy a house here. How would you like us as neighbours?' She gazed at Steve wide-eyed.

He looked her up and down. 'It sure as hell would improve the scenery.'

* * *

Carey dislodged herself from the senator's wife and found Sunday.

'I know we can't get involved in long talks now, but tell me, are you happy?'

'Happy?' Sunday replied. 'Does one ever really know at the time? I think I'm happy. I *know* Steve is.'

'You certainly surprised us all. I mean everyone thought he was much too slippery to get caught again.'

'I didn't *catch* him. I didn't set any traps. He wants to marry me.'

'Of course he does. All I'm saying is that you were clever the way you played it. Like very smart.'

'Carey, I haven't been playing any games. I haven't even slept with him yet.'

'*What?*'

'Oh, don't worry, tomorrow's the big day. I'm not fool enough to marry a man I don't know sexually.'

'You've been going together two whole months and you haven't slept with him and *that*'s not playing games! Wowee you've got to be made of stone.' She started to laugh. 'I've really got to hand it to you.'

'Don't you dare say a word to anyone. Not anyone. Steve would kill me if he thought I had mentioned it.'

'You know you can trust me. What's he been doing for action?'

'You're beginning to sound like Dindi. Nothing. That's one of the things I like about him, he's been prepared to wait.'

'*Come on.* Steve Magnum?'

'Yes. Steve Magnum.'

'If you say so.' But Carey wasn't really prepared to believe that. He must have had *something* going for him.

'Anyway, what about you?' Sunday asked. 'Have you decided about Marshall yet?'

Carey looked sheepish. 'Gee, I just don't know, it's so *difficult*. He's sweet and nice when you get to know him, but marriage . . . we've got a lot of problems going for us that other people just don't have.'

'I hope you work it out. I think the only place one can really be safe is in a good marriage, and one that's not based entirely on sex.'

* * *

155

Later, Max took Sunday into a comer and studied her hand. 'It's all here, you know,' he said, 'a very strong man, a powerful influence. I just didn't see it as marriage. But of course, it is so.'

'Do you see children?' she asked anxiously.

'Perhaps, after a while.' Sunday's hand perplexed him; there was this strange break, something . . . 'Yes, I see children eventually. Two.'

She smiled. 'You know, Max, since I came to visit you that day I've felt like a new person.'

He nodded. He knew he had the power to reassure people, relax them. It pleased him. 'Tell me, my dear, do you know the senator? I'd very much like to meet him.'

Max felt he *should* meet the senator. He adored to acquire people and watch them fall under his spell – as he told them about themselves. The senator could be an important acquisition. Max was rather upset at the way Branch was treating him. He had attempted to make a rendezvous but Branch had brushed him off edgily. The fact that he had done this only made him more interesting. 'Such a sexy boy,' Max muttered under his breath, 'what muscles!'

It was a shame, he reflected, that he couldn't predict his own future.

* * *

Branch was steering well clear of Max Thorpe. It seemed every way he turned there was a fag lying in wait. Even the director of the film he was doing was one, with a wife and three children tucked away somewhere.

It disgusted Branch. He only did it for his career and to get on. When he was a star, they had better not come sniffing around.

He watched Sunday with lovesick eyes.

Why hadn't she waited for him?

* * *

Dindi followed Steve carefully, stationing herself in nearby groups and keeping her eye on him. When he went upstairs she was a discreet distance behind. He went into a room and shut the door.

After a few minutes she followed. The room was a study which led into a black marble bathroom.

He was in the bathroom taking a leak.

'Oops, excuse me,' said Dindi, 'I was looking for the powder room.'

He finished what he was doing, and then casually zipped himself out of sight. 'Yeah?'

'Well, really,' she giggled, 'I was following you.'

Ignoring her, he peered at himself in the mirror, combing his hair and deciding whether to take a quick eye-bath as his eyes were bloodshot from all the booze he had put away.

'I was following you because I like you, and I thought, well, you're not going to be a bachelor much longer, and well, y'know, you have the *wildest* reputation, and I thought maybe it would be fun – for you as well as me – if we had a little sort of goodbye-Steve Magnum fuck!'

He started to laugh. 'You're a hell of a friend.'

'I'm not *really* Sunday's friend. In fact, I don't even know her. I came here with a guy. She'd never find out.'

'Forget it, baby.' He turned back to the mirror.

Dindi walked out of the bathroom and locked the door in the study. She took off her clothes, leaving only the long chains she was wearing around her neck. Then she went back into the bathroom and said, 'I hear you *adore* being whipped. Maybe one last time . . . ?'

Chapter Twenty-Seven

It took Herbert Lincoln Jefferson time to adjust. The fact that his wife Marge was involved in some kind of sexual black magic was bad enough, but before he had made up his mind to do anything about it, he was stunned by the news that a young girl had been murdered on Miller Drive. Her description fitted the girl he had picked up the previous evening.

He was shocked. He couldn't have killed her: it was impossible. He had only knocked her around a little, given her the sort of treatment she deserved. She wasn't the first woman he had hit, and with the others it had always been all right. Someone else had probably come across her after he had driven off.

There was a picture in the paper of two policemen standing at the spot where she was found. The report said she was about eighteen or nineteen, a heroin addict, victim of a brutal beating, naked but with no signs of sexual assault. She was unidentified. The police claimed to be working on several leads.

Herbert went cold with fear when he read about it. If the police got him he couldn't stand it. It would mean prison and filth. He had heard about what went on in the prisons, with men raping other men.

Was there anything to connect him with the girl? Had anyone seen her get in his car? Had they noted the number?

He had left the car in the Supreme Chauffeur garage. Her

fingerprints must be inside it. What if the police went there and found them? He must clean them off at once.

Shaking with fear, he hurried upstairs and dressed. Marge was still asleep, snoring and seeming to smile.

He shook her awake. 'If anyone comes here asking where I was last night, I was here with you from nine o'clock until twelve when I took the car back. Understand?'

'Wassamatter?' Her sleepy eyes opened.

'I was with you,' he shouted, 'all night.'

'But you was working last night,' she whined.

Controlling an impulse to drag her out of bed and shake her, he said, 'I was here with you. That's what you tell them. No matter what. OK?'

'Are you in trouble?' she asked suspiciously.

'Maybe,' he muttered. 'But you'd better say what I told you to say, otherwise you'll be good and sorry.'

'All right. Where are you going?'

'I have to go to the garage. They have an early job for me.'

'But you're on night shift.'

'Now remember, I came home nine o'clock because I finished early. Then I took the car back at twelve and came straight home again.'

'OK.' She shifted her bulky body out of bed and reached for a bar of chocolate on the dressing table.

* * *

When he was gone she got up. Herbert *was* in trouble, she knew that. But how could she be his alibi when she had been next door all evening? She would have to talk it over with Louella Crisp. What a wonderful neighbour she was, so kind and understanding. Thank goodness she had come to live next door and rescued Marge from a life that consisted merely of eating, watching TV, and Herbie.

She shuffled downstairs to make her usual breakfast of eggs, toasted muffins and low-calorie chocolate malt. She was trying to cut down, she had promised Louella she would. It was so wonderful of Louella to let her join her 'circle of friends', as she called them. The previous evening had been her initiation, and it had involved sex with each of the five men present. But Marge didn't mind. Louella had explained to her that she had to submit to become part of the group; every new member did the same thing.

'It's a great honour,' Louella had told her. 'We select very few people. The men who will be with you are very respected members of the community.'

Thrilled, Marge had looked covertly at their faces, hoping to recognize a movie star at least. She was a little disappointed for they hadn't *looked* very important, mostly ageing and nondescript. But all the same it had been so long since Herbert had touched her that it didn't really matter what they looked like.

She picked the paper off the kitchen floor where Herbie had left it, and glanced at an advertisement for a fake mink hat. Then she read about the murder of a hippie girl, sinking her teeth into a fat fuzzy peach as she did so.

* * *

Herbert arrived at the Supreme Chauffeur Company in record time.

'What are you doing here, Jefferson?' the man at the desk asked him. 'You're not on nights *and* days, are you?'

Herbert shook his head, his eyes shifting uneasily. 'No. Lost me cigarette lighter. It's valuable. Thought I'd better look for it right away. Is the Caddy I had last night still in the garage?'

The man consulted a book. 'Nope. Went in for a service this morning. Be back at six.'

Herbert felt sweat form on his body. 'Where's it gone?'

'Usual place on La Cienega.'

Herbert turned and walked out. If it was being serviced it would finish up with a thorough clean inside and out. But he didn't dare take a chance. He would have to go to the garage, and examine it. Maybe the girl had dropped something in the car.

He quickened his step to the bus stop and cursed the fact that he still had no car. You were dead without one in Los Angeles, the public transport system stank.

It was a hot smoggy morning and he felt in desperate need of a shower. How he hated to feel dirty. When his mother was alive she used to beat him if he tried to skip his nightly bath. 'You dirty little bastard,' she would scream, 'you're filthy, like your father.'

How pleased she would be if she could see him now, showering two or three times a day.

* * *

On the bus he took care to sit alone, scowling out of the window at the passing people.

He thought about the letter he had posted to Sunday Simmons. It made him feel good.

He thought about her supposed engagement to Steve Magnum. Of course it wasn't true – just publicity because they were acting in a film together. Herbert imagined himself wise in the ways of Hollywood.

He thought about Marge and the strange scene he had witnessed next door. He hated the whole idea of it. God, when this business of the murder was off his mind he was going to do something about it. He wasn't having his wife mixing with a bunch of perverts. Meanwhile he would leave Marge in ignorance, let her think he knew nothing.

* * *

The car was up on a block, a workman poking about underneath.

'I have to get in there,' Herbert said abruptly.

'Yeah?' The man looked him over.

'I'm from the Supreme Chauffeur Company. A customer lost something inside the car, and I have to look for it.'

The workman's eyes narrowed. 'I didn't take anything.'

Herbert nodded impatiently. 'I know you didn't, I just have to look. It might not be there, but I have to look – now.'

Complaining, the man lowered the car and Herbert got inside. He sat behind the wheel, gripping it tightly, and forced his eyes to look slowly around. Having done that, he got out and tipped the seats forward, bending down to study the thick pile rugs, first the driver's side, then the other.

He searched carefully, his mean brown eyes covering every inch. Satisfied, he was about to stand up when his eye caught the glint of something stuck down the side of the carpet. He picked it up. It was a fine gold chain with a small disc attached. On the disc were three tiny diamonds with the word 'DAD' engraved.

He pocketed it quickly and strolled away from the car.

The workman was busy talking to another mechanic as he left.

* * *

Louella Crisp, a sharp bird-like woman, stared piercingly at Marge Lincoln Jefferson. 'You've got to find out what he's done,' she said for the third time.

'I don't know how I can,' Marge whined in reply. 'He never tells me nothin' unless he feels like it.'

'I'm telling you that you *must* find out. Don't you understand that he *has* to tell you if he wants *you* to tell people he was with you.'

'I'll try,' Marge said reluctantly.

'See that you do.' Louella clapped her hands together. 'There's to be another gathering next Saturday. There will be other men that will initiate you. Soon you will be one of us absolutely. I'm afraid that I must ask you again for the five hundred dollars membership token. Do you have it?'

Marge fidgeted uncomfortably. 'Gee I'll give it to you soon. I have it, but Herbert's got my bank book. I'll get it from him by Saturday.'

'I hope so, otherwise it will be impossible for you to continue to come to our little parties.' Louella put a thin hand on her shoulder. 'I like you very much, Marge dear, but if the other members find you haven't paid, well – whatever I say, I'm afraid they won't want you.'

'I'll get it, I swear I'll get it,' Marge said quickly. Now that she had found Louella and her circle of friends, she was terri-fied of losing them. There was fifteen hundred dollars in her bank book, money she had saved before she even met Herbie. He had tried many times to get her to take the money out, but she had refused. It was all she had. Furious on one occasion, he had grabbed the book and said that if he couldn't have it, neither could she. He had hidden it, but she knew that she must find it and get the money for Louella.

Chapter Twenty-Eight

Roundabout was finished.

Serafina and the children had returned to London.

In the big house there were only Charlie, Dindi, George and the servants.

In the garage there was a new white Lamborghini Miura.

In the study the latest camera equipment piled high, some boxes containing Leicas and Rolleiflexes unopened.

Charlie was depressed. The completing of a film always left him strangely melancholy and alone. It took him days, sometimes weeks to adjust, get rid of the character he had been playing and become himself. Fortunately the character in *Roundabout* had not been too complex. Mr Everyman. Ordinary Schmuck caught in extraordinary situations. Charlie had captured him to a T. The man-in-the-street was one of his most masterly comic exercises. Everyone at the studio agreed it was probably one of his best performances. The film was destined to be a huge moneymaker.

Angela Carter was adequate, but it was Dindi on whom everyone commented. She came over as pretty and appealing, the Baby Girl she had played for Charlie on their first date. She was lucky to have Marshall as her agent.

'I'm amazed,' Marshall confided to Carey. 'She really comes across as cute on the screen. Even the women like her. Cy wants her for another picture at once.'

Since Las Vegas relations between Dindi and Charlie had been strained. They lived together, hostility cutting the air like a knife. One of Dindi's most constant moans was how could he have left her with the Allens, his mother and a gardener!

'You can look after yourself,' Charlie had said when she telephoned in a rage from Las Vegas.

'You bet your ass I can, and just you watch me!'

Reports of her liaisons with the hotel manager came back with both Serafina and Natalie.

'It was disgusting and humiliating,' Serafina wailed. 'Your wife, Charlie, *my son's* wife, going everywhere with another man.'

Natalie was more subtle. 'I think I should tell you, Charlie, as a friend. I know she's very young, but really, she was practically having an affair with this third-rate gangster-type in public.' Natalie gazed at him sympathetically and laid an understanding hand on his arm. 'You need a more mature woman, Charlie, a woman who appreciates you.'

'You're right, love. I made a horrible mistake,' he admitted.

Natalie smiled. Soon it would be right for her to step in.

She was dismayed to find herself pregnant shortly afterwards. Clay had ruined her plans. Why did she have to be the one woman in God knows how many whom the pill had let down?

Clay was delighted and refused to let her do anything about it. 'Old Max Thorpe, the bum, was right,' he whooped. 'Don't you remember he told us at that party of Charlie's you were going to get knocked up again?'

Thin-lipped, Natalie considered how long it would be before the whole thing would be over and she was back in shape. At least a year. Would Charlie wait that long?

She sighed. What an infuriating twist of fate! Just when Dindi was on her way out too.

* * *

Shortly after returning to London, Serafina was taken ill.

Charlie was unsure what to do.

'How bad is she?' he demanded of her boyfriend, Archie, who had phoned to tell him.

'Pretty bad,' Archie replied glumly. 'They took her to the hospital today. She was asking for you.'

'What hospital? What's her doctor's number? Is she in a private room?'

Charlie telephoned the doctor and established that she had suffered a mild heart attack. 'Should I fly in?' he asked.

'I don't think that's necessary,' her doctor replied. 'Although, of course, she's getting on in years a bit, and you never know.'

Charlie hung up, despondent. If he were not so scared of flying he would get on a plane without hesitation. But the thought of sitting captive on an aeroplane, a piece of machinery that to his mind could disintegrate at any moment, was just too terrifying. He had already decided that when he did return to London it was going to be by train and ship.

The doctor's words hung in his ears – 'She's getting on a bit.' 'You never know.' He was in an agony of indecision.

Later that day Dindi returned from Acapulco. She burst into the house, laughing and chattering. 'Acapulco was absolutely great, you should have come. The party was lovely, I met all sorts of people—'

'Serafina's very sick,' he said gravely.

'Oh, is she? By the way, what do you think of this idea. In *All the World Loves a Stripper*, you doing a sort of guest appearance, like a one-day shot as a gag? The publicity would be great. Jerry suggested it. I think he's the greatest publicity guy ever, he really knows where it's at. Do you know—'

'Dindi, didn't you hear me? I said Serafina is very sick.' He stared at her in a white-faced rage.

'I heard you. She's sick. So what do you want me to do – a chorus of "Dixie"? Too much screwing at her age, that's what—'

He slapped her hard across the face. Her hat fell off and the imprint of his hand blazed across her skin.

'You bastard,' she sobbed. 'You lousy English bastard. What did you do that for?'

'That's my mother you're talking about.' He started to shout. 'My mother is a fine woman and I don't even want to hear her name coming out of your mouth. You are a tramp, Dindi, a tramp. Don't think I don't know what went on in Las Vegas after I left. Serafina was ashamed of you, ashamed!'

'That old bat was ashamed of *me*. Why, I was embarrassed to be in the same company as that over-made-up old crow! How dare you talk about *me*, when she was screwing a fuckin' gardener! That's a hell of a mother you've got there, a real old—'

'Out of my house. Pack your bags and *get out*.'

'You're kidding, aren't you? This is California, baby, and you can get the hell out of *my* house.'

In disgust he turned his back to walk away.

Grabbing a silver-framed picture of Serafina from the piano, Dindi hurled it at him. 'That's what I think about your old mother,' she yelled.

The photo frame shattered on the floor, Charlie bent to extract his mother's picture. In a fury Dindi snatched it from him and ripped it in half. He slapped her again, and she spat at him, tears rolling down her cheeks. 'I know you tried to get me cut out of the film. I know you're jealous of my success. You're an old has-been with no friends. No friends, you hear me. Everyone on *Roundabout* hated you.'

Slowly he picked up the torn picture of his mother. 'You know I'm very lucky.' He forced his voice to be calm. 'Very lucky that it didn't take me too long to find out what a *cunt* I married.' With that he walked out of the room, out of the house, got into the Lamborghini Miura, and drove off.

Dindi followed him, yelling insults until the car disappeared from sight. 'Bastard! Prick!' she muttered, until gradually the tears stopped and the mind started to work. It wasn't too bad, it wasn't too bad at all. And the publicity would be great. She could picture herself in court, blue eyes wide and innocent, demure little powder-pink dress. 'Yes, he beat me, I know it was because he was jealous of my success. I put up with it as long as I could.' The statement could be interrupted with a choked sob at that point.

'I'll fix that limey sonofabitch!' she muttered. 'I'll fix him good!'

* * *

Charlie drove to the Beverly Hills Hotel. His mind was very clear, very calm. He phoned George at the house and told him to pack a bag for London. Then he made a reservation on the evening jet over the Pole. Next he called Marshall K. Marshall and obtained the name of the best lawyer in L.A.

He was able to see him before he left.

'I want a divorce,' he stated. 'I don't care what it costs, but I want to settle a lump sum and I want her off my back.'

Knowing Dindi's love of money, he was sure her natural greed would persuade her to accept an outright payment and he wanted nothing more to do with her. The thought of paying alimony every month disgusted him.

'It's going to be mighty expensive,' the lawyer said.

'I know,' Charlie replied. 'Do it.'

* * *

Serafina's face was worth the long hours of terror while strapped into his seat above the Atlantic.

'You're a good boy,' she crooned.

He was shocked to see her without make-up. Ever since he could remember her face had been ornamented with blue eyeshadows, thick creamy pan-stiks, bright vermilion lipsticks.

Now she lay in the hospital bed, her skin a deathly mottled green, her eyes sunken and lifeless. For the first time he realized just how old his mother was.

'I'm going to be all right, son,' she said, 'Archie's looking after me.'

Archie, a shabby little man hunched in the corner, nodded eagerly. 'I'm looking after her, Charlie boy, not to worry.'

Charlie knew she was going to die. Her tired, beaten face told him that. But he smiled and said, 'Where's all that life and vitality I was always hearing about? I thought you'd be dashing around making some tea.'

She managed to show her cracked, decayed teeth. 'Soon, Charlie, soon.' Then she appeared to fall into a sleep, and later that night she passed away.

* * *

Charlie went to the big house in Richmond and wandered around.

Downstairs it was in beautiful order, with the smart modern furniture put there by the decorator he had commissioned.

Upstairs the only two rooms that seemed to have been used were Serafina's bedroom, and an adjoining dressing room where Archie slept.

Her room was flooded with pieces of her life. There were photos of Charlie everywhere. Pictures of him as a boy. Smiling blandly beneath a mask of pancake on his first stage appearance. Growing up to be a fat young man. Marrying Lorna, two blank un-lived-in faces setting off on life. A rare photo of his father, stern-faced. Serafina at the age of sixteen, a thin lively girl with luxuriant red ringlets.

Then came the photos of Charlie Brick – star. Meeting the Queen. Receiving an award. Going to a première – They were all there, a pictorial record of his life.

In her wardrobe hung her old stage dresses, musty and faded with age, but still smelling of the old days, the theatres, and greasepaint.

Charlie buried his nose in them and was assailed by so many memories that a lump formed and stayed in his throat.

It was hard to believe that Serafina was dead. His Serafina. His mother.

He slept that night in her big four-poster bed, and the next day he arranged the funeral and comforted Archie, who had broken down completely.

Charlie regretted not having brought him to Hollywood with Serafina. He had had no idea how much the funny little man cared.

* * *

Lorna phoned at once when she heard.

'Do you want me to bring the children over?' she asked.

'No, I don't think so. I'd like them at the funeral. It's tomorrow. If you came to the house at ten perhaps we could all go together.'

'Yes, of course. And Charlie, I'm really sorry. Serafina and I were never the best of friends, but she was a wonderful old lady, the children adored her.'

'Thank you.' He hung up, near to tears.

* * *

Lorna arrived the next day on time. It had been such a long time since he had seen her and she had changed. Her hair was longer, fluffier, and she had put on weight, but of course she had just had a baby.

She kissed him on the cheek, and the smell of her old familiar perfume made him think for a moment that nothing had changed between them.

'My goodness, you're thin,' she exclaimed.

He hugged the children. Little Cindy was crying. 'I want Serry, Daddy,' she said.

Serafina had insisted that they never called her Grandma. 'Do I *look* like a grandmother?' she was always demanding of people.

George arrived in time for the funeral. He had been left behind to transfer Charlie's personal belongings from the house in Bel Air to the Beverly Hills Hotel, and had then caught the next plane over. He decided not to mention that Dindi had thrown a huge party for what seemed like every dead-beat in L.A. the evening Charlie had left. He was merely relieved that his boss had caught on to her fairly quickly.

'How long are you going to stay?' Lorna asked Charlie as they drove to the cemetery.

He shrugged. 'I suppose I'll go straight back. I'm starting another film on the thirtieth. Besides, there's nothing for me here.' He looked at her pointedly.

'I – I was talking to Jim, and he said it would be fine if you could come to our house for dinner before you go.'

He bit back a sharp retort. After all, she *was* trying to be nice. 'No, love, sorry, I don't think that would work out.'

'If you change your mind we have an old place in Islington. We've got lots to do to it, but it will be lovely when we finish.' She squeezed his arm impulsively. His cold, unaffectionate Lorna actually squeezed his arm. 'I'm glad we can be friends, Charlie. I want to be friends. Jim and I are very happy, and I'm glad you remarried. Natalie wrote and told me she's very pretty.' Lorna laughed with no bitterness. 'I was never pretty enough for you, Charlie.' He went to interrupt but she continued, 'No, don't start telling me lies. As soon as you became a film star I could see all the new people we met thinking, "Huh, not so hot, he could do better than that."'

'Not true,' he objected.

'Oh yes, it is. *You* know how bitchy everyone is in show business. We were at a party once and there were two girls discussing you in the loo. "Charlie Brick's quite sexy," one of them said – of course they didn't know who I was – "Yes," replied the other one, "and available too, with that wife he's got tucked away somewhere. I've never seen her but I hear she's a dog."'

'I don't believe you.'

171

'Don't. It doesn't really matter, not now anyway, but it is true.'

They sat in silence the rest of the way to the cemetery, the children strangely quiet in the front seat.

It was probably true, Charlie reflected. People were bitchy if your wife wasn't some kind of raving beauty. With regret he could even remember doing it himself, meeting a star and thinking – Well, the wife's not much.

Why did people rest so much importance on physical attributes? He did so himself. That was why he dieted so strenuously, and only took out dozey starlets and models, and finally married one. The lovely Dindi, who had absolutely nothing to offer except her looks.

Perhaps that was why he still wanted Lorna, because she was an ordinary person who had known him when he was a nobody. He didn't fancy her, there was nothing sexual left, but he still wanted her.

*　*　*

The burial was depressing. It seemed that relatives whom he never knew existed appeared from all over the country.

Serafina's elder sister, Lily, fell upon him, crying and moaning. He knew for a fact that they never got along, and had not even seen each other for five years.

'They're all jealous,' Serafina had once said, 'jealous of my youth and vitality and my famous son. I was always the queen in our family.'

Serafina had seven sisters and three brothers, and they all appeared with their respective sons, daughters, sons-in-law, daughters-in-law, and grandchildren. Charlie hardly knew any of them.

The service was brief. Serafina had never been a religious woman. Then everyone walked across to the cemetery to see the coffin lowered into the ground.

Charlie gritted his teeth. He decided funerals were unnecessary. People should be allowed the dignity of dying in private and peace. He made a decision to write in his will that he was to be cremated immediately and that there was to be no funeral.

Lorna stayed by his side, both in the church and at the grave. They held on to a child each. She squeezed his arm once, and he squeezed her back. He had never felt so close to anyone in his life.

After the funeral there was the disturbing business of entertaining all the relatives back at the house.

They came in their Morris Oxfords, and Mini Minors, and battered old Fords.

They descended on the table of refreshments like locusts.

They oohed and they aahed. Three children fell into the swimming pool. One of Serafina's brothers started telling dirty jokes. Lily asked Charlie what was going to happen to all Serafina's things. Family gossip was rife. Serafina was forgotten.

The last Mini Minor was finally on its way at five o'clock.

'What a joke!' Charlie exclaimed. 'What a bloody horrible joke. Serafina would have had a fit if she'd been here.'

'What are you going to do now?' Lorna asked with concern, as she found the children's coats and prepared to go.

'Don't worry about me, love. Archie and I will have a bite together.'

'Are you *sure* you wouldn't like to come to dinner?' Shyly she added, 'I'd like you to see the baby. She's sweet. We call her Gemma.'

'I'm sorry. I haven't even asked about your baby.'

'There's nothing to ask really. A baby is a baby, and everyone thinks theirs is the most beautiful. Actually she looks a little like Cindy.'

Charlie debated whether this was a dig at him, but decided it wasn't. Then because he wanted to please her he said, 'I've decided to fly back to Hollywood tomorrow. Maybe next time I'm here I will come over.'

'My goodness, flying everywhere without a second thought nowadays.'

'I suppose you get over everything in time, love.'

George cooked bacon and eggs for Charlie and Archie. They sat in the kitchen and Charlie noticed how shrivelled Archie had become since Serafina's death.

There but for the grace of success go I, Charlie thought – a shabby little stand-up knock-down comic, who Charlie saw now had really cared for Serafina.

'I'll be out of here tomorrow before you leave,' Archie said, his eyes red-rimmed and sad.

'Where will you go?'

'I don't know. I'll travel around a bit. There's a club up in Manchester wants me back.'

'Look, Archie,' Charlie said impulsively, 'you don't have to go, you were good to my mother. I want you to have this house. *She* would have wanted you to have it.'

'No, Charlie, no.' Archie shook his head slowly. 'You don't have to give me a house because I looked after Serafina. Besides, I couldn't live here without her.'

'But I want you to have it. Sell it, do what you like with it, it's yours.'

Archie rose from the kitchen table with dignity. 'No. I said no and I mean no. I'll be going to bed now, see you in the morning.'

The little man departed, leaving Charlie alone. Depressed, he too went up to bed, Serafina's bed. He slept badly dreaming of plane crashes. He awoke in a cold sweat at 4 a.m. and was unable to get back to sleep.

In the morning Archie was gone. No forwarding address, nothing – he had packed his one suitcase and left quietly.

Charlie was upset. He had wanted to give him some money at least.

George helped him pack all of Serafina's personal things, which were sent off to storage.

Agents were instructed to put the house on the market.

By 4 p.m., fortified with Mexican Gold, and protected from prying reporters by George, Charlie was on a plane back to L.A.

Chapter Twenty-Nine

The morning after the engagement party, Sunday awoke to the sound of the telephone. It was Carey phoning from the airport.

'I'm sorry I have to dash off like this, but you and Steve don't need me around anyway and I'm expecting some important contracts.'

'Couldn't you stay at least a couple of days? I've hardly seen you.'

'I know, but work calls. Now, when are you naming the big day? Don't forget, I want to be the first to know.'

'Don't worry. I'll call you at once if we decide before we come back. By the way, if things work out tonight I expect I'll move into his house.'

Carey chuckled. 'With Steve Magnum at the wheel and you in the driver's seat, I'd like to take a little bet that things will *definitely* work out.'

Sunday smiled. She hoped so. She needed a man so badly now. She needed Steve.

It was a beautiful morning. A clear hot balmy day. Steve had promised to telephone her when he woke up. That probably wouldn't be until late, for the party had still been going strong when she had left at 4 a.m. with Marisa and Woody.

There had been so many people. Steve had many friends. She had found him playing craps with a bunch of men. Quietly she kissed him and whispered, 'I want to have dinner in tomorrow night, just the two of us.'

He was drunk. He laughed and shouted, 'Say goodnight to my princess.' Then he fished in his pocket and pulled out a small package. 'Open this when you're in bed.'

She had done as he said. The package contained the figures of a man and woman, their hands joined. They were about two inches high, exquisitely made in solid gold. The female figure had two bright round diamonds for breasts and another pear-shaped diamond strategically placed. The male figure was practically all diamond.

A note was enclosed. All it said was, 'I don't want to boast but . . .'

Sunday laughed. It was the most vulgar gift she had ever received.

* * *

Breakfast was a mango and some peaches by her small private pool. Then she swam, cleaning away the slight hangover. Next she did her daily exercises underwater.

'My God, aren't we the energetic one!' It was Dindi, hidden from the world by a huge cowboy hat, tinted sunglasses, and a yellow pant suit. 'I was sure you'd be up, so I thought I'd drop by before leaving.'

Sunday climbed out of the pool, shaking water out of her hair and hitching up the bottom of her bikini. 'Are you going too? What a pity. Carey just called me from the airport. I suppose you have to get back to Charlie.'

Dindi hooted with laughter. 'You're kidding, aren't you? I have to get back for work, darling, hard work. Did I tell you I'm starring in *All the World Loves a Stripper*? My reviews for *Roundabout* say I steal the whole film.'

'That's great. Can't wait to see it.'

'I'll have it run for you,' she said airily. 'When are you coming back?'

Sunday shrugged. 'I don't know. Whatever Steve wants.'

Dindi took off her hat and threw her face back to catch the sun. 'I think I should tell you, after all we are friends and I'm not one for keeping secrets. Anyway if it was me I would want to know.'

'Know what?'

'Well, I guess it was my fault too,' she admitted, 'but I *was* sort of stoned, and you know what I'm like when a guy comes on strong, and I *was* curious.'

'What *are* you talking about?'

'Sunday, I don't want to hurt you. I know how uptight you are about sex, and Gods knows you had a bad enough time with that freaked-out first husband of yours. But I must be honest, and I do think you would be better off knowing.'

Coldly Sunday said, 'Please don't call my first husband names. He was sick, that's all, sick. Why, you hardly even knew him.'

Dindi sighed. 'I suppose I should have told you before. I knew him very well. As a matter of fact, Benno used to make me have scenes with the two of them. I was mad about Benno. I rather fancied myself as a Roman princess. He was, like all men though, a first-class shit, and after Paulo died he was so miserable he kicked me out. You know, of course, that Benno and Paulo were making it?'

White-faced, Sunday said, 'You must be out of your mind.'

Dindi shrugged. 'Believe me or don't believe me, it doesn't make any difference. Fly to beautiful Roma and ask Benno yourself. I thought you must have known, everybody else did. All those tall blond Roman counts and princes swing both ways, it's in their blood. Listen, the three of us were holed up in a hotel for three days the week before he died.'

Very quietly Sunday said, 'I think you had better go.'

'Oh shit,' Dindi exclaimed, 'I'm doing you a *favour*, telling you the truth. I think you live in a little ivory tower or something. Anyway, that's not even what I came to say. I thought you knew all that. What I *wanted* to tell you was about your new boyfriend, Mister Magnum.'

'I don't want to hear anything else you have to say, Dindi. Can't you understand that I—'

'Yeah – I can understand that you're trying to shut yourself off from life. Well, whether you like hearing it or not, the fact is I screwed your big movie-star boyfriend last night. They're all bastards, baby, and Steve Magnum ain't no different. He screwed me at *your* party while you were chatting politely to *his* guests.' She sighed. 'In this life you have to look out for number one, you're always alone in the end. You may think I'm a bitch, but I like you, and I figure you're better off knowing what kind of guy you're marrying.' She stood up. 'Well, there it is, I'm sorry if you're upset, but that's show biz.' She put on her hat. 'By the way, he's a fantastic lay!'

For a while Sunday sat in silence. Instinctively she knew that Dindi had spoken the truth. She pushed the information about Paulo to the back of her mind to be dealt with later.

Steve Magnum.

Goodbye.

She didn't want to listen to his lies.

Quickly she hurried into the bungalow, packed, and ordered a limousine. Then she called Carey's secretary in Los Angeles and dictated a brief statement to be given to the press.

'I'm going away for a week or so,' she told the girl.

'Tell Miss St Martin that I'm fine. I don't want to be disturbed, and I'll call her in a couple of days.' She took the two gold figures Steve had given her and replaced them in their box. Then she wrote a short note saying, 'I understand you're fantastic.' Next she enclosed her large diamond engagement ring.

The Mexican driver arrived and began to load her suitcases into the car. She handed him the package and note. 'After you have taken me to the airport please deliver this to Señor Magnum.'

The driver nodded, his eyes fixed firmly on her bosom.

Chapter Thirty

'You're a real friend. With friends like you I have no need of enemies.' Charlie sat in his Beverly Hills hotel bungalow and stared Clay down. 'I mean what the hell was all that bit about you met her with her mother? You laid her, didn't you? Her mother – what a load of crap. And the horrible thing is I'm sitting here like a right schmuck, believing you!' He shook his head. 'Thanks a lot, *friend.*'

Clay gulped his scotch down quickly. 'What did you want me to say, for Christ's sake? Oh yes, I *have* met your wife, I fucked her with a drunken Italian in Rome. After all by the time I saw her again you were *married* to her.'

'Bullshit! We've been friends long enough. You could have told me.'

'What good would telling you have done? I thought maybe she had reformed. After all, if I'd told you then, you might have ended up hating *me*!'

'That's great, you weren't concerned about me having made a right berk of myself marrying some ding-dong, you were just concerned about yourself. You're a selfish bastard.'

Clay helped himself to another scotch from the bottle on the table. 'Come on, Charlie. Let's forget about it. Everyone's allowed one mistake in life. Why did you marry her anyway?'

'Who knows? I was stoned, getting over Lorna. She looked like some pretty innocent little angel, and she gave great head.'

'So do half the hookers in Hollywood,' Clay remarked wisely.

It was 10 p.m. Charlie had been back in Los Angeles a week, and he and Clay had just been to see a special rough cut of *Roundabout*. Natalie was at home.

'She has a bad attack of morning sickness all day and all night,' Clay remarked with a laugh. 'It's going to be a boy this time, I can feel it in my balls!'

After viewing the film, they returned to Charlie's bungalow, chatting and drinking. It was the first time Charlie had been out since getting back. He had holed up in the hotel, working on a script, and playing with his tape-recorders and cameras.

Dindi had derived the maximum amount of publicity out of their forthcoming divorce, giving forth with several conflicting statements and posing for innumerable pictures until her lawyer had forced her to be silent.

Charlie merely produced that well-worn quote: 'No comment.'

Along with the Sunday Simmons/Steve Magnum engagement breaking up, Dindi and Charlie were the show-business talk of the week.

'What do you say we go out and have some fun?' Clay suggested. 'It's not often I get a night off.'

'Where do you want to go?'

'Cruising. We could cruise a bit and pull two lovely little darlings.'

Charlie laughed. 'You haven't changed much, have you? Remember the first time we ever met?'

'Could I ever forget!' Clay exclaimed. 'Vietary Studios. I was banging a real hot one in the dressing room and you barged in. She pulled up her knickers so quick, I thought she had taken my cock with her!'

'You always were a randy old bastard,' Charlie said with an admiring chuckle.

'You came in calm as you like and said in that camp faggot accent you were using then – "Oh, did I come at the wrong time?" I could have killed you! The bird scampered off, and I ended up with nothing!'

'The start of a beautiful friendship.'

'Yes. Well, we've both come a long way from those days, haven't we? Of course, you're in the best position. Famous film star. You can pull more or less anyone you want. When you were having that fling with Michelle Lomas, I don't mind telling you I was goddam jealous.'

'Were you?'

'Sure I was. Any fellow worth his balls would have been.'

Charlie laughed modestly. 'Michelle was a fabulous woman.'

'Come on, let's have another drink for Serafina, she was always fond of a drop of scotch. I'm going to miss that grand old lady.'

Solemnly they re-filled their glasses and toasted Serafina.

Clay said, 'Fancy dropping into a disco?'

Charlie shook his head. 'You go.'

'Come on, it will do you good. Anyhow, I fancy having a ride in that flash car of yours.'

* * *

The discotheque was jammed as usual. Charlie had only ever been there once with Dindi. The place made him uncomfortable. It was jammed with starlets and beach-boys and actors and young celebrities and a few old celebrities who figured they were still young, and hookers of both sexes.

Clay pushed his way through and found them a place at the bar. He immediately started to chat to a blonde in a gold catsuit who looked completely stoned.

Charlie wished he hadn't come. Clay meant well, but this really wasn't his scene.

'You're Charlie Brick, aren't you?' a smaller, not so pretty version of Dindi asked him. She had the same flaxen hair and big blue eyes. 'I'm here with my boyfriend, but I wanted to tell you that you really turn me on.' She fidgeted in her see-through mini and abstractedly stroked her small breasts. 'Your glasses are so sexy. What star are you?'

'Virgo,' Charlie replied, fascinated as he watched her nipples harden under her own touch.

'Hmm,' she cast her eyes heavenwards, 'I thought so. I'm Aquarius. I'm an actress.'

As if I didn't know, he thought.

'Well, I guess I'd better get on back to my boyfriend. Shall I call you?'

'Don't call me, I'll call you.'

'Huh?'

'Nothing. It's a joke. Yes, do call me. I'm at the Hilton.'

She flitted away, and Charlie turned to see how Clay was getting on. He was doing nicely, whispering in the blonde's ear.

'Er, I think I've had enough of this place,' Charlie commented. 'Shall we move on?'

Reluctantly Clay agreed, scribbling the blonde's phone number in a small notebook.

Then he suggested they cruise down the Strip to inspect the action there. 'If I'm lucky, I might find myself a fourteen-year-old drop-out,' he joked.

Charlie had lost all enthusiasm for the trip. They might just as well have phoned for a couple of hookers, because whoever they found wandering about at this time of night was bound to be one anyway. He wasn't sure if he even felt like getting laid.

'Slow down, get over to the side,' Clay said excitedly.

Two girls were walking towards them, both dressed in tight chinos and clinging sweaters, both swinging fringed suede handbags and chewing gum. They edged towards the car as it stopped, first having a good look around for any cops.

'Looking for a little action?' the first girl asked, leaning down to the open window and peering in at Clay. 'We're available for any trips you care to take.'

He started to reply, but Charlie suddenly jammed his foot down on the accelerator, sending the car racing away.

'Hey, what's the matter?' Clay asked indignantly.

'For God's sake, the pair of them stank. Hopped up to the eyeballs on top of the stink!'

'I didn't realize we were on the look-out for Miss Clean America.'

'Fuck you.'

They rode in silence.

'What do you want then?' Clay finally asked.

Charlie shrugged. He was tired. What he really wanted was to go home to bed. They were passing by a strip joint. 'Let's go in here,' he said, swerving the Lamborghini into an adjoining parking lot. It was certainly better than cruising up and down like a couple of hicks.

'Good idea.' Clay's face brightened.

Charlie thought, What's this all about? What the hell are we looking for? A quick flash of tit like a couple of high-school boys? He was annoyed with himself and annoyed with Clay.

The place was sleazy, with plain wooden tables arranged around an L-shaped stage. A waitress, wearing black tights and a tired red bra, took their order.

A girl was up on the stage, going through her routine. She was wearing a bathing suit and a sash saying 'Miss Hot California'. She had flaming red hair and an enormous bosom. California packed in more enormous bosoms, thanks to all the doctors using silicone injections, than any other state.

She moved energetically, wriggling out of the bathing suit before you knew it, wearing just the sash and a red-white-and-blue G-string.

'Get a load of that!' Clay exclaimed happily.

Charlie sighed. The girl looked unreal. Two great globes of upstanding flesh. He ordered a bottle of scotch, which he proceeded to empty fast.

The next performer had piles of raven hair and a low-cut purple beaded evening dress. She was introduced as Crazy

Harold, and the music blared 'Big Spender'. She bumped and grinded her way automatically around the stage.

Charlie found the whole thing completely asexual. Clay was as excited as a schoolboy getting laid for the first time.

Between strippers, a comedian told weak blue jokes in a straight out of Brooklyn accent. Charlie studied the voice. He found it much more interesting than the girls. It had a particular nasal twang that he wished to capture exactly for the character he was playing in his next film.

'Now I give you a coupla wild mustangs! Little Skinny Sackcloth and Fantastic Fat Fanny!' the comedian said.

The way he said 'Mustang' knocked Charlie out. He muttered it under his breath, trying to get the intonation right.

Clay was roaring with laughter, along with the rest of the room, as the two new strippers appeared.

Little Skinny Sackcloth was a Twiggy-type girl, extremely pretty and wearing a pink mini shift.

Fantastic Fat Fanny was also pretty, but a mountainous balloon of a girl from her wobbling double chins to her jelly-like legs. She too was wearing a pink mini dress.

They paraded the stage to the strains of 'Hello, Dolly'.

'Christ!' Clay muttered. 'I always fancied having a fat girl.'

Charlie was getting through the scotch and feeling no pain, but even in the most stoned of conditions he could never have fancied the fat one. The little skinny one was a different proposition. She was rather appealing, with her wispy yellow hair and fawn-like eyes.

The girls removed their clothes in unison. First the skimpy mini shifts, under which they were wearing bras, panties and stockings clipped to old-fashioned suspenders.

Fat Fanny was grotesque, rolls upon rolls of uncontrollable flesh, quivering and shaking in time to the music. In comparison, Skinny Sackcloth was a skeleton, with ribs sticking out of an emaciated ribcage.

The combination of the two female forms was almost obscene. Their bras unclipped down the front, and now rolling their hips in time to a honky-tonk arrangement of 'Hard-Hearted Hannah', they undid the clips.

'I've got to have the fat one,' Clay groaned.

If Natalie could only see him now, Charlie thought, amused at Clay's enthusiasm. Fat Fanny looked like some sort of gross animal. Big boobs flopping and falling, nipples the size of the skinny one's entire little buds.

They ended the show. The comedian leaped up on the stage, cracked a couple of stale jokes, and promised everyone a brilliant new show in exactly one hour's time.

Clay grabbed the man on his way to the bar. Charlie called for the check and paid it. He was going to drop Clay off at his car and go to bed. Any more cruising Clay could do on his own.

Clay fumbled in his pocket and handed the comedian money.

Charlie got up. He had taken off his glasses, as no one ever recognized him without them, and who needed to be recognized in such a dump? 'Come on,' he said patiently.

'It's all arranged,' Clay said excitedly. 'All fixed.'

'What's all fixed?'

'Fantastic Fat Fanny and the Skinny bit. I gave the fellow two hundred dollars and we're to go across the street to their apartment. They've only got an hour. How about that for organization?'

'Two hundred dollars for those two freaks. I think you're going soft.'

'Soft I'm not. Let's go.'

Reluctantly Charlie trailed behind. Natalie had always said that Clay would screw anything, but this was ridiculous.

Little Skinny Sackcloth opened the door of the apartment. She was wearing a black chiffon ostrich-feather-trimmed dressing-gown and a vacuous smile.

The apartment was one room, and reminded Charlie of his first sexual encounter so long ago in a dingy dressing-room with a sister act. It had the same smells: cheap perfume and stale sweat.

Clay pushed eagerly forward. 'Got any booze?' he asked.

Skinny looked at him blankly. 'Jake didn't say nothin' 'bout booze bein' part of the deal.'

A toilet flushed and Fat Fanny emerged from the bathroom. She was wearing the same style dressing-gown as the skinny one. Immediately she took control. 'You want scotch, it's ten bucks a piece. Take your pants off and make yourselves at home, not too at home, we've only got an hour. Any rough stuff is extra, you read me – extra. And if you both want to make it with me at the same time, that's also extra.' She spoke very quickly in a fluffy light voice that didn't match up to her size.

Clay looked at Charlie and Charlie looked at Clay and they both burst out laughing.

'Well, *you* might be able to get it up but I certainly can't,' Charlie said.

'For two hundred dollars I'm going to try,' Clay replied, unzipping his pants and stepping out of them.

'I think I'll just watch,' Charlie said politely as the skinny girl approached him.

The fat one shook off her dressing-gown and lay on a couch. Clay mounted her, a foolish grin on his face.

'Tell my friend I'll wait in the car,' Charlie said to the skinny one, and quietly slipped out.

Chapter Thirty-One

Sunday caught the first plane out of Acapulco airport. Destination – Mexico City.

She wore her hair scraped back, dark glasses, and bought her ticket in the name of Miss Sands. She hadn't decided where she was going, but she had to move fast before the barrage of publicity broke.

Getting engaged to Steve Magnum had catapulted her into the public eye. And how she had to get away – especially from Steve. She knew if he found her there would be excuses and apologies and finally insults. She didn't want to go through that.

Once in Mexico City she scanned the next flights out. She didn't want to travel too far. Then the idea of Rio occurred to her. Why not Rio? She had not been back since her parents died, and this was the perfect opportunity. There was a plane leaving within the hour.

* * *

The small boy stood wide-eyed by the boarding-gate. Sunday noticed him immediately, because for one thing he seemed much too young to be travelling alone – about five or six – and secondly, he was the most beautiful child she had ever seen. He had long dark hair framing his face like a halo, and huge black eyes set in an olive-skinned oval face. If I ever have a child, she thought, I would like him to look just like this.

The boy stood very still, occasionally darting his huge eyes anxiously around, obviously expecting someone.

When the flight was called he started to cry, not in a whining, snivelling way; tears just seemed to form in his big black eyes and trickle down his cheeks.

She went over to him. 'Are you waiting for your mother?'

He shook his head.

'Is someone coming for you?'

The child nodded. '*Oui, Papa.*'

'Are you French?'

'Yes, he is French,' a bored masculine voice said behind her. 'And he is quite all right, thank you, so you may now leave him alone.'

The man took the boy firmly by the hand and they set off for the plane, leaving Sunday standing there.

She followed them, catching up as they entered the aircraft.

'I'm sorry,' she said, 'I thought he was alone. I was only trying to see if he needed any help. He was crying.'

'Crying?' the man's voice was amused. 'Jean-Pierre never cries.'

'Oh, you're Claude Hussan, aren't you?' She could have bitten off her tongue, she sounded like some cloying fan.

He ignored her, just took his seats without giving her another glance.

She realized that he obviously didn't remember her. She had been all dressed up and at her most glamorous when they had met in Acapulco. Now she was hidden behind glasses and her hair was a mess. Still, he *was* a rude man, and the child *had* been crying. 'Jean-Pierre never cries.' What a ridiculous and typically masculine statement to make about a five-year-old boy.

The plane taxied down the runway and was suddenly airborne. Sunday loved flying. It was so exhilarating, so powerful.

She felt relaxed and in a way relieved. Steve Magnum had not been the right man for her. She had accepted him for all the wrong reasons. Down the aisle Claude Hussan was chatting to a stewardess who was smiling and flashing even white teeth. He wasn't being rude to *her*.

The journey went fast. At the stopover Sunday bought the newspapers, but there was no report yet about her and Steve Magnum. She had a coffee, went to the ladies' room, and again noticed the little boy standing alone. She smiled at him, and he grinned back. His two front teeth were missing and he looked like a little urchin.

She wondered where his father was – probably in a bar somewhere, getting drunk.

She re-boarded the plane, and shortly before take-off Claude appeared with Jean-Pierre. She turned her head away as they went past.

* * *

Carey arrived at her office direct from the airport. She was tired and hot, and the copy of a Saint Laurent suit she was wearing had crumpled from the journey.

Marshall – who had flown in with her – had spent the entire journey trying to convince her they should get married immediately. He had suddenly – for some unknown reason – blown his entire cool after she had slept with him for the first time following Sunday and Steve's party. Instead of saying 'Think about it', 'Take your time', 'I know I'm much older than you', he was now saying, 'Name the day, Carey, and make it soon; in fact next week would be perfect.'

She sat behind her desk and chewed on a pencil. There was a stack of messages which she didn't even bother to look at.

Marshall had been great in bed. Surprisingly so for a fifty-six-year-old man. In fact, better than the twenty-three-year-old actor who had been her last encounter.

It was funny going to bed with Marshall. Old Marshall with

whom she had worked for seven years. It had seemed almost incestuous at the time, and she had had to get well and truly drunk before they went back to their hotel.

There was definitely a lot to be said for the older man's technique in bed, which certainly beat stamina any day.

She giggled quietly to herself. What was to stop her getting married now? She was twenty-eight years old, she had been around, she was ready to settle with one man, and Marshall had told her that she could keep on her business.

Of course, her mother, who lived in a nice house in Pasadena with her married brother and his wife, would have a fit. Whenever Carey visited them they were always trying to fix her up with nice up-and-coming lawyers or accountants. She would be the disgrace of the family if she married a white man. But so what? She wasn't prejudiced.

She buzzed her secretary. What the hell? If she didn't take the plunge now, she never would.

'Sue, get me Sunday Simmons in Acapulco.' She decided Sunday should be the first to know.

'She won't be there, will she?' Sue said. 'I've got Steve Magnum for you.'

'Put him through.'

There was a pause and then Steve's voice crackled urgently across the line. 'Where is she, Carey?'

'Where is who?'

'Don't be smartass. Where is she?'

'Steve, I just got in. I had a lousy trip and I don't feel too great, so please stop shouting. If you're looking for Sunday I spoke to her just before I left, and she was in bed. Why don't you two move in together and then you won't be so anxious every time she pops out to go shopping or something.'

'Cut the shit,' he said coldly.

Sue, who had a habit of listening in on all Carey's calls, suddenly came dashing into the office and picked up the top message on Carey's pad. She waved it under her nose. Carey read it quickly.

'What the fuck is going on?' Steve demanded. 'Are you going to tell me where she is or not?'

'What happened?' Carey said. 'Everything was fine when I left, but my dumb secretary's just shown me a message from Sunday.'

'What message?'

'It seems she called in a press release I'm supposed to give out, and she said she was fine and would call me in a couple of days.'

'What's the press release?'

'It just says "Sunday Simmons and Steve Magnum have decided to call off their engagement by mutual agreement".'

'Mutual agreement, shit,' he snapped. 'Have you given it out?'

'I told you, I just this second saw it'

'I don't want you to give that announcement out.'

'*You're* not my client, Steve.'

'I am now, honey, I'm sending you over a large retainer.'

'I'm sorry. If Sunday wants me to give out that statement, I'm going to have to do it.'

'If there's one thing I can't stand it's a spade with integrity.'

There was a short silence, during which she contemplated hanging up.

'Aw – I'm sorry,' Steve said. 'I'll tell you what, I'm going to hire you anyway.'

'What happened between Sunday and you?' she snapped.

'What happened – who knows. Sunday is a funny lady. I was bombed last night and I guess I did something I shouldn't have – according to her mixed-up standards.'

'What did you do?'

'It was nothing much.' He hesitated. 'Anyone else would have laughed it off.'

'What was it, for God's sake? It must have been something for Sunday to call everything off.'

'I had a scene with some nothing broad – a five-minute fuck.'

'And you *told* Sunday?'

'Are you crazy? Of course I didn't tell her. But somehow or other she must have found out; She sent back the ring with a note and just took off. By the time I got up today she was gone.'

'Dindi?'

'Huh?'

'It was Dindi Sydne, wasn't it?'

'I don't know who it was. Those broads all look the same to me. Some little blonde who's married to the English actor – whatshisname – Charlie Brick. A real freak-out.'

'Yes, that's Dindi. I bet she couldn't wait to tell Sunday all about it. Honestly, Steve, what made you do it?'

'A hard-on, honey, a plain old-fashioned hard-on. Do me one big favour – don't release that statement for twenty-four hours. Once I find her I'll talk her round.'

'I don't know, Steve, I should really—'

'Twenty-four hours, for Chrissake, I'm not asking for ten million bucks. I really love the girl. Give me a break.'

'All right. But only twenty-four hours, and then, if I haven't heard anything, I'm going to have to give it out.'

'You won't regret it when you're flower-girl at our wedding. Just keep this quiet. I've got a detective flying in from L.A. and he'll track her fast.'

'Well, of course *I'll* keep quiet, but I can't say the same for Dindi Sydne.'

'Don't worry, I'll take care of her. Keep in touch if you hear anything.'

He hung up.

Great, thought Carey, a great situation. Knowing Sunday, Steve Magnum had lost already.

She sighed. Looking at it from a purely business point of view, the publicity was invaluable.

Chapter Thirty-Two

Marge Lincoln Jefferson sat nervously in the bank manager's office. Her palms were wringing wet. She wiped them surreptitiously on the cotton skirt of her dress.

Louella had been over time and time again how she was to behave, what she was to say. But still she was nervous as she waited for the man to respond to her speech. 'So, Mrs Lincoln Jefferson, you've lost your bank book, I see. You should be more careful, you know; bank books must be looked after, put away, then we can just add all that nice fat juicy interest on without any trouble.'

When he said fat and juicy, his eyes considered her large floppy breasts sagging beneath the cotton dress in an old dirty bra. She was saving her only good one for the gathering on Saturday.

'Yeah, I know,' she said, gathering courage. 'But I gotta have five hundred dollars quickly, I gotta have it today.'

'Today? Hmm, I certainly don't think you can get anything today. We do have a seven-day withdrawal period, you know. However, I'll take specimens of your signature and details, and then if you come back in a week everything should be fine.'

What would Louella think of that? She might not even let her go to the gathering on Saturday night.

Marge squeezed out two fat tears. 'I *gotta* have it today. A week's time might be too late. I gotta go into the hospital, woman's problems, y'know?'

The bank manager flushed. He didn't want to hear about this gross woman's intimate problems.

Marge remembered what Louella had said, 'Any sign of trouble, and you sweet-talk the guy.'

She got up and leaned over his desk, resting her vast bosom on the desk top. 'You gotta give me a break,' she said, remembering the line from an old Mae West movie she had seen six times on television, 'er – you be good to me and I'll – er – be good to you – you know what I mean?'

The bank manager knew only too well what she meant. He cleared his throat and coughed nervously. 'I'll see if we can make an exception, Mrs Lincoln Jefferson. Would you please wait a minute?' Anything to get this awful woman out of his office.

Marge sat down and waited. If Herbie knew what she was doing he would kill her, but Louella had said it was all right. Louella had told her she had to do it, otherwise there would be no more circle of friends, no more meetings, no more parties and fun.

A secretary came in and smiled at Marge. 'Would you sign these forms please?' she requested. 'Mr Marvin has had to slip out, but he has authorized me to hand over five hundred dollars from your account.'

* * *

Two days passed and nothing happened. Herbert went about his business as normal. He scanned the papers every day, looking for more news about the murder, but there was nothing after the initial item. Murders were everyday occurrences in Los Angeles, and nothing to get excited about unless there was some additional news potential, such as the victim being famous or the crime particularly horrendous.

Marge kept asking in her whiney nasal voice: 'Whadid you

do, Herbie? Why *do* you want me to tell the police you was here?'

He ignored her. He took more showers than usual, and thought in a dreamy way what he would have done if it had been Sunday Simmons instead of that stinking dirty hippie – Sunday Simmons taking her dress off and offering herself to him.

He took the bus to work as usual, trying to find a seat on his own, and deciding that as soon as he got paid he would put a deposit on a car. He couldn't stand travelling on the bus, what with the smell and the people. He needed to pay the rent on his house which was two months overdue. He also had to meet the monthly payments on the television and refrigerater, but a car was more important. A car was a basic necessity.

It was a pity Marge didn't go back to work; although she could no longer get a job as a topless waitress.

Herbert coughed in disgust. He didn't want her any more. She had been useful to cook his meals and wash his clothes, but he could get a day maid to do that. No, after what he had witnessed the other evening, he didn't want the dirty bitch around.

Divorce was an expensive business. He thought carefully of other ways to dispose of her . . .

* * *

'I got the money,' Marge announced triumphantly.

Louella, sitting tight-lipped in her old green Chewy, took it from Marge's outstretched hand and counted it. Then she put it in her purse and smiled. 'What a clever girl. Now you are *really* one of us.'

They drove back to Louella's house. She made some herb tea, then she went through the last two days' papers with Marge, showing her all the items she had underlined.

There were forty burglaries, twelve muggings, a bank holdup, thirty-three rapes, and two murders.

'It must be one of these,' Louella said. 'I want you to read everything carefully until you are familiar with them all.'

'Do I have to, Louey? My readin ain't the greatest.'

'If we want to know what your husband has been up to, you have to. If we find out for instance that it was him that raped that woman alone in her house, then he can never boss you around again. We will be in control.'

Marge giggled. 'I guess you're right, but Herbie would never rape anyone.'

'How do you know? What you must do is familiarize yourself with these cases and mention them to Herbert. When you hit on the right one you will know at once by his reaction.'

'But what if it's not any of these?'

Louella shrugged. 'Then we think of another way to find out what he did.'

'OK, Louey. Gee, I don't know what I'd have done if you hadn't of come and lived next door. You're so nice to me, letting me join your "circle of friends" and everything.' She gripped Louella's arm with a warm, pudgy hand. 'You've changed my whole life, I really mean that.'

Louella smiled, the smile never reaching her small violet eyes. She regarded Marge in the same way that Herbert did, as a lumbering, brainless idiot. But it was stupid women like Marge who enabled her to make a living.

What would Marge do if she knew that the 'circle of friends' consisted of a lot of kinky business men who could only make it by pretending they were at some sort of black-magic orgy? Lonely women were so easy to find in Los Angeles – widows, divorcees, actresses who had never got further than the studio gates. Without exception, once Louella found them and befriended them, they were only too happy to join the circle of friends, and none objected to the so-called sexual initiations. It boiled down to the fact that they all wanted to have sex, and putting a respectable name to it and charging *them* five hundred dollars made everything all right.

Louella found the women. Her husband collected together

the male misfits, who paid fifty dollars each and attended only once. Had Marge been offered to them as a prostitute for fifty dollars, they would probably all have baulked, but the very bizarreness of the situation made everyone happy.

After two months, by which time Marge would have been initiated by over fifty men, Louella and her husband would quietly vanish with the best part of five thousand dollars, leaving Marge bewildered and suddenly friendless again.

In four years they had treated nearly forty women in this fashion, and the future looked bright, for they hadn't even half covered the State of California. None of the women ever complained. What could they say? It was as simple as that.

A lucrative sideline, Louella had discovered, was getting something on the victims, something in their past they wished to hide. This could often produce a few hundred dollars more.

Louella sensed that if she could pin something on Marge's husband, she could pry the rest of their savings away from them. Herbert Lincoln Jefferson looked like a shifty character. A rapist at least.

* * *

When Herbert reported for work at the Supreme Chauffeur Company on Saturday night, the man at the desk said, 'Jefferson, you're wanted down at the main office.'

'Me?' questioned Herbert stupidly.

'Yeah, you, there's been a complaint or something.'

Herbert's body broke out in a cold sweat. A complaint?

He tried to decide what to do. It must be the police. They must have found out about the girl. Should he run? Where to? He had only a few dollars on him and without a car he wouldn't get very far.

No, the best thing to do was to stay and deny everything. Marge would back him up with his alibi. At least he hoped she would.

The only thing that could possibly connect him with the

case was the girl's neck-chain he had found on the floor of the car, but he had carefully hidden that under the mattress of his bed. Marge hardly ever made the bed, so there was little likelihood of her ever finding it. It was quite safe where it was. He wasn't even sure that it had belonged to the girl; any of his passengers could have dropped it.

In the main office Mr Snake, the manager, lolled in a black leather chair, his feet up on the desk in front of him. He was on the phone and ignored Herbert when he was ushered into the office by a secretary.

Herbert stood ill at ease in front of the desk and thought about sitting down. Mr Snake hadn't indicated that he should, and in the face of employers Herbert always liked to do the right thing. At least the police weren't present, which was something to be thankful for.

Mr Snake finished his conversation, banged the receiver down, fumbled for a cigarette, and snapped, 'Have you been taking a leak in our customers' swimming pools, Jefferson?'

'What?' Herbert questioned, his sallow skin reddening.

'You heard me. Right or wrong?'

'Wrong,' he said quickly. That was something they couldn't prove.

'You're fired. I gave you a chance to tell the truth and you blew it. Some kid was taking a film of his mother before she went out, and through the glass doors there's you taking a piss in their pool, calm as you like. I saw the film myself this afternoon. Pick up your things and get out of here. The cashier's got your check made up until today.'

Mr Snake picked up the phone again, and by the time Herbert turned to leave he was deep in conversation.

Chapter Thirty-Three

After the incident with Clay and the two strippers, Charlie went into a deep depression. He shut himself in his hotel bungalow with the ever-faithful George, and refused to see anyone except on business about the film he was due to start. The film, a comedy, was called *Fred*.

The main girl's part was to be played by Laurel Jones, an ugly-pretty girl who had been nominated, but had not won, the previous year's Oscar for best supporting actress. She came to dinner with Charlie at his hotel, bringing her husband of two months, a long-haired member of a currently successful pop group called 'Sons'.

Charlie liked them both. They were full of talk about politics, drop-outs, world air pollution, world starvation. To Charlie it made a refreshing change from conversation consisting of either the film industry or who was laying whom.

Laurel and her husband, Floss, were vegetarians and planning six months off work to become involved with a World Starvation project in India.

'That's where it's at, man,' Floss said, 'helping people who can't help themselves.'

Laurel nodded, her eyes shining with agreement.

'Yes, but what about your careers?' Charlie asked. 'You're

both sort of at the start. I mean I know you're doing very well, but if you just throw it up right now—'

'We worked it all out,' Floss said.

'Yes,' Laurel joined in, 'Floss and the boys are going to record enough stuff and tape appearances to keep them going, and I've got another movie to do after *Fred*.'

'Man, if you can't spare six months of your time to help other human beings I just don't know.' Floss shook his head sadly.

Charlie tried to recall what *he* had done to help other people. He always, gave George his old clothes, and he had given over fifty thousand dollars to various charity organizations in the last few years. That was tax deductible, of course. He had been approached some months back to make a public appeal for the homeless, but had declined to do so, not because he didn't believe in the cause, but because it embarrassed him to appear in public unless he was acting. He had signed a petition along with many other prominent people to legalize pot. Laurel and Floss, both nineteen, made him feel very old.

After dinner he suggested maybe they could all turn on and listen to some sounds.

Laurel and Floss exchanged smiles. 'We gave it up,' Laurel said.

'Yeah, either you need it or you don't, and we figured we had reached a point where we just didn't need it any more.' Floss ran his hand through his long blond hair. 'You go ahead,' he added.

Sheepishly Charlie put away the joint he had taken out. 'No, I don't need it,' he said, 'I just thought you er . . .'

'Everybody thinks all we do is fly on drugs and trial marriages and all that stuff. Laurel and I want to show people that our main concern is for the future of the world we live in. Every day we both meditate for an hour. That's the greatest. Throw off your clothes, man, and meditate, it's better than getting high.'

After they left, Charlie took off his black-ribbed turtle-neck sweater and pants. How did one meditate?

He sat cross-legged in the middle of the floor, contemplating. Then after five minutes he said, 'Fuck it!', lit a joint, put on some sounds, and went to bed.

* * *

Apart from Laurel Jones there was supposed to be six gorgeous girls in *Fred*. Charlie, who had casting approval, told Cy Hamilton Junior to hire whomever he wanted. They were only small parts, and Charlie simply couldn't be bothered to audition a load of starlets.

Cy said on the phone, 'Come on down to the office, shmuck, I've got more delicious cooze passing through here than you've ever seen.'

Charlie wondered what kick it gave men like Cy and Clay to be on the continual look-out for available girls. They were married, so what was the point? How many girls could you screw at once? When he had been married to Lorna he had never bothered to look around; there had only been Michelle. But on thinking it over, he had to admit that before Dindi he had been exactly the same – searching for the prettiest face, the biggest breasts, the longest legs. It didn't matter if they were all raving idiots, he had been concerned only with outward appearances. Underneath all the lions' manes of hair and false eyelashes had there lurked one reasonable brain?

'I have definitely learnt my lesson,' Charlie confided to George, who was used to receiving intimate revelations from his boss. 'No more dumb starlets,'

George nodded wisely. He wouldn't have minded a few of Charlie's cast-offs.

* * *

The first day on the set Charlie was working with a six-foot two-inch redhead named Thames Mason.

She smiled and widened her large hazel eyes. 'Mr Brick, it's such a delight to work with you. I've simply adored all of your movies. You don't know what a thrill it is for me today.' She spoke a heavy Southern drawl.

Charlie drew under cover of the character he was playing and became Fred. Although the accent was fascinating, he had no plans to become friendly with anyone on the film. They would know him as Fred, and that was all – except for Laurel. She and Floss began to see a lot of Charlie, who enjoyed listening to them.

He visited their house and met their friends. They were a different group from the film crowd – young record producers, singers, musicians. Most of them favoured hippy-style dress and they accepted Charlie quite easily. What he liked was that nobody seemed impressed by who he was; in fact he wasn't at all sure if anybody knew or cared. He was just another friend of Laurel's and Floss's.

He took to going to see them almost every night after work. They held open house for their friends.

A Mexican couple took care of the house and there was always plenty of food.

Charlie took his own supply of pot, because although Laurel and Floss didn't turn on, they didn't object to their friends doing so, and most of their friends did.

It was a good scene as far as Charlie was concerned. He got himself some long flowing tops, baggy trousers, and love beads. He stopped wearing his thick horn-rimmed spectacles and switched to granny glasses. He couldn't grow his hair because of the movie, but he planned to as soon as it was finished.

'You look great, man,' Floss told him. 'You're really part of the seventies scene.'

Charlie smiled. He was sitting on the floor in their living room watching slides of butterflies projected onto the wall, and listening to a new album. He passed the joint he was holding to the fair-haired boy beside him, who in turn passed it along to a girl.

'You really should get on to the meditating kick,' Floss remarked. 'Laurel was a mess until I put her on to it.'

Charlie nodded. 'Yes, I will try it.' He had been coming to their house for ten days now, and Floss was always on at him to meditate. About eleven o'clock every night Laurel and Floss, and whoever else wanted to, solemnly stripped off and sat cross-legged and silent in the middle of the room for at least half an hour.

Charlie couldn't really see the point of it. He had never been enthusiastic at the idea of mass nudity.

Laurel had a perfect body. Everything was very small and compact. Floss was muscled and rangey.

Sex in Laurel and Floss's house appeared to be a very casual event. There were two bedrooms for their friends to use, and often a couple would stroll off to one, spend an hour or so and then re-emerge.

Charlie had his eye on a girl. She was English, and he had only seen her at the house once before. She wasn't pretty. She had a ratty, sulky face with suspicious eyes, but in any discussions she always spoke intelligently. She was young, very skinny, with long coarse light brown hair.

Charlie had not actually spoken to her, but she accepted a joint from him, and caught him staring when she took off her clothes to meditate. She was so thin that her ribcage stuck out, and she had tiny upturned breasts with crushed nipples.

When she dressed he sought her out. 'You're English,' he remarked.

'I would have thought that was obvious,' she replied, eyeing him with suspicious eyes.

'Yes, well of course it is. London with a touch of the north.'

'That's right. Why didn't you meditate? And why were you staring at my body? I'm not beautiful.'

'Er – well, love – well – er – you're certainly not ugly.'

She laughed suddenly. She had little-girl teeth. 'I'd love something sweet. Do you think there's any chocolate cake around?'

'Let's go and get some.'

'OK.'

They left silently. She made no comment on his car, just acted as if she'd been climbing into Lamborghini Miuras all her life.

'Go to the market on Doheny,' she instructed.

He drove there and they picked out chocolate cakes, cookies, pecan nuts, different flavoured ice-creams, and some candy bars.

'What a feast!' she exclaimed.

Poor kid, he thought, she probably hasn't eaten. More than likely she was eking out an existence in some crash pad on the Strip. 'Shall we take it back to Laurel and Floss?' he suggested.

'Whatever you like.'

I'd like to get laid, he thought. There had been no one since Dindi. But the hell with it, he wanted more than a quick lay, he wanted some sort of relationship with a girl to whom he could actually talk.

The following night he learnt from Laurel that the girl was Lady Phillipa Longmead, and that she was visiting her mother and stepfather who had a house on Beverly Drive.

Whilst he was talking to Laurel, having caught her just before the hour of meditation, Phillipa was sitting on the floor, shovelling handfuls of chocolate cake into an effeminate boy's mouth.

Charlie went over and said, 'Are you going to meditate tonight?'

She shrugged. 'I might, if there's nothing else going on. Are you going to?'

He quickly shook his head.

'Ashamed of your body?' she asked casually.

'Certainly not.'

'Let it all hang out,' the effeminate boy sang.

'I could take you home,' Charlie ventured.

'Who, me?' the boy asked.

Phillipa shoved the last of the chocolate cake into the boy's mouth. 'I don't usually go home this early, but if you've got any grass I'll come to your place.'

During the drive to the hotel she discussed the latest student riots. 'It's just sad the way those kids get beaten on the head.' Then she talked about a big open-air rock festival being held near San Francisco the following weekend. 'Laurel and Floss are going. I may go with them.'

At the hotel she flicked through his record albums with an air of dismissal. 'Don't you have any new sounds? No, I suppose you don't.' She finally selected a Rolling Stones album of which she approved. Then she put her dirty feet on a table and smoked the joint he gave her. She took very strong, deep pulls, closing her eyes and letting the smoke snake slowly out of her nostrils.

Charlie sat opposite her. He felt a very strong need to have this girl approve of him. He wanted her to realize that he might be over thirty but that he wasn't one of the dreaded older generation; he was still young, still hip.

They listened to the Stones in silence. When the album was finished she said, 'If you want some sex, just ask me. I don't particularly care for it myself, but I don't mind.'

He was immediately excited. 'No, no,' he said. 'Don't worry, it's the last thing I was thinking of.'

'I suppose you don't find me very desirable after all those beautiful big-busted freaks you mix with. Personally I think sex is all a mental thing.'

He nodded. 'I agree.'

'Do you?' She was surprised. 'Do you really?'

'Yes, well I could never really fancy a girl – go to bed with her I mean – unless I could talk to her. Sex for sex's sake is just . . .' he trailed off, searching for words. Oh, if Clay could only hear me now, he thought.

'I think that's so commendable of you, I really do. Most old men think quite differently. My stepfather's friends are always trying to touch me, it makes me sick.'

Most *old* men!! Charlie was choked. Did she think he was old? He was only thirty-nine, thin as a rake, in perfect condition, dressed in the latest style. How could she possibly think he was old?

'How old do you think I am?' he asked.

She shrugged, her favourite gesture. 'I don't know, how old are you?'

'No, come on, seriously, take a guess. How old would you say I was?'

'If I guess too old you'll only be angry, and if I guess too young I'll be flattering you.'

'How old?'

She studied him through narrowed eyes. 'Thirty-nine,' she said at last.

'You're kidding?'

'No, why? Younger or older?'

'Spot on, you're spot on. How did you know?'

She shrugged. 'You look thirty-nine.'

'I look thirty-nine?'

She smiled a peculiarly evil smile. 'I told you you'd be angry.'

'I'm not angry,' he said quickly. 'Why should I be?'

She stood up and bit her nails silently for a few moments. 'I'm eighteen and I feel old, so I can understand it must be pretty dreadful to be your age.'

'I'll drive you home,' he said abruptly. The girl was an idiot.

'You don't have to bother, I'm not going home yet anyway, I have to meet some friends on the Strip.'

She was worse than the fawning starlets with her offhand manner.

'Fine,' he said coldly. 'The desk will call you a cab.'

'See you,' she said. 'Thanks for the pot.'

Charlie then phoned Thames Mason, whose number he had taken just in case.

She was with him in less than half an hour, her six-foot-two body clad in floral lounging pyjamas. She plugged her career for ten minutes, suggested that maybe her part could be built up in *Fred*, and then stripped off to reveal an Amazon body.

Charlie made love to her quickly and inefficiently and sent her home with a promise of another scene to be written in for her.

When she left he felt more alone than ever. If he had not been who he was, she wouldn't have come running over.

So-called actresses, they weren't worth shit!

Chapter Thirty-Four

Sunday checked into the hotel directly from the airport. She was tired and angry. What a fool she must have been to trust a man like Steve Magnum! It worried her that she had even been planning to marry him. What kind of relationship could a girl expect with a much-married movie star?

The trouble was she had not been leading a normal life. She had arrived in Hollywood depressed and withdrawn, done two films in quick succession, and Steve Magnum had made a play for her at the right time.

She undressed and ordered a hamburger and a milk shake in her room. She also had the newspapers sent up, but there was still nothing in them about her and Steve. If it didn't appear the following day she would just have to phone Carey and find out what was going on.

She brushed her hair at the window, admiring the view. Was it worth flying to Rome to find out the truth from Benno? No, of course not, because Dindi had been speaking the truth, and somehow, now that she knew it, everything fell into place. Paulo had never really seemed to enjoy making love to her; he had always seemed a little distracted, sometimes bored. The only times he was genuinely passionate were when he could persuade her to go down on her knees in front of him while he admired his long blond beautiful body in the mirror.

The two men in her life – Raf and Paulo – had never given her any real satisfaction.

Thinking about it, she felt her body become warm. Angrily she got into bed. She knew only too well what frustration meant. When the Steve Magnum affair was over she would go out like other girls, and have an affair with the first man she liked well enough.

She couldn't sleep. Thoughts kept crowding in on her. After an hour of tossing and turning she took two of the sleeping pills that had been given to her in Rome after Paulo's death. This was the first time since then that she had had cause to take them. She disliked taking medicines after seeing what drugs had done to Paulo, but she needed sleep desperately.

At last she slept, a deep heavy sleep, because the pills were strong and she was unused to them. She dreamt of Steve. He was in bed with her, pulling her nightdress off and moulding her breasts with rough hands. She moaned in her sleep. He was pinning her arms down and entering her roughly, and she was gasping and curling her legs around him, and raking her nails down his back. Then she was on a roller-coaster of sensation, her whole body taut, nerve-ends ready to explode in a fantastic climax. Nothing mattered any more except reaching the top of the mountain, and as she hit the peak she started to laugh, and the relief and the joy of it was incredible.

Then she opened her eyes in time to watch Claude Hussan roll off her.

She lay there for a moment, her mind in a fog.

Calmly, he was lighting a cigarette. Puffing on it once, he handed it to her.

She brushed it away, the truth of what had just happened dawning on her. He had somehow or other *got into her room and raped her*, and she hadn't even woken up – or had she?

'What are you doing here?' she asked in a low voice, realizing how ridiculous the question was even as she asked it. 'How did you get in?'

'I have my ways. I was merely answering your invitation on the plane.'

'What invitation?'

He laughed. 'My dear lady, I knew what you wanted, even if you may not have known yourself.'

She was ashamed. Had it been so obvious that she needed a man?

Her body was in a soft state of abandon and fulfilment.

His hands started to use her again. 'If I was wrong I'll go,' he said.

She sat up quickly. 'Get out of here!'

He wound his hand in her hair and pulled her back beside him. Then he kissed her long and hard. 'It's better this way,' he said. 'Now we can have an honest relationship without going through all the *merde* of dating, and juvenile things like that.'

She moaned, responding to his body. What did she have to lose? It was too late for outrage and cries of rape, and since their first meeting in Acapulco she had been attracted to him. 'All right,' she muttered, surprising herself.

'You're a clever woman, Sunday,' Claude said, only a trace of a French accent in his voice. 'Now I shall make love to you while you're awake, and tomorrow we will get to know each other.'

* * *

By the time Steve Magnum's detectives tracked Sunday down, she and Claude Hussan were inseparable. Steve was furious. He was sure that the reason Sunday had run out on him in Acapulco was because of the French director. He snarled at Carey to release the statement to the press, which she did at once, sparking off much speculation and gossip.

Steve immediately started dating every available girl in town. He even stopped blaming Dindi, and saw her too. She attached herself like a leech, gradually getting rid of rivals and moving in on him as his constant companion.

Carey shuddered at Sunday's latest choice in men. Claude

Hussan had the reputation of being a mean, cynical, bastard, who enoyed great success with the ladies. His wife was a lesbian, and he had two mistresses in Paris who had both borne him children. He was a brilliant director, but apparently murderous to work with, and completely ruthless when it came to other people's feelings. Rumour also had it that he was prepared to indulge in any sexual deviation, especially orgies.

Carey shook her head. He didn't sound like Sunday's sort of man at all. She wished that Sunday would at least telephone her. She hadn't heard one word and although she left messages at the hotel in Rio her calls were not returned.

Marshall said, 'Don't worry. As long as she's back in time for her next movie it's not your business. She's your client, that's all.'

'She's also my friend,' Carey replied, and continued to worry.

* * *

Claude Hussan was in Rio to interview two actors he wanted for his film. As it was to be his first American film he wanted every part perfectly cast.

He gave Sunday the script to read. She was excited about it. If only he would consider her for the woman's role; it was a wonderful part.

'Who do you have in mind for Stefanie?' she asked casually one night.

'An actress of great strength,' Claude replied. 'A woman like Bancroft or Woodward. An American Moreau.'

She was silent. He would obviously never consider her, although she was sure she could play the part. Stefanie, a rich Beverly Hills wife who lives in a mansion with her husband, an ageing voyeuristic banker. One day their house is broken into by two boys, who make love to Stefanie, forcing her husband to watch. They stay, keeping the couple prisoners, until gradually Stefanie's loyalties switch from her husband to the boys and she becomes like them.

'I have to get back to L.A. soon,' she remarked later that evening, 'I really should let Carey know I'm on my way.'

'I'm not stopping you,' he said brusquely. 'Our arrangement is to do what we want when we want to.'

'But I don't *want* to go. You know I signed for a film.'

'A film? Is that what you call those flimsy pieces of garbage you make?'

They had been together only two weeks. She knew she must be in love because it didn't seem to matter what he did, she just wanted to be with him. He was incredibly rude to everyone – waiters, maids, the hotel receptionists, he treated them all like dirt. He had a contemptuous attitude towards everyone.

One day she asked him, 'How can you talk to people that way?'

'If they have no more ambition in life than being a servant, they deserve whatever treatment they get,' he snapped.

She was embarrassed by his behaviour. She smiled at the waiter he had recently screamed at, tipped the maid he threw out of the room, chatted amiably to the temporary nurse he had hired to take care of his son.

Jean-Pierre was a lovable little boy, although rather quiet for a five-year-old. Claude hardly seemed to notice his existence, but Sunday spent a lot of time with him. She took him to play on the beach, for walks, and started to teach him English.

'Why is he with you?' she asked Claude one day. 'You never give him any attention. Where is his mother?'

He ignored her, a habit he had when he did not wish to answer a question.

She sighed. He was an impossible, difficult, spoilt man. But when he made love to her every night it was so thrilling and beautiful that she chose to ignore his faults.

She knew she couldn't put off contacting Carey any longer. She had been reluctant to phone her, knowing she would criticize, but it had to be done as she had to get back to Los

Angeles. It wouldn't be so bad. Claude was flying to Paris for a week and then he too would be in L.A.

'Are you bringing Jean-Pierre back with you,' she asked. 'Or will he stay in Paris with his mother?'

'His mother does not want him with her,' Claude replied shortly. 'Usually he stays with his grandmother, but she is sick, so I suppose I shall have to keep him with me.'

'It makes me very sad the way you treat him,' she said. 'You take no notice of him. Don't you care?'

'He is with me, isn't he? That should mean that I care, shouldn't it?' He was angry. 'I could have arranged to leave him, but I bring him with me.'

'Shall I take him back to L.A. with me tomorrow?' she asked on impulse. 'We get along very well. I think he likes me, and after all, you will be with us in a week.'

He turned away from her. They were lying in bed, resting before a dinner engagement.

She touched his back gently. 'Please let him come with me, Claude, it would be like having a little piece of you near me. I'm going to miss you so much. We could phone the nurse now and tell her to prepare his things. I don't leave until the afternoon, there's plenty of time.'

He kicked the covers off and lay on his back. 'Make love to me the way I like it, and if it's good, we'll see.'

Chapter Thirty-Five

Charlie's lawyer telephoned him on the set. 'She's agreed to an outright payment,' he announced. 'Her lawyers advised her to stick out for alimony, but she decided to accept your offer.'

'Natural greed got the better of her,' Charlie said, relieved. 'I knew it would. Finalize the whole thing as soon as possible.'

He hung up, delighted. The money he would have to pay was worth it – anything to cut Dindi Sydne completely out of his life.

Dindi was also delighted. Charlie Brick had served her purpose, and to get rid of him *plus* receiving a large cash settlement was more than she had hoped for.

Everything was going her way. *All the World Loves a Stripper* was well into production. She was receiving a great deal of publicity, and not only from the film. In the columns her name was constantly mentioned as the girl who was consoling Steve Magnum after his broken engagement. And it was true, she *was* consoling him; nothing consoled him more than a long raunchy session with the whip. She didn't mind that, though. In fact, she really quite enjoyed it, and on the side she was banging a beautiful pale blond pool boy who came to her house three mornings a week, serviced her, and then serviced the pool.

It was really very convenient the way everything had worked out – Sunday getting hooked up with Claude Hussan, and Steve blaming *him* for Sunday's behaviour. Of course Dindi was smart enough to know that Steve was carrying one big torch, but that was only because he hadn't had an affair with Sunday, a fact he had admitted to Dindi one drunken night.

Secretly Dindi admired Sunday. Miss Simmons certainly knew how to grab a guy by the balls.

She wondered how she was making out with darling Claude. Once, in Rome, Dindi had had a scene with his wife while he sat fully dressed on a couch, watching. He had never spoken to her, just paid her the money she had been promised by the agent who had taken her there. Sunday certainly believed in getting mixed up with weirdos!

When her film was finished Dindi planned to visit Las Vegas with Steve on his once-a-year gambling stint. At the same time she could get a quick divorce from Charlie. She was just as anxious to be rid of him as he was of her, and if she played her cards right, maybe – hopefully – there might be a chance that Dindi Brick – née Sydne – might just possibly become Mrs Steve Magnum.

* * *

'I hear you're all going up to that rock festival,' Charlie said to Laurel casually.

'Yes,' she agreed, 'it's going to be so great. We've hired a bus to take us, and we're going to sleep out in tents. Floss says it's going to be a beautiful experience. Hey, why don't you come?'

'No, you don't want me along, it's going to be all you kids—'

'Charlie, *please* come. You know we'd love to have you with us. Floss will be knocked out if I tell him you're coming.'

'Perhaps I could drive there, maybe follow your bus in my car.'

She grimaced. 'That would look sort of funny. Can't you come in the bus with us? Mick's coming, and Tina, Rex and Janie, Phillipa—'

'Well, if you're sure there's room.'

'I'm sure. We'll have a great time. We'll leave Friday straight after shooting.'

He nodded. Why shouldn't he go? He was one of the crowd; they had accepted him. Besides which, he wanted to see Philippa again, to prove to her that he wasn't as old as she seemed to think.

When they finished work that night he had George drive him to the latest psychedelic shop, where he browsed among the ponchos, army jackets and T-shirts, emblazoned with 'Don't go to pot – take it'. He finally chose a white canvas Indian-style shirt and a fringed suede jacket, similar to one Floss was always wearing.

Outside in the Mercedes, George wondered how long *this* phase would last.

Charlie decided against going to Laurel and Floss's house that night. He had George drive him straight back to his hotel. There were several scripts he wanted to read. He just felt like relaxing and being on his own.

There were a lot of messages from people who wanted him to contact them. Natalie Allen had left her name several times over the past week, and Marshall K. Marshall requested that he telephone him at home as soon as possible. They were the only two calls Charlie felt obliged to make.

He phoned Natalie first, feeling guilty because he hadn't spoken to either of them since his night out with Clay.

'Well, well, stranger,' she said, 'what *have* you been doing with yourself? I've been trying to ring you for days.'

'I'm sorry, love,' he replied warmly. 'Been so busy on the film, just haven't had a minute.'

'You certainly had a minute for Clay the other night. He came staggering home at four a.m., smelling like a brewery. What *were* the two of you up to?'

He changed the subject. 'Why don't you visit the set one day, have a spot of lunch? I'll send George to fetch you.'

'I'd love to but I'm absolutely exhausted, I just can't be bothered to leave the house. Why don't *you* fix up a night, *now* while I've got you on the phone, to come over to dinner. How about tomorrow?'

The next night was Thursday and he wanted to prepare himself for the weekend trip. 'Can't make that.'

'Friday then, or better still come for the day Saturday and stay for dinner.'

'No, I can't, love, I'm off for the weekend.'

'Oh! Off where?'

'I'm going to that – er – big rock festival thing.'

Natalie laughed. 'You're doing what?'

Defensively Charlie said, 'The rock festival out in the open. Should be great.'

'Who on earth got you to go to that? It will be full of freaks. I saw the television show on the last one and it was unbelievable. All those filthy-looking kids, you'll hate it, Charlie.

How did she know what he would hate and what he would not hate? The trouble with Natalie was that she didn't move with the times.

'Is Clay around?' he asked.

Still laughing, she said, 'Just a minute, I'll get him.' Then he heard muffled conversation and more laughter as she explained to Clay where he was going.

'Off to the flower people, I hear,' Clay said, joining in the fun. 'Find me a little thirteen-year-old darling.'

'Yes, and don't you wish you were going with me?'

'I do. Natalie wants to know about dinner Monday.'

'Fine.'

'Have a good time, see you then.'

Next Charlie phoned Marshall K. Marshall.

'I'd like to have a meeting with you,' Marshall said. 'Bad news, I'm afraid.'

'Bad news? What?'

'I'd sooner meet with you, Charlie, have a proper discussion.'

'What is it, for Chrissakes? If there's one thing I can't stand it's suspense.'

'Look, if you're going to be free for lunch tomorrow I'll come to the studio.'

'What about now? Can't you come over now?'

'No, I can't,' Marshall snapped, 'I've put in a heavy day and I'm in bed.'

'Can I come over to see you? I mean if it's *that* important.'

'It's not a matter of life and death, it's just a business discussion I think we should have, and the sooner the better.'

Like all actors Charlie couldn't wait. When it came to his career he was supersensitive. 'If you don't mind, I'll be with you in half an hour.'

'All right, you're the client.'

Marshall hung up and studied the sleeping Carey, lying beside him. She had the most beautiful skin he had ever seen, a rich warm milk chocolate. He shook her awake. They had fallen into bed at five o'clock and it was now nearly eight.

She awoke smiling. 'You're never satisfied, are you? You're worse than a nineteen-year-old high-school boy. If I marry you, you're going to wear me out in no time flat, and—'

He brushed his chubby cigar-stained hands across her hard taut breasts. 'Relax, I've got Charlie Brick coming over, so shift your sexy ass and go home and decide what day next week it's going to be, and I *mean* next *week*. No more stalling.'

She smiled. 'The thing I love about you is you still talk to me like I'm the little secretary you hired way back.'

It was his turn to smile. 'What's so different about you now?'

'I'm making it with the boss – sorry – ex-boss.' She dressed in the copy of a pink Cardin suit she had worn to the office that day. 'I'm meeting Sunday at the airport in the morning, so I'll call you when I'm back in the office.'

Downstairs the maid was just admitting Charlie Brick as Carey was about to leave.

Marshall came downstairs in a plain maroon dressing gown. Carey blew him an affectionate kiss and left. '*That* is one hell of a girl,' he remarked.

'She's very attractive,' Charlie agreed. He had heard rumours that Marshall was planning to marry her.

They went into the living room and Charlie accepted a brandy. 'Well, come on,' he said, hardly able to contain his annoyance, 'what's all this bad news then?'

'I didn't want to talk on the phone,' Marshall said. 'You never know who may be listening in, and in this town news travels fast enough without giving it a boot up the ass. The fact is, Charlie, your next picture has been cancelled.'

'What?'

'Yes, I know, it's screwy as hell. *Roundabout* is going to make a lot of money and I hear that *Fred* couldn't be going better, but you know what the industry's like now, everyone's running scared. Money is very, very tight. They can't get the deal together, and frankly I never was impressed with that script.'

'But it doesn't make sense. My films make money, I haven't had a flop yet. I'm still one of the top-ten box-office stars. It's ridiculous.'

'Sure it's ridiculous, and they're going to realize it. Listen, it's not going to affect you too badly. Your working schedule in Europe is crammed anyway, I should think you would be glad of some time off.'

'I don't like not working,' Charlie said stiffly. 'I don't enjoy sitting around on my backside while newer, younger, actors push themselves forward. Find me something else to do – an independent, a low-budget art film. I wouldn't mind a change of pace. I'll drop my price if it's something I really like. Take a piece of the action.'

'OK, Charlie.'

'I might even be prepared to finance something myself.'

Marshall shook his head in disbelief. 'You actors – you're all the same, you'll even pay to see yourselves on the screen!'

Chapter Thirty-Six

'What's with the kid?' Carey asked, her mouth open in astonishment.

Sunday, looking incredibly beautiful in a yellow dress, her hair wild around her suntanned face, smiled. 'Jean-Pierre, meet Carey. Carey, this is Jean-Pierre Hussan.'

The small boy stared up at Carey solemnly and extended his hand.

'Wow,' Carey sighed, 'if the father looks anything like the son, I can understand your hang-up.'

'The father is just as beautiful.' Sunday laughed. 'Oh, Carey, I'm so happy!'

'You look like you are, in fact you look great. I want to hear all about it, but first let's get to the car before some wandering photographer spots you and pounces. By the way, why did you tell me no press at the airport?'

Sunday nodded at the boy. 'Claude insisted. Anyway, they would only be asking me stupid questions about Steve Magnum.'

'We have to go straight for fittings. You were needed two weeks ago.'

'I'm sorry, but everything's been so marvellous, I couldn't come before.'

'I understand.'

After the fittings they drove to the Château Marmont where Sunday collected the rest of her luggage. There was a lot of mail that she had told them to hold for her.

'I don't know why you didn't have it all forwarded on to you in Acapulco,' Carey said. 'It's ridiculous, there might be something important.'

Sunday shook her head. 'The only letter that could even be remotely important will be from my aunt in England, and she only writes twice a year. In fact I can't imagine who all these letters are from.'

'You'd be surprised who you get letters from when you're famous. Probably other agents trying to steal you away!'

Sunday laughed. 'I'll open them at the house. I'm so excited about it. Jean-Pierre's going to love it with the ocean right there, aren't you, sweetheart?'

She gave the little boy a hug and he smiled, something he had only just started to do.

Carey said, 'I checked the house out yesterday, it's all in order. I got in some groceries. I really can't understand why you want to be stuck down in Malibu.'

'I'm not stuck down in Malibu. I'm going to be in a great little house overlooking the sea, away from all the smog and phoney social bit. I think Claude will love it.'

'Is Claude going to be moving in with you?'

'I hope so. Carey, I *know* you'll like him, I can't wait for the two of you to meet. I want to have a little barbecue dinner when he arrives, just maybe you and Marshall, Branch, if he's back, and perhaps Max Thorpe.'

'Sounds like a fun group. Why not ask Dindi and Steve to make it *really* fun?'

'Are they going together?'

'Rumour and Joyce Haber has it. I hear that he's so tanked up that it's an effort for him to get it up any more!'

'You're really disgusting!' But she was laughing, and once more Carey marvelled at the change in her. Good, bad or indifferent, Claude Hussan had certainly brought out a new Sunday.

221

They stopped off at Carey's apartment to fetch Limbo. Then they drove straight down to the house.

'It's so great,' Sunday exclaimed. 'Much better than I remember. Why don't you borrow a suit and we'll have a swim? Come on, Jean-Pierre, get changed.'

She opened his suitcase and threw him a small pair of bathing shorts. Limbo was running around, going mad with excitement.

'I can't stay,' Carey said wistfully, 'I'd like to, but I've been out of the office all day and there's things to be done. Now, tomorrow your press conference is at two p.m. I'll have a car pick you up at one. I do think it would be a good idea not to bring the child. The maid comes in tomorrow at ten; have her look after him. There are several interesting offers I'd like to discuss with you, so I thought maybe dinner tomorrow night at Marshall's house.'

'I want to hear all about that. Is there going to be a wedding?'

'Listen, kid, I must rush, I'll call you later. There's a list of local services in the kitchen in case you need anything, and I'm always available on the phone.'

'We won't need anything. We're going to have a swim, something to eat, and an early night.'

The ocean was warm, throwing up big waves that knocked Jean-Pierre flat and sent Limbo scurrying in mad circles on the shore. Sunday set the little boy firmly on her shoulders and waded in.

Later, after the child was in bed she unpacked a few things, fed Limbo and wandered around, exploring the house. Carey telephoned and they had a short chat. Claude didn't, although he had promised.

She wondered how he would like the house. It would be peaceful for him, a place where he could really relax. He was so involved in his work, always planning and flunking about it, having discussions and meetings.

That was a good thing, she decided. A man should be dedicated to his work. She didn't care if she ever worked again. If things worked out with Claude, perhaps she wouldn't: it would be enough just to be with him, look after him and have his children, lots and lots of them, all looking like Jean-Pierre.

She sighed. It was a dream. He was still married, and even if he were single, she knew he wasn't the marrying kind. Well, she didn't mind that. They could just live together, and still have children. She wouldn't tie him down.

What was her career all about anyway? Nobody cared about her as an actress, a person. All they cared about was the maximum exposure of breasts, legs, and anything else that was going. Even if she became a star, that was still all they would care about.

She sat down and started opening her mail.

Carey was right. Two letters from agents, offering her their services; circulars about cars, televisions and household equipment; a short letter from Aunt enclosing an English press clipping and complaining about Sunday's lack of clothes in the photograph.

There were three bulky envelopes, all addressed in the same scrawly hand. She inspected the postmarks and opened the oldest one first. A plastic bag fell out. '*Sunday – when will you—*'

'Oh God!' she groaned. It was full of obscenities about what the writer wanted to do to her, imagined doing, and said they would soon be doing.

She read it briefly in fascinated horror.

'*I promise not to keep you waiting too long, we will be together soon, so keep your lovely—*'

She tore it up.

The other two were the same, the ravings of a sick mind.

It was very depressing, and because the man seemed so certain they would be together, a little frightening. She was glad the writer didn't know where she was now; at least he only knew the hotel where she had been.

She telephoned the Château in a panic, and told them not to give out her address.

It was nothing to worry about. Carey said that all actresses got these kind of letters.

She went to bed feeling sick, and looked forward to the brightness of the morning.

Chapter Thirty-Seven

It was Herbert's third shower of the day. The water trickled lukewarm down his thin hairless body.

His eyes were clenched shut, as he thought about what he had caught his fat whore of a wife doing. Legs spread, she had been next door taking on all comers. Of course from the window where he had crouched watching, he didn't have the best vantage point, but he certainly knew what was going on, oh yes, he certainly knew.

It was good he had not told Marge about getting fired from the Supreme Chauffeur Company. Now he was free to spy on her. In fact he was free to do what he wanted all day and all night.

As he had been working night shifts, he left the house at the usual time. Then he would either spend the evening at the movie theatre where the Jack Milan film with Sunday Simmons was playing, or he would go to a topless bar and watch the scenery with his cold hard eyes.

He knew when Marge was planning to go out. She became jumpy and nervous, fussing around him, trying to hurry him out of the house. He obliged by leaving quickly, but then he would return and watch her disgusting behaviour through his neighbour's window.

Money was running short. He would have to get another job soon. He wasn't worried, because long before being fired he had been prudent enough to steal some Supreme Chauffeur notepaper, and had written himself several glowing references.

When he found a job he would leave Marge – just walk out and leave her. Why should he work hard to put food in the mouth of such a filthy woman?

First he decided he would draw out her savings and buy himself a car. He would trick her into signing something, giving him access to her money, or he would forge her signature. That shouldn't be too difficult.

'Are you gonna be in there all day, Herbie?' Marge whined outside the door.

She was always whining about something, asking him stupid questions about bank raids and women getting raped. Only that very morning she had said to him, 'Herbie, isn't it kinda difficult to rape a woman unless she wants it?'

'You think of nothing but sex,' he had replied in disgust.

'There's nothing wrong with that, is there? I can remember when your tongue used to hang out when I worked in that place with my titties all bare. You loved it.'

'I don't love it now, you're a fat cow. Aren't you ashamed of your body?'

Marge banged loudly on the bathroom door. 'I'm gonna pee in my pants if you don't let me in.'

Reluctantly he climbed out of the shower and, covering himself with a towel, opened the door.

She bounced in, and with a flash of fat thighs plonked herself on the toilet.

'Hey, Herbie, remember that murder up on er – Miller Drive – just off the Strip? Remember it? Some young girl.' She paused. 'What's the matter?'

He had turned white. The towel had fallen from his hands and he stared at her in horror. She *knew*. The bitch knew!

With a sense of triumph Marge realized that she had hit on something at last. Louella had been right! Her plan had worked! All the studying of newspapers and remembering names of streets, banks and victims had paid off.

'What do you know?' he demanded harshly.

'Enough,' she replied, remembering Louella's advice to stay quiet. 'Enough to put you behind bars for life.' She added the last line on impulse; it sounded good. Lana Turner had said it on the late movie two nights before, and the guy she said it to had crumbled, buried his head in his hands and begged for mercy.

Herbert did neither of those things. He just stood there in his hairless nakedness, chewing on his bottom lip and narrowing his small mean eyes.

Marge felt good. In all their years of marriage Herbert had treated her like a piece of furniture, bossed her around, and even beaten her up. No wonder she had let herself get fat. For years before meeting Louella, she had hardly been out of the house except to go to the market. And there had been no sex at all after she lost the baby. Not that Herbert had been any great shakes at it – in and out like a rabbit and straight into the shower – but it had been better than nothing. Later Marge had harboured a grumbling resentment against him, especially when she found the filthy letters he was writing to all those fancy movie stars. The letters had helped, though; instead of Herbert, she took the letters to bed and imagined he was talking to her.

Herbert's mind was racing. How had the bitch found out? Did he talk in his sleep? How did she know? And more important, what did she want from him?

'What are you going to do?' he asked, picking up the towel and wrapping it around himself, trying to stay calm and cool and not beat the fat bitch in case perhaps she had told someone else. Maybe she had told that crabby neighbour, or one of the men she had been with at those disgusting sex orgies.

'Don't worry.' Marge shifted herself off the toilet. 'Why should I do anything? You're my husband, aren't you? And husband and wife should stick together.' On impulse she put her arms around him and did a little wriggle against his body.

With horror he knew what she wanted.

'Yeah, you're my husband and I'm your wife, so even if I *wanted* to go to the cops it wouldn't seem right, would it?'

She suddenly pulled off her cheap cotton dress, dragging it impatiently over her head. Then she released her mammoth bosom from a pink bra and shook it at him. 'I guess we should do some of those things married people like to do together, huh? I guess that would be a lot of fun.'

She tugged at the towel round his waist. He stood quite still. If he did *that* with her he could catch something. He had seen her with all those other men; she must be *crawling* with germs.

But she didn't want him to do that. She wanted him to do something to her much more intimate, something she had tried to get him to do when they were first married but he had refused.

He couldn't refuse now. Bile rose in his throat and he went to work.

Later when Marge had gone out, smiling, triumphant and unwashed, Herbert wrote to Sunday Simmons, pouring out all his desires and needs, and charged his frustration into a clean plastic bag. She was all he had in life, the only beautiful thing.

He went out, posted the letter, and then went to see her in the Jack Milan movie, where he spent the rest of the day, watching it four times. He left after slipping his hand up the leg of an unsuspecting woman. Before she could complain he was gone.

He bought a newspaper and sat in a coffee shop studying the jobs vacant. He circled several possibilities. Tomorrow he had to get a job. There was no money, and with Marge knowing what he had done he could hardly walk out and leave her; she'd have the cops after him in no time.

The only answer, he realized, was to get rid of Marge – get rid of her once and for all.

It needed planning, but it could be done.

Chapter Thirty-Eight

'I wouldn't have thought this would be your scene at all,' Lady Phillipa said. She was sitting next to Charlie on the bus, her long hair wispy around her unmade-up face. She was wearing a purple patterned flowing dress and no shoes.

'Why ever not?' Charlie asked, feeling very much part of the group in his new outfit.

'Well, you're part of the whole film star bit, aren't you? Big cars and houses. Surrounded by possessions. Possessions are your hang-up, aren't they? You probably use women as possessions too. Tell me this, a woman is a sexual object to you, is she not?'

'No, she's not,' he replied sharply. This ratty girl had a great knack of making him angry. 'And possessions are not my hang-up, as you put it. I don't even have a house of my own.'

'Tough shit.' She started to laugh. 'Don't even have one little house of your own, that's really bad.'

'Is there something you don't like about me?' he asked tightly.

'Nothing about you personally. Just you generally. I mean you're part of the so-called establishment, you're one of them, not one of us. Why are you hanging around with us?'

'I'm not hanging around with you – I'm taking a trip with friends, Laurel and Floss and the others. Why does that upset you?'

'Because you belong to a different generation. You're my mother's whole scene. You don't belong here.'

The different-generation crack hurt Charlie. He stared out of the window and wished he hadn't come.

After a while Phillipa said, 'I could do with getting high. Got anything?'

'Oh, I'm all right for supplying you with pot, am I?'

'Yes. If you like I'll pay you by sleeping with you.'

'That's the second time you've offered me sex. Haven't you got any money?'

She flushed. 'I told you I don't like sex much, money's more important to me, so I offered you the least important.'

'Bully for you!' Maybe one was better off with a big-breasted dumb girl. 'By the way, I don't even know your mother.'

'You don't *have* to know her. You're part of the great show-biz world, aren't you?'

'So are Laurel and Floss,' he pointed out mildly.

'They're different.'

He produced a joint and wondered if it was all right to smoke it on the bus. He didn't feel like it, but he wanted to keep Phillipa company, so he lit up and in two minutes Floss was by his side, hissing, 'Are you crazy? If the cops should stop us there'd be no trip of any kind.'

'Sorry,' said Charlie, quickly stubbing out the cigarette.

Phillipa laughed. 'Everyone's so uptight. Get pleasantly happy on a little hash and that's bad.'

'I'm with you,' he agreed.

'Yes, but the rest of your neurotic age group aren't.'

There she went again, another dig about his age.

'They don't want to see the young enjoying all the things they never had. They hate to think of us doing what we want, wearing what we want, turning on and having sex without feeling guilty about it.'

'You feel guilty about sex.'

'I do not.'

'Yes, you do – otherwise you'd enjoy it.'

Patiently she explained. 'I do not enjoy sex because I cannot achieve any type of orgasm. I'm built that way.'

'How do you know?'

'I just know. Now go on and tell me that you're the one and only man who can bring me to a full and beautiful climax.'

'Maybe I could.' He started to feel a bit horny. Maybe he could.

She laughed mirthlessly. 'Do you know how many old men have told me that?'

'How many *old* men have you *had*?'

'Four – well, five, if you want to count my stepfather, and he was lousy. It's an interesting fact that he told me my mother doesn't achieve orgasm either. How about that? And she's been married twice and had countless boyfriends.'

'And I thought you were a modern girl! But you're really charmingly old-fashioned, even down to knocking off your stepfather. Couldn't you have at least made it your father?'

She shrugged. 'I really don't care whether you believe me or not. I'm way past the stage of bothering about what people think of me.'

He wondered how long it would take George to drive up and collect him. Lady Phillipa Longmead was a screwed-up adolescent, and that was not what he needed in his life.

Laurel came down the aisle. 'Isn't this fun,' she enthused, her face alert and flushed. 'Only three more hours to go, and then a beautiful night under the stars. Charlie, I'm so glad you came with us. Did you remember your sleeping bag?'

'You didn't tell me to bring a sleeping bag.'

'Didn't I? Sometimes I'm so forgetful. Philly, can Charlie squeeze in with you?'

'I think that's what he had in mind anyway.'

Laurel smiled. 'I love you both. You know that, I truly love you.' She touched them both on the shoulder as if she were a faith-healer, and carried on up the aisle.

'We were at school together in Switzerland,' Phillipa remarked. 'We learnt French, cooking and masturbation.'

'What do you do now?' Charlie asked.

'I bum around. I'm supposed to be studying modern design, but right now I'm taking a holiday to get over my abortion. I don't have to do anything really; I've got plenty of money – trust funds and things. When I get back to London I'm buying a house somewhere in Hampstead or maybe the country, and turning it into a commune. People will be free to come and go and do their own thing. No rules, just a lovely uncomplicated life.'

'And you footing all the bills?'

'Why not? I've got the money. Why shouldn't I use it on other people. What do you do with all your money?'

'I pay taxes, look after my children, and pay bills. Sometimes I buy myself a car or a camera or anything I fancy.'

'Including a woman, a sexual object.'

'For someone who's not interested in sex it does seem to be your only subject.'

'My mother doesn't know where it's at. She's like you, always trying to be smart. She's sending me to an analyst here. You go in to see this man and he makes you take off all your clothes and lie on a couch. Everything has to come off. He says he can see the tension points on the body that way. How about *that*? He got a bit of a shock when he first saw me; he's used to all those Beverly Hills rich ladies with big boobs and flat stomachs and sexy thighs. I think he was choked when he got me. Nothing to feast his greedy little eyes on.'

Charlie laughed. He could imagine the scene. 'Why do you go?'

'My mother's a trustee. I don't get my money until I'm twenty-one, so meanwhile she doles out what she thinks I should get. Actually she can't stand me; it's mutual. Would you care to meet her? She'd *love* to meet you.'

'Are you inviting me?'

She yawned. 'Aren't you bored with me yet? I usually bore people quite early on in a relationship.'

Well, she *was* different.

231

* * *

The festival was being held in the grounds of a large old farm-house. Acres and acres of green land, swarming with the thousands of young visitors who were steadily appearing by the hour.

It was quite a sight. They were arriving on foot, by car, motorcycle, bus, and train. A colourful procession; some of the girls carried babies, and a few toddlers moved along with the crowd. Nearly everyone had long hair and flowing clothes. Ordinarily dressed people were regarded as suspect.

A few policemen were to be seen, travelling in pairs, looking grim and tough in their dark uniforms.

It was just beginning to get dark. Laurel and Floss with their whole group moved steadily through the crowds to find a good vantage point to spend the night.

Hot-dog, hamburger, and ice-cream stands were dotted around. Tents were being erected for the night. Some people just had blankets to lie on.

Phillipa walked silently beside Charlie, who carried her heavy sleeping bag. This wasn't quite the way he had imagined it. Laurel had quite definitely mentioned tents, and he thought they had the whole matter arranged. He had imagined luxurious tents set up on a hill overlooking the crowd, certainly not sleeping bags down among the herd.

He was tired from the day's work at the studio, the hot dusty bus ride, and now this long trek. He was also starving hungry, and anxious to take a leak.

A dreamy-looking girl was sitting on the grass, breastfeeding a rather large baby. Two teeny boppers recognized Floss and giggled around him. A group of leather-jacketed boys swaggered past, all greasy hair and sneery faces. Over everything there hung the acrid bitter-sweet aroma of marijuana.

Laurel and Floss finally found a place to settle, and Laurel went around asking all their friends sweetly, 'Is this OK for you? Are you *sure*?'

Phillipa said to Charlie, 'I have to go to the loo.'

At last, a common interest! They went off together to find the convenience tents that Floss assured them couldn't be far away. In fact, they walked for ten minutes before they found them, by which time it was dark and Charlie wondered how they were going to find their way back.

'Wait for me right outside,' he commanded Phillipa.

She smiled a rare smile. 'You know you're not all bad. I can't see my mother doing this.'

Great, he thought. I should have gone after the mother!

In the badly smelling men's convenience a bearded boy was giving himself a shot, an old belt tied tightly around his arm, the vein bulging. Two characters sporting beards lounged around, watching. Charlie got out as fast as he could.

Phillipa took her time and then emerged ruffled. 'You wouldn't believe the scene in there,' she remarked. 'There's a couple of lady fuzz searching everyone for acid or pot or something ridiculous. What a nerve!'

Charlie was glad they hadn't been where he was. He could see the headline now: 'Actor caught with marijuana at pop festival.'

'We're never going to find our way back,' she complained.

He took her hand and led her through the crowds. He had always had a good sense of direction.

What would she say if he suggested they get the hell out of this and go home?

It started to spit, fine warm rain, that was hardly noticeable.

'I'm hungry,' she moaned.

How would a sleeping bag be in the rain, Charlie wondered. He stopped and bought two hot-dogs – ruinous for his diet – and they kept looking for their group.

'There they are,' Phillipa yelled at last. 'There's Janie and Rex. Hey, where's everyone else?'

Out of the busload only a few were left.

Janie, a fat girl dressed like a gypsy, said, 'Everyone's chickened

233

off. They didn't like the scene. The cops are patrolling round with great big dogs and it's just not cool. You can't even get high in peace.'

'Where have they gone?' Charlie asked, furious at having been left behind.

'Some party one of the groups is having. They'll all be back tomorrow for the show. We're supposed to keep the pitch. How about a bite of your hot-dog?'

'Didn't Laurel or Floss leave a message for us?' Charlie demanded furiously.

Janie shook her head. 'Guess not.'

'Come on.' He tossed the remains of his hot-dog at the fat girl, and gripped Phillipa's arm. 'Let's get out of here.'

Chapter Thirty-Nine

Sunday's press conference went smoothly. She countered questions about herself and Steve Magnum with charm and tact.

Carey had decided that the best way to present Sunday to the press was at a cocktail party where she could circulate freely among the reporters.

She was a hot property. On the strength of the Jack Milan movie alone, she was receiving a huge amount of fan mail.

Carey had several firm offers to discuss with her. It had been a good move to hold off signing anything while the word spread. Sunday could now pick and choose.

'What about you and Claude Hussan?' an alert girl columnist asked.

Sunday smiled. She wanted to say 'We're in love and I hope we will always be together', but Carey had warned her to say nothing about him beyond the old worn-out quote that they were merely good friends.

'We're just friends,' she said lamely.

'But you were in South America with him and his son?' the girl persisted.

'Well, yes.' She was surprised, no one was supposed to know about that.

'Is it true he's divorcing his wife?'

'I don't know. Is he?'

'I thought if anyone would know it would be you.' The girl's voice was sarcastic. She didn't like actresses. She had been one herself and had failed miserably.

'Excuse me,' Sunday said politely. 'They need me for a photo.'

'Just one more question before you go. Could you love a man like Claude Hussan? Isn't he just another Steve Magnum with a French accent?'

Sunday blinked. 'You'll have to excuse me,' and she edged away.

* * *

Later there was dinner at Marshall's house, just the three of them, and they discussed the various offers.

'I don't want to make any decisions until I talk it over with Claude,' Sunday stated.

Carey shrugged. 'Fine. But my personal opinion is that we should accept the new Milan film. After all, it's an equal part and a marvellous script. Then we could follow it up with the Constable movie, he's such a great director.'

Sunday nodded. None of the propositions particularly excited her. They all called upon her to look fantastic, and the money was good, but was it too much to expect that her parts should require some acting ability?

'You know the industry is in a crazy state,' Marshall said. 'Hardly anyone's working, it's tough all round. You seem to be the golden girl of the moment. Enjoy it, sweetheart – while you can.'

Sunday got up to leave.

'Don't forget fittings and make-up tests at ten tomorrow,' Carey reminded her. 'A car will collect you at nine. By the way, when is Claude arriving?'

'The end of the week. He was supposed to call me but I guess he's been too busy. He works so hard, sometimes he forgets to eat.'

Carey and Marshall exchanged glances.

* * *

The next day Alert Girl Reporter wrote in her widely syndi-cated gossip column: '*Sunday Simmons is the beautiful new Sex Goddess of our ever-searching tinsel city. I met her last night and she told me confidentially – batting foot-long false eyelashes and tossing her fall of auburn hair – that as far as she is concerned, rumoured new love of her life, notorious French film director Claude Hussan, is merely another Steve Magnum with a French accent. Our Steve, as you may recall, is a recent fiancé of the up-and-coming Miss Simmons. This lovely girl with the Raquel Welch-type body and Mickey Mouse quotes should go far.*'

Sunday was dismayed. What if Claude should see it? It made her look such an empty-headed little idiot.

She raged at Carey. 'No more press parties. I don't care if my name never appears in a gossip column again. I won't talk to any more of these bitchy, frustrated women!'

'Fine,' Carey soothed. 'But they're not all like that. It's not so terrible. People just remember they saw your name, not what it said about you.'

'That's what you think,' Sunday replied shortly. 'I always remember what I read, and anyway, how do you think Claude's going to feel?'

'Claude's not even going to see it unless you show it to him.'

* * *

That evening Sunday had dinner with Branch. He took her to their favourite health restaurant. Over coffee Max Thorpe appeared, plump and red-faced with his streaky bleached-blond hair. He greeted Sunday warmly and joined them. 'I told you we'd come by the house later,' Branch said peevishly.

'I know, I know, but I couldn't wait to see the beautiful Sunday Simmons,' Max enthused. His watery eyes darted all over the place and came to settle on Branch. 'You don't mind, do you?'

Surly-mouthed, Branch shook his head.

'He's doing so well,' Max said, patting Sunday's hand.

'Yes, I know.' She smiled. 'I think the television series will be wonderful for him.'

'Did he tell you he's moving in with me? So stupid for him to pay all that money to a hotel when I have such a big house.' Max shifted his hand from Sunday's to Branch's, where it lingered. 'It gets quite lonely there at times; it will be nice to have some company.'

Branch looked miserably at Sunday. She felt the tension between the two men and feigned a yawn. 'Sorry, everyone, but I think it's time I was off. Early call tomorrow.'

'I don't like you driving back to the beach alone,' Branch mumbled. 'This town is full of nuts.'

'Don't be silly. I have a perfectly reliable rented Ford, full up with gas, and I'll close all the windows and lock all the doors.'

Branch grunted and called for the check, which Max paid. They all strolled to the parking lot where Branch left with Max in his white Rolls Royce, and Sunday set off for the beach in her pale blue Ford.

She drove fast, keeping to the middle lane and not glancing around when she was held up at traffic lights. If you so much as peeked left or right, it was odds on that you would catch a man's eye and he would take that as an immediate invitation. Los Angeles was the sort of city where women, especially women who looked like Sunday, rarely drove alone at night.

Claude hadn't phoned, and she was worried about him. She didn't even know for certain what day to expect his arrival.

She thought about Branch and Max. Carey and Marshall.

She did not notice the old grey Buick following her. Its licence plate obscured by mud. Its driver hidden behind heavy dark glasses.

She was too busy thinking, so she noticed nothing. Not even when she turned off along the lonely beach road and the old grey Buick was right behind her.

Chapter Forty

'How long have you been here?' Natalie asked, her polite phrasing hardly hiding the distaste she felt towards the skinny barefoot girl whom Charlie had brought to dinner.

Phillipa yawned openly, not concealing her gaping mouth with her hand, but treating all to a full view of her tonsils. 'Long enough,' she said in her flat, slightly northern voice. She had made Charlie promise that he wouldn't tell them who she was until after dinner. She wanted to prove to him the change in people's reactions when they found out she had a title.

Natalie choked down some prawn cocktail. Who did the little bitch think she was? Some pick-up from that awful hippy freak-out Charlie had gone to!

'I like your outfit,' Clay remarked. 'Very lovely, very unusual.'

'Thanks.' Phillipa flashed a rare smile. 'I picked it up off a junk stall in Portobello Road.'

She was wearing a rather tatty, nearly see-through, dress. It was embroidered with lace in places, and hung open to her waist. Her small bosom stayed hidden, only emerging when she stretched for her wine. Clay watched, fascinated.

'How was the concert?' Natalie asked. 'I saw on the news that a girl had a baby there.' She patted her own small bulge protectively. 'It must have been terrible for her.'

'Worse for the onlookers, I should think,' Phillipa said, removing a prawn from her mouth and examining it before abandoning it on the side of her plate.

'Something wrong?' Natalie asked when the ratty girl did the same thing with a second prawn.

'I think they're off,' Phillipa replied offhandedly.

Everyone stopped eating and Natalie glared. If there was one thing she couldn't stand it was to see food wasted. 'They can't be off,' she said quickly, 'I got them from the market myself this morning.'

Clay pushed his plate away. 'Let's not risk it, darling.'

Natalie's eyes filled with angry tears.

'What's next?' Clay asked.

'Roast lamb,' Natalie replied tightly.

'Ah, folks,' Clay said, 'the Allens will now treat you to some rancid roast lamb.' He roared with laughter.

'You're not funny,' Natalie said coldly, and banging the dishes together, she stamped out of the room.

'I don't know what's the matter with her,' Clay said glumly, 'she's so bloody sensitive lately.'

'She's pregnant,' Charlie said quietly. 'Women are always touchy when they're pregnant.' For a brief moment he remembered Lorna when she was carrying his two children. It had been the happiest time of his life. She had been soft and warm and affectionate. Women were beautiful when they were pregnant. He followed Natalie out to the kitchen.

Phillipa picked on a hang nail and Clay filled her glass with wine.

'Where did you and old Charlie meet up?' he asked.

'At an orgy,' Phillipa replied, and concentrated on her nail.

After dinner they went out to the patio for coffee. Natalie was calm and happy. Charlie was being especially sweet to her. His unbelievable girlfriend had lapsed into an hour-long silence.

There seemed no point in telling the Allens that plain Phillipa was actually Lady Phillipa Longmead. Charlie was sure it would make no difference to them.

'I hired a chauffeur today,' Clay remarked. 'A nice quiet chap. He can take Natalie around. The doctor said she's got to give up driving – her back or something.'

'I wish you had let *me* interview him,' Natalie said. 'After all, it will be I who is with him most of the time.'

'You were asleep, darling. Anyway I was lucky to get him. *They* interview you. He'll be here at ten in the morning, so you'll see him soon enough. His name is Herbert Lincoln Jefferson. Are you ready for that name?'

* * *

They sat in the Lamborghini in front of Phillipa's parents' house.

'Your friends, didn't like me and I don't care,' she said.

'Well, you weren't exactly charm personified were you? Telling Natalie the prawns were off. You should have just kept quiet about it.'

'Why?'

'Because it would have been the polite thing to do.'

'Oh Charlie, don't be so uptight and antiquated. That's the trouble with your stupid generation, you're all so busy being polite that you don't even see what's going on under your nose. Wars and violence, people starving, young kids being sent off to get their brains blown out, and worse – if it's an arm or a leg they lose, they just get dumped in some lousy army hospital and left to rot like garbage.'

'I don't want any of your lectures. I know what's going on. I don't like it any more than you do, but it's life, you have to accept it.'

'Accept it?' Her lip curled sarcastically. 'That's just what we're *not* going to do.' She got out of the car and walked into the house without a backward glance.

Charlie sat glumly, watching her disappear. She was a strange girl. She made him feel guilty. She made him feel that his life was small and useless and that he wasn't *doing* anything.

However, at least she could open her mouth and talk. She was aware, and that was a commendable quality.

He gunned the car into action, and feeling depressed, drove back to his hotel.

* * *

Charlie and Laurel were hardly talking. He could not conceal his anger at the way she and Floss had just taken off at the rock festival. Neither of them mentioned it, but there was a cold barrier between them which everyone noticed. He stopped going to their house. He was busy reading properties anyway, looking for something he could do in the gap left by the cancelled movie. He had no reason to return to England before the end of the year.

He saw Phillipa. She came to his hotel most evenings and sat around while he read. Sometimes she read scripts for him. She had surprisingly bright criticisms, and as he got to know her she relaxed and was a much more pleasant person to be with. It remained a purely platonic relationship. He didn't really fancy her sexually, so he didn't push it. Of course everyone thought they were at it day and night. Apart from the fact that Clay dropped by occasionally, they saw hardly anyone.

One day Phillipa said, 'My mother is having one of her parties. She wants me to bring you.'

Charlie looked at her in surprise. 'I thought you hated parties.'

'I do. But she's been on and on about you, so in a weak moment I said yes.'

'I didn't know you *had* weak moments.'

She flushed. 'It's tomorrow night at eight. Will you come?'

'If you want me to.'

* * *

Phillipa's mother, Jane, was in her early forties. She was slim, tall, perfectly groomed, with a typically English prettiness. She looked nothing like her daughter. She wore a long red dress, and two thin diamond bracelets on each wrist. Her hair was swept back into a chignon, and in contrast to her husband she was the blueprint of good taste.

Husband Sol, short and paunchy, with a giant cigar shoved obscenely between his lips, made no concession to the fact that they were having a party. He wore a gaudy Palm Beach shirt and baggy brown trousers.

Jane extended an elegant hand and said, 'I'm so delighted to meet you, Mr Brick. Phillipa talks of you all the time.'

Sol shifted the cigar to the side of his mouth and rasped in pure Brooklynese, 'Hey, Charlie, baby, good t'see ya. Name your poison.'

Phillipa was nowhere in sight.

Charlie made himself comfortable at the bar and chatted to Angela Carter and her escort.

It was an hour before Phillipa appeared. Charlie hardly recognized her. Her normally long flowing hair was arranged in the semblance of a style, and instead of shaggy robes, she wore a white Victorian dress and shoes! Her face, with the small amount of make-up she had applied, was less interesting but more attractive.

'You look great,' he said, smiling.

'Do I?' Suddenly she seemed like a rather shy eighteen-year-old and not the tough independent hippie he was used to.

Her mother descended and threw up her hands in horror. 'Phillipa, what *are* you wearing? Honestly, Mr. Brick, I just don't know what to do about this girl, she always looks such a frightful mess.'

A look of pain flitted quickly across Phillipa's face and was just as quickly gone. She stepped out of her shoes defiantly. 'Sorry, Jane, I know you hate the smell of my feet, but it's so much more *healthy*!'

Jane smiled. 'Such a *young* girl, she'll learn won't she, Mr Brick? Or shall I call you Charlie? After all, when we were her age we had to go through this silly Bohemian phase too, I suppose, but it's so *boring* while it lasts. Don't you agree?'

They stood on either side of him: Phillipa, eyes sulky and defiant; Jane, confident and poised. They waited to see whose side he would take.

He sidestepped the issue and said, 'This is a really lovely house. Have you lived here long?'

When Jane went off to talk to other guests, Phillipa whispered, 'Let's go. This is really awful. I can't stand all these phoney people.'

Charlie was just about to agree when he spotted Dindi at the door. She was in a white satin pyjama-suit slashed to the waist, her suntanned bosom barely concealed, her blonde hair fluffy around her pouty face. She was with Steve Magnum and his entourage.

Charlie felt a jolt of outrage at the sight of her. He would never forget the way she had spoken of Serafina the day before his dear mother died. He loathed her, and it also galled him that she was becoming so successful. She had used him, a fact he would always remember.

Abruptly he downed the rest of his drink and said to Phillipa, who was absently picking at her long hair, 'One more drink and we'll be on our way. OK, love?' He wasn't about to slink out the moment Dindi appeared.

Across the room she had noticed him, and in a loud voice she said to Steve, 'Who on earth is Charlie with?'

'Charlie who?' Steve asked, swaying slightly.

'You'd think he could do better than that,' Dindi giggled, 'I guess times are bad. I heard that they cancelled his next movie.'

Steve wasn't listening. He was hugging Jane, with whom he had once had an affair.

Dindi headed across the room towards Charlie. 'Hello,' she said loudly.

He wanted to ignore her, but sensed that that would give her more satisfaction than a cool greeting. He nodded at her coldly. 'Dindi.'

'Putting on a little weight, I see.' She giggled in her customary manner.

He smiled tightly. She had hit him where it hurt – his ego.

Jane joined them at that point, kissing Dindi on both cheeks and gushing, 'But of course you two know each other, don't you? Really it's quite difficult to keep up with who was married to whom in this town.'

'You manage,' Phillipa muttered under her breath.

'What, dear? Oh Dindi, darling, have you met my little girl? She makes me feel quite ancient. Phillipa, this is Dindi Synde.' She smiled prettily at Charlie. 'Mr Brick's ex-wife, or *are* you divorced yet, one never knows?'

Silently Charlie surveyed the three women: Jane, so sure of herself, a hint of bitchery gleaming in her flat grey eyes; Dindi, bursting out of her top, all blonde hair and nasty curled lips; Phillipa, flushed and a little panicky.

He gripped Phillipa by her boney arm, saying, 'I just remembered a very urgent appointment, thanks so much,' and steered her across the room, through the hall, and out of the front door.

'Thank God you did that,' she exclaimed. 'I don't think I could have stood it in there one more minute. Were you really married to *her*?'

'It's a short story,' he mumbled quickly. 'Let's go back to the hotel and light up a nice big fat relaxing joint. I need to get the smell of that cow out of my nose.'

'Who – Jane or Dindi?'

'Both of them – they go together beautifully.'

Later, when they were both pleasantly high, and the voice of Nina Simone filled the room, Charlie undressed her.

It was time. They had been together weeks without really being together.

She was painfully thin, and stiffened in his arms, although she never spoke a word of objection. She was rigid with distaste, tight, dry, unwelcoming.

He produced a jar of Vaseline and she shied away in disgust. The whole thing was a mistake. It was wrong.

Charlie felt all the desire drain away from him and he told her to get dressed.

She muttered, 'I'm sorry. I *told* you I didn't like it. I *warned* you.'

He shut himself in the bathroom and stared at his reflection in the mirror. Slowly he took off the trendy glasses he was wearing and snapped them in half. What was he trying to prove? That he was a young swinger? She would have liked it well enough if he had been some young stud.

When he came out she was gone.

Chapter Forty-One

Claude Hussan arrived in town and checked into the Beverly Hills Hotel.

Sunday found out about it by reading the *Hollywood Reporter*.

She was furious, and immediately called Carey from the set. 'Can you have lunch?' she asked. 'I need your advice.'

'Sure, I'll be there at twelve.' Carey hung up thoughtfully. She too had read the trades.

The director was patient with Sunday that morning. She fluffed lines, dried up, and several times cut in on other actors. It was very unlike her.

Carey was first in the studio restaurant. She smoked a cigarette and thought about what she would say.

Sunday rushed in fifteen minutes late. She was wrapped in a pink silk housecoat, her long tan legs attracting everyone's attention. She flopped down, ordered an orange juice and an egg salad, then said, 'I just don't understand it, it's quite ridiculous. I've called the hotel but they say he left orders not to be disturbed. Carey – I don't even care about me, but I've got his *child*! He hasn't even called me *once* since I left Rio. That's *two* weeks ago.'

'Calm down.' It was the first time Carey had seen Sunday blow her cool. 'Just take it easy and I'll give you the facts.'

'What facts?'

247

'He arrived yesterday morning with his wife. He's apparently busy casting and interviewing all day long. Marshall has three clients seeing him today. As you know, his movie should start in three weeks and he still hasn't gotten a star.'

Sunday bit her lip. 'His wife? But I thought they were separated, getting a divorce—'

'Did he tell you that?'

'No, but I just assumed. He never spoke of her except to say that she didn't want Jean-Pierre. I just can't believe they're together. Why doesn't he phone me – explain?'

'I didn't want to burst your bubble before, you seemed so happy. But this is a real mean guy. He has a horrible reputation, and frankly I was amazed at you getting caught up with him.'

'You *always* think the worst of people. Claude is a beautiful, sensitive man.' But even as she said it the words rang false. It wasn't true. Claude was a surly, difficult bastard but she loved him.

'Then why hasn't he phoned you?'

'There must be a reason. I'm sure there's some perfectly logical explanation. Why, I'll probably get home and find him playing with Jean-Pierre on the beach.'

She picked at her egg salad.

'How's the movie going?' Carey asked. 'I thought I might spend some time on the set tomorrow morning.'

'OK. By the way I've been getting more of those sick letters I told you about. Three this week – and whoever it is has my address.'

'I've told you, tear them up and take no notice. It's probably your friendly milkman. Those nuts never do anything. You get a stack of dirties at the office too.'

'But this is the same person who was writing to me at the Château, I think I should—'

'Hello, Carey.' Charlie Brick stopped by the table. 'Where's Marshall?'

'We're not always together, you know. I expect he's slaving away at the office. Charlie, do you know Sunday Simmons?'

'Er, yes.' He smiled at her; then remembering she was a friend of Dindi, his smile froze.

'I sneaked onto your set the other day,' Sunday said. 'You were marvellous. When I was a kid I was a tremendous fan – in fact I still am.' Why did it always sound so stupid when you were admiring someone?

Christ Almighty! Was his life to be fraught with oblique references to his age? When she was a kid indeed! He had only been making films for ten years. 'Thank you. Come over again, I'll buy you a coffee.'

'I'd love to. Next time I have a break I'll be there.'

'He's very attractive in that funky English way,' Carey remarked after he left. 'When he's playing himself, that is. I really dig that kind of subtle appeal. Marshall has it. I think we may actually get married any day now. He's finally persuaded me.'

'That's wonderful. You never told me.'

'Why should I? You've got enough problems. Anyway, I have made the fateful decision and now all I have to do is name the day. My mother will kill me!'

* * *

Sunday finished shooting early. The director cautioned her to go home and get a good night's sleep. She drove twice past the Beverly Hills Hotel, trying to decide whether to go in. She knew it was the wrong way to approach Claude, yet she desperately wanted everything to be all right. Frustratedly she drove to Malibu.

Jean-Pierre was playing on the beach with Katia, the young Mexican girl she had hired to look after him. Mr Hussan had not called.

* * *

Jack Milan arrived at six, for a drink, his youngest child, Victoria, with him. He owned a neighbouring beach house and had telephoned Sunday to ask if he could talk to her.

'Good to see you. I was only saying to Ellie the other day how we should call you up and ask you over for dinner,' he said.

She smiled. 'Drink?'

'Fine. I'll take scotch on the rocks.' He prowled around the tiny house. 'Nice place you've got here, very cosy.'

'I like it.'

'Yeah, you know I just found out you have a kid. You certainly know how to keep a secret.'

'He's not mine. I wish he was. I'm just looking after him for a friend.'

'Sure,' Jack said disbelievingly. 'It's a shame about you and Steve, you would have been great together. I was congratulating myself on playing Cupid.'

She smiled again and wondered what he wanted. She was sure this was not a social call. The phone rang and automatically she picked it up.

'I want to fuck you,' a voice whispered. 'I want to—'

She quickly slammed down the receiver. 'Oh God!' The day had become too much for her and she burst into tears.

'Hey, honey, what's the matter?' Jack was embarrassed.

'Jack, please go. I'm just tired, everything's getting on top of me. Please understand.'

The child was watching her with unconcealed interest.

Jack got up reluctantly. 'Are you sure there's nothing I can do?'

'Nothing. I'm really sorry. Forgive me.'

'If you promise to have dinner with us next week. Ellie will call you.'

'That would be nice.'

He left and she called the Beverly Hills Hotel, but Mr Hussan was unobtainable, so she left her name and number and went to bed.

Outside an old grey Buick cruised slowly past her house.

Chapter Forty-Two

Getting the job with Clay Allen was easy. Herbert answered the advertisement in the paper, went along wearing his one and only suit, showed the glowing references he had written himself, and he was in.

It was an easy job. He spent most of the day lolling around the Allen's kitchen, for neither of them seemed to go out much. As often as not, Clay spent most of the day writing in the poolhouse, and Natalie made only an occasional trip to Saks or Magnum's. She sent the maid to the market, and sometimes he had to take the nanny and their child over to someone's house. He kept himself to himself, communicating with neither the maid nor the nanny.

Clay paid him an advance and he purchased an old grey Buick.

If it were not for Marge, he would have been reasonably happy. She had become unbearable, bossy and demanding, nagging and shrill. Worst of all, she required his services sexually. This amazed him, after what he continually observed going on next door.

Now that he had a car he made careful plans about how to do away with her. The first thing was to move away from those stinking neighbours, to somewhere where they were unknown. It would be no easy move, and Marge would be furious, but he had a plan, and now with a job and a car things were looking up.

He found time to track down Sunday Simmons. He had read about her arriving back from Rio, and it was a simple matter to wait outside Carey St Martin's office and follow her until she led him to Sunday and the house at the beach. After that, he followed her whenever he was free. He knew what time she usually left the studio, and if possible he was there. Sometimes he spent the night sleeping in his car near her house and he would follow her again at seven in the morning when she drove to the studio.

She even looked beautiful at that hour with her hair pulled back, and big tinted sunglasses.

One day he watched Sunday leave, and then waited for the Mexican girl to take the child shopping. It was easy for him to break into the house through the patio. He wandered around, sniffing anxiously through her belongings. He wrote down her phone number and took some pictures from a large stack lying on a table. In her bedroom he pocketed a lacy bra and panties; then he left as stealthily as he had arrived.

In his mind he knew that with Marge out of the way he and Sunday would be together. It never occurred to him that she would refuse him once he revealed himself to her.

He wrote her many letters, each one better than the last. On two occasions he even risked telephoning her, but she had cut off instantly both times, so he decided it was better to wait until he was in a position to present himself personally.

* * *

Marge waited two weeks before she told Louella of her discovery. She was having a good time. Herbert was doing what she wanted and she didn't need it spoiled in any way.

Why *should* she tell Louella anyway? It was none of her business. Sometimes Louella was almost as mean as Herbert, especially last Saturday night when she had made her accept one of the 'circle of friends' in a most unspeakable manner.

'I don't like to do it like that,' Marge had protested. 'It hurts!'

'Do you want to leave the circle?' Louella demanded coldly. 'There are plenty of other women who would be happy to be in your position.'

Marge agreed, hated it, and was reduced to tears.

Louella had laughed in front of everyone. 'You're behaving like a sixteen-year-old virgin,' she had jeered.

Later she had been sorry and made Marge hot milk and chatted sweetly to her.

It was only pride of accomplishment that made her finally reveal to Louella what Herbert had done. *Her* accomplishment at being clever enough to find out. As she was telling Louella, the enormity of it struck her for the first time. Herbert had *killed* a girl, *murdered* her. It was unthinkable.

She started to blubber and cry and panic. Perhaps by even knowing about it she was an accomplice.

Louella confirmed her worst fears. 'Of course you're part of it,' she remarked. 'Just by not going to the police makes you as guilty as him.'

Marge jumped with fright. 'You know too,' she blurted out.

'Yes, but I might go to the police.'

Marge's face crumpled in horror. 'But – but you wouldn't do that.'

'Perhaps I should. I didn't realize how serious this would turn out to be.'

Marge started to cry loudly. Why had she ever interfered? Why had she ever become friendly with Louella Crisp? She had been happy watching her television and eating.

'However,' Louella continued, 'maybe as your friend I can help you. Of course it will take money. How much do you have?'

'A thousand dollars,' Marge stammered. 'It's *all* I've got, though, kind of my savings for my old age.' She gave a sickly grin. 'What do you need money for?'

Louella clucked her tongue. 'If you're going to ask stupid questions I don't think I can help you. We need professional advice and of course there's my friend at police headquarters.

A thousand dollars won't be enough if we're to get this matter dropped, the investigation quashed.'

'What investigation?' Marge squealed in alarm.

'I didn't want to worry you before, but I suspected what Herbert had done, so I made some discreet enquiries and I found that they are pursuing this case very strongly.'

'Oh!' Marge went white and her mouth hung open in a strange disjointed way.

'Of course, with, say, three thousand dollars I think we can settle everything.'

Marge started to cry again. 'I don't have three thousand dollars.'

'What about Herbert?' Louella's mind was racing. Was three thousand dollars too much to ask for? Marge, the silly bitch, believed her story, but would Herbert see it for the blackmail it was? He was probably smarter than Marge, but how much smarter could he be, having married her in the first place?

'Herbie doesn't have any money,' Marge whined. 'We're always behind, catchin' up on payin' for somethin' or other.'

'You had better talk to him.' Louella said coldly.

'I can't do that! He'd kill me.'

'Then there is nothing I can do to help you. I shall have to go straight to the police, otherwise I'll find myself in the same position as you, and I don't want to spend the rest of my life in jail.'

Marge shuddered. 'I'll get you my thousand dollars,' she said quickly, 'and I'll talk to Herbie, he'll think of something. Is that OK? Will that help us?'

Louella nodded. 'I should think so. Only I don't expect my friend can wait too long for the rest of the money.'

*　*　*

Herbert didn't go home that night. He had found a way to I get onto the patio on the beach side of Sunday's house. By crawling along on his hands and knees, then resting on his

254

stomach, he could peer through a chink in the curtains into her bedroom.

He waited two hours after the lights went off, to be sure everyone was asleep. He was especially nervous that the little dog would wake up, start yapping, and give him away.

He inched himself slowly and silently towards her window, then raised himself to look inside.

His luck was in. She hadn't bothered to pull the drapes at all, and he had a clear view of her sprawled across the bed, covered only by a thin sheet. One long brown leg was thrown over the sheet, and a bare arm.

It occurred to him that she was naked beneath the sheet, and that if he waited patiently she would throw it off altogether. His mouth went dry at the thought, and his breathing became laboured and heavy.

It would be so easy, he thought, to force the safety-catch on her window and let himself in. He was confident that once he identified himself as the writer of the letters, she would welcome him with open arms. But it was too soon. He wasn't ready. He had to be free.

Chewing on his lower lip, he crouched uncomfortably, watching her until dawn. Then he made his way back to his car and dozed until she emerged at seven o'clock and set off for the studios.

He followed her. Only when she was safely inside the studio gates did he go home to Marge.

Chapter Forty-Three

Charlie was in a depression. His birthday came and went and he celebrated it alone at his hotel.

He had not telephoned Phillipa since the night she had walked out on him. He had given up the struggle as far as she was concerned.

He took out Thames Mason, who bored him with talk about the number of magazine covers she had appeared on that year. He took out a mousey studio secretary, who bored him, period. He took out a pseudo-intellectual magazine writer, who wanted to be tied up and raped. He took out a blonde pretty ding-a-ling, who unfortunately reminded him of Dindi. He took out a different woman every night.

One evening, sitting in the back of the Mercedes with a Swedish starlet, he complained to George. 'You drive this car like a bus, can't you get a move on?'

George glanced in the rear-view mirror. It was very unlike Charlie to be picky with him, when in any case he was already exceeding the speed limit.

Charlie leaned back in the car, trying to avoid the onslaught of words from the Swede. She hadn't stopped all night. After five minutes of her company he had been ready to slit her throat, and now they had been together for two long hours.

'So the producer said to me, "You are a beautiful girl, Lena, and the star refuses to have you in the same scene with her. Can you blame her?" he said. So they cut me out. Of course I can understand it, Clara is ten years older than me and—'

Charlie tuned out. Enough was enough. He would phone Phillipa the next day.

'Come on, George, I've got a seven o'clock call tomorrow,' he said irritably.

George put his foot down and the big car surged forward. They were approaching a changing light and, sensing his boss's impatience, George pressed his foot down even harder. They could just make it across the light.

That was the last George remembered before the accident. He never even saw the Cadillac coming the other way.

In the split second before the cars hit, Charlie knew what was happening, and he grabbed the girl, covering her with his body.

He woke up two days later in the Cedars of Lebanon Hospital.

It was the strangest feeling to open your eyes and not know where you were or what was happening. There was a tube attached to his arm, but apart from that he couldn't feel or see any sign of injury.

He was in a plain white room. A nurse sat next to the bed, knitting, her head bent in concentration.

'Nurse,' he tried to say. His voice came out as a dried-up croak, just enough to attract her attention.

She dropped the knitting and jumped up. 'Mr Brick,' she fluttered, 'you're awake, that's wonderful. Please don't move, I'll call for the doctor.'

'Must have some water,' he gasped. His throat felt swollen and intolerably dry.

She lifted his head and allowed him a few sips, although he could have drunk the whole pitcher twice over. Then she departed, returning with a doctor and two more nurses.

* * *

Slowly, he pieced together the story. The two cars, travelling in opposite directions, had both been trying to jump the light. The passenger in the front seat of the Cadillac died. The driver and George were both suffering from multiple injuries. Charlie, by protecting the girl in the back, had smashed his head on the side and been unconscious for two days. The girl – Lena – had escaped with a few bruises.

Charlie had a bump on his head the size of an egg, and a nasty cut across his forehead. He felt relieved to be alive. It had been a close call, and the doctors had been unable to predict how long he would stay unconscious. It could have been weeks or even months.

'I never realized so many people cared,' Charlie told Clay a few days later. 'You should see some of the letters I've had, it's bloody marvellous.' He was thinking in particular of a letter from Lorna, a letter full of all the love and affection she had never given him in their marriage. God, she had changed. But then so had he.

'There were a lot of people thought you might not pull through,' Clay remarked. 'Those head injuries are very dodgy things.'

'I've seen the papers. Christ, the English ones are almost obituaries. But I feel good. In fact I never really felt anything except a diabolical headache when I woke up. It's poor old George I'm worried about. He's broken about everything there is to break. They say he'll be OK although it will take some time. I don't know what I'll do without him.'

'I wanted to talk to you about that. We've got this great chauffeur who we never seem to use. Natalie is too tired to go shopping now, and I prefer to drive myself anyway, so he's all yours.'

'Wait a minute, I don't want to—'

'No argument, Charlie. You don't need all the drag of inter-viewing and finding someone, this guy will do you fine. His name is Herbert. I'll have him meet you tomorrow. In fact I'll come with him.'

* * *

Charlie was anxious to leave the hospital. The doctors had insisted that he stay there for at least a week's observation, but he was bored and jumpy and felt he didn't need to. Besides there was the film he was shooting; the delay was costing a lot of money. He knew that while he had been unconscious there had been talk of a replacement. The director and producer had both been to see him, and he had reassured them that he would be back within a week.

He had received a stream of visitors.

Laurel and Floss came, friendly and anxious, bearing a gift of chocolate cake heavily impregnated with pot which Charlie, unknowingly, had given to the nurses, who had never been quite the same since.

He was glad to see Phillipa, serious and apologetic about the last evening they had spent together. After all, there were more things to a relationship than sex.

The Swedish starlet who had been in the car wreck with him was basking in all the publicity. She came to visit him with two photographers. He saw her, but banned the photographers. She was furious.

At his age, and in his position, he knew it was ridiculous to run around with little starlets just so people would think what a swinger he was. Why should he care what people thought?

True to his word, Clay arrived with his chauffeur to take Charlie home.

Home was his suite at the Beverly Hills Hotel, which seemed depressingly quiet and empty without George pottering about.

Clay had invited him to stay a few days with Natalie and himself, but Charlie declined. He wanted to finish the movie and then take a holiday. In a way things had worked out for the best. Now he was not committed until the end of the year and could do what he wanted.

He fell once more into the routine of working at the studio all day, and seeing Phillipa in the evenings.

He made good use of Clay's chauffeur, but found him cold and withdrawn and could not establish any contact with him. This disturbed Charlie, who needed some sort of rapport with the people who worked for him.

Phillipa complained that Herbert was always staring at her in a strange way. Charlie replied that it was because most of her long hippy clothes were transparent.

'I've seen him somewhere before,' she said, 'I wish I could remember where. I don't like him. I hope you get rid of him soon.'

The next day Charlie gave Herbert a hundred-dollar bonus, and sent him back to Clay.

Clay, who really no longer needed him, gave him a month's salary and dismissed him.

It was nearly a week later when Phillipa remembered where she had seen him. 'It was on the Strip one night, several months ago. He was cruising along in a big black car and he picked up this girl. I didn't know her but we had all been chatting – she was in a bad way – needed money. Anyway this creep in the car picked her up and the next day she was found murdered in the hills.'

Charlie laughed incredulously. 'That's ridiculous.'

'Why?' Her face was tight and serious. 'It was him, I'm sure of it.'

'Oh, come on, you sound like a bad movie, love. Anyway, if it had been *that* important, you would have remembered him before.'

'I think we should do something.'

Charlie laughed. 'What did you have in mind? Phone up Clay and say, "Hey, about your chauffeur – Phillipa just remembered she saw him pick up a girl several months ago who was later found murdered"?'

'I can't stand you when you're flippant, you remind me of my mother.'

She knew how to put the boot in.

'All right, if it will make you happy we'll call the police, and you'll find out the case was solved the next day, and Herbert what's-his-name will sue you for a fortune.'

'Forget it, Charlie, let's just forget it.'

Chapter Forty-Four

A week after Claude's return he telephoned Sunday. She could hardly keep the hurt and anger out of her voice.

'I've been so busy,' he complained.

'Didn't you get my messages?' she asked.

'Come up to my hotel this evening. We'll have dinner, I'll explain.'

'Don't you want to come to my house and see Jean-Pierre?'

'He's fine, isn't he?'

'Yes, of course.' She bit her lip, hating and loving at the same time. 'But I thought you'd want to see him.'

'Another time,' he said brusquely. 'Tonight I want to talk to you. Be here at eight.'

He hung up, leaving her angry and confused. She knew that if she were smart, she would give him back his child and walk away from the relationship. And she planned to be smart.

* * *

Claude opened the door of his suite. He was wearing an all-black outfit and tinted glasses. He smoked a short black cigarette.

Sunday couldn't help thinking how much he looked like a

French movie star. The compelling, almost ugly face, the long rangey body. She felt her reserves start to crumble.

The attraction, she reminded herself, was purely physical. He had come at her with his body first, and that was all he had ever given.

'Hello.' He kissed her briefly on the cheek.

She brushed her hand in her hair nervously, determined to stay unaffected. 'Hello, Claude, you're looking well.' Everything she wanted to say sounded like an accusation, so she remained silent. What she wanted was a drink, an exchange of small talk, and then a discussion about when Jean-Pierre should be delivered back – nothing dramatic, no hysterics.

'Your breasts are getting smaller,' he remarked, rubbing his hands familiarly across them.

She backed away angrily. With a sudden sickness, she realized that merely his touch made her desire him, and she knew that he knew it too.

Would it matter if she went to bed with him one last time? Men behaved like that continually. After all, she was a grown woman, and there was nothing wrong in wanting sex.

As if reading her thoughts, Claude said, 'Let's screw first and talk after.' He was already peeling off his black silk turtle-neck sweater.

She hesitated. She wanted very much to be able to say no.

'Come on.' He stood naked in front of her and roughly fiddled with the thin snake-skin belt on her brown trousers.

She stood still while he stripped her item by item, until her clothes rested in a small pile beside them.

Then he was on her, knocking her on the floor, his hands and mouth rough.

She was silent, listening to the stream of obscenities uttered in French and English. It reminded her in a frightening way of the letters she had been getting.

Her body responded to his, but her mind remained above them, a detached onlooker.

Afterwards, when Claude went into the bathroom, she

huddled on the floor, feeling the bites and scratches he had given her. *Why did she still love him so much?*

He emerged in good spirits. 'You've changed,' he said. 'You're better at it now. Who's been teaching you?'

It insulted her that he did not care if she had been with other men.

'I want you to do my film,' he said abruptly. 'You're probably a terrible actress, but I'm a director who can do something for you. I don't believe in false modesty. If you do it, it will make you as an actress. But you have to put yourself in my hands entirely. You have to *live, eat* and *breathe* Stefanie.'

She had read the script. She knew she could do the part, but she hadn't thought in a million years he would ever think of her.

She stared at him for a long thoughtful moment, then she nodded. 'Thank you, Claude, I know you won't be sorry.'

* * *

Carey was not excited at the prospect of meeting Claude Hussan. She regarded as a no-good bastard any man who could treat Sunday the way he had done. She was also sceptical about Sunday doing his film. Was it the right vehicle for her? She read the script, and wasn't sure. Sunday was too young and beautiful to fit the part. More important, was she a good enough actress? It was heavy stuff, and Carey wasn't sure if Sunday could manage it. There were also explicit sex scenes. In the hands of an American director they would cause no embarrassment, but who knew what Hussan would expect his leading actress to do?

Sunday had phoned that morning, bubbling over with delight. As far as she was concerned, there were no uncertainties. She would make the picture, and that was that. Carey had to insist on having the script sent over at once, since Claude wanted to settle contracts and money that very afternoon.

'Accept anything,' Sunday had said. 'I *have* to do it.'

Carey would have been a lot happier for her to do the film with Jack Milan. Now came this bombshell, Claude Hussan's first American film.

He had insisted on meeting Carey in his suite, although she would have preferred to see him at her office.

A secretary answered the door, a girl typical of the many out-of-work actresses who also typed. She asked Carey to take a seat, then disappeared into the bedroom.

Carey leafed through a copy of *Films and Filming*.

The secretary re-emerged shortly, now clad in a polka-dot bikini. She collected some papers from the desk, said 'Mr Hussan will be right with you,' and wiggled out the door.

Carey's first impression was of Hussan's eyes. They were the eyes of a man who had made it, but done many things along the way to get there. Then she took in the rest of him, and suddenly Sunday's hang-up became clear.

'You want a drink?' he offered.

She said no, annoyed at the fact that he neither bothered to introduce himself or even acknowledge the fact that he knew who she was. But she was being silly. Of course he knew who she was.

He lounged in a chair opposite her and stared.

She tried to establish control. 'I'm not sure if this is the right part for my client,' she began.

He interrupted her. 'Neither am I. She's probably a terrible actress, but in my hands that doesn't matter. I know what I want and I am prepared to take a chance. This film will make her.'

'She's already made. I could sign contracts for her tomorrow that would keep her working solidly. She's very much in demand.'

'Crap, that's all she's done, commercial crap. *I* will develop this girl, and as an actress, not as a big-breasted wonder.'

'I can't argue,' Carey said stiffly. 'Sunday has made up her mind, as you well know. Her price will be high, the usual stipulations that she approves all publicity stills and material about her, no nude scenes, no—'

JACKIE COLLINS

'Don't waste your breath. We will pay her fifty thousand dollars, plus she signs a personal contract with me. If I want her naked hanging from a light fixture, I'll have her that way. Don't you worry about it, just tell Sunday, she'll agree.' He went to the desk and picked up some papers. 'Here's the contract. I want it signed and back here tomorrow.'

* * *

Carey, shaking with anger, drove straight to the studio.

'You can't do it,' she told Sunday when she came off the set. 'He won't pay your money, nor allow you any special clauses. You'll be completely in his hands. He could ruin you.'

'Relax, he won't ruin me. Have you seen any of his films? He's brilliant.'

'But your money – if you drop your price now it will be bad. I *know* I can get you good money on the Milan film, and maybe even a piece of the action. I—'

'Don't knock yourself out, Carey. I love you and appreciate everything you've done for me, but whether you like it or not I just *have* to do Claude's film.'

Carey sighed. 'This man has some hold over you, and I bet I know where it is. Right between the legs.'

'You're wrong, it's not that. Just be patient and go along with me. I *know* this film is right for me, and if it's not,' she smiled softly, 'then I'll get out of this business.'

Chapter Forty-Five

Lena, the Swedish starlet, was suing Charlie for three million dollars.

'All she had was a couple of bruises,' he told his lawyer incredulously.

'She's suing for back injury, permanent headaches, a scar on her leg and blurred vision.'

'Why doesn't she throw in a broken neck while she's at it? Christ, these money-grabbing little hookers are unbelievable!'

'Of course you're not responsible. Insurance will cover you. I'll keep you informed.'

'Thanks a lot.'

He had finished shooting the movie, and was staying in a rented house in Palm Springs with Phillipa.

Under doctor's orders he had to relax and take things easy for a few months. He didn't know how he was going to do *that*, for after only a week of inactivity he was going mad.

Phillipa was no great help. She was there and that's about all there was to the relationship – no sex, just companionship, and a strange companionship at that. She rarely spoke except to comment on some disaster somewhere in the world.

He often wondered why, if she were so concerned, she was not out doing something. She seemed quite content to exist with him in the very luxury she was always criticizing . . .

His day was routine. Up at nine, a work-out, a sauna, a swim. Then he read the papers by the pool until lunch was served by the maid. After lunch he had a sleep upstairs and then from four until dinner at seven he would potter about with his stereo sets or cameras.

Phillipa was a reluctant model for his photography. He had to shift her, complaining, out of her chair, and move her around almost by force. It made him laugh. It clearly showed the difference between actresses and other girls. Actresses were only too delighted to pose for innumerable photos, changing their clothes, their expressions, their hairstyles, anything just to continue their love affair with a camera lens.

He remembered one day he had started taking pictures of Dindi early in the morning and she had posed happily until eight o'clock at night. She had changed her outfit forty times!

After dinner they watched television, usually smoking a little grass.

Charlie wished he could do something creative, perhaps write or paint, but his talent lay strictly in performing.

He had never looked so good in his life – thin, suntanned, in great shape.

He spent a great deal of time on the phone, talking to his children, or chatting to George in hospital to cheer him up. He spoke to Lorna, who was obviously embarrassed about the letter she had sent him when she thought he might not recover. Their conversation was short and flustered.

Was she happy? he wondered. Or did she miss him and the excitement of their life together? Although what excitement had she really had? It was always *he* who was doing everything. *She* was usually stuck at home with the kids.

She was certainly making more of a go with her second marriage than he had done with his. Maybe he should have knocked Dindi up, that might have kept her quiet and at home. But how did you knock up a girl who used a diaphragm *and* took the pill?

There were a lot of invitations – parties, dinners, barbecues

– but Charlie was content to go nowhere, and Phillipa was certainly no social butterfly.

He felt, unconsciously, that their relationship was doing neither of them any good. She seemed to have opted out of everything, and while his day was full of minor activity of sorts, Phillipa just appeared in the morning, flopped out in a lounging chair in the shade, and slept the day away.

Then there was sex. She didn't want to try again, and he didn't want to force himself on her, but things were getting a bit desperate. His physical fitness seemed to increase his sexual appetite.

It was a tricky problem. He didn't want to upset Phillipa, of whom he was very fond in a brotherly way, but his need was becoming more demanding every day.

He finally decided to have people to stay for the weekend: Natalie and Clay; Marshall and Carey; and Thames Mason, with a butch-looking queen called Marvin Mariboo who had worked in publicity on the last film. That should solve everything for the benefit of Phillipa, and with the promise of a part, Thames could be relied on to be discreet.

* * *

The weekend got off to a bad start. Carey turned up on Friday morning without Marshall. She said he was working and would arrive the next day. Clay arrived in the afternoon without Natalie, who felt queasy and had decided to stay at home. To make matters complete, Thames drove in on Friday night with the news that Marvin had been beaten up by a sailor and wouldn't be coming at all!

Dinner on Friday night consisted of Clay chatting up first Carey and then Thames. He obviously fancied them both strongly.

Phillipa sat silently at one end of the table, making faces at Charlie, her way of telling him that she didn't approve of any of his guests.

Carey put Clay down at every turn. She made it quite clear that he was going to get exactly nowhere with her.

Thames, however, found his line of chat particularly fascinating, especially when he said what a wonderful idea it would be to write a television series for her.

'I'm surprised no one has suggested it before,' he said, leaning closer to her across the asparagus. 'Any idiot can see that you have great comic potential. You could be a young beautiful Lucille Ball.'

Thames visibly preened.

'That's you, Clay, old love, any idiot!' Charlie said, furious at the sure-fire conclusion that Thames was going to be sharing Clay's bed that evening, not his.

'I'm going for a walk,' Phillipa announced, suddenly getting up.

'But dinner's not finished,' Charlie protested.

'I'm not hungry. I'll see you in the morning.'

He realized she was miserable. She knew why he had organized this weekend, and she obviously didn't want to sit around and watch Clay and him bicker over Thames. He laughed out loud. The situation suddenly struck him as terribly funny.

'What's the matter?' Carey asked.

He noticed what a fantastic coffee-cream colour her skin was. 'Nothing, love, just thinking.' She was very womanly. He had never had a . . . He stamped on his thoughts quickly. She was Marshall's.

After dinner he went to the study to select some tapes.

Clay followed him, drunk and happy. 'You don't mind, old boy, do you?' he asked. 'She's ripe and ready. Where on earth did you find her? Thank Christ Natalie didn't come.'

Like everyone else, Clay imagined that Charlie and Phillipa were having an affair. It didn't occur to him that Charlie had invited Thames for himself.

'Go right ahead,' Charlie said. 'Do what the fuck you like.' He was disgusted with Clay. Somehow it didn't seem quite fair when your wife was lying at home, pregnant.

'Of course, I really fancy the spade,' Clay continued, 'but there's no free pussy being handed out in *that* direction.'

'Tough,' Charlie said, putting on Miles Davis good and loud.

* * *

The four of them sat in the living room, drinking, talking and listening to the sounds.

Charlie got out some pot and they all turned on, including Carey. She really wanted to go to bed, but she hadn't smoked in a long time as it wasn't quite Marshall's scene. She felt like it. Having made the decision to marry Marshall didn't mean that she had to stop living.

Thames was a mass of giggles. She would have let Clay strip her and have her in front of everyone if he had been so inclined, but he dragged all six feet of her off to his bedroom with a sheepish goodnight.

'Where's Phillipa?' Carey asked.

'I don't know.' Charlie was irritable. 'She's a funny girl. Probably walking around the desert.'

'Do you know Claude Hussan? He's a sonofabitch, a real mean bum,' Carey's thoughts became disjointed when she was stoned, and she switched from one subject to the next, never even waiting for an answer.

Charlie on the other hand, if he wasn't involved in sexual activity, became rather melancholy and morbid. 'What's it all about, love?' he suddenly asked. 'Where are we all running to?'

'Marshall likes you,' Carey remarked. 'Put on Aretha Franklin.'

He changed tapes to Carey's request. He felt a very strong urge to make love to her. She was lying back in a chair, her eyes closed.

'Didn't you ever want to be an actress?' he asked. 'Most beautiful women, especially in this town, see it as their life's ambition.'

271

She shook her head. 'Hell, no. Who needs that shit? I could never have handled myself like Sunday. She really knows where it's at, or at least I thought she did until Claude.'

'What's she like?' he asked, with only vague interest. After all, he was thinking, Marshall isn't *that* close a friend, and if we had a scene who would know?

'Sunday is a marvellous girl. Very young in some ways, yet old in others. Sometimes she – *Charlie, what are you doing?*'

He had approached her from behind and now he bent over, plunging his hands inside the neckline of her dress. She was wearing no bra and he was able to pop her small bosom out of the material before she could object.

She stood up quickly. 'You bastard! I'm not some little Hollywood hooker, you know. How dare you!'

He hadn't expected such a reaction. Being a movie star meant that most ladies were ready and willing.

'Sorry,' he mumbled sheepishly, and moved quickly away from her. 'I, er, just thought . . .'

'Well, think again.' Her anger was caused by the fact that she fancied him and was furious with herself. She had made up her mind that when she married Marshall, she would be faithful; there would be no screwing around on the side as was the case with *all* the unhappy married couples she knew.

He buried his head in his hands. 'I have always found,' he said sadly, 'that the women I want in life are usually the ones I can't have. I want a woman I can come home to and say, "Fuck you," and she just says "Yes, darling, that's right, let's go to bed." Sometimes I think it's better to go with a hooker, at least you know where you are. All they want from you is your money.'

Adjusting her dress, Carey listened quietly. 'You're wrong, Charlie,' she said. 'There are plenty of girls who don't just like you for who you are. You're a very attractive man.'

'Do you mean that?' His face brightened.

'Yes, I mean it. The trouble with you is you mix with the wrong people. I bet all your friends are show biz. That way you only meet people looking to be with a star. What about you and Phillipa?'

'Platonic. Purely friendship. She's a nice girl, but very young.'

Carey kissed him on the cheek. 'I'm going to bed.'

He held her lightly around the waist. 'No hard feelings?'

'It's forgotten. Let's be friends, Charlie.'

'All right, love, I'd like that, I really would.'

Chapter Forty-Six

It bothered Sunday that Carey didn't approve of Claude. She knew that he wasn't the most likeable of people at first acquaintance, but she was sure that if they met socially, the atmosphere between them would become less strained.

Of Carey, Claude said, 'She's just mad because she won't be making much commission out of you. Only *you* would have the only black agent in town. She starts off with a chip on her shoulder.'

'Carey doesn't care about the money,' Sunday defended. 'She's honestly not sure the part is for me.'

It was the weekend, and they were lying on Sunday's patio. She had finally succeeded in getting him to come to her house, and he seemed to be enjoying himself lazing around and doing nothing. At first Jean-Pierre had been shy with him. Now he had gone off to swim with Katia.

'The boy likes you,' Claude remarked, 'better than his mother.'

Sunday wanted to ask, 'Was it true she was here with you?' But instead she bit her lip, and said, 'Don't you think he should go back with you? The nanny is very good, she'll stay.'

'Fed up with him?' he chided.

'Don't be silly, of course not. I would love him to stay here; I was just thinking of you.'

'Think of the boy, he's happier with you.'

'What about the Palm Springs location? Shall he come with me or you?'

'We'll leave him here with the nanny. You are going to be working, creating a character. I don't want you to have a child hanging around. It's not going to be another easy piece of shit with the crew admiring you and you just showing your tits and looking beautiful. By the way, we'll live at the house.'

'What house?'

'The house in Palm Springs I'm shooting the film in.' He yawned. 'It will be good for you, you'll see.'

Later she reflected on their conversation. She wasn't sure how she felt any more. Did she love him, or was it just a very physical attraction? He was spoilt, arrogant, rude, a bastard. How could she love a man like that?

She resigned herself to the fact that their relationship was transient and would probably only last as long as the movie.

I'm getting hard, she thought, I'm thinking only of what's good for me. In a way I'm using Claude, but then he's using me, so I suppose that makes us even.

* * *

The weather in Palm Springs was unbearably hot. The idea that Claude had of living and shooting in the same house was bizarre.

The house, surrounded on all sides by acres of desert, was nice enough. It had a swimming pool, tennis court, sauna, billiard room, all the usual extras that Los Angeles executives expected in their cosy desert retreats. However, Sunday found that Claude wanted them to sleep in the actual bedroom in which he was filming. It was horrible to sleep in a bed with a camera looming across the room, arc lights, cables, sound equipment everywhere.

'I can't stand this,' she announced the first night. 'We have no privacy, it's like being in a shop window.'

He stared at her. 'You want to be an actress for once, try and live the part without bitching.'

He was tough to work with, demanding, critical, rude.

Every detail had to be just so, every take perfect.

There were only three other actors on the location – the man who was playing her husband, and the two young men who broke into the house and raped her.

Claude's eye for casting was uncanny. The three men fitted their roles perfectly. The husband was pot-bellied, weak and greedy-eyed. The first boy, thin, blond, Southern, with a slow evil smile, had green eyes. The second boy, the actor Claude had gone after in Rio, was dark, about twenty. He had long-lashed black eyes, a panther-like walk, and was intent, beautiful. His name was Carlos Lo.

Claude allowed Sunday no contact with them except when they were doing a scene together.

It was a clever move that worked beautifully.

The four actors became the characters in the film, and Claude merely manipulated them as he wanted.

Chapter Forty-Seven

Herbert read that Sunday Simmons was going to Palm Springs. Maybe he would follow her. Marge could be fobbed off with the excuse that the Allens were going, she was under the misguided impression that he still worked for them.

Perhaps this would be the answer to all his problems. He would find an opportunity to present himself to Sunday, who, with her money and influence, would be able to help him, perhaps take him to Europe, far away from Marge and her accusations.

The idea appealed to him.

That evening he trailed Sunday to Malibu. To his disgust she had a guest. Sitting in his parked car, he watched with annoyance as a long black Cadillac pulled up at her house and a man emerged. This meant she would not be going to bed early as she usually did, and he would have to wait for the man to leave before he could crawl along the side of the house and watch her while she slept.

He settled back in the driving seat, aware, with a slight sniff of distaste, that he needed a shower. It would have been good to have gone home earlier and taken one, but he was avoiding Marge as much as possible now that he was expected to perform disgusting sexual acts as soon as he entered the house.

The blowsy hag had become insatiable. Bile entered his throat at the very thought of her.

'I've gotta talk t'ya, Herbie,' she had whined that very morning. 'Try and get home early.'

He was no fool. He knew why she wanted him home early.

He must have dozed, for when he looked at his watch it was one o'clock, and the Cadillac was still there, although the house was now in darkness.

His body was stiff and cramped. He slid out of the car and edged towards the house. It was silent. He crawled along the side, and crouched in his usual position at Sunday's window.

She was asleep, lying on her back, naked. Beside her, one dark hairy arm thrown casually across her belly, was a man.

Herbert's first reaction was pain – a pain so deep that he was forced to belch to get rid of it. He didn't move, he just stared, his eyes taking in the contours of her perfect rounded breasts, her long tanned legs, and the thin white space where her bikini had covered her.

The pain convulsed him and he stayed very still and quiet until it gradually subsided and turned into a deep vicious hate.

Bitch! Why hadn't she waited for him?

How he would love to see her face if he confronted her now. She would squirm, apologize, beg his forgiveness. It would all be too late.

He was suddenly seized with a great excitement, a feeling too difficult to hold back. With a convulsive jerk he relieved himself in his trousers. Then stealthily, silently, he crawled away, back to his car, back to Marge.

* * *

Marge was propped up in bed watching the late movie and determinedly eating her way through four Hershey bars, a giant-size bag of popcorn, three packets of nuts, and two bananas.

She needed it all. It presented some sort of defence against the barrage of fury that would come from Herbert when she told him that Louella knew everything.

She couldn't postpone telling him any longer. Although she

had given Louella the thousand dollars, Louella was pressing for the rest.

Eventually she fell asleep, the television still on, a half-peeled orange in her hand, the juice oozing slowly on to the bedspread.

Herbert, arriving home much later, was annoyed to see the lights still on. He had wanted to creep in unseen, dispose of his ruined trousers, and take a good hot shower. Now Marge would start fussing and grabbing him.

He was pleased to see she was asleep, and he crept about stealthily, hoping not to wake her.

It was very hard for him to believe that he had seen Sunday Simmons lying in the arms of another man. He knew that occasionally women – even respectable women – needed sex. But Sunday surely needed nothing more than the letters he had been sending her. *She should have been prepared to wait.* He had told her quite clearly that they would eventually be together. She deserved to be punished.

As soon as he switched off the television Marge awoke. Her mouth and eyes clogged with sleep, she immediately started to tell him the truth.

'Herbie, I done a stupid thing, well, aw, it really ain't all that stupid, I mean it was you that was stupid in the first place. Y'see . . .'

He listened in grim silence, his anger only slightly abated by the fact that at least he would no longer have to have sex with her, that he was once more in charge of the marriage. *She* was as frightened of Louella as *he* should have been. But he would find a way to deal with the blackmailing bitch next door.

Marge was blubbering and crying. He asked her very coldly, very matter-of-factly, who were all the men with whom she had been fornicating next door. She told him, between sobs, about Louella's circle of friends.

He started to hit her, heavy, hate-filled slaps across her face and body.

She cowed under him, frightened to scream, and he continued to beat her until he felt better. Then he sat on the end of the bed and inspected his hands, thin white hands with carefully clipped nails.

Slowly ideas were forming in his head. Ideas that would take care of everyone. He could punish Sunday and at the same time pay Louella the two thousand dollars, get her off his back.

It was a bizarre idea, but one that could quite possibly work.

Chapter Forty-Eight

Inactivity did not agree with Charlie. He became uneasy and unsure. He needed the reassuring eye of the camera on him.

As far as he was concerned the doctors were full of crap, and after two tedious weeks of Palm Springs sunshine, he phoned Marshall to tell him so.

Marshall was unsympathetic. 'You're supposed to rest,' he reminded him. 'Anyhow, there's nothing for you to do now.'

'I'll do a guest appearance,' Charlie insisted. 'A few days on something for a gag. How about a TV special?'

Marshall was quiet for a moment. 'You wouldn't enjoy it.'

'For Christ's sake, love, there must be *something*.'

It had taken Phillipa two days to return after walking out of the dinner. She waited until the house guests left and then she came back.

'Where were you?' Charlie stormed:

She looked dirty and unkempt. 'I stayed with some friends. We tripped out for two days non-stop, it was a beautiful experience. I got you some great hash.'

Her eyes were wide and starey and he knew she had been tripping on acid. He didn't approve. Smoking pot was one thing, but anything else was playing with fire.

'I've made a very interesting discovery,' she said. 'If I mix pot and speed I think I can make it.'

'Make what?' he asked sharply.

'Fuck, of course. Have sex. You know what I mean – the thing you had that great fucking beanpole down here for.'

'I think it's time you went back to Mother. If you think I'm flattered by you telling me that you can only make it with me by being stoned out of your head, then think again.'

'Well, you were so bloody desperate to get laid, and that horrible friend of yours, Clay what'sit, and that Carey woman, I *hate* your friends, they're all phoney shit!'

'And so are you, Phillipa, sweetheart, so are you. In fact, you're a lot phonier than they are because you pretend to be something you're absolutely not. You're really screwed up, you know that, don't you?'

'You *old* man,' she jeered. 'You *stupid old man*. How about you, then? Dieting, and growing your hair, wearing freaky clothes, and *only* being accepted because you're a movie star. People laugh at you. You're ridiculous, so think about *that*.'

The call to Marshall was desperate. Being alone in the Palm Springs house was murder. If Marshall didn't come up with something within the next few days, he thought seriously of going home to London.

It saddened him that every time a relationship ended he seemed to get snowed under with abuse. Even Phillipa had thrown in the crack about him only being accepted because he was Charlie Brick, film star. He had somehow never thought she regarded him in that way.

Dozy starlets or otherwise, they were all sisters under the skin, and it was a hell of a lot more fun with the starlets as far as sex was concerned.

* * *

Carey was in town and Charlie took her out to dinner.

She was seething. 'That French superstar sonofabitch director is going to ruin Sunday's career. He has her locked up in that house, and won't even let me *talk* to her for more than ten minutes. He thinks he's God.'

'Carey, love, you've got to speak to Marsh, I'm going spare down here. I've worked all my life and this doing nothing bores the shit out of me. I'm fit as a fiddle. Tell him to fix up *something* for me.'

'But the doctors said you were to rest.'

'Fuck the bloody doctors, love, I *have* to work.'

'I'll talk to Marshall. I know he thinks you should take it easy for now: after all, you have two movies to do at the end of the year. Now, you are coming to our wedding?'

'Wouldn't miss it. Hey, love, I've got a *marvellous* idea. How many people are you inviting?'

'Fifty. We're going to insult most of Hollywood, but I just can't stand a gang war. It's strictly family and close friends.'

'Why not have it here?'

'Where?'

'In my house here. In this highly expensive rented shack. The garden would be marvellous. We'll hire a preacher. Bring everyone in on a special plane. It's a great idea. My wedding present to you and Marsh.'

She laughed. 'It's a wild idea. Why not? We haven't arranged anything.' She leaned forward and kissed him on the cheek. 'I think it will be wonderful. Can we get it all together by Saturday?'

'Leave it to me, it will give me something to do.'

* * *

Charlie wanted the wedding to be special. He had known Marshall for years and was very fond of him – and he liked Carey a lot.

He hired a secretary called Maggi to handle all the details, and issued instructions about what he wanted. She was a pugfaced redhead, covered in freckles. She stayed, keeping him company. She was a good listener and didn't talk too much. Charlie had decided conversations were *out*.

Chapter Forty-Nine

'Take these pills.'

'I've told you I don't take pills. They make me sick, and anyhow I don't *need* sleeping pills.'

Sunday was lying in bed with Claude, the camera looming over them like a third person. It was three in the morning and she was tired enough to close her eyes and fall into a deep sleep.

Claude had been in a strange mood all evening, talking to her about the film, the characters, what it all meant. Then at one o'clock he had wanted to make love, and she had never known him better, so controlled, so commanding. He kept on bringing them both to the brink, and then stopping, lighting a cigarette or prowling round the room for a few moments. Finally it was breathtaking. Now she felt very relaxed, and he was nagging her to take sleeping pills.

'I want you to take them,' he insisted. 'There is a very important reason.'

'What reason?'

'Look, I have told you if you work well tomorrow morning, you can go to your friend's wedding. OK. I do something for you – you do something for me. Now take them, and stop arguing like a baby.' He thrust the two turquoise capsules at her.

'No, Claude, I will not take pills. That's it. Besides, if we're to start shooting at seven I'll still be asleep.'

He sighed. 'Clever girl, *half* asleep, that's how I want you, half asleep and groggy. I was going to surprise you, but since you're being difficult . . . We are shooting the rape scene tomorrow, first thing. I don't want you to get out of bed.'

'Oh, come on!' She didn't believe him. 'With unwashed face and dirty teeth?'

'How the hell do you think Stefanie *was* when the boys broke in? She was in bed, wasn't she? Asleep, wasn't she? And she took sleeping pills, didn't she? And that, my dear, is how we are going to shoot it. If you want to be an actress, then do it my way.'

Reluctantly she swallowed the pills and closed her eyes. There was no dialogue to the scene, just a lot of struggling. She wondered vaguely how Claude would shoot it. Close-ups, that would be his way, close-ups of her face, that's why he wanted her to look real.

She fell asleep unworried. He was a brilliant director. She trusted him.

The first sensation was one of the covers being pulled off, and then weight, something heavy crawling on top of her.

She tried to move. Then tearing, her nightdress coming off.

She tried to open her eyes, but her eyelids felt stuck together. Hands were covering her breasts, clumsy hands, rough hands. She heard a loud whirring noise, the camera. Where was Claude?

She managed to open her eyes but the blinding lights forced her to shut them quickly. She said, 'Get *off* me,' and in a haze opened her eyes again and stared bewildered at Carlos Lo's face. He sat astride her, his hands on her bosom, his breath coming in short excited gasps.

Beside him the other actor crouched over her, laughing softly.

'What is this?' she protested. She felt weak, without strength, half asleep. 'Oh, the bastard,' she muttered, 'the lousy bastard.

He's shooting this for real. He's actually going to let these two punks rape me.'

She started to struggle but there was no strength to her movements.

One of the actors pinned her arms down, while the other forced her legs apart, and at the moment of entry Claude was above her with a hand-held camera, the lens as close to her face as was possible.

'You bastards!' she screamed weakly.

Then it was the thin one's turn, evil green eyes smiling at her. She lay back. There was no point in struggling. She was no match for two of them.

He licked her face while he did it. Then he climbed off and the camera wandered over her like another lover.

She lay very still, very quiet, spreadeagled on the bed, the way they had left her.

'I'll never forgive you for this, Claude,' she said, '*never.*'

'Maybe when you read your glowing notices you might.' He casually put his camera down and she noticed that the big camera was still going. The two actors had left.

'By the way,' Claude said, 'I want you to meet my wife.'

A woman stepped out from behind the big camera, a thin pale blonde in her early thirties. She smiled good-naturedly. 'Don't worry about this, dear. It is Claude's way. The end result is all that matters, I'm sure you agree.'

Sunday sat up, hugging her knees to her, rocking back and forth in disbelief.

'We always knew you were right for Stefanie. You have a beautiful body. Claude is a very lucky man to have had the pleasure of that. But now, alas, things are different. I am sure you understand. Perhaps while we finish the film we can come to some new arrangement. Three can be – how you say? – *très compatible*. I am sure I would be able to show you a few things that even Claude couldn't manage.'

'You don't honestly think I'm going to stay and *finish* this film?' Sunday asked, trying to control her voice.

'You would be a very silly girl if you didn't. You would have nothing to gain and everything to lose.'

She laughed incredulously. The whole thing was like a bad dream, and she still felt groggy and half asleep, too tired to argue.

'You really have no choice *but* to finish the film,' Claude's wife continued. 'Firstly, we have a contract. Secondly, if you refuse, the film that we just shot will be used – you know what I mean – not in connection with this production, just Sunday Simmons off the set. That sort of thing has a big market.'

Sunday stared at Claude. 'Why?' she cried.

His wife replied for him. 'Because Claude is an artist, a genius, everything must be perfect. In the stuff he shot this morning he will just use your eyes, your face. It will be perfect. You will be acclaimed as a great actress. You wait, my dear, when this film comes out you will be *thanking* us.'

Shakily she got out of bed. She felt dirty and used. She just wanted to get away from these two sick people. She just wanted to get out of the house.

She pulled on jeans and a sweater.

'Where are you going?' Claude asked, as she walked unsteadily to the door.

'A wedding.'

'Fine. But we work tomorrow as usual. I'm sure when you think about it, you'll see how right everything is.'

She picked up her big bag and left without another word.

Fortunately her car was outside. She leaned her head on the steering-wheel and tried to think where to go. It was too far to attempt to drive to Los Angeles, at least in the state she was in. Yet she had nowhere else to go. It was seven o'clock in the morning. A hotel?

Suddenly she thought of Charlie Brick, He had a house. Carey was getting married there that afternoon. She fished in her bag and found the address, then drove to the nearest filling station and asked directions.

Chapter Fifty

Charlie always woke up early. He liked to swim before it got too hot. This morning in particular he was anxious to check everything out, to inspect the patio and the archway of flowers specially erected for the wedding, to test out the platform where the couple would stand to be married.

Long white trestle-tables stood ready to be laden with food. Striped awnings, hung with flowers, protected them from the sun.

He put his two movie cameras, the Japanese Argus and the Bolex, carefully on a special table. Next to them went the stills cameras, the Leica, Rolleiflex, and Pentax, and a neat pile of film.

Carey was arriving at eleven, the caterers at twelve, the preacher at one, the guests at two.

The wedding was planned to take place at two-thirty. There was plenty of time.

He glanced at his watch, it was just past seven. There was not much left for him to do. He had decided what to wear. Perhaps he should give old Marsh a call, wake him up and tell him to come over for coffee. Marshall was staying with friends nearby.

Then he heard a car arriving, and he strolled out to the driveway to see who it was. The car screeched to a halt and Sunday Simmons jumped out.

At first he didn't recognize her. Her hair was uncombed, wild, and there were deep shadows under her eyes. Then he looked at the rest of her and remembered. There was no one else built like that!

'You're a bit early, love,' he said, and then noticing how her eyes couldn't quite focus, he quickly went over to her and took her arm. 'Hey, what's the matter?'

She leaned on him, not quite sure how she had ever found the house, feeling sick and tired. 'I think I'm going to throw up,' she muttered. He got her inside and over the downstairs toilet. He held her while she vomited.

What was it all about? Was she a drinker? Had she been on a bad drug trip?

She was wearing nothing under the thin sweater. She had probably had a bad scene with her boyfriend. But why come to him?

When he could see she was all right, he left her alone, went into the kitchen and told the maid to make tea and toast. He drank a big glass of apple juice, and took two spoonfuls of wheat germ and honey. He was on a health kick.

She didn't emerge for twenty minutes. She had washed her face and brushed her hair back.

He took her hand, led her into the breakfast room and made her drink the hot sweet tea waiting there.

Neither of them spoke.

She leaned back in the chair and stared out of the glass doors at the wedding preparations.

He thought he had never seen a woman quite so beautiful.

'This is the best cup of tea I've had since I was in London,' she said at last. 'Can I have some more please?'

He poured her another cup. 'I always bring me own tea,' he replied in a funny Cockney accent. 'These bleeding Yanks got no idea when it comes to tea.'

She smiled softly.

The phone rang and she signalled wildly that she was not there.

It was Marshall. Charlie kept the conversation short and told him he would call back later. He turned to Sunday and said, 'Don't you think I should know what's going on?'

She nodded. 'I suppose you should, since I came and dumped myself on your doorstep. It's a long story and I feel pretty awful. What I'd really like to do is have a bath and a sleep. I came here because I didn't want to miss Carey's wedding. I don't want her to know about any of this, I don't want to spoil her day. You see, she was right all along, she warned me that—'

She stopped abruptly as Maggi came bouncing in, clad in a short towelling beach jacket, her red hair in bunches. 'Ooops, sorry, am I interrupting something?' said Maggi brightly. 'I thought I'd get up early and help.'

'That's all right, love.' Charlie was secretly choked. Maggi had never risen before ten yet. She was just bloody nosey.

'Maggi, this is Sunday Simmons.'

'Hello,' Maggi said, and sat down, grabbing a piece of toast.

'I expect your room's ready now,' Charlie said to Sunday. 'Y'know, love, it's really a nice surprise you were able to get here so early. Come on, I'll show you the way.' He led her upstairs. 'Take no notice of Maggi,' he said, 'she's an idiot. Have you got anything to wear for the wedding?'

Sunday shook her head. 'I don't even have shoes.'

'If you write down your sizes I'll send someone to Saks for an outfit.' He took her into a guest suite overlooking the garden.

'You've been really kind,' she said. 'I'll explain it all to you later, but please, promise me, don't tell Carey.'

'I've got nothing to tell her, have I? She'll be here at eleven, but I'll put her in the other side of the house, and if you stay here, I'll come for you before the wedding. OK?'

'Fine. Thanks again, Charlie. I just don't know how to thank you.'

I do – he thought – I know the ideal way. Bye, bye, Maggi, it was short and sweet.

* * *

Carey had a mild case of panic coupled with a bad attack of nerves. She arrived accompanied by her sister, a fat girl dressed entirely in pink. What a mistake to have brought Mary Jane before the others. She didn't understand, or even approve of the whole scene. To marry an older man was bad enough, but a white one was worse. Carey's whole family presented a united front of ill-concealed disapproval.

She cornered Charlie. 'Listen, it's not that I usually turn on before lunch, but if you don't want a collapsed bride on your hands, please – just a little smoke.'

He grinned. 'What a marvellous idea, love, come along to my bedroom.'

'Let me just get rid of my sister and I'll be there.'

They sat on his bed, giggling a bit, and Carey said, 'Isn't this silly? Why should I be afraid of getting married?'

Charlie agreed, dragging on the joint and passing it to her.

When they came out Maggi was hovering. 'What have you two been up to?' she accused.

'Nothing that would interest you, my love,' Charlie replied, deciding that one couldn't make a bloody move in his own house without Maggi poking her nose in. He was half tempted to tell Carey about Sunday. After all, Carey was his friend, and surely his loyalties lay with her? But there was something about Sunday that inspired his confidence and he knew he wouldn't give her away.

* * *

The wedding went off beautifully. Carey made a stunning bride in a short gold brocade dress with flowers in her hair. Marshall was nervous and flustered. The place was thick with relatives from both sides, and although black and white made no difference to Carey and Marshall, both sets of relatives bristled with prejudice and resentment.

The ceremony itself was short and simple, and then there was champagne, a cold buffet, and a huge wedding cake inscribed '100 per cent at last!'

Charlie tried to keep an eye on Sunday, but shortly after Carey and Marshall departed for their honeymoon and the guests started to thin out, he couldn't find her. She had taken her car and gone.

Chapter Fifty-One

Sunday hoped that no one noticed her departure as she slipped out just before Carey and Marshall. She felt badly about Charlie Brick. He had been extremely understanding and kind, and maybe she owed him an explanation, but why involve him in her life? She had a decision to make, and only she could make it.

She was filled with anger, and disgusted with herself for being such a fool. Hadn't she learnt *anything* about men? She should have seen Claude Hussan for what he was at the very beginning. What kind of a man was it who broke into a hotel room and made love to a woman by way of introduction? And what kind of a woman was it who responded to an introduction of that sort?

'A frustrated one,' she muttered. 'And he knew it and just walked right in.'

She drove the car hard and fast, heading for Los Angeles and sanity.

Did Claude and his wife *really* think she would accept what had happened and continue with the film?

She wished she could have told Carey, but Carey had gone to Hawaii for a week, and she didn't want to spoil her honeymoon. Knowing Carey, she would have cancelled her trip and stayed to sort things out.

Actually there was nothing to sort out. Whatever happened, whatever harm it did her, Sunday had made up her mind not to finish the film.

Claude would lose too. He had gambled on the fact that her career meant more to her than her pride. She was an actress after all, and actresses *always* put their careers before all else, didn't they? Through all the hurt there was at least a slight sense of satisfaction that she could hurt him too. Her decision was to go home and wait. Claude had to make the first move. He was the one who had created the situation.

Of course there was the boy, Jean-Pierre. Still at her house. She was quite willing to keep him, indeed she would do anything rather than give him back to Claude and his wife.

She entered the city on Sunset tired and hungry. She pulled the car into a drive-in and ordered a tuna sandwich and a glass of milk.

'Hey, Sunday, I can't believe it!' It was Branch Strong. He looked suntanned and brawny in T-shirt and jeans and was carrying four large milk-shake cartons balanced on top of one another. 'I thought you were still in the Springs. When did you get back? Why didn't you call?'

'I just got back. I'm on my way home now.'

'You drove? Alone? If you had asked I'd have come and fetched you.'

She smiled. 'Where are you going with all those milk shakes?'

He looked embarrassed. 'Well – er, these are for Max. He's got a craving for them right now, he's like an old lady. Hey, why don't you come back and see him. He'd like that.'

Branch knew perfectly well that Max would hate it, as at that very moment he was probably preparing himself for Branch's return by draping his naked body on the new fur bedspread he had bought. Max liked milk shakes followed by sex, and he didn't like varying the routine.

'I'm just grabbing a sandwich, then it's straight home. I'm really exhausted.'

Branch shrugged, disappointed yet relieved. 'Listen, I want

to ask you to do me a *real* big favour. There's a première of *The Twelve Guns* tomorrow night. I only have a small part – but important – like it could mean a lot for me. It's a big première – everyone's going to be there – will you be my date?'

'I just got back – I don't know – I hate premières – I don't think so.'

His face fell. 'Hey, Sunday – like, please. I need you there. It would be so good for me to walk in with you. In fact I told the studio you were my date. They gave me great seats.'

'How could you do that? You didn't even know I'd be here.'

He looked sheepish. 'I know. I figured I'd say you couldn't get away at the last minute. It was really kind of a stupid thing for me to do. Your name is advertised with the list of stars that are going. How about it? A helping hand, huh?'

'Oh, all right.' Let Claude see that she didn't give a damn.

They made arrangements and parted.

Branch was elated. He ran whistling into Max Thorpe's house. Max, as expected, was reclining nude on the fur bedspread.

'Bad news,' Branch mumbled, placing the milk shakes carefully on a bedside table. 'I just ran into Sunday and she came back specially to go to the première with me. She saw all the ads and figured she should be here.'

'What?' Max said, going red in the face. 'But what about me? You promised the ticket was for *me*.'

'Yeah, I know that. But I had to tell the studio I was taking a girl, and it was *your* idea I said Sunday as she was away. Well, now she's back.' Trying to hide a smirk, Branch unzipped his trousers and pulled off his T-shirt before joining Max on the fur bedspread.

Max waved him peevishly away. 'I don't want you tonight,' he said in a petulant voice. 'What about my violet dinner jacket? Brand new and wasted.'

Branch shrugged, quickly getting up and pulling on his clothes. 'Sorry, it's not my fault.' He was fed up with Max, bored with the whole faggoty scene.

He liked girls. How much longer before he could tell Max Thorpe to get stuffed?

* * *

Sunday was surprised, there were lights and music coming from her house. She glanced at her watch; it was nearly eleven. What was Katia up to? She had been hired because she seemed quiet and responsible.

She walked into her house, into a sea of strange faces, most of them Mexican, dancing to a James Brown record, colourfully dressed and noisy.

In the midst of the crowd she saw Katia pressed up against the wall by a young man, her face soft and smiling. She was wearing a blue dress that belonged to Sunday, and nearby, curled up in a corner, his knees tucked under his chin, was Jean-Pierre, his big eyes gravely watching.

'Hey, baby, who are you?' A boy grabbed Sunday's arm. 'Where did *you* spring from?'

Angrily, she snatched her arm away.

A perfect ending to the day!

She strode over, picked up Jean-Pierre, and turned on Katia. The girl's eyes had become big and frightened and she was stammering something about it being her birthday.

'Get everyone out of here right now,' Sunday said and, carrying Jean-Pierre, she marched into her bedroom.

All her clothes were spread out across the bed. A spilled bottle of perfume dripped from the bedside table.

'Are you all right?' She hugged the little boy.

He nodded shyly, burying his head on her shoulder.

She moved the clothes off the bed and put Jean-Pierre beneath the covers.

There were sounds of doors slamming and cars starting up.

Sunday brushed her hair back wearily and sighed. Would this day never end?

Chapter Fifty-Two

Herbert Lincoln Jefferson confronted Louella Crisp the day-after Marge had told him about the deal – and the money Louella had to have. They had never met, although of course he had seen her through the window when he was spying on Marge. She had stringy breasts and short veined legs and rolls of fat around the belly of her otherwise skinny body.

He prepared himself carefully, showering, shaving, combing his straight dark brown hair for a long time. He cleaned his fingernails, and had Marge polish his shoes, a job she had given up because of her recent triumphs. He wore a grey suit recently returned from the cleaners, and a sickly yellow sports shirt with a green wool tie.

He considered he looked immaculate, and admired himself for quite some time in the bathroom mirror.

Louella Crisp would soon see she was dealing with a man of substance, not a pathetic fool like Marge.

Louella in fact took one look at Herbert and decided that here was a mean sonofabitch. She didn't want to mess with him: she wanted to grab the money and run. Maybe she might even forget about the money. He had such evil little eyes, cold, empty and spiteful.

He sat down in her living room and stared at her. 'I'm not Marge, you know,' he said at last. 'You've been taking advantage of Marge. I know what's been going on. I've seen the things you do in this house.'

'Never mind what you've seen,' Louella said quickly, making up her mind that she *would* get the two thousand dollars out of him. 'What about the things *I* know. Personal things about you, things my friends in the police department would be interested to hear about?'

His eyes stared at her, flat and expressionless. 'You're not talking to Marge. I'm not a fool. The money's for *you*. Two thousand dollars, and that's the end of the matter. I can get it for you, but I'll need your help.'

'In what way?' she asked suspiciously.

'In a way you'll like. In the way you make your money now.'

'What are you talking about?'

He reached into his jacket pocket and produced two glossy photos of Sunday Simmons which he had stolen from her house. Across one he had scrawled, 'Any time you call – Love, Sunday.'

He handed the pictures to Louella, who looked at them blankly. 'Who's this?'

'A friend of mine,' he said briskly. 'A very *close* friend of mine. In fact, we're so close that she'd do anything for me.' He paused meaningfully. 'Anything.'

Chapter Fifty-Three

When the last guests departed Charlie felt depressed. He had sent Maggi packing during the afternoon. She had started to say things like, 'All my friends say I should be an actress, what do you think?'

'I think you'd better go home,' he had replied.

Now he was alone again and miserable. So miserable in fact that on impulse he climbed into his new black Ferrari and started to drive to Los Angeles. He felt in need of company, a change of locale. He planned to check into the Beverly Hills Hotel and telephone Clay.

It was two in the morning when he arrived, and he thought better of disturbing Natalie. He called Thames Mason because he was lonely.

She dutifully got out of bed, came over, got into bed and consoled him. She told him all about her scene with Clay, laughing all the way. Then she finished by saying, 'Man, is that guy hung!'

Charlie immediately felt inadequate and sent her home, but not before she made him promise he would take her to the première of *The Twelve Guns* the following night.

He wondered if she discussed what he was like in bed, and decided to ask Clay.

He slept fitfully and had a weird sexual dream involving

himself, Natalie, Thames, Sunday, and his mother. He awoke feeling lousy, and went down to the pool.

It was too early for anyone else to be there, and he swam undisturbed. He had made up his mind to go back to London. There was no point in hanging around, going mad doing nothing. He decided to return and build a house, put down roots somewhere. It would keep him busy, and when the house was finished he would tell Lorna that he wanted the children every weekend. They would love it. He would even let them design their own quarters.

He phoned Clay, who was happy to come over for breakfast. On impulse he told him about Sunday.

Clay said, 'Well, I reckon she fancies you, and when you've finished I wouldn't say no to that one.'

'If she fancied me she'd have hung around, wouldn't she?'

'Women are funny creatures. She probably thought you didn't fancy *her*.'

Charlie shook his head. 'Your logic! How's Natalie feeling?'

'Fat. She'd love to see you. Why don't you have dinner with us tonight?'

'Can't. Taking Thames Mason to a première.'

Clay whistled. 'Now *there's* a raver!'

'Yes, you're telling me.'

'I didn't know you'd been there.'

'You don't know everywhere I've been.'

* * *

Later he dressed for the première in a new Doug Hayward dinner suit. He inspected himself in the mirror and was forced to admit that the rest had done him good. He was thin, in great shape, with a nice dark tan. He had abandoned the John Lennon specs and was back in his horn-rims. His black hair was just long enough to curl slightly over the back of his collar.

He drove the Ferrari to Thames's apartment.

She lived in typical Hollywood bachelor-girl style in an

apartment building on the Strip. There were photos and stills of herself everywhere.

'I must photograph you,' he said, accepting a scotch in a green plastic glass with 'I like you' printed on the bottom.

'Oh, I'd love that,' she cooed, 'I'm *very* photogenic. In fact I've been told I have *perfect* features. Maybe we could do a whole bit for one of the fan mags. You know – *you* photographing me and *them* photographing us.'

She looked spectacular in thigh-high silver boots and a silver body stocking with intriguing patches of material missing.

'I'll probably be going to London this week,' he confided.

She was not the least bit interested. 'Do you think my eyelashes look too thick?' she asked anxiously.

He peered at her. It was difficult to tell; her eyes were surrounded with silver shadow. 'I don't know, love, I'm not much good at make-up, but you look great.'

'Do I?' She twirled around in front of him. 'It should be a fantastic première, *everyone* will be there, and everyone will notice me with you.'

He could hardly see how they could miss her, with him or not. A six-foot-two-inch redhead who looked like Thames Mason was hardly an everyday occurrence.

'Would it matter if I wasn't Charlie Brick? If I was just Joe Nobody, would you still want to go with me?'

She frowned. 'Who's Joe Nobody? I've never heard of him . . . Oh, I see,' she giggled, 'trying to put me on, huh?'

'Come on, we'll be late.'

Outside her apartment, Thames surveyed the Ferrari with a slight sneer.

'Don't you have a Rolls and driver?' she asked in surprise.

Charlie was beginning to count to ten under his breath. Would he *never* learn? This was positively the last starlet.

Chapter Fifty-Four

Sunday hated scenes. She hated firing people, but Katia had to go. The next morning she paid her two weeks money in advance and told her to leave.

The girl was sullen about it, but her departure didn't seem to bother Jean-Pierre. He was so delighted to have Sunday back that he never left her side.

They went to the market and stocked up, for Katia had left a refrigerator full of cold chilli beans and rancid hot-dogs.

'What have you been eating?' Sunday asked Jean-Pierre. He grinned and sat in the supermarket trolley, picking out blocks of ice cream, apples, chocolate, cookies, all his favourite things.

Limbo was thin and jumpy. Sunday was furious with herself for having gone to Palm Springs and left them. It was Claude's fault. Everything was Claude's fault.

Branch phoned at lunchtime. 'What time shall I pick you up?' he enquired. 'I've got a limo.'

'Oh!' She had forgotten all about the première, and what was she to do with Jean-Pierre now? 'Look, Branch, I don't think I can make it. I had to fire my maid and I've got no sitter for Jean-Pierre.'

'You *have* to make it. You promised. *I'll* find you a sitter, don't worry about it, just make yourself real beautiful and I'll call you back.'

She was stuck. She didn't want to go, but how could she let Branch down?

* * *

For the première she decided to wear a filmy chiffon top over harem trousers tucked into satin boots. Her hair was loose, not quite concealing gold gypsy earrings. She looked very beautiful.

Branch was on time, bringing with him Esmé Mae, Max Thorpe's long-time maid. A fat placid lady, she made immediate friends with Jean-Pierre and fussed around Limbo.

Sunday departed quite happy with the arrangement. She left instructions where she would be and emphasized the importance of contacting her immediately if she were needed. In her mind was the vague thought that Claude might arrive to take Jean-Pierre away.

Branch wore a white fringed leather suit, and a big ten-gallon hat. He was laughing and pleased with himself. 'I may only have a small part in this here movie, but I'm sure as hell gonna get me noticed, walkin' in with you.'

She decided Branch was a typical good-looking hunk of Hollywood idiot. Sweet and nice, but dumb.

Suddenly she found herself thinking about Charlie Brick and how different he was. How warm and amusing and – yes attractive, in an off-beat way. She wished that she attracted men like that instead of all the bastards.

'How's Max?' she asked, making conversation.

'He's fine,' Branch replied with false enthusiasm. Max wasn't fine at all. He had been in a bitchy fury since Branch had told him that he couldn't take him to the première, and today they hadn't spoken at all.

Sunday sighed and leaned back in the limousine.

She wished that the evening were over.

Chapter Fifty-Five

Planning the operation had not been easy, and until Herbert read in the newspaper that Sunday Simmons was attending the première of *The Twelve Guns*, he had been uncertain how to achieve his purpose. When he read that she was to be there, everything fell into place, and he picked that night as *the* night.

His only worry was that she might not return from Palm Springs, but the newspapers said she would be at the première, so he just had to take a chance.

Louella had been getting impatient and making cracks, but she seemed satisfied when he gave her the date and told her to go ahead with arrangements.

Marge was sulking. Nobody would tell her what was going on. Louella simply stopped contacting her, and Herbert was rude and bad-tempered. What really upset Marge was the fact that Louella and Herbert kept meeting. She found her only solace in the local supermarket, and successfully gained ten pounds. Fortunately they gave credit.

Herbert got up early on the day of the première. There was much to do. The previous evening he had spent parked outside Sunday Simmons's house at the beach, and had been rewarded by her return home quite late in the evening.

He was delighted when all the people in the house left shortly afterwards. Her Mexican maid was a little bitch. He had telephoned several times during Sunday's absence, and when he gave her the pleasure of a few poetic utterances, she had hurled a stream of foreign abuse at him and hung up.

Marge said, 'You wanna have breakfast?'

He cast her a look of contempt, 'No.' Did the fat cow not realize that this was the last morning they would ever spend together? Of course she didn't! In fact, not even Louella knew of his plans for Marge.

He showered and put on a clean shirt and trousers. Then he went next door to see Louella.

'Is everything prepared?' he asked.

'Yes. Are you *sure* she'll do it?'

'You keep on asking me that.' He replied in an irritable voice. 'She *said* she'll do it. We have a *very special* friendship. I told you she will do anything for me.'

'Why doesn't she just give you the money, then? Why's she going to go through with this?'

'Because she wants to.' He replied patiently. 'How many men will there be?'

'Fourteen guys at a hundred and fifty bucks apiece. They're all lined up hot and ready, so don't think you can pull a fake on us. They're going for a lot of money, so you had better produce the genuine goods.'

'She'll be here. Nine o'clock, I'll bring her in. She doesn't want conversation or anything like that, just a normal circle-of-friends evening, everything the same as usual. The men will take their turns exactly the same as with Marge, and then I'll take her home.'

Louella shook her head. 'I wouldn't have thought a movie star would have wanted to do this sort of thing.'

'Oh, she'll want to do it all right.' He narrowed his cold mean eyes. 'She's very good at it.'

Later that day he dressed in his chauffeur's uniform and went by bus to the car lot, where he had arranged to borrow a black Lincoln Continental. The car was perfect for his purpose, as it had belonged to a pop star and was fitted with black-tinted windows and various locking devices on the doors and windows which ensured complete privacy. It had also been tuned to a very high degree and could go extremely fast.

The man at the car lot had advertised the car and was delighted when Herbert appeared and told him he worked for Charlie Brick. He had been happy to make an appointment for Herbert to borrow the car for an evening to get Mr Brick's approval.

Herbert was a convincing liar.

He collected the car and drove to the beach. There, at a deserted spot, he changed the licence plates and worked on the interior speakers for a while. Then he fixed the glass panel which separated the front seat from the back in such a way that it could only be opened from the driver's position. He also altered the interior mechanism so that all doors would lock automatically. Anyone getting into the back seat would be a prisoner, unable to get out until he released them.

Satisfied with his work, he drove to Sunday's house and waited.

Soon she would come out, and he could go in and get what he wanted.

And then the final steps.

Chapter Fifty-Six

Two huge revolving searchlights lit up the sky around the Cinerama Dome on Sunset where *The Twelve Guns* was being premièred.

Police held back the hordes of oohing and aahing fans who spilled across the sidewalk, craning for a glimpse of their favourite stars.

A television unit was set up in the foyer with Jack Julip of the Jack Julip show doing quickie interviews with anyone who mattered.

Anxious cameramen milled around, flashes at the ready to catch the overflowing cleavage and long ripe legs being paraded before them.

Stu Waterman, head publicity man for Now Productions, disappeared into the men's room for the fifth time in twenty minutes to gulp another slug of whiskey from his very useful gold-plated present-to-himself hip-flask.

Things were not working out as planned. Carol Shipman, who had worked ass-naked for ten days on *The Twelve Guns*, had refused to arrive at the première in the buff on a horse – refused because she didn't think it dignified. Dignified indeed, coming from some little English hooker who showed her pussy to anyone who asked!

Stu was incensed. As an alternative, he had had to settle for

Cindy Lawrence, a starlet with forty-two-inch boobs who had never appeared in anything.

Cindy wore a long flowing wig that covered nothing, and a lot of poster paint saying *The Twelve Guns*. Stu helped get her on the horse at the back of the cinema, and she set off round to the front with her escort of five cowboys.

Stu dashed through the cinema, lining up the television cameras and lensmen.

He was just in time to see Cindy arrive. The horse, nervous from the screams of the crowds, immediately bolted, and Cindy fell off, breaking an arm and exposing a lot more than even *she* was supposed to.

Somehow, a blonde with a forty-two-inch bust, sprawled naked in an ungainly position on the sidewalk, did not have the impact that was originally intended.

Carol Shipman arrived in what appeared to be a nun's habit, wearing no make-up and her hair scraped back. Stu had to nudge his own photographer to take her picture. Jack Julip was not even interested.

'I thought I told you to look sexy?' Stu hissed.

She stared at him, not even bothering to reply.

He bit his lip angrily. Where were all the new stars? These little fuckers couldn't even bother to run a comb through their hair.

Angela Carter arrived, all red hair and white furs. The crowd pressed forward, the flashes started, Jack Julip grabbed her anxiously.

Stu sighed with relief and darted off to the back to see what was happening. His assistant – Mike – was helping a round-assed brunette up on to one of the horses.

'Who's that?' Stu hissed.

'I don't know,' Mike replied. 'She's with Brad Lamb and *he* won't get on a horse.'

'Well, get her off. The whole point of this gimmick is to have the *stars* arrive on the horses. I didn't set this up for a load of unknown cooze.'

Mike helped the girl off. She glared at Stu as he took another swig from his flask, and dashed back to the front.

Just then a white Bentley drew up and the chauffeur opened the door to let out Dindi Synde and her escort.

'Hello, Dindi, sweetheart.' Stu wrapped his arm around her. She was wearing little more than a pair of black leather shorts, a gold-studded bra and thigh-length boots. 'I've got a little stunt planned that you'd be just right for.'

'Name it, baby.' She giggled. 'You know I'll do anything.'

* * *

'You were right,' Charlie said irritably to Thames, 'I should have had a Rolls and chauffeur tonight.'

They had been stuck for ten minutes in a line of traffic approaching the cinema.

Thames was studying her face in a giant-sized compact. 'We'd still be stuck here, chauffeur or not,' she remarked.

'We could get out and walk,' he suggested.

'With that crowd? Are you kidding? They'd mob me!'

She laughed briskly, shutting her compact, delighted with her appearance.

An official approached them, checking the pasted number on the windscreen of their car.

'Mr Brick?' he asked.

Charlie nodded.

'Mr Brick, sir. Please turn off at the next side turning. We have arranged a quicker way for you to reach the cinema.'

'But I've got a driver meeting me at the front.'

'It's all been arranged, sir.'

Charlie shrugged. Anything was better than being stuck in traffic, which was one of his pet hates. He did as the man asked, and was shortly stopped by another official.

'Lookee at all those horses,' said Thames. 'I guess it's some kind of stunt.'

Mike hurried over, extending a nervously sweating hand.

'I'm Stu Waterman's assistant,' he said. 'Stu thought it would be nice for you and the lady' – he peered at Thames – 'to arrive on horses, or both on one horse if you like.'

'One horse would be fun,' Thames cooed.

Charlies laughed out loud. 'Not me, mate, the only time I ever got on a horse I was being paid, and I ended up flat on my backside.'

'I don't think there's any fee,' Mike said earnestly. He wished Stu would return. It wasn't fair sticking him round the back with the horses, which nobody seemed to want to ride.

'Oh, Charlie,' Thames cooed, 'it would be fun. Please let's do it.'

'Forget it,' he replied tersely.

'You would have an escort of five cowboys,' Mike said. 'It will be very effective. Everyone's doing it.'

'Yes, well I'm not,' Charlie said. 'But I'm not stopping you,' he added to Thames.

'I can't do it alone,' she said sulkily. She didn't want to miss the opportunity of arriving with Charlie.

*　*　*

Branch said, 'What a *wild* idea!'

The thought of drawing up to the cinema on a horse, with Sunday up there with him and an escort of five cowboys, appealed to him immensely.

Sunday was not so impressed. 'You go right ahead, Branch. I'll meet you in the lobby.'

'Hey, honey, what do you mean? You're with me. I'll hold you tight, won't let you go.'

'It's not that I'm frightened of falling off. I just – er – don't want to do it.'

Stu Waterman had been listening patiently. He took Sunday persuasively by the arm. 'Sweetheart, think of the publicity, think of the TV cameras, think of—'

She shook her arm free. 'I think it's a stupid stunt.'

Branch coughed in an embarrassed fashion. 'Hey, Stu, maybe I should do it alone, and Sunday can kinda come out and meet me.'

'I'm not doing that either,' she said quickly. She was sick and tired of being pushed into things.

'Now listen, baby,' Stu Waterman said, 'you made it on publicity and you're only just there, every little bit helps.'

'I'm sure it does help *you*, Mr. Waterman.' She climbed back into the limo and said to Branch, 'I'll meet you inside.'

Torn between a desire to be seen arriving with Sunday or drawing up on a fine white stallion, Branch shuffled uneasily.

Stu solved the problem. 'Come on, boy,' he said, 'you'll make all the papers tomorrow – the Warren Beatty of the range!'

* * *

Herbert, having attended to his business at the beach, parked the limousine several blocks away from the Cinerama Dome, locked it, and headed on foot to join the crush of people milling about outside. He shoved his way through to the front, oblivious to all the insults hurled at him as he squeezed and groped his way forward.

In the front line he squashed between two elderly queens and a group of teeny boppers.

The queens were shaking their heads sadly and saying, 'Who is there to compare with Joan Crawford today?'

The teeny boppers were screaming, 'There's Randy! It's *him*! Doesn't he look fan-*tas*-tic!!'

Herbert slid his hand onto the backside of one of the jumping girls. She didn't seem to notice. She was wearing very tight rolled-up blue jeans and a skinny-knit sweater that ended around her ribs.

Herbert contemplated the fact that it was disgusting the way mothers let their daughters parade themselves. He squeezed her bottom ever so slightly, and she stopped jumping and looked around. She nudged a girlfriend, whispered something, and they both giggled.

Herbert stared ahead, noting with hardly a flutter the arrival of Angela Carter, who had once been the recipient of his letters, but who had never had the good fortune to meet him. That was to be Sunday Simmons's privilege – and tonight.

* * *

Charlie saw Sunday arrive while he was talking to Jack Julip.

She walked in alone, slightly hesitant. The cameramen leapt forward. Jack was already ending the interview with Charlie, and nodding at an assistant to bring Sunday over next. He shook hands with Charlie, a clammy insincere shake.

Thames, who had been silently pushed to the sidelines, muttered, 'That guy's a bum, his show stinks and so does he.'

Out of the corner of his eye Charlie observed Sunday refusing to be interviewed. The look of amazement and shock that spread over Jack Julip's face was classic.

In his confusion Jack grabbed Thames, announcing, 'And this lovely young lady, accompanying Charlie Brick, is none other than rising star . . .' He left her to name herself.

'Thames Mason.' She preened and waved to the crowd. 'You're a doll, Jack, I *looove* your show!' She then proceeded to bore everyone with details of how she took off her clothes in her latest movie, all in the cause of art.

Charlie went over to Sunday. 'You owe me an explanation; not to mention,' he added jokingly, 'the money for the outfit I got you – hundreds of dollars worth of—'

'Did you arrive on a horse?' she asked.

'No.'

They both laughed.

'In that case I'll pay you.'

'Who are you with?' he asked.

'Branch Strong. *He's* arriving on a horse any second.'

'If I had known, we could have done a swop. Thames was longing to get in the saddle.'

She smiled. 'I'm sorry about running off. I should explain; you were very kind and understanding.'

'How about later? Thames has a nude scene she can't wait to rehearse and I'm not in the mood.'

He was sorry as soon as he said it. She froze up immediately, giving him a cold little smile and saying, 'Sorry, but I'm busy. If you can tell me how much I owe you, I'll see you get a cheque tomorrow.'

'I don't want the money, I was joking.'

'But I owe it to you, I insist.'

An intrepid photographer was taking shots of them together, and as soon as her interview was over Thames came striding to join them.

'I guess we should wander on in,' she said, gripping Charlie's hand possessively and glaring at Sunday.

'Plenty of time, love. Do you two know each other?'

* * *

Satisfied, Herbert watched Sunday Simmons arrive. She was safely in the cinema now, and everything was progressing smoothly. He checked his watch, and slowly started to ease out of the crowd.

Chapter Fifty-Seven

Inside the theatre, people jostled for their seats. There was much neck-craning as positions were checked out. It was important to be sitting in the right place, not shoved to the side or the back or in the cheaper seats.

Charlie had good seats and Thames was delighted. Most premières she attended were with two-bit actors. She was usually given the tickets, which were invariably bad. The film companies wanted her at their premières for the publicity she might get posing in the foyer, but they were not prepared to give her good seats.

'Isn't Jack Julip just great?' She enthused, licking her lips and smiling at a wandering photographer who had managed to get inside.

Sunday and Branch sat a few rows back in aisle seats.

Branch was nervous and sick to his stomach. Two rows in front of him sat Maxwell Thorpe in his new violet dinner-jacket, and next to him was Oliver Ritz. In appearance, Oliver was frail and intense, darkly handsome, like Branch, he had a small part in *The Twelve Guns*, but everyone knew he was a raving fag. Until that very week he had been openly living with a very famous male star.

Branch swallowed a lump in his throat. He liked Sunday very much, but not enough to wreck his whole future. If he had known that Maxwell would plan this revenge, there would have been no question who he would take to the première. Goddamn it, he *liked* living in a big Hollywood mansion. He *liked* being able to have a choice of an Excalibur or a Lincoln to drive. He *liked* walking into Cy Devore and ordering whatever he wanted.

Would it all still be available after tonight? Or was this Maxwell Thorpe's way of telling him he was out?

Sunday shut her eyes and wished the film would begin. She hated all the phoney ballyhoo, the gushing hellos from people who wouldn't even talk to her when her career crumbled flat, as well it might if Claude Hussan had his way.

She had already decided that she would not go with Branch to the party afterwards. She would plead a splitting headache, and she didn't really care if he believed her or not. She was through being nice to people at cost to herself.

Branch meanwhile was wondering if he could redeem the situation with Max by getting rid of Sunday and taking Max to the party instead. He could make some excuse to Sunday and send her home with the chauffeur.

He had almost decided to edge his way over to Max and invite him, when the lights faded and the movie began.

* * *

Outside in the lobby, Stu Waterman was saying to Mike, 'I don't give a fuck what you do with the horses, just get 'em out of here!'

The television crews were removing their equipment. The photographers had already left. The crowds had trickled away, and the policemen gone.

Stu took a swig from his flask and swore with disgust when he found it empty. He needed a vacation, his ulcer was killing him. Working for actors was a lousy way to make a living.

* * *

Herbert sat in the car. His palms were sweating but he remained outwardly calm. It was most important to behave in a normal everyday manner.

He started the big limousine, which rolled slowly forward.

He glanced at his watch once more. *The Twelve Guns* had been on for exactly one hour.

He drove the car to the cinema's parking lot, and got out. Then he unlocked the trunk and removed a brown paper bag, which he placed on the back passenger seat. He locked the car carefully, and went into the theatre.

* * *

Charlie just couldn't believe that anyone could talk so much.

All through the movie, speaking out of the corner of her mouth like some bizarre Southern gangster, Thames kept up a running commentary.

'You see that guy – we were at drama school together; and that one – baby, what a swinger – living with two chicks and balling day and night . . . now she's got the worst body I've ever seen, where they ever found her I don't know – just look at those boobs, hangin' down like grandma's!!'

'*Will you be quiet*,' he hissed for the twentieth time.

Pouting, she paid attention to the screen for a minute, then, 'Pubic hair in *Westerns*! Whee! What next?'

'*I am telling you*,' Charlie said angrily, 'if you don't shut up I am going to leave you here to talk to yourself. I *can't stand it*.'

Thames chewed on a fingernail. Jack Julip had promised her a spot on his regular TV show if she could manage to come by his house later and discuss it. It was tempting. Much as she wanted to go to the party with Charlie, maybe a television show would be better exposure.

'Hey,' she said, 'look at that guy's ass, there's more bare ass in this movie than *Oh Calcutta!*'

316

* * *

Sunday was finding the film boring and distasteful. It was a strong combination of violence and sex, and apparently nothing else.

Branch was mesmerized. He had just appeared in close-up, and boy was he photogenic! Even the chicken-pox scar next to his mouth looked good. This was his best scene in the movie: four close-ups, ten lines.

* * *

Herbert strolled through the lobby. It was very quiet. He walked over to the box-office, where a girl sat silently filing her nails and thinking how much prettier she was than all the movie stars she had seen that evening.

'I have an urgent message for Miss Sunday Simmons,' Herbert said. 'Do you know where she's sitting?'

The girl inspected Herbert, ordinary and neat in his chauffeur's uniform. One had to be very careful nowadays with so many lunatics wandering about. She had a special security button by her foot which she was supposed to press if she were robbed or attacked or if any maniacs appeared. This man was certainly all right.

'I don't know where she's sitting,' she said. 'I did see her come in. Maybe the boy who took the tickets would know. In fact I'm sure he would, he always notices the celebrities.'

'Where can I find him?' He could not control a quick glance at his watch.

'Oh, he'll be standing at the back. The tall boy.'

A five-dollar tip and the tall usher immediately accompanied Herbert to where Sunday was sitting.

On screen Branch was slowly unbuttoning his shirt, his eyes staring at the camera.

The usher leaned across Branch and said in a loud stage-whisper, 'Miss Simmons, I'm sorry to disturb you, but your chauffeur is here. He says it's very urgent.'

'Urgent?' Sunday said in a startled voice.

On screen Branch was slowly unbuttoning his jeans, his eyes staring at the camera.

Sunday stood up and nudged Branch, who was apparently mesmerized by his image on the screen. He didn't budge, just gave her a hurried push as she squeezed to get past him.

The camera was moving in on his face, which now filled the whole screen. He wondered how Max felt now. He hardly even noticed Sunday leave.

* * *

Thames said, 'That guy sure is one hell of a piece of beefcake. I hear he's a faggot, isn't that a waste? I bet I could . . .'

Charlie got up. There was no reason on earth why he had to stay and put up with this. Let her call him all the names she wanted: he was going.

* * *

Once in the lobby Herbert took over. He brushed the usher aside who was searching in his pocket for a pen to get her autograph, and said quickly, 'Miss Simmons, we must hurry. It's the boy, he's had an accident. They sent me for you at once.'

Sunday went white. If Claude Hussan had laid one finger on that child . . .

'Is it bad?' she asked, the words sticking in her throat.

Herbert nodded gravely, rushing her through the foyer and out to the parking lot.

Politely he held open the door of the car while she climbed in. Then he allowed himself a short sigh of relief.

So far so good.

She was in the trap.

Chapter Fifty-Eight

Sunday sat back in the car and closed her eyes tightly. If anything had happened to Jean-Pierre because of her . . . it didn't bear thinking about.

She couldn't see a thing in the car. The chauffeur was blocked off by black glass, and the side windows were tinted in such a fashion that she was unable to see out of them. She groped for the button to release the glass between her and the chauffeur, but although she pressed it sharply several times, it didn't seem to work.

She leaned forward and tapped on the glass. The car glided smoothly on.

Slowly it dawned on her that perhaps this was Claude's idea of a joke.

* * *

In the driving seat Herbert permitted himself a fleeting smile of triumph. It had all been so easy. Masterly planning on his part, of course.

He heard her bang on the glass and his smile widened. He would not reveal too quickly who he was. Let her imagine things. It would do her good to worry a little. Women were much too secure nowadays, everything handed to them on a plate.

When *he* had finished with *Miss* Sunday Simmons, she would *know* who the *master* was.

* * *

The car slowed. A traffic light? As soon as it stopped she tried to open the door. It was locked tight. Then the car was off again.

She wasn't frightened. Nothing Claude could do would frighten her. It was the child she was concerned about. Was the idea to blackmail her to finish the film? She wouldn't put it past them. She wouldn't put anything past them.

Damn Branch for sitting in the cinema so entranced by his own image on the screen! He should have come with her. He shouldn't have let her leave by herself.

She sat back in the seat and composed herself to meet Claude.

* * *

Once in the lobby Charlie had second thoughts. Wasn't it kind of shitty to leave Thames on her own?

Well, a girl like Thames would not be on her own for long. Besides, it was her own bloody fault. The girl had driven him *mad* with her inane chatter.

As he walked towards his car he thought he saw Sunday getting into a black Lincoln. There was something vaguely familiar about the chauffeur. Wasn't it Herbert something-or-other whom Clay had loaned him?

He quickened his step. They had both agreed on the fact that it was a rotten film, so maybe she would have dinner with him after all.

Before he could reach the Lincoln it moved off in the opposite direction. He got in his Ferrari. Maybe he would just follow her for a bit, see where she was going. After all, he had nothing else to do.

320

* * *

Herbert switched on the speaker and spoke into a small hand microphone.

'We have the boy. He is quite safe and will remain so as long as you do everything we say.'

'Who *are* you?' Sunday asked angrily. 'Where is Mr Hussan?'

Herbert paused, momentarily taken aback by her anger. He had expected her to be cowed, frightened.

'We have the child,' he continued. 'His safety depends on your behaviour. *Mr* Hussan can't help you now. You are in our hands. You must be obedient and quiet, otherwise the child will end up the same way as the dog.'

'What dog?' She asked, a sinking feeling taking hold of her. She had heard the man's voice somewhere before.

'Look in the package on the right-hand corner of the seat'.

Abruptly interior lights went on. She looked around. God!. It felt as though she were imprisoned in a black cell. The car sped forward and she could see nothing through the opaque black glass.

On the seat there was a brown paper bag. She touched it. It was damp. She reached inside, looked, felt, and screamed.

The package contained Limbo's head.

* * *

Marge Lincoln Jefferson stuffed another chocolate in her mouth. She was fed up. Ever since she had told Herbert about Louella wanting the money, she had been cast out by both of them.

Louella fobbed her off with excuses when she tried to see her. She found it impossible to get beyond the front door.

'What about the circle of friends?' Marge whined. 'When will the next evening be?'

'I can't say,' Louella had muttered hurriedly, and slammed the door in her face.

Herbert was no better. He had always been a difficult man to please, but now she could do nothing right, and he snapped and snarled at her the whole time.

She was reduced once more to just the television for company, and they were threatening to take that away, because Herbert had not made the last payment.

Marge sat and brooded. She knew they were up to something, for that morning Herbert had been surprisingly cheerful, and when he went out he had produced a large box of chocolates which he gave her. She had been amazed beyond words.

She had noticed activity at her neighbours' – Louella and her husband carrying packages and suitcases out to their station-wagon all day, loading up as if they were going on a trip.

Marge popped another chocolate in her mouth, and went to the window again. She had a good view of what was happening. If there was going to be another circle-of-friends evening, she planned to be in on it.

* * *

'Listen carefully,' Herbert said. They were nearing their destination and it was time to give instructions.

Sunday huddled on the back seat as far away from the grisly package as she could get. The fact that she could not see the owner of the flat grey voice seemed to make matters worse. She was frightened, but determined to try to remain as calm as possible.

'Who are you?' she asked again. 'What do you want?'

'Just listen,' Herbert insisted gruffly. 'If you listen and do as you are told, everything will be all right. If you *don't* do as I tell you, the boy will die like the dog.'

'How much do you want? I have money, I can get more. How much?'

He paused. It hadn't occurred to him that he could get money from her. The thought was appealing, but it was even more appealing to go ahead with his original plan.

'Money can't help the boy. We are going to a house. At this house you will do as you are told. You will not speak to anyone but me. *One* word in the wrong place and the child will die. At a signal from me there are people who will act, so don't try and get away with anything. Do you understand?'

'Yes, I understand.' She desperately tried to remember where she had heard his voice before. 'And what am I supposed to do?'

'Nothing that you haven't done before and enjoyed. You should have waited for me. If you had waited for me I wouldn't make you do this.'

'Waited for you? Do I *know* you?'

'Oh yes, you know me.'

It was like a continuation of the bad dream in Palm Springs. She felt sick and trapped. This must be Claude Hussan's doing, although how could he involve Jean-Pierre? And who was the madman driving the car? She knew his voice . . . who was he?

* * *

Charlie was getting bored. Following Sunday had been a ridiculous, childish thing to do. He was not even positive it was she in the car; he had only caught a glimpse. And where the hell were they going? Away from Beverly Hills and down into dreary little streets with rows and rows of shabby houses.

Twice he decided to stop and twice he changed his mind, because having come so far he might as well see where she was going. Of course he wouldn't let her see him; it would be too embarrassing to let her know he had followed her.

It occurred to him that he must fancy her. No, it was stronger than that. There was something about her . . . just something about her.

* * *

Esmé Mae peered once more at Jean-Pierre. He was fast asleep in bed, his long black lashes curling over innocent cheeks. Where was that little bit of a dog? She had looked for it everywhere. Its dinner was waiting, and Miss Simmons had said to be sure that the dog came in for its dinner.

Well, it must have run off up the beach somewhere, for Esmé Mae had shouted herself hoarse.

She pulled the covers up over Jean-Pierre and waddled into the kitchen for a good hot cup of coffee.

Chapter Fifty-Nine

The car stopped.

The voice warned, 'Now just remember everything I've said. If you do as you're told, you'll be getting back in this car in a couple of hours. We'll collect the boy and I'll take you both home. If you *don't* co-operate – well, you know what to expect. The boy's life is in your hands.'

She waited silently for the voice to present himself. There was no point in trying to scream or run. If he had Jean-Pierre, she would just have to do as he said.

The door opened and she saw they were in a quiet street. Herbert's eyes avoided hers as he took her by the arm and helped her out of the car. She was almost sure she had never seen him before.

He walked her silently up the pathway to a small shabby house and rapped sharply on the door.

A woman answered it, small and brittle in a green satin dress with loads of fake jewellery.

They didn't speak to each other, but her eyes darted over Sunday inquisitively.

Herbert hurried her up creaking stairs into a bedroom, and quickly shut the door. He was breaking out in a sweat. His clothes felt too tight, his skin clammy. He longed for a shower.

He leant against the door. 'Take your clothes off,' he said, 'and put that on.' He nodded at a black robe lying on the bed.

She stared at him.

'Get your clothes *off*,' he snarled.

Slowly she bent and pulled her boots off first; then turning her back to him, she slipped off her trousers and chiffon top. Underneath she wore flesh-coloured panties and bra. She put the robe over her head.

'Everything off,' Herbert stated. There was an uncomfortable tightness in his trousers.

'Tell Claude the joke's gone far enough,' she said weakly. 'I'll finish the goddamn film, I'll do it.' She started to cry.

'This is nothing to do with Claude – this is *me* – *me*. Don't you know who I am?'

'What do you want from me? What have I done?'

'Stop snivelling and take the rest of your clothes off. It shouldn't worry a whore to take her clothes off.'

Slowly she pulled the panties off under the robe. He took them from her and stuffed them in his pocket.

She fumbled with her bra and he said, 'Take the robe off. I want to see you naked.'

She wondered if he would kill her. He had such blank and evil eyes. She shivered uncontrollably. 'Who are you?' she asked. 'Why are you doing this to me?'

'*Take the robe off*,' he muttered. He felt stifled, enclosed. A vein throbbed in his throat. His eyes were glazed.

She lifted the robe over her head and faced him.

He stared at her, filled with hate. His eyes roamed shiftily over her naked body.

Then before it was too late, he commanded, 'Turn round and *don't look back*. If you look back the boy will die!'

She turned away from him, shutting her eyes in terror. Clenching her body in anticipation of what was to come.

He ripped open his pants, his hands clumsy in their haste, and with a low anguished groan he relieved his desire into her panties, which he snatched from his pocket.

He made no attempt to approach her. Let her wait, let her suffer a little in waiting for his touch.

She heard him fumbling with his clothes, and then the short anguished groan. She caught her breath in disgust. She knew what he had done.

And *then* she knew who he was. It was the maniac who had written her all those obscene letters. It had to be! And the voice – now she was almost sure it was the same voice that had muttered obscenities to her over the phone.

Herbert felt strong again. Once more he was in control. He glanced guiltily at his watch. Louella would be waiting.

'Put the robe on and follow me,' he said.

* * *

Charlie parked on the other side of the street further down from the Lincoln.

He watched Sunday as she was hustled into the faded little house by the chauffeur.

It was all very odd. Why would she leave a première halfway through to come dashing down to this place? Perhaps this was where her family lived. But vaguely he remembered Carey telling him that she came from South America and that her parents were dead.

It was none of his business, of course, and she would probably be embarrassed and upset is she ever discovered he had followed her. Yet maybe he ought to stay around for five minutes. There was something not quite right.

He lit a cigarette, and wondered at his sudden hang-up with Sunday Simmons. She was only another actress. Beautiful of course, but just the sort he had sworn to stay away from. Mmm . . . there was definitely something different about her. He wanted to see her, to get to know her, to spend time together.

Of course she probably wouldn't want to know about him. She probably had every guy in Hollywood after her. Clay literally drooled whenever her name was mentioned.

He shrugged and decided to drive off, but he hesitated, because while he had been sitting thinking about her, nine men had gone into the house and there was another one arriving now.

What was it, a party? If so, where were the girls?

He decided to wait just a little bit longer.

* * *

Marge knew what it was all right. It was a circle-of-friends evening. She bit her pudgy nails and muttered under her breath.

Louella thought she was so smart-assed clever. *And* Herbert, the two of them plotting and planning to deprive her of her rights.

Well, they weren't as clever as all that. It was *her right* to attend *all* circle-of-friends meetings. She had paid, hadn't she? She was a member, wasn't she? She would *exercise* her rights and join in.

The only problem was that she didn't feel well. She had a nagging pain in her stomach, but she wasn't going to let *that* stop her. She found a bottle of brandy and took a few deep swigs. Then she popped a couple more chocolates in her mouth to take away the taste. Her head was throbbing and she felt dizzy from the alcohol.

To hell with Louella and Herbert. She was on her way.

* * *

Herbert whispered sharply to Sunday. They stood outside a closed door in the hallway of the house.

'Now remember, whore,' he said, 'not one word or the boy gets it. Just do as your told. I'll be watching you all the time.'

She shivered, cold in the nearly transparent black robe.

He opened the door and they walked in.

The room was lit by long black candles, and all around stood naked men, naked except for masks covering their faces.

The woman who had let her in approached them with arms outstretched. She was naked too, with stringy breasts hanging down. 'Welcome to the "circle of friends", my dear.'

Sunday shrank back as she tried to embrace her, and Herbert dug her sharply in the back.

Louella took her by the hand and led her over to what seemed like a board, covered with black velvet and propped against the wall. It was surrounded by black candles and reminded Sunday of a coffin.

The atmosphere was horribly weird – all the silent naked men in the flickering half-light, with Herbert hovering, still fully dressed.

'Divest yourself of your robe, my dear,' Louella said soothingly. 'Take off your clothes and you take off sin.'

Almost in a daze she allowed the robe to be pulled off, and then Louella and a man assisted her on to the board, where she lay.

Louella murmured some kind of chant. The men repeated it after her.

She dipped into a pot of black cream and rubbed it on Sunday's nipples until they were black and greasy.

Shivering with disgust and horror, Sunday tensed her body, trying not to feel Louella's short stubby fingers. She attempted to clear her mind of all thoughts and become just a body. A body was all they wanted. If she could only disconnect her mind then it wouldn't matter. Nothing would matter. They could do what they wanted and not even touch her.

She lay very still. Whatever happened she had to be sure they wouldn't harm Jean-Pierre.

Louella was chanting again. They were all holding hands and walking slowly around her.

Masked faces and naked bodies were moving closer – closer . . .

Chapter Sixty

The fat woman intrigued Charlie. She had emerged from next door, approached the front door of the house Sunday was in, changed her mind, peered in through a side window, gone back to the front door, changed her mind again, and now she was standing on a straggly bit of grass at the front seemingly indecisive about what to do.

Charlie got out of the car. He intended to stroll casually around the house and then leave. The whole thing was becoming ridiculous. Sunday probably had a very good reason for being where she was, and anyway it was none of his business. He only knew her slightly, and he had no right to be spying on her like this.

Marge staggered. She had a pain in her gut. It was so uncomfortable she could hardly breathe. She wanted to march into Louella's house and surprise them – but she had to wait a minute, catch her breath, let the pain subside. She could see nothing through the windows. They had pulled heavy drapes.

She knelt down on the grass, and suddenly to her surprise, she fell right over.

She lay there stupidly, hoping that she would soon feel better.

Charlie saw the fat woman fall, and realized that here was his chance to get into the house if he wanted to. He hurried over to her. 'Are you all right?' he asked. 'Here let me help you up.'

She looked at him with sick yellow eyes and decided he was a member of the circle of friends. 'Take me in with you,' she mumbled, 'I'm gonna get my rights.'

'Certainly,' he replied soothingly. The woman looked very sick indeed. He propped her up. God, she was a weight. 'Come on, dear,' he said, 'make an effort.'

She heaved herself up. 'That little bastard's not gonna get away with it,' she announced, weaving and swaying.

Together they reached the front door. 'I've gotta key,' she said. Louella had given it to her some time ago and forgotten to get it back.

Charlie opened the front door. Then it struck him that Sunday might not be pleased to see him. She would know he had followed her, and he would look like a fool.

Marge had a grip on his arm. 'Come on,' she mumbled, 'we'll surprise 'em.' She dragged him over to a door and flung it open.

He could hardly see anything. The room was lit only by candles. Then his eyes accustomed themselves to the flickering gloom and he saw everything.

Marge began to yell. 'I've come for my rights. Don't think you can get rid of me you bastards . . .'

There was Sunday, so pale and beautiful, resting on a black board, surrounded by a circle of naked, masked people.

Herbert, the chauffeur, started to smack the fat woman viciously round the face.

Oh Christ! Charlie thought. It's some black-magic scene. She's involved in a weird fucking cult. Oh shit!

Marge fell in a heavy heap on the floor, groaning.

The naked men started running for their clothes, all piled in a corner.

A short nude woman pleaded with them. '*Wait*, everything will be fine. *Wait*. We'll get rid of her.' She indicated the heap that was Marge. 'It's my sister, she's drunk – *wait*.'

Nobody took any notice of her. The scene was confusion.

Charlie stood by the door. Nobody appeared to notice him.

331

He shook his head in disbelief. He knew Hollywood was full of kooks, people ready to do anything for a kick, but he just had not figured Sunday as one of them.

She hadn't moved. She lay as if hypnotized, completely beautiful, completely blank.

He shrugged. There was nothing for him to hang around for, and yet he had a strange feeling that he should go to her, persuade her to come with him, get her out of this crazy scene.

Herbert looked around in panic. What had happened to his plans? *Why was Marge here?* He had given her the chocolates, hadn't he? If she had eaten them, she should have been dead by now. Dead and out of his life! Each chocolate had been carefully treated. He had used enough arsenic to kill an elephant.

Maybe she *was* dead. She was lying awfully still. It was time to get out . . .

Sunday remained motionless. She had forced herself into a self-induced state of oblivion which a doctor would call severe shock. Perfectly still, she waited for the inevitable. The only important thing was that Jean-Pierre remain unharmed. She noticed the chaos around her as if from a great distance.

Just as Charlie decided that he would try to talk some sense into Sunday, Herbert grabbed her. He caught her roughly by the arm and commanded, '*Move!*' propelling her towards the door, towards Charlie.

The hell with it, Charlie thought, he had gone this far, why not all the way? He stepped forward, blocking their path. Before he could say anything, Herbert kicked him swiftly in the balls, and dragged Sunday out of the house.

For a brief moment she saw him, her eyes focused, recognized, and she began to scream as reality hit.

Charlie was doubled over in agony. He couldn't move. The pain was intense. Now Sunday was screaming uncontrollably.

Louella heard the screams. She had pulled on an old dressing-gown and was darting around the room, trying to restore some kind of order. She ran to the window. Something was horribly wrong. Marge was too still on the floor. If Sunday Simmons had come of her own free will why was she screaming?

She remembered how this whole evening had come about. *It was because Herbert had murdered a girl.*

Charlie was trying to stand.

'You'd better stop him from taking her in that car,' Louella yelled at the few remaining men, struggling with trousers and jackets. 'He's mad. He'll kill her!'

Charlie was the only one to move. He made it to the front door in time to see Herbert shove Sunday in the back of the Lincoln. He reached the car just as it sped off.

The pain was lessening. He ran across the street to the Ferrari and threw himself in.

It was all so clear now. The man was Herbert Lincoln Jefferson, the chauffeur Phillipa had made the unbelievable accusations about. And he had laughed, told her not to be so silly.

And now the man had Sunday.

* * *

There was applause at the end of the movie. Branch was pleased, proud to have been a part of it. He looked around to receive Sunday's congratulations, and realized she had left.

Where *had* she gone? He vaguely remembered someone coming to fetch her in the middle of the film. He thought perhaps he should telephone to check that everything was all right, but just then Maxwell Thorpe walked by with his new young actor, and Branch leapt to his feet.

'I sent her home,' he whispered. 'I want to take *you* to the party.'

Maxwell smiled. 'You're a little late, my dear, but you may come with us if you wish.'

'Fine, Max, I'll do that,' Branch said eagerly. 'How did you like the film? How did you like *me?*'

He had forgotten all about Sunday.

* * *

'I know who you are,' Sunday said. She tried to make her voice sound calm and collected, although in fact she was terrified as she huddled, still naked, in the back of the car.

She wasn't sure if the speakers were on. She wasn't sure if he could hear her, but she was determined to appear in complete control. It was important, she sensed, with this madman, not to break down. 'Can you hear me?' she asked. 'I'm cold. Give me something to put on.'

There was silence.

'You wrote me the letters, didn't you?' she continued. 'Answer me. You wrote them, didn't you?'

There was no reply.

She bit her lip hard. Where were they going? What now? Was Jean-Pierre all right? And the biggest question of all – where had Charlie Brick appeared from?

* * *

Herbert drove wildly. He had to take her somewhere quiet.

He was thirteen years old and jerking off when his aunt walked in the room. She was much younger than his mother, and skinny, with pointed tits that she never bothered to conceal. She stood and looked at him, hands on skinny hips, and then she started to laugh. Her laughter went on and on as she pointed gleefully at his penis and said, 'You don't wanna waste all that on yourself, sonny.'

She slipped off her skimpy gown and made him lie down. Then she straddled him and moved herself up and down, up and down on top of him – in and out, up and down – laughing all the time.

Afterwards he stood under the shower for hours, scrubbing, scrubbing; but it was days before he could get rid of the smell of cheap perfume.

He left home, grew up, and there were whores, lots of them,

but none of them could help. The only way he could do it was by himself.

Then he met Marge with the great wobbling breasts. She served him tuna fish on rye and a cold beer and ended up marrying him.

She reminded him of a picture he had been using in his fantasies. The picture was of a nude girl in thigh-length black boots, climbing on to a horse, one leg in the stirrup. When he managed to identify the girl in the picture with Marge he was able to perform, so well and often, that soon she became pregnant. She lost the first baby, and the second. After that he just couldn't do it any more.

He would have liked a baby, a little girl to play with and take for walks, but it was not to be. It was back to the pictures, and then the letters and the telephone calls. He found them satisfying enough, but every once in a while he wanted to try again, and before the hippie girl on Sunset there had been several whores, all of them beaten up in a frenzy of frustration and hate.

Now he had Sunday Simmons, the pinnacle of his desires. If he couldn't perform with her, there was no hope, and nobody else was going to have her. If he drove high enough into the hills, he could park the car safely, and she was in the back, naked and ready. If it worked they would go away together.

If it didn't work, well then, what was there to lose? A woman would never be satisfied if she wasn't getting it. She would never stay with him.

He knew a spot high above Hollywood where he could send the car whirling over the top. Both of them together.

It was the only way.

Chapter Sixty-One

Charlie felt a sense of unreality. Things like this only happened in the movies. But he had *heard* her scream. He had seen her pushed naked into the car.

He felt a sense of exhilaration, as though very pleasantly stoned.

He got behind the Lincoln and stayed there. They were heading back to Hollywood.

It occurred to him that he should call the police. He had a phone in the car, conveniently placed near his right hand. But what could he say. How would it all sound?

'Hello, this is Charlie Brick. I'm following some madman who's got Sunday Simmons stripped off in the back of his car.'

'Oh yeah?' he could hear the reply. 'And I'm Mickey Mouse.'

But what if he *didn't* call the police? Eventually the Lincoln would stop, the nut would get out, and what then? Charlie was not renowned for his strength, and what if Herbert had a gun?

At the first opportunity he dialled the operator. It was difficult to remove his hand from the wheel for a minute, because the Lincoln was jumping lights, stop signs, everything.

They were bolting up La Cienega heading for the Strip. 'I want to report a kidnapping,' he said, when he was put through. 'It's Sunday Simmons.'

'Oh yeah,' said the cop, 'and I'm Donald Duck!'

* * *

'I'm cold,' Sunday pleaded again. '*Please* stop. Give me something to put on then we can talk.' She paused. 'We can talk about your letters.'

There was still no reply. The car rushed maddeningly on. If only he would *say* something. She felt a rising sense of panic.

There seemed to be no air in the car. 'Stop, please stop,' she begged. 'I think I'm going to faint . . .'

* * *

They were nearly there.

Herbert licked his lips, which felt dry and cracked. He reached in his pocket for some lip-salve and felt the locket, the thin gold chain that had fallen off the neck of the girl he had murdered. He planned to give it to Sunday as a present. He stuffed it back in his pocket, found the lip-salve, and liberally applied it round his mouth.

He was unaware of the Ferrari close behind. He slowed down as the Lincoln twisted and turned higher and higher into the Hollywood Hills.

Nervously, his hand unzipped his pants and he stroked himself, steadily, stealthily, almost as if he were petting a snake.

It was nearly time. They were reaching the spot he had been seeking. It was off the road up a makeshift driveway. There was a house, half built, jutting out over the peak.

He took the car to the edge, and stopped. Then he got out and opened the back door of the car.

Sunday stared at him in the dark. She could see his outline as he peered in at her. The only sound was of crickets chirping. She could smell grass and damp earth.

Herbert climbed in the car, leaving the door open. His hands fell upon her breasts like scavengers, the fingers twitching and kneading.

She shrank back as his lips fastened on one breast.

337

She started to struggle, to pull herself free.

He pinned her down. He was strong.

They fought silently. He prised open her legs. She clawed and raked at his face.

'Whore!' he muttered, and slapped her.

Then, as she felt him about to enter her, there was a sudden release of pressure and he was pulled off.

* * *

Charlie stopped the Ferrari when the other car turned off the road. He left it with a special red light flashing, and followed the path of the Lincoln by foot. To say he was nervous was putting it mildly.

He didn't have far to go before reaching the car. He could hear the wordless struggle, the grunts and groans. He didn't hesitate, and plunged straight in, grabbing Herbert by the back of his shirt, hauling him off.

Charlie had never been in a fight, but he followed his instincts, and when Herbert rushed him, he tripped him with his right leg and followed that up with a hefty kick to the crotch.

'That will pay you back for the one you gave me, mate,' he muttered. 'One good kick in the balls deserves another.'

Herbert rolled on the ground.

Charlie pulled Sunday out of the car. 'Let's move before he does,' he said, and taking her hand, they started to run back to the Ferrari.

'Just hold it right there, mister.' A cop stood by his car, his gun pointed straight at them.

Chapter Sixty-Two

A week later Charlie and Sunday sat on the big jet, side by side. They held hands, his protectively over hers.

They were the most publicized couple in the world. Beyond the endless headlines, speculation and rumours, people wondered what had *really* happened that night.

All of Hollywood had its own theory: 'They both belonged to this weird black-magic cult, and it got out of hand.' 'She was *always* at orgies.' 'He's a well-known pervert.'

Marge Lincoln Jefferson was found dead of a massive dose of poison.

Herbert Lincoln Jefferson was arrested, and charged first with attempted kidnapping and rape, and then, after the discovery of Marge, with murder.

Louella Crisp was tracked down with her mild little husband in Arizona and brought back for questioning. Later she was charged with being an accessory.

Carey and Marshall flew back to Los Angeles when they heard the news.

Sunday was under sedation in hospital. She was perfectly all right, but still suffering from shock.

Charlie had taken over. He dealt with the police and the press. 'She is not to be bothered with *anything*,' he informed Carey.

'Of course,' Carey agreed. 'But I sure have got a lot of questions to ask you . . .'

Claude Hussan arrived from Palm Springs to collect his son from the beach house. He came to see Carey at her office.

'I'm sorry, I'm cancelling Sunday's contract. We are recasting.'

'You're kidding?' Carey exclaimed. 'You must have read what happened to her, she's on every front page in the world.'

Claude shrugged. 'It's unlucky. *She* left the film. Anyhow, you may give her my regards and this message – just tell her the extra footage is useless and we won't be using it.'

Carey glared at him. 'If you're not using her, why would you use extra footage anyway?'

'Just give her the message.' His eyes lingered and again she felt their physical pull. 'Goodbye,' he said abruptly.

Carey was not sorry about his film, but she wondered how Sunday would feel. Why *had* she returned to Los Angeles?

* * *

After two days Sunday came out of hospital. Besieged by photographers and reporters, she fled to the comparative safety of Carey and Marshall's house. They protected her as best they could.

She had made many decisions in the past week. She told Carey she never intended to appear in another movie. In a way she felt responsible for the whole mess. Carey couldn't believe it. 'What will you do?' she asked.

'Whatever I do, it will be something private.'

* * *

It had been announced that Dindi Sydne was to replace Sunday in Claude Hussan's film.

Carey was surprised at the way Sunday took the news. She just smiled and said, 'I think he's got the right girl now.'

Something had happened between Claude and Sunday, but Carey did not feel it was the right time to pry.

Charlie visited Sunday every day, and sat and talked with her in the garden. He made her laugh; he made her happy. And when he asked her to come to London with him she accepted. She felt low, depressed, and only Charlie made her feel good. He said, 'No hang-ups, we'll see what happens . . .'

* * *

'I'm going to take you to Manchester,' Charlie said. 'It's a funny place, but I was born there. Serafina nipped in the hospital and had me between shows.'

Sunday squeezed his hand. 'I wish I could have met her, she sounds like such a grand old lady.'

'Yes, she would have liked you. Isn't it funny, love? Here we are, side by side, like we've known each other all our lives. What a lot of time we wasted.'

'Nothing's ever wasted in life, Charlie. You always learn something.'

'Yes,' he looked at her intently. 'I suppose you do.'

* * *

The jet was swooping in to land.

'Stay behind me like a Japanese housewife and leave the press to me,' Charlie said. 'I'll answer a few questions and tell them you're my secretary.'

She smiled softly. 'Now that would be a good job for me. I *can* type, you know.'

'Yes? Good God – hidden talents!'

They both laughed.

Chapter Sixty-Three

Cedric Homer peered into the driving mirror of the sleek silver Rolls Royce parked outside the arrival gate at London airport. He combed his straight dark brown hair. He was an ordinary-looking man, thin and sharp-featured. In his grey chauffeur's uniform he seemed to blend in with the car.

He finished combing his hair and stared rudely at a passing girl in a mini skirt.

'Little scrubbers!' he muttered. 'Going around flashing their bums at everyone.'

His eyes followed the girl out of sight, then he got out of the car and stood beside it.

He thought about the previous evening, which he had spent with his mother in the old flat they shared in Islington. It had been a good evening. They had looked through his collection of photos and cuttings. He had every item that had ever appeared about Sunday Simmons in the English papers and magazines. She was so beautiful, so lovely, even his mother agreed with him.

Then later that evening he had shut himself in his own room, and the evening had been even better . . .

A policeman strolled up to the car. 'This is a no-parking zone,' he said. 'You've been here fifteen minutes, you'd better move along.'

'My party will be here in a minute,' Cedric said. 'I'm meeting Charlie Brick.'

'Oh, Charlie Brick. That's all right then, I suppose. Coming in this morning, is he?'

Cedric nodded. It was good luck that his boss had picked him to be the driver to meet Charlie Brick at the airport. Charlie Brick knew Sunday Simmons. If he told Charlie, explained that he wanted to write a letter of admiration, then he was sure Charlie would give him her address.

Cedric hummed softly to himself . . .

About the Author

There have been many imitators, but only Jackie Collins can tell you what really goes on in the fastest lane of all. From Beverly Hills bedrooms to a raunchy prowl along the streets of Hollywood; from glittering rock parties and concerts to stretch limos and the mansions of the power brokers – Jackie Collins chronicles the real truth from the inside looking out.

Jackie Collins has been called a 'raunchy moralist' by the late director Louis Malle and 'Hollywood's own Marcel Proust' by *Vanity Fair* magazine. With over 400 million copies of her books sold in more than forty countries, and with some twenty-eight *New York Times* bestsellers to her credit, Jackie Collins is one of the world's top-selling novelists. She is known for giving her readers an unrivalled insider's knowledge of Hollywood and the glamorous lives and loves of the rich, famous, and infamous! 'I write about real people in disguise,' she says. 'If anything, my characters are toned down – the truth is much more bizarre.'

Visit Jackie's website www.jackiecollins.com, and follow her on Twitter at JackieJCollins and Facebook at www.facebook.com/jackiecollins.